*For my family, without whom
I never would have had the courage
to begin this journey...*

There was once a worthy man who married for his second wife the haughtiest, proudest woman that had ever been seen. She had two daughters, who possessed their mother's temper and resembled her in everything.

Her husband, on the other hand, had a young daughter...

Charles Perrault, *Cendrillon*

∾

PROLOGUE

*N*o expense was spared, at least not where anyone could see. Black velvet shrouded the gold-inlaid casket, cloaked the silent forms of the pallbearers, and muffled the hooves of the matched sable cobs that drew the funeral caisson. Despite the cold of winter, crimson roses fell in a blanket over the coffin's lid, strewed the cobblestones with their petals, and nestled fashionably in the arms of the grieving family.

The wake had been lavish and well attended, more out of curiosity and avarice than fond memory. Lord Percival Colbourne had begun with money and ended with more, well on the way to realizing his dream of building a merchant empire. Though his fortunes had suffered of late from the political climate, he had remained both a prominent figure in commerce and a notably doting father until the last moments of his regrettably shortened life. But when the usually hale Lord Percival succumbed suddenly to ague, he left behind far more of interest to the world than he took from it. Four unprotected women were his legacy, women now in mourning, but all with a potential share in the wealth and prospects of a rich and influential man.

Lady Malisse Colbourne was his widow, a petite blonde beauty nearer thirty than forty. She seemed far too young, too delicate, and too innocent to have not one but two daughters approaching marriageable age. Anya and Darya, fourteen and thirteen, as blonde and blue-eyed as their mother, were considered heirs to both her impeccable form and her exquisite sense of style. On this tragic occasion, the two youngest members of the Colbourne family paced demurely behind the coffin, porcelain complexions unmarred despite their polite tears. Lord Percival had not perhaps been their father by birth, but they understood the demands of dowry. The man who had secured you an agreeable future with a sizeable marriage portion deserved gratitude, if not quite devotion.

The tableau might have been perfect had there not been another mourner, one who had not stopped to contemplate the lovely contrast of her unbound hair against her black satin gown. She had not noticed the roses, except where the thorns pricked her skin, and cared nothing for the solemn dignity of the procession. Trystan Embrie Colbourne had thrown herself onto the caisson with the casket and refused to be moved. Her chestnut curls were snarled and her face was a wreck of redness and tears, but she pressed it to the cold black lid with a scandalous ferocity of grief. Her father, friend, and only family was dead, and the world was without light or color.

The response to this display was, not surprisingly, varied. Society matrons shook their heads and pronounced her spoiled. Gentlemen feigned shock that ladies should possess such powerful emotions. Miss Colbourne's stepmother and stepsisters seemed determined to pretend that their fourth did not exist.

Perhaps the only persons with warmer emotions towards the sufferer were those far to the rear of the funeral train. These were, primarily, servants, who had known the fiery child for all her fifteen years, and may not have expected much restraint from one loved and indulged since her earliest moments.

Though a funeral might seem like the end of a story, it is also the beginning of another. Trystan's story began at the darkest moment of her life, when hope was dead and everything good seemed burnt to ashes. But buried deep within those ashes were the embers of something quite unexpected, of a day when Trystan Embrie Colbourne would set out to get what she wanted, and find what she needed instead.

CHAPTER 1

*S*omewhere in the darkness between too late and too early, Trystan jerked and opened her eyes. For a long moment she blinked into the dark, then sat up in her wide, curtained bed, frustrated by the unshakeable notion that she had forgotten something important.

It was not likely to be true. There was little in her life that seemed worth forgetting, let alone remembering. Aside from embroidery and lessons in etiquette, the only activity her step-mother seemed to think appropriate for young ladies was dancing, an improbable thing to have forgotten in the middle of the night.

Trystan flopped back onto her pillow and groaned. It was just her rotten luck that boredom was considered genteel, while profitable labor was not. Of late, Trystan's days had grown so tedious, she had begun to daydream of aiding the household staff in their chores. The thought was lovely, but laughable, as there was little chance of her being permitted to engage in something so vulgar as work. Ladies, according to Malisse, were intended to be decorous, not useful. She no doubt feared that if Trystan were to be discovered performing servant's work, someone might get the wrong idea about the Colbourne estate and assume the family had fallen into penury. Anya and Darya's marriage prospects would suffer and the poor lambs would go into a decline. Had it been an option, Trystan would have performed a great many chores for the privilege of observing such a spectacle.

By that time, Trystan was far too disgruntled for sleep. Grumbling under her breath, she threw off her blankets and shivered her way across the room to light a candle. Malisse had only yesterday complained about Trystan's excessive consumption of candles, but Trystan had chosen not to admit the cause. The lack of purpose in her days had left her unable to sleep at night, and she was not fond of the dark.

Thankfully, even though the room was cold, there were still enough coals in the banked fire to light a taper. Trystan coaxed her nub of a candle to sputtering life and set it on her dressing table, where the thin, wavering light could be reflected across the room. Then she glared at the mirror and wondered for the thousandth time what she should have done differently.

In her dreams, she had a family. A father who was still alive. A mother of any sort who cared whether she existed. Extended family who visited and were loud and annoyed everyone excessively until they left and were sorely missed. But somehow, all of these ordinary things had eluded Trystan's grasp.

Her father had been slipping away from her even before he died. She had no extended family that she knew of, and her stepmother and stepsisters would prefer she not exist. Many of the servants Trystan had known since childhood had been dismissed after her father's death, and since that day a stiff formality had fallen over the household. The remaining servants were kind, of course, but they were, after all, paid to be kind so it was difficult to place much confidence in their affection.

Trystan was likewise lacking in friendship, a fact she had neither noticed nor cared about until after her father was gone. By then, however, her stepmother had forbidden her to go out in society, so Trystan had little chance to discover whether it was even possible for her to make friends. And because she met no one besides her family, such as it was, there were no marriage prospects either, which, to be fair, probably owed as much to her lack of dowry as her lack of social opportunities.

So much for general evils. In her present mood, Trystan expanded her list of life's trials to include more particular misfortunes. Her last pair of clean stockings had a hole in them and would have to be darned. There was unfinished embroidery lurking downstairs, next to the current dreary collection of moralizing tales her stepmother would expect her to read after luncheon. Which meal, unless Trystan had mistaken the smell of the delivery wagon last night, would consist of some variation on the theme of fish, just in case she had become too comfortable in the midst of her other tribulations.

And then, of course, she remembered. Remembered the nameless something that had awakened her well before dawn.

Today was her birthday. She was eighteen years old.

Suddenly the fish seemed a grave injustice.

Trystan sat back down on the edge of her bed, near tears and aching with the knowledge that no one else was likely to remember. It would simply be another ordinary day.

It ought to have been the happiest of her life. She should indeed have been awakened long before dawn, but by the laughter and excitement of friends. There should have been a grand party. Presents. Perhaps even a selection of suitors, who would, of course, have been found entirely unsuitable by her fondly indulgent father.

If he hadn't been dead. Her father had not, Trystan recalled rather acidly, bothered to think of these things before deciding it was necessary to oversee a shipment of goods in person. On a boat. Across the ocean. In the middle of winter.

The resulting ague that claimed his life a few weeks after his return seemed also to have altered his mind, and his will. Everything he owned had been left to Malisse, who would rather shave her eyebrows than spend a penny on Trystan.

Trystan imagined it would have been immensely comforting to reflect that she didn't need money. That because of her innate goodness and staggering beauty, someone was bound to fall in love with her. But she was reasonably intelligent and mostly realistic. And she had a mirror.

Hers was not, she reflected, the sort of face that inspired legions of admiring swains. Pretty enough to complement a fortune, but not sufficient to disguise the lack of it. Her hair was an unfashionable shade, somewhere on the red side of brown. Her eyes were a plain light brown. Height? Average. Figure? Average. Worse than average if she made the mistake of standing next to her stepsisters.

No, it wasn't likely that anyone would be willing to ignore her penniless state. And it would be even harder to ignore the rumors that Trystan had ceased to mingle with society because she was shockingly unhinged by grief. Thanks to her stepmother's malicious gossip, Trystan was generally considered to be a spoiled brat who lost her mind when her father died.

Spoiled? Well, perhaps she had been. A little. Lost her mind? Not quite yet. Though it seemed a daily possibility. Trystan's days were filled with so much nothing it was probably a miracle she had not yet lent truth to her stepmother's stories. She was permitted to engage only in appropriately feminine activities, and sometimes reading, provided her stepmother approved of the material. Strenuous exercise (anything more taxing than a decorous stroll) was prohibited, and Trystan was rarely allowed to leave the house.

Heaving a sigh that sounded rather affected, even to her own ears, Trystan decided she might as well dress for the morning. Her plans for the day did not include moping about her bedroom in a nightgown.

As she pulled on trousers and a long woolen shirt, Trystan berated herself sternly. There was no use being maudlin. She didn't truly need friends. And she was an adult now. A woman. She had never bothered much with other people before, and it seemed silly to start now. She should be quite self-sufficient.

But on this day, a day that should have been filled with laughter, with hope for the future, with the congratulations of loved ones, Trystan could not reason away a stinging sense of regret. It would have been nice to share the day with someone. Anyone. But even if, by some miracle, her family remembered, none of them were likely to care.

After buttoning the over-large shirt, Trystan completed her unconventional ensemble with a broad leather belt and not-quite-clean overcoat, then surveyed herself thoughtfully in the mirror. She appeared entirely disreputable, exactly as she intended. No respectable lady wore trousers, or left the house unescorted before breakfast. The combination would no doubt inspire swooning fits should her family happen to catch sight of her. Which was, unfortunately, not her intention, as attractive as she found the idea of Malisse in a dead faint.

As if on cue, the distant rattling and crunching of carriage wheels came faintly to Trystan's ears. Despite her rather grim mood, a grin twitched at the corner of her mouth. With growing impatience, Trystan waited, until she heard the unmistakable sound of the front door opening, followed by the echo of disaffected argument.

Her family had returned to Colbourne Manor.

"… what you thought you were doing. I'm sure I never taught you such indelicate methods of securing a man's attention." A sweetly girlish voice cut in, over the sounds of the indeterminate squabbling that so frequently characterized Anya and Darya's conversational exchanges.

Malisse. After an entire night of social revelry, she still managed to sound as fresh and innocent as a child escaped from the nursery. Trystan found it terribly annoying.

"Well if Darya hadn't been behaving so scandalously, I'd have had no need, Mother," Anya returned cuttingly. "I swear if she had a heavier fan, Lord Ervin would have a broken arm by now."

"It's not my fault, and anyway I wasn't the one pretending to be ill just so Tavender would catch me, and besides, it's none of your business what I was doing with Lord Ervin." Darya's whining always seemed to get worse when she was tired. And it was nearly unbearable to begin with.

"Mother, she has no right to spy on me and you said we shouldn't encourage Lord Tavender because he's not even the oldest, even if it was just to make the Earl jealous."

Trystan leaned against her door and closed her eyes to enjoy the scene.

"Girls!" Malisse's iron control slipped just a hair. "Must I remind you? Second sons are not even to be trifled with. Unless you have conceived a fondness for being considered coquettes, you will restrict your attentions to those gentlemen I have pointed out as appropriate choices. And really, need I comment on the remainder of your actions this evening?" A pause. She would be glaring down her nose, despite the fact that both her daughters towered over her. "Apparently I have failed in my duty to impress upon you both the value of subtlety in social exchanges."

Darya's shrill protest was likely matched by an offended look from her sister. Trystan could picture it clearly, the hand on her hip, the roll of the eye, the affronted pout. Her ear still pressed to the door, Trystan savored the sound of their disgrace with a smile on her lips.

As the bickering began by degrees to ascend the stairs, Malisse could be heard giving instructions to whoever had stayed up to admit them. Probably Hoskins, the butler. No breakfast, no noise, and luncheon in their rooms. It was perfect.

While she waited for everyone to stumble into their beds, Trystan bent down to rummage carefully under her own. Eventually, after a few muttered curses, she located her leather gloves, a crumpled and rather shapeless hat, and her riding boots, amidst a rather impressive collection of dirt, hay and other unmentionable substances which combined to produce a lingering pungency of horse. It was hardly what one would expect to find under a well-brought-up young lady's bed, but it was really the only place Trystan had been able to think of to hide such contraband articles. The chambermaid never bothered to clean under the furniture, or Malisse might have discovered Trystan's secret months ago.

A quick glance out the window confirmed that it was very nearly dawn. Trystan sat on her bed and watched the light grow steadily stronger as the last sounds of her family making their way to bed died into silence. Only after the silence had reigned unmolested for nearly a quarter of an hour did Trystan determine it was safe for her own day to begin.

Holding her boots in one hand, Trystan eased her door open cautiously. There was still a small chance of discovery. One of the maids might be up and about her chores early. Anya or Darya might discover a need for warm milk to put them to sleep. But in Trystan's experience, neither of these was probable. After a long night of dissipation, it was difficult to imagine her family rousing before midday for any reason, excepting perhaps a fire. Or rodents. Or a rich, handsome suitor come to carry one of them off. None of which were likely. Unfortunately.

The house remained silent as Trystan left her room and padded down the hall, past her sisters' bedroom doors to the stairs, keeping a wary eye out for the servants. Though most of them were unlikely to blab to their mistress about her stepdaughter's unconventional habits, Trystan had no intention of staking her freedom on such a supposition. These stolen mornings were far too necessary to her sanity to risk them on the uncertain loyalty of anyone hired by Malisse.

The older servants were another matter, but there were so few left now. Though Trystan had rarely taken the time to notice them before her father's death, they had since begun to seem like the only familiar objects in an unfamiliar world, the last remaining links to a happier time. It was absurd, no doubt, to find consolation in such a thing, but Trystan did not have much to choose from.

Distracted by her musings, Trystan paid too little attention to her descent and missed the last stair. Desperate to avoid a fall, she grabbed hastily for the post at the end of the bannister, but missed, and struck the ornamental knob atop the post instead. To her horror, the carved ball of mahogany was only resting there, unsecured by anything stronger than gravity and inclination. It flew off under her hand and bounced twice on the polished marble floor before caroming off the legs of a delicate enameled table. In the silent, high-ceilinged hall, the sound seemed deafening.

Someone had to have heard. Trystan covered her mouth and felt nearly sick with disappointment as she listened for any hint of approaching footsteps. If she was discovered, her chance for escape would be ruined. But before she could even begin to feel hopeful that the echoes of her disastrous misstep had been missed, a new disaster threatened: the flower-filled vase atop the abused table was teetering noticeably.

Her heart pounding in her ears, Trystan dropped her boots and leaped for the fragile piece of porcelain, struggling to swallow an undignified squeak of terror. Miraculously, she moved fast enough to catch the vase before it smashed into several million pieces, but not before it relieved itself of most of the water inside.

With the vase in one hand and yesterday's rather pathetic flowers in the other, Trystan looked around in frantic haste for some way to mop up the evidence. Unfortunately, no one seemed to have left a towel in the front hallway. Not even a strategically dropped handkerchief. It was most wretchedly inconvenient.

But time was not on her side, and even if the entire household was improbably and momentarily deaf, someone was bound to be up and moving about before too long. Trystan was not about to be found standing in a puddle before breakfast wearing trousers and a guilty expression. She set the vase down in the middle of the table, plopped the flowers back inside, picked up her boots and bolted for the safety of the kitchen.

~

Trystan could always smell the kitchen long before she entered it. Somehow, it was the smell of safety and comfort, even now that she should no longer need either of those things. It was also the smell Trystan would always associate with Vianne, whom Trystan used to appreciate chiefly for her cooking, and later for her habit of never requiring explanations. It wasn't until Trystan was older that she realized Vianne had no need for explanations because she already knew everything.

Taking a deep breath to fortify herself, Trystan pasted a smile on her face and strolled through the doorway into the kitchen as nonchalantly as possible. In comparison with the silence of the rest of the house, the kitchen was a veritable hive of furious activity, warm and fragrant from the preparation for the day's meals. The scullery girls scrubbed industriously at already clean fixtures, while the kitchen maids bustled about looking both flushed and flustered. The bread was rising, a compote was stewing, and the tea things were set out in anticipation of the morning's demands, despite the fact that no one was likely to use them.

Vianne was in her usual chair by the fire, reviewing her notes while keeping a sharp eye on her domain.

A solid, unflappable woman with iron-gray hair and a firm sense of discipline, Vianne had been employed at Colbourne Manor since before Trystan was born. Her stern expression and long wooden spoon were the terror of the household, and a constant source of irritation to Malisse, who resented the fact that she found her own cook intimidating. Even when very young, Trystan had refused to be frightened, but she had always afforded Vianne a sort of awed respect. Though the cook was not what Trystan would call genial, her presence had been an unwavering fixture of Trystan's childhood. And most important of all on this occasion, no one who worked for Vianne would dream of betraying Trystan to her stepmother.

"Child." Vianne's greeting was noncommittal, as always. Her face betrayed no sign that she found anything odd in Trystan's appearance.

"Good morning, Vianne." Trystan returned the greeting with her blandest expression. "Breakfast?"

One of the harassed-looking kitchen maids scurried up with a plate and a steaming mug, obviously prepared in advance.

Pleased to find herself expected, but in far too much haste to sit down and enjoy it, Trystan drank her tea. Perhaps a little too quickly. It burned her tongue, but at least it was hot and sweet. The mornings were not yet comfortably warm, and the tea would fortify her until sun and exercise banished the early spring chill. After returning the mug, Trystan turned her attention to the plate and wolfed down a piece of yesterday's bread. She might have even grinned a little to herself as she imagined her stepmother's horror at each enormous bite. As the last morsel disappeared, Trystan wiped the crumbs from her mouth and nodded her thanks, her mouth too full to actually say the words.

Before she went out by the scullery door, Trystan lingered in the warmth long enough to pull on her boots and braid her hair. The thick braid went under her coat and was covered by her shapeless, short-billed cap. Her disguise would never defeat a determined inspection, but she had never allowed anyone to get close enough to suspect her identity. They would, she thought with a secretive smile, have to catch her first.

As Trystan stepped into the scullery doorway, Vianne stopped her with a word.

"Wait," she said. Trystan turned back, eyebrows lifted in

curiosity. The cook's expression remained unreadable. "Blessings of the day, child. You need not be back until dinner." Trystan blinked and stared uncertainly. "I've arranged everything," Vianne continued, not bothering to explain the details, "but be sure you return in time to change."

It really didn't seem possible. "Vianne, I…" Trystan stopped. Considered. Surely she couldn't be gone an entire day. Someone would notice. There would be outrage. Indignation. A brief trial followed by a beheading. But somehow, none of that seemed quite as important as what the cook had *not* said.

Vianne remembered. She knew what this day meant to Trystan. And not only had she remembered, but she had ensured that it would not be as terrible as Trystan feared. But how? And even more importantly, why? It could not have been a simple undertaking. Excuses would have to be made, stories rehearsed and alibis invented. If anyone in on the deception proved untrustworthy, Vianne's job could be at stake. Why would she risk so much for someone who had never been anything but a charge on her responsibility?

"Vianne, I…" Trystan tried again. "Did you…" How did one ask such a thing without sounding ungrateful?

"Child." The cook frowned disapprovingly. "Stop mumbling at once." She looked sternly at Trystan from under lowered brows. "And do not ask me to explain after all this time."

Trystan's mouth hung open briefly, but closed again. She had the uncomfortable thought that she might be about to cry. Or laugh. The unfamiliar feeling in her chest seemed to demand both. "How can I…" She started to say something, she hardly knew what, when Vianne, appearing almost amused at her inability to complete a sentence, held out a sack with Trystan's lunch.

"Don't be late."

Trystan took the sack, feeling suddenly warm and a trifle overwhelmed. An alarming impulse took her by surprise, but she did not dare do something so forward. One simply didn't hug a servant, and Vianne would not thank her for such demonstrative behavior. Instead Trystan said the words she had never said as a child, words Malisse would never utter, words that were completely inadequate to express what she felt.

"Thank you."

Vianne's eyebrows rose just a fraction, as near to an expression of surprise as the cook had likely ever permitted to cross her face. Trystan turned and slipped out the door before she could give way to any other strange impulses.

≈

Trystan shivered as she left the warmth of the kitchen behind, but it was only partly due to the cool morning air. A sense of giddy anticipation lent her an energy that seemed impossible to contain. A full day to spend as she chose! It was a luxury she had not experienced for some time, and had barely even dared imagine. For the first time in what seemed an age, she was happy and no one was watching, so Trystan gave in to temptation and jig-stepped her way through the kitchen garden. She twirled past the compost heap and skipped around the beds of freshly tilled earth without losing sight of her destination: the only other place at the Manor where she could still find some measure of comfort.

Trystan had always loved the stables. She spent many hours underfoot there in childhood, where her education in all things horse had been seen to, not by her father, but by Andrei and Alexei, the quiet, dark-haired brothers who still ran the

Colbourne stable. They rarely approved of anyone who didn't have four hooves and a tail, but for some reason, they approved of their employer's daughter.

It had been an educational experience for everyone, Trystan recalled with a small smile as she trailed rather muddy footprints across the stable yard. She had learned to respect both horses and fences, and to apply herself for the sake of accomplishment with a zeal she had never shown towards dancing, drawing, or embroidery. Once she had proven her ability to manage even the most difficult of his hunters, Trystan had begged and pleaded and cajoled until Lord Percival permitted her to join him on hunts, despite his second wife's objections. The ensuing disagreements were a source of great satisfaction to Trystan, who resented her stepmother's attempts to interfere as deeply as she scorned the woman's notions of propriety.

But Trystan's youthful triumph had been short lived. When Malisse took over the estate and banished her stepdaughter from the stables, Trystan had been terrified that she would lose the closest thing she had to freedom. Without the cooperation of Andrei and Alexei, her stolen morning rides would be impossible. But even when Malisse had ordered the sale of most of Lord Colbourne's prized horses, and the brothers could easily have found better, more lucrative opportunities elsewhere, both men chose to stay. Trystan had been so relieved that she refused to speculate about their reasons. Three years later, she still couldn't bring herself to ask them why.

After pausing to wipe the worst of the mud off her boots, Trystan stepped through the open stable door, stopping only for a moment to close her eyes and breathe deeply. The aromas of leather and hay and horse blended together to produce a smell she loved so much it almost hurt, but today that ache was comforting. It reminded her of other birthdays that had not been so cold and lonely, and she found that she preferred the hurt of memory to feeling nothing at all.

When she opened her eyes again, it took a few moments for them to adjust to the gloom, but she could just make out the tall, shadowy shape of her horse, shifting his weight restlessly in the center of the long stable aisle. As she drew nearer, she noted that he was already saddled and waiting, his ears swiveling towards her in response to the sound of her arrival.

Theron had been one of her father's favorite hunters, a leggy gray gelding with speed, energy, and a boundless enthusiasm for hurdling anything that would stand still. He was a handful, but the only other options were Anya and Darya's placid saddle horses or one of the four matched bays that pulled the coach. None of them were acceptable mounts unless the rider fully intended to fall asleep in the saddle, which was hardly Trystan's style.

For the first time, Trystan thought to wonder why her step-mother had chosen to keep Theron at all. Or whether Malisse even knew that he had been kept.

Andre and Alexei waited quietly next to the horse, watching Trystan's approach. The brothers knew of her morning excursions, of course. There was no way they could not, and Trystan trusted them without question; but they hadn't saddled her horse for her in years. Not since she was tall enough to do it for herself.

"Ah, good morning?" Trystan was beginning to wonder whether anything about her day was going to go as she expected.

The brothers, who were not forthcoming by nature, doffed their caps and nodded in return.

"And a good morning t'you, m'lady" said Andrei, with as much deference as he might have shown to Lady Colbourne herself. Trystan's brows shot up inquiringly.

"Since when does our relationship merit such exquisite formality?" She looked curiously from one brother to the next, curiosity shifting to suspicion when the men shared an amused glance. "Did Vianne have something to do with this?"

"Couldn't say, m'lady," Andrei offered with a straight face.

"Nor can I, m'lady," added Alexei.

"And you can just stop m'lady-ing me like a couple of lackeys!" Trystan retorted, with an eye-roll of exasperation. "We haven't stood on ceremony since you picked me up out of the manure pile when I was five!"

"You're not five anymore, Miss Trystan." Alexei spoke quietly, as he always did, but his manner seemed unusually direct. He and Andrei exchanged minuscule nods. "This is for you." Alexei reached out, took her unresisting hand, and pressed something into it. Something small, and tightly wrapped.

Trystan stared at her hand, too shocked to respond. She looked up at him, her question in her eyes. Alexei's face proved too enigmatic for her to read, so she glanced at his brother.

"In honor of the day," Andrei explained. Alexei nodded, a faint smile crossing his lips.

"I believe it is customary," he added softly.

It was a birthday present. They had given her a birthday present. She supposed she should, as befitted her station, be appalled. Young ladies did not receive gifts from servants. It was an affront to her dignity and her station. But Trystan did not feel appalled; she felt like crying, at yet another unexpected proof that she had not been entirely forgotten. It was astonishing and thoughtful and actually rather embarrassing, but she would not cry. She would not.

"Thank you," she said instead, looking at the brothers in turn, wondering what else she could possibly say. "I didn't realize anyone remembered. I didn't expect… you shouldn't have, you know… but I really…" Words failed her yet again.

As if recognizing her dilemma, Andrei reached over and handed her Theron's reins.

"Have a pleasant day, m'lady," Alexei said

"Had you considered the Kingswood, m'lady?" Andrei asked. "You'd have time to ride to the Tree today." Trystan swiveled slightly to face him with her mouth hanging open.

"How could you have known about that?" she asked him incredulously. "It was such a long time ago. And I never told anyone."

It had been six years. Six interminable years since she and her father had picnicked under the King's Tree for her birthday. Just the two of them together. The last outing they shared before Malisse had come between them.

"You were happy that day." Alexei's voice brought her out of that train of unpleasant memories. "Perhaps if you went back, you'd remember." Trystan met his eyes and was staggered by what she saw. Sadness. And compassion. For her, of all people.

"Thank you," she whispered. For the third time in one morning. This time, perhaps, she meant it the most deeply.

Compelled to look away before she broke down completely, Trystan cleared her throat and fumbled with the reins. Both men replaced their caps and Andrei busied himself with checking Theron's girth. As soon as he nodded that all was ready, Trystan led Theron out of the stable and over to the mounting block in the yard. She had best leave before anyone else contrived to surprise her; she wasn't sure she could bear any more thoughtfulness.

It was the work of moments to swing into the saddle, secure her saddlebag, and set her feet in the irons. Glancing back, Trystan saw Andrei standing in the stable doorway. He smiled at her, and touched his cap in farewell as she gathered the reins and trotted off alone into the foggy spring morning.

~

The Kingswood was a broad, well-tended forest that stretched miles to the south and east of Colbourne Manor. The forest lay on Crown lands, and was tended by the king's foresters, but had always been freely used by the nobility for parties and excursions. No one suspected the rich of poaching deer.

Near the center of the wood, in the midst of a quiet glade, was a vast oak known as the King's Tree. No one knew how old it was, or how it came to be there, but it was a strangely peaceful place. The way had seemed long, when she was a child, but Trystan's memory placed it well within the reach of a day's ride. She could eat her lunch at the Tree, and still return before dinner.

It was strange how swiftly a day's outlook could be altered. Trystan had begun the morning feeling lost and forgotten, and yet here she was, hacking briskly through the cool, morning air, embarking on an adventure that bore all the markings of a conspiracy. One involving more than just a few people.

Vianne's involvement made sense. The cook had always looked out for her welfare to a certain degree. Andrei and Alexei she had thought somewhat fond of her, but only because she loved the horses as much as they did. The few other servants who had known her since childhood reserved more warmth of manner for Trystan than they did for her stepmother, but she had supposed it to be out of habit, rather than any true affection.

She had certainly never suspected them of harboring deeper feelings.

Even Trystan could admit that she had not been an easy person to like.

She felt a twinge of conscience as she bent to open the last gate, the one that marked the edge of her father's estate. Beyond it lay a rutted lane, which ran between low stone walls. In one direction lay Colbourne village, in the other, the wide Crown road which led all the way to Evenleigh and beyond.

She was interested in neither. Roads begat traffic, which Trystan studiously avoided. Her path lay a mile or more across the fields, where the edge of the Kingswood butted up against seldom-used pastureland. It was a direction she had taken many times while hunting, during a time when all had been right with her world and no one's wishes were more important than her own.

Everything had changed after the wedding. It had all gone so very wrong. Her father's affections began to grow distant and vague and Trystan had been forced to wonder if she had made a mistake by shutting other people out of her life. But she had still not really tried to make friends. She had been too pre-occupied by her anger at the disruption of her perfect world, too busy trying to set it right. She had only wanted her father back. Until that terrible day he returned from his journey sick and shivering and never left his bed again.

It still ached. Even three years later, those memories filled Trystan with the familiar leaden drag of loss.

As she urged Theron into a brisk trot across the damp, fog-shrouded field, a bitter echo of the same useless questions kept time with the drum of his hooves. Why her? Why him? How could he die and leave her alone?

Caught up in her recollections, Trystan realized how tense she had become only when Theron's head tossed uncomfortably and he began to jig beneath her. She slackened her grip on the reins and released the rigidity in her legs until he subsided. If only her own troubles could have been so easily resolved.

Once the funeral was past, by the time her anger and grief had diminished, and by the time she realized she had no power against Malisse, it had been too late. Between her own pride and her stepmother's restrictions, she was left utterly alone.

Or so she had always thought. She was beginning to suspect she had been entirely mistaken.

When the eaves of the forest finally appeared through the mist on the far side of the field, Trystan urged Theron into a canter, eager to leave the familiar fields behind. She had thoroughly explored the pastures around Colbourne years ago, but avoided the woods since her father's death. There had never been enough time, and it would have felt strange to go there without him. But Alexei was right. She needed to go back. Perhaps it would help her find a way to move forward.

The edge of the field was marked by a brush fence, thick and tangled, which Theron hurdled with ease, though it was much more difficult to convince him to pull up afterwards. He had not yet had a chance to expend much energy, and did not appreciate being forced to walk until they found their way through the brush to the nearest of the forest paths.

Once they pressed through the edges of the wood, it proved more pleasant, due to the efforts of royal foresters to keep the paths and the underbrush cleared. Their vigilance provided a shady haunt for picnics or royal hunts, which Trystan knew occurred primarily during the long summer months, when bored nobility descended in droves on the nearby court at Evenleigh.

Fortunately, she was unlikely to have much company on such a cool spring morning, especially at an hour which fashionable society considered closer to bedtime than breakfast.

Trystan's memory proved adequate to the task of finding her way into the wood, but, sadly, it failed miserably in the matter of navigation within. Where her mind recalled broad, open paths laid out in a neat pattern, she found instead a maze of narrow trails, none of which seemed to lead in a predictable direction.

It was a pleasant enough place to be lost, unless one wanted to be elsewhere and was mounted on a horse that had decided to be silly about trees. The farther they went, the more nervous Theron seemed, blowing anxiously and flicking his ears at every sound.

The sun rose higher, filtering sporadically through the foliage overhead, indicating to Trystan that she had perhaps been unforgivably foolish. She had simply assumed her memories would guide her, but it had been too long, and no doubt the forest trails had changed.

Inwardly cursing her failure to consider this probability before attempting such an unwise expedition, Trystan was on the verge of returning the way she had come when she heard the improbable sound of hoofbeats. She pulled Theron to a stop and listened, hoping they had been an echo, but they continued.

Trystan had no desire to discover what sort of person besides herself had a taste for cold morning rides. While the frequent presence of green-clad king's foresters made criminal activity unlikely, even an innocent rider could prove disastrous for her.

Turning Theron's head, Trystan quickly left the trail behind, moving deeper into the wood at as fast a pace as caution would allow. After a brief period of ducking under low-hanging branches and hopping over the occasional downed tree, she slowed and listened, certain the other rider would have remained on the path. To her surprise and dismay, she heard hoofbeats again, and turned to find the rider just coming into view between the trees.

Trystan felt intolerably stupid. She should have stayed closer to home. Not risked her anonymity on such a chancy venture. There were no good reasons for another rider to follow her, and precious little she could do now except run.

Clinging close to Theron's neck, she spurred him on faster, choosing paths that led through thicker brush and changing direction without warning. Despite the cool air, she began to sweat beneath her voluminous coat, while her stomach clenched apprehensively each time she turned to look and found the other rider far closer than she'd hoped.

Just when Trystan was nearly convinced that her worst fears would be realized, the trees began to thin. The light broke through and the brush parted as they finally reached the edge of the forest. A steep, grassy hillside rose up in front of them, unfamiliar but welcome, and Trystan found herself grinning with fiercely relieved anticipation.

Within moments, they gained the top of the hill, revealing only rolling downs ahead, green and rippling in the morning sun. It was perfect. On open ground, Theron would leave the encroaching rider in the dust, wishing his horse had wings. Trystan gave Theron his head, shifted her weight and tapped him with her heels. He needed no further encouragement, but shot forward, as if eager to leave the forest behind.

Caught up in the glory of sun and speed, Trystan's first warning of danger was Theron's ears, pinned tightly to his head. Glancing back, she received an unwelcome shock. The other rider was no more than ten lengths behind and gaining. He was also clearly male and intent upon catching her.

A thrill of fear shot through her chest. Whether he meant her any personal harm or not, she must not be caught! It became a race in earnest, and Trystan used any advantage she could. Theron was unmatched in the hunt, so she took every opportunity to lead the breathless chase over stone walls, brush hedges, even once a narrow brook, but with little success.

When it became evident that her horse could go no farther, Trystan pulled Theron back to a trot, and then a stumbling walk. His sides were lathered and heaving, and her own legs were trembling with weariness. There would be no outrunning the trouble she was in this time. All she could do was pray she'd be able talk her way out of it instead.

Sliding gracelessly from the saddle, Trystan was forced for the first time in years to steady herself against Theron's shoulder. She caught up his reins and kept walking, pretending to ignore the horseman who drew up on her left, determined not to acknowledge her unease at his proximity. His horse, she noted with some satisfaction, was also sweating and breathing hard, only marginally better off than Theron.

"What the devil was that?" her pursuer demanded, clearly too angry to bother with conventional social niceties. No 'good morning' or 'how do you do.' The arrogant clod actually thought he had a right to question her. Irritation overwhelmed instinct, and Trystan stopped to glare up at him in spite of herself.

The man appeared perfectly ordinary. He was perhaps a few years older than herself and of middling height, with a square-shouldered, workmanlike build. Trystan noted that he carried himself well in the saddle, with a good seat and light hands. Short, wind-tousled brown hair and direct gray eyes dominated what might have been a rather nice face, had it not been hard and set with anger. She could not immediately identify his station, at least not by his dress. His clothes were not so dissimilar from hers, of simple cloth and cut, in an unremarkable color. Probably not a forester.

It occurred to her at some point during her perusal that the man was returning her scrutiny. An expression of surprised uncertainty dawned across his features as he studied her. Trystan felt an unwanted blush spread across her cheeks as she realized that he was far too close to be fooled by her attire. Some of the anger faded from the man's eyes, though he still looked piqued.

"Were you trying to kill a perfectly good horse or just break your neck?" More reproof than question, his words stung Trystan into making a reply.

"I don't know you and I don't care for your company," she answered coldly, returning her gaze to the landscape with what she hoped was evident disdain. "How I choose to care for my horse is my own affair, which I'll thank you to stay out of."

Silence was the only immediate reply. Trystan discovered an irrational urge to know whether the man felt appropriately reprimanded, but refused to give him the satisfaction of appearing to expect a response.

"What were you doing in the king's forest?" Perhaps he'd been silent out of a need to restrain his temper, because his question echoed with command rather than contrition.

"And what business is it of yours?" Trystan snapped back, now well beyond irritated. "The forest has always been free, unless you care to accuse me of poaching." She swung to face him and held up empty hands to indicate her evident lack of stolen game. "As that is clearly ridiculous, I hope you'll acknowledge your discourtesy and leave me in peace."

The man's scrutiny grew momentarily more intense, but ended abruptly with shrug and a brief quirk of his lips. "You are, in fact, correct," he acknowledged with a nod. "I apologize. You appeared out of place, and as I regularly visit the woods, I felt it my duty to investigate." He let out a deep sigh that sounded like concession. "As you say, your errand is your own. Please forgive me for frightening you."

Somewhat mollified, but still feeling the vulnerability of her position, Trystan was no less determined to get rid of the encroaching stranger. If nothing else, perhaps she could ignore him to death.

Subsiding into a dignified silence, she turned and walked away. Theron needed time to recover from his headlong flight, and without encouragement, perhaps the other rider would simply give up and move on. She walked on for several minutes, trying to recapture some sense of peace. The sun was warm, and there were no sounds but birds overhead and hooves in the tall grass. It ought to have been a pleasant interlude, but it proved difficult to feel very pleased when her companion showed no signs of growing bored. If anything, he gave every evidence of complacent enjoyment of the situation, trailing in her wake with a loose rein while chewing on a grass stem. Trystan had no choice but to stop and glower at him in bemused frustration.

"Why are you still here?"

The strange man looked back with an expression of mild surprise. "I suppose I'm still hoping you'll accept my apology." His quick and slightly rueful grin made him appear more mischievous than apologetic. "Or satisfy my curiosity. Or perhaps both, if I can manage to be sufficiently contrite."

Trystan could not immediately produce a response. She had only limited experience with men in general, and owed much of what she did have to the occasional observation of her stepsisters' prospective suitors. They tended to be foolish and self-absorbed, far more adept at flattery than honesty, despite the benefit of wealth and education. This man, though he was dressed as poorly as she, seemed to possess both authority and wit. Neither a fool nor a flatterer, he was far more dangerous to Trystan's peace of mind than any other man of her acquaintance, narrow though it was.

At this point, her forward progress was impeded by a stone wall, which Theron was clearly too tired to hurdle. Rather than walk alongside it, Trystan decided to pretend that the wall had been her destination all along. With only a small effort, she pulled herself up and sat on the wide top, swinging her reins idly as if to rest.

The strange rider rested both hands on his pommel as he watched, then rewarded her efforts to ignore him with a self-deprecating laugh. "Do you know, it has been some time since I have been quite so determinedly repulsed," he admitted, in an alarmingly cheerful voice. To Trystan's dismay, he proceeded to dismount and seat himself a few feet away from her on the wall. "But," he continued, "I daresay poor Parsifal here could use the rest."

Despite her consternation, Trystan could not help eyeing his tall bay mare with some surprise. She darted one brief glance at his face to see if he was, in fact, serious.

"Yes," he replied to her unspoken question, with a sheepish look that suggested he knew exactly what she was thinking. "Parsifal. I'm afraid I let my cousins name her, and was too preoccupied to assert beforehand that she was a *girl* horse."

Trystan laughed before she had time to think better of it. She'd had no intention of encouraging the man, but it felt like a very long time since she last laughed. "Girl horse or not," Trystan found herself admitting, albeit grudgingly, "I've not seen many who could keep up with Theron. She's beautiful."

Her companion grinned like a proud father. "She's something, isn't she?" He patted the mare's nose fondly, then threw a quick, sideways glance at Trystan. "Though I confess I've not met many young women who could tell a hunter from a hack."

So he was admitting that he had seen through her disguise. Trystan's apprehension, nearly forgotten in the midst of laughter, came surging back. She fell stiffly silent and wondered if she should simply get up and walk away.

To her surprise, the man seemed to sense her uneasiness. "I don't intend to eat you, you know." Startled by this absurdity, Trystan turned her gaze on her companion, whose wry expression made Trystan wonder if he had read her mind. "I only devour young maidens when there's no other food to be had," he promised solemnly, "and as I likewise have no designs on your virtue, can we be friends?"

His expression was so hopeful that Trystan could not quite bring herself to walk away. Yet. It was tempting to return his disarmingly lopsided smile with an amused smile of her own. And to wonder what it might be like to actually have a friend. What a pity that her need for anonymity prevented her from taking the idea seriously.

"You're a complete stranger who began our acquaintance with intolerable rudeness," Trystan answered, not entirely certain whether there were any actual guidelines for behavior in situations such as this. "I don't know your name and I'm not about to tell you mine, and in any case, there is no one suitable to introduce us. I don't see how we can be friends under the circumstances." She could not explain, even to herself, the strange and illogical desire to not rebuff him completely.

She needn't have worried. The young man waved a dismissive hand, apparently unmoved by her objections.

"I'm certain there is a way to resolve these difficulties," he assured her. "It is perfectly within the bounds of etiquette to refer to you as 'my lady' or perhaps to hail you from afar as 'hey there, you with the gray horse!' I'm sure we could hold perfectly logical conversations if you would only consent to provide such titles for me in return." The gravity of his expression was ruined by a gleam of what Trystan suspected was amusement in his eyes.

"Perhaps," Trystan replied, in a suitably prim voice, "but I was taught to be polite. I couldn't possibly call you any of the things that have thus far come to mind." To the man's credit, he appeared to try very hard to remain solemn, but failed, his expression dissolving rapidly into delighted laughter.

"I begin to think you disapprove of me," he offered, as soon as he was able, though he did not seem much distressed by the possibility.

"Yes," Trystan answered baldly, "and I can only hope the experience will have an improving effect on your manners. Though," she added, "I suspect the opposite will prove true."

"No doubt you're right," the man returned, with unquenchable cheerfulness. "But I do believe you are stalling. If we're to continue this conversation with even the slightest pretensions to decorum, we must establish what form of address you mean to use for the duration."

"Oh, very well," Trystan folded her arms and feigned disgust. "I suppose I could find some sort of label for you. If you insist." She paused as if to consider. "I'm partial to 'disagreeably inquisitive' myself, but 'self-satisfied prat' would serve just as well. I'll let you decide." She shoved her nose in the air and tried to look haughty, but the effect was rather spoiled by the grin that pulled irresistibly at the corner of her mouth. For some reason, it was suddenly very difficult to remain angry. Or serious.

Instead of being quite reasonably affronted, her companion only choked on another laugh. "I confess, I find it rather lowering to be thought disagreeable, or self-satisfied, but I am quite unable to argue with your other sentiments. And so, my lady," he continued hopefully, "might I inquire whither you were bound this fine morning?"

Trystan raised an eyebrow at his formal tone. "You are welcome to inquire, but I'm not likely to answer," she admitted. "I try to avoid being seen, for obvious reasons." She gestured to her clothing. "In truth, I'm probably a fool to be talking to you at all. Before too long, I'm sure to say something I shouldn't. Well," she amended, "something else I shouldn't. Your conversation seems to bring out the worst in me."

Her companion feigned an expression of affronted dignity. "But I've been the very model of propriety," he protested, "and I said I wasn't going to eat you. If I'd had any dishonorable intentions, which I didn't, let me assure you I'm now much too terrified to act upon them. What are you afraid of?"

Trystan was tempted to smile, but she could not afford to let him distract her again.

"Nothing." She tried to brush the question aside, while admitting to herself that what she was doing was dangerous. She could not remember seeing the man before, but what if he had seen her? What if he could guess who she was? By his dress and demeanor, he was probably some young lord's groom, a man who might have crossed her path during past hunts with her father.

Then again, his cousins had named the horse, so possibly he was the young lord himself, slumming in the Kingswood before breakfast. The idea almost made her smile in spite of herself. But her continued silence would do nothing to dispel suspicion. She had to say something. Anything, as long as it wasn't the truth.

"Do you know"—she turned and accosted him abruptly—"I think it's most unfair that you've been asking all the questions." Which was true, she realized. He had been friendly, but hardly forthcoming. "It seems unchivalrous to expect a lady to declare her name and intentions first." Unfortunately, it sounded like exactly what it was: an attempt to deflect the man's persistent curiosity.

"Not very sporting," he noted, "but not precisely unjustified, either." He sighed, looked off across the downs, then glanced at her and offered what sounded oddly like an apology: "It seems I'm not so very anxious to lose my anonymity either. I suspect we are at a social impasse."

Trystan was surprised by his acuity, but not his reluctance. A young nobleman, if this was in fact his secret, would hardly want a wild young woman of uncertain origins showing up to embarrass him in front of his family.

"Perhaps I should assure *you*," she said dryly, "that you have nothing to fear from me."

He looked at her in surprise, then appeared stricken as he realized what direction her thoughts had taken. "Don't be daft," he said, swinging the tips of his reins at her in mock retribution. "That wasn't meant to warn you off."

"Then why?" Trystan asked, her curiosity getting the better of her tongue. "And don't pretend that you fear censure. Young men are encouraged to be independent. What would it matter if you were known to have committed the terrible crime of chasing mysterious persons across a cow pasture before breakfast?" Her slightly bitter tone failed to get a rise out of her companion.

"Because, for me as much as for you, the whole point of being out here is to be unknown. To be free of life's burdens, if only for a few hours." He shook his head at her. "Don't make the mistake of believing that all young men are at liberty to do as we please. We may bear different expectations, but they are binding just the same."

Abashed, Trystan considered an apology, but her companion's expression held no judgment.

"It is nothing to do with you, I swear it," he promised solemnly. "On a day like today, I would refuse my name to a squirrel." Trystan choked on a laugh as he continued. "I know it seems a rather pathetic rebellion," he admitted, "but sometimes I tire of being what I must. I have judged it better to risk my reputation than to risk becoming a tiresome, predictable curmudgeon before I'm thirty."

It was an echo of Trystan's own, scarcely understood fears. What if she never escaped her life? What would she become if she lost even the freedom of these occasional rides? Could she survive without any hope that life might someday be different?

An unguarded glance at her companion produced an entirely unexpected rush of emotion she could not readily identify. It might even have been liking. Though it should have been impossible to feel such a thing for an inquisitive, self-satisfied prat.

"I fear," Trystan said lightly, hoping to disguise her own consternation, "you may be too late." He looked startled. "But even a tiresome, predictable curmudgeon is entitled to the occasional day off."

The man put on a pained expression and pressed a hand to his heart. "You wound me, lady. How have I offended thee, to deserve such callous disregard?"

Trystan giggled. "Stop making me laugh," she protested. "It isn't dignified, especially when we've only just met."

"Dignity," he replied, "is highly over-rated. Besides, how can we have just met? We never once spoke of the weather or complimented one another on our sartorial splendor. It seems obvious to me that we've known each other for ages."

He was joking of course, but the joke was not without truth. Perhaps she did not feel as though she knew him, but she did feel as though she wanted to. Which was ridiculous. They both had too many secrets.

And, as she had to keep telling herself, she couldn't possibly like him. This unfamiliar feeling was nothing but her own longing for a friend. Someone who could know her, and someone who could be known in return. This man could not possibly be that person. They may have shared feelings, but they did not even dare share their names. There could be nothing here for either of them but pretense, which would likely end in pain. It was long past time for her to leave the stranger behind.

Without making any reply, Trystan hopped off the wall and looped her reins back over Theron's ears in preparation to retreat. The gelding was still tired, but if they kept to a walk he would cool off in time. Grasping her stirrup, she realized too late that she would have to climb back on the wall if she hoped to mount. Muttering under her breath, she turned around and caught the eye of her companion, who was, curse him, watching her with a look that was both hopeful and worried.

"Did I offend you?" he asked suddenly. "I assure you it was not my intention to be insultingly familiar. If I have frightened you again I apologize."

Trystan drew a quick breath, astonished anew by both his perceptiveness and his readiness to apologize to a woman whose appearance and manner gave him no reason to assume her a lady. "I am neither offended, nor insulted, nor frightened," she said as evenly as possible. "Merely struck by the absurdity of this conversation." She flung up an arm in frustration. "We speak to one another like friends, but dare not reveal our names! It is irrational and untenable and…" She hunted for a better word. "Utterly pointless!" Not her most eloquent moment. "I have only this one day to escape my life and I am not willing to spend it in a way I might regret."

She spoke heatedly and too hastily and realized as she finished that her words could easily have wounded, but the man on the wall did not reply angrily or walk away. She met his gaze without meaning to, and it held only a look of grave concern.

"You are right, of course," he said, descending from his own perch on the wall and running a weary hand through already rumpled hair. "We should be about our own pursuits." His mouth quirked ruefully. "I hope my detaining you has not marred your day beyond repair?"

Trystan looked back at him with a hopeless mixture of confusion and amusement and what she admitted to herself was regret. She wished he was someone she could have known.

"My peace of mind, perhaps, but not my day. And if only I had a mounting block even my mind might be significantly restored." She feigned a cheerfulness she did not feel, but neither of them was fooled.

Expecting an equally inane reply, she was taken aback when the strange man only walked to the side of her horse, knelt there in the grass, and cupped his hands for her foot, much as Andrei or Alexei might have done.

Trystan backed away, unable to conceal her shock. "No! You cannot... I'm not... stop it!" It was unnerving, how he seemed to confound her expectations at every turn. And how he managed to look so unruffled, kneeling there in the dirt, making her feel so provincial for her protestation.

"I don't see why not," he replied reasonably, "unless you mean to insult my ability to support such a tiny creature as you, in which case I protest. Strenuously." He meant to make her laugh again. She would have laughed had she not been undone by his selfless act of courtesy. Open mouthed, she stared at him for long enough that he lifted a brow at her in mock annoyance.

"My lady, are you going to mount up or not?" he demanded. "My knee is getting wet."

Trystan blushed, hated herself for blushing, and hastily put her left boot in his hands, wincing mentally at the worn muddiness of it, hating herself again for noticing. She actually closed her eyes in confusion as he tossed her up, as easily as if she were a bird instead of a girl. Hiding her embarrassment by fiddling with her reins and stirrups, she turned to thank him and depart, only to find that he had mounted his own horse and sat looking at her expectantly.

"Thank you," she forced out, "for..." she stopped. What *was* she thanking him for?

"For chasing you, waylaying you, delaying you, and irritating you? You're welcome."

She glared at him, but without actual heat. He was, in a way, absolutely accurate. So why had she felt compelled to thank him? For making her smile? For making her laugh? For taking her outside of her life if only for a few sunlit moments on a stone wall in the middle of... The middle of where?

She took a look around her and swore, rather forcefully, as

she realized what he had probably already figured out. She was lost. Her headlong flight had left her solidly in the middle of unfamiliar farm country, miles from recognizable landmarks, with an exhausted horse.

When she looked back at him, the wretched man only raised his eyebrows and grinned in appreciation of her less-than-decorous language.

"Dare I observe," he stated carefully, "that you may in fact be in need of directions?"

"I don't know," Trystan responded irritably. "Do you dare?" It would have been so very satisfying at that point to ride off in a huff, but it would most likely only prove more embarrassing later. Perhaps she should settle for being grateful that someone was there to point her in the right direction. Sighing in resignation she turned Theron around. "All right, fine," she answered without much grace. "I'm lost. But I'm obviously not going to tell you where I live. So," she conceded, "would you be so kind as to direct me to the King's Tree?"

The man's eyes widened fractionally, while he tried not to smile. "Ah..." He took a moment to clear his throat conspicuously. "Where exactly did you expect the Tree to be?"

Trystan reddened yet again. She was certain she had never in her life blushed so many times in a single day. "It's hardly my fault that some strange man attempted to waylay me in the middle of the Kingswood," she groused back, loathe to admit her stupidity. "One cannot simply ask any suspicious-looking person they should happen to encounter for directions."

Her newly appointed guide favored her with a quirky expression, not of triumph, but of genuine, good-natured amusement. "Not to worry, my lady." He accompanied his words with a bow that managed to appear courtly, even from the saddle. "It so happens that I was headed in that very direction myself when we met, so... ah... precipitously? I would be delighted to make amends for causing you dismay."

Trystan hesitated. She knew very well she should say no. She should ask him for simple directions and ride away, leaving behind her embarrassment, her uncertainty, and a man who was so unexpectedly kind that she could not bear to deny him again.

Resigned to her own foolishness, she nodded, carefully ignoring the silly little leap of happiness in her chest.

"I accept," she said.

CHAPTER 2

*H*is Royal Highness Prince Ramsey Donevan Tremontaine rode homeward through the Kingswood at a brisk trot, feeling rather guilty. His clandestine early-morning exit from Evenburg Castle had been nothing if not un-princely, but he had been desperate. The past week had been more than usually exhausting, both mentally and physically, and he would have done far worse than sneak out of his rooms for the privilege of a few hours alone to clear his head.

Ramsey had always been a private person, and the past ten years of his increasingly public life had taught him the true value of solitude. It was the one prerogative of his position that he protected with every resource at his royal command. When royal command was no longer enough, he was more than willing to resort to subterfuge.

The plan had been simple: instruct his valet that he was officially still asleep, steal away, ride to the woods and return before the court finished breakfast. As long as he returned by mid-morning, no one else would be awake enough to miss him.

It was a good plan, and one that Ramsey had frequently put into practice during the busiest seasons at court, when the constant barrage of people and their concerns fatigued him beyond bearing. Even when court was nearly empty, the incessant arguments between councilors, guild leaders and the king occasionally drove him to make his escape. After a few hours of peace and quiet he would return, to silently resume the burdens of a life he had never wanted. As long as he was careful, Ramsey's escapes hurt no one, and ensured that he was able to meet his numerous obligations with at least the appearance of equanimity.

But those escapes had never before resulted in such a shameful neglect of his responsibilities. It was now well past luncheon. Ramsey had missed at least two meetings and a formal presentation, and by this time was no doubt the subject of a great deal of speculation.

He was supposed to be the reliable one. The respectable one. The prince who didn't make mistakes. As much as he regretted the lapse, Ramsey considered that perhaps this would teach the court to remember that he was human.

As the path they followed emerged from the wood and approached the crossroads, Parsifal dropped to a walk and swiveled one dark ear in her rider's direction. To return, or not to return?

Ramsey's lips quirked in wry amusement. Even his horse could tell how badly he wanted to escape his life. With a gentle nudge of his heel, the prince directed his mare down the broad, smooth Crown road towards Evenleigh. Towards home, and whatever dire consequences awaited him.

The king was going to be furious. Ramsey's father had been perpetually irascible for weeks, probably due to the crippling combination of intransigent guild leaders and a resurgence of gout. The king's patience was short at the best of times, which these were emphatically not. This particular transgression would doubtless lead to an irate lecture about the dignity and safety of the crown, among other things.

If Ramsey was very careful, he might get through it without yawning.

It wasn't that he didn't care. The gods alone knew how deeply he cared about his kingdom and what became of it. But there were times that he wished he was someone else. That the weight of his people's every trouble, every quibble, every squabble, could have fallen on another set of shoulders. As it should have done.

A familiar bitterness rose in Ramsey's throat. No one seemed to understand that he had never cared for the dignity or privilege of his position. Even as a boy, he had desired little more than a quiet, private life, a life he had been taught to believe would be his. As the younger son, he had been considered largely expendable. A spare, in case of emergencies.

Unfortunately, Prince Rowan Tremontaine had turned out to be an emergency.

The clatter of wheels on the road behind him prompted Ramsey to rein his mount closer to the grassy margin of the thoroughfare. He turned to look over his shoulder as an elegant black barouche barreled past him at a smart clip, bearing a fashionable set of young people—one gentleman and three ladies. Two of the ladies turned to look at him as they passed, wearing puzzled looks that Ramsey suspected would soon turn to horrified recognition.

Had they really just seen their crown prince, riding alone on the side of the road like a common stablehand? Ramsey mentally added "behavior unbefitting" to the very long list of the day's misdeeds. It would no doubt be discussed at length during his upcoming tongue-lashing.

Where he was sure to be reminded of his most important duty: to remain above reproof. To retain the confidence of his people. After his elder brother's scandalous career, there was little room for Ramsey to err.

Urging Parsifal into a trot, Ramsey continued down the road in the wake of the now-distant barouche, mentally bidding his solitude farewell. He was not far now from the edge of the city, and the road would not remain so empty for long. Already, the houses grew more numerous and clustered more closely together. Soon, houses would give way to businesses, to the tightly-packed and thickly-peopled streets of Evenleigh. Even thinking of it made Ramsey feel tired.

But not as tired as before. Even his guilt stung less when he considered the events of his entirely unexpected morning.

A smile crossed Ramsey's lips, unbidden, as he imagined telling the tale at court. They would never believe him. Who, after all, would credit the notion of a prince who chased miscreants about the wood on horseback? Even worse would be their dismay should he be fool enough to relate the aftermath of that indiscretion. The confrontation. The conversation that followed. And the woman, who had so inexplicably lightened his heart.

She was completely unlike the other women he knew. And it wasn't as though he lacked experience. Ramsey may have been quiet and reserved, but he was also royal. Since being declared heir to the throne he had been introduced to an uncomfortable number of females, many of whom seemed to cherish fond hopes of marrying their way into a crown. At least to Ramsey's mind, their assiduous and utterly insincere attempts to capture his attention made it rather difficult to tell one from another.

But this young woman had been nothing if not original, a bundle of contradictions that Ramsey had not yet managed to decipher.

She had ties to a noble house, of that Ramsey was sure. Her blithe assurance of free passage through the Kingswood betrayed origins that were well-connected, if not legitimate. But neither her clothing nor her mount had matched her manner.

Dressed in some stable-boy's cast-offs, riding a magnificent hunter as though born in the saddle, she had been one moment as imperious as a duchess, and the next embarrassed by a simple courtesy. She spoke with the educated accents of a young woman of rank, though she seemed to possess none of their irritating conversational habits. Her demeanor had been neither coy nor cold, but rather disconcertingly straightforward, favoring honesty over flattery and argument over flirtation. And yet she had somehow managed to hide more than she revealed.

As he drew closer to town, Ramsey was forced to devote more of his attention to navigating the bewildering crowd of riders and wheeled vehicles. It was mid-afternoon, and the traffic would be at its peak. Parsifal, fortunately, was unimpressed by crowds or noise, and cared nothing for assessing, sidelong glances. Of which Ramsey could expect a fair number. The people in and around Evenleigh knew him by sight, and would be watching his progress through town with avid curiosity.

Ramsey hated being stared at. Hated the scrutiny that came with his position. Which, he could admit, probably accounted for much of his fascination with the woman he had met that morning. He was not accustomed to conversing with women unburdened by the shared knowledge of his identity. Her apparent ignorance of his rank had presented a rare opportunity to converse freely, without wondering what the other person might want from him. The experience had been immensely refreshing.

But the freedom he felt had involved more than the simple novelty of anonymity. Ramsey could not yet account for the bizarre conviction that he knew this girl. Not that he had met her before, but that they understood one another. For perhaps the first time in his life, he had talked to a female his own age and their conversation had been something more than a painful search for a topic that suited both participants.

Since leaving her, Ramsey had failed miserably in his efforts to achieve the peace of mind he had sought when setting out that morning. Instead, his stubborn mind insisted upon returning to a girl who tried unsuccessfully to hide beauty behind shapeless clothes. To disguise deep vulnerability with a fiery temper. She had met his eyes, amber to gray, and left him shaken. She had seen him, truly seen him, and the result could only be painful for both of them.

Ramsey knew she could be nothing to him. He was pragmatic enough to admit that she was probably an illegitimate child, or perhaps the daughter of an indigent nobleman. An unnamed woman wearing a man's clothes and riding unescorted through the Kingswood was hardly an acceptable friend for a prince who could not afford to make mistakes.

Prince Rowan, despite his insouciance towards the succession, still had his supporters. They were few but vocal in repudiation of their favorite's disinheritance, and would exploit any weakness on Ramsey's part without a moment's hesitation. This unknown girl's acquaintance was precisely the sort of transgression they would take great delight in pointing out. If their objections could even be heard amidst the din of his own father's explosive objections.

And anyway, the girl was gone, and had given him no encouragement to pursue the acquaintance. He would never see her again, and would no doubt forget her quickly enough as he became ever more absorbed in the pressing details of economic unrest, his brother's indiscretions and his father's impatient temper.

Ramsey couldn't afford distractions. Especially not attractive female distractions with exquisite taste in horses.

Reduced to rolling his eyes at his own idiocy, Ramsey pressed his mare forward and tried to think about something else. Anything else.

∽

Too soon, Parsifal's hooves echoed on cobblestone, as they made their way slowly through the crowded streets of the city. Too soon Ramsey spotted the stocky, gray-haired and green-coated guardsman waiting at the next corner for him to draw even.

Brawley. Looking harried and resigned.

"Your Highness, you promised." The horses fell in beside each other without a fuss.

"No, Brawley, I didn't," Ramsey answered wearily. "I said I'd think about it, and I did."

"This is thinking about it?" Brawley had been the captain of the princes' guard since Ramsey was five, and the years had worn their exchanges to a blunt familiarity Ramsey treasured. Most of the time.

"This is me *not* running mad, Brawley. The rest of the world can either deal with it or stop pretending I'm supposed to be a saint."

"I never asked you to give up riding, Your Highness." Brawley's persistence was one of the man's most useful characteristics. When it wasn't being used against his prince. "Only that you tell me when you go and take a guard."

"Which would necessarily defeat the purpose of being *alone*," replied Ramsey, "and therefore be a waste of time for all of us. Stop worrying. I only ride in the Kingswood and you did train me to take care of myself."

Brawley eyed his charge with evident disgust. "I tried," he snorted. "About the only thing I can say for you is that you paid more attention than your brother."

Ramsey sensed defeat in this admission and decided to exploit it, hoping to cajole his guard captain into a better mood. The last thing he needed was another lecture. "You were an impeccable teacher," he insisted, "and you know I was a better than average student." He offered Brawley a disarming grin. "And of course there's Parsifal to consider. If you can name me one horse that can outrun her I'll repent."

Brawley's lips twisted sourly. "No, Your Highness, you would go out and buy the other horse and keep disappearing."

Ramsey shrugged, a tacit admission of agreement, containing not a shred of repentance. He regretted disappointing and inconveniencing his keeper, but the two of them had had this discussion many times in the past few months. Especially since the economic troubles had fueled further discontent over the issue of the succession.

Prince Rowan was not only the elder, but had always been more popular amongst the younger, more ambitious members of the peerage. Of late their stridently vocal minority had grown, both in size and volume. They now numbered among their ranks a startling percentage of the merchant nobility, who claimed to fear the precedent of passing over a legitimate and healthy heir. Considering that none of them had shown much inclination to care ten years ago when King Hollin first announced his decision, their current complaints seemed as spurious as they were suspicious.

Despite the lack of any discernible uniting force amongst the dissenters, the increasingly volatile rhetoric had convinced the king and his advisors that there was some danger to the heir's well-being, and Brawley took this suspicion very seriously. Ramsey remained unconcerned. Andar was a relatively peaceful kingdom, and wars had been rare throughout its history. He could not really imagine anyone committing violence against his person for the sake of his unconscionable brother. Especially since Rowan had never indicated publicly that he was anything less than pleased with the present situation.

Which made the outcry for his reinstatement all the more absurd. While Ramsey would be the first to agree that his own abilities were not an ideal match for his position, he also knew his brother too well to consider abdicating. Ramsey might not have wanted to be king, but neither could he stomach the idea of his kingdom's fate resting in the hands of a charming, opportunistic wastrel.

"Anything I should know before we get back?" Ramsey asked his captain, not really wanting the answer, but knowing his daylong absence had no doubt provoked some degree of chaos.

Brawley didn't answer for a few moments, never a good sign. "The guilds are restless," he finally reported. "I know that's not news, but I think His Majesty needs to take it more seriously. This morning's collection of petitions sounded more like demands."

Ramsey groaned in exasperation. "They always sound like

demands. I think they're required to include a threat of some kind, even if it's worded politely. What are they fussing about this time?"

Brawley just looked thoughtful. "Well, the Vintners Guild is politely requesting that if you are to be the heir, you must give more serious consideration to securing the succession."

Ramsey muttered a few half-hearted curses under his breath. Someone or other had been trying to force him into marriage since he had come of age at eighteen. He had managed to put it off for seven years, and resented the effort to bully him into it now. That he agreed it was probably time was no consolation. "That's nothing new, Brawley. If you remember, I had my first betrothal offer when I was five. What else?"

"A coalition, of sorts," Brawley answered, looking and sounding perplexed. "I'd have said the guilds would never agree on anything but it appears I'd have been wrong. As you know, there's been more agreement than usual on several issues that have come up the last few months, and now…"

Ramsey waited. Given time, Brawley could usually see to the heart of a matter, oftentimes better than the councilors who were paid to do just that.

"Four guilds have banded together, put their names to a single petition."

Ramsey's eyes narrowed in thought. "I'm guessing they want trade concessions?"

Brawley nodded in brusque approval. "Yes and no," he answered, obviously pleased that his prince had guessed correctly. "It's actually worse. Probably the most direct challenge your father has ever faced."

"Challenging Father?" Ramsey whistled in disbelief, or possibly admiration. He'd not thought the guild representatives possessed so much temerity. "Don't they know he's been in a mood for the past month? Or that he and Rowan are clashing worse than usual right now?"

"Aye, they do," Brawley growled darkly, "and it's plain they don't care. They've pulled together, put on a convincing show of solidarity, telling His Majesty, not asking, that they want him to relinquish responsibility for the laws governing imports and exports."

Ramsey was prince enough to prevent his jaw from dropping, but only just. "They want... have they gone mad?"

Brawley shook his head grimly. "My sources suggest not. They actually seem to have won the support of better than half the guilds with an interest in foreign trade, though most of them are waiting to see how the king responds before they go public."

"They want complete control over trade law!" Ramsey's brows lowered ominously. "They can't possibly think Father would be fool enough to grant it. There's something else they're after." He considered for a moment. "This is about Caelan, isn't it?" Brawley was silent. "Caelan..." Ramsey continued, his expression thoughtful. "They're going to ask for a reversal on the ban, aren't they?" Brawley still said nothing, but he didn't have to. Ramsey could read the grim expression on his captain's face. "Half-wits," Ramsey muttered, making little effort to quash his annoyance.

Caelan was their neighbor to the east, a large, powerful country that had all but ignored them for years. Andar had always been too small, too poor, and too surrounded by mountains. There had never been much point in conquest, even if one of their neighbors had been inclined to try. But a few years before Ramsey was born, all of that had begun to change.

Silver was discovered near the south Andari coast. Vast deposits of it. A new class of merchant nobility had emerged, and with it a sense of economic discontent. While the wealth had vastly improved the people's standard of living, it had also given rise to several unpleasant consequences.

The luxuries market, until that point fairly small, had expanded enormously, almost overnight. Fine wines, exotic furs, elaborate jewelry, and fabulous delicacies had become the greatest concerns amongst the wealthier classes, and their burgeoning appetites had engendered a growing clamor for access to an ever wider range of commodities. The answer, of course, was trade. Andar had quickly established diplomatic relations with several nations eager to benefit from their neighbor's new prosperity. But not with Caelan, despite the polite overtures of numerous Caelani ambassadors. King Hollin had flatly refused to even discuss the possibility.

The king did not object to trade, or to prosperity, but he did object to slavery, and Caelan had long been known as a place where you could buy or sell anything, including men, women and children. King Hollin remained adamant in his insistence that Andar not gain from such a disgusting practice, either directly or indirectly. Unfortunately, all that most of the court could see was the king's obstinate refusal to permit them access to the most convenient source of fantastic and exotic goods from all corners of the known world. He had even closed the borders and put guards on the passes that led through the eastern mountains. This unyielding stance had proven to be a matter for increasing contention and concern. The merchant guilds were showing a swiftly diminishing degree of deference in their demands to have the ban reversed. And there were other, clearer heads amongst the nobility who feared that Andar's refusal to appease their larger, hungrier neighbor might lead to far more dangerous consequences than the petty wrath of a few blustering guild leaders.

Had Andar not been bordered on three sides by mountains and on the fourth by an easily defensible ocean harbor, Ramsey might have shared their worries. As it was, Andar was still too small, too isolated, and possessed of only the one commodity. He could not imagine anyone risking war for so little gain.

Ramsey glanced over at Brawley, trying to guess from his captain's expression just how much chaos was waiting for him at home. "Is Father howling for my head?" Ramsey ventured to ask.

"Only since just after sunrise."

"What joy is mine," the prince groaned. "I suppose I'd better go face my doom."

"Your just desserts, more like," Brawley responded acerbically. His prince didn't answer, only exhaled wearily and pushed his horse just a little faster up the rising road towards home.

Evenburg Castle and its grounds sprawled self-consciously at the top of a gradual rise in the terrain, backed up against the gentle green hills of crown lands. The rise on which it was built had, over the centuries, been covered by the haphazard sprawl of Evenleigh Township.

The gray stone walls and towers of Evenburg had been Ramsey's place of residence for much of his life. He had also spent several years in the country, at Tremontaine House, a rambling brick manor which he considered far more truly his home. The castle was pleasant enough to look at, but it was often cold, somewhat drafty, and the near-perpetual presence of the court made it difficult for Ramsey to feel quite comfortable there.

Especially now, when the two most visible members of his family were so much at odds with each other.

As Parsifal trotted leisurely through the always open gates, Ramsey was greeted by waves, salutes, and more than a few mocking cheers by both guardsmen and acquaintances, indicating he was probably in even more trouble than he had anticipated. Dismounting reluctantly, he handed off the reins to a hastily arrived groom, just as a short, stocky blond man in training leathers fell in beside him.

"All I can say is, I hope she was worth it."

Ramsey stopped walking across the bailey to stare, bemusedly, at his smirking friend. "Kyril, what the devil are you talking about?"

"Whoever it was kept you out all day." The younger man's grin threatened to split his ears. "Had to have been a woman. And here's your father having one of his gouty days." He cocked his head to one side as if considering. "Though if she's promised to marry you he may forgive you for everything."

"My friend, one of these days your imagination is going to get you into trouble of a sharp and metallic nature," Ramsey muttered, feeling a bit shaken by his friend's lucky guess and not at all willing to admit that it had hit the mark.

"And you, Your Liegeness, are going to have such a headache when your father and advisors are finished with you that you're unlikely to remember promising to do me bodily harm."

Ramsey took a swing at the insouciant young nobleman, and missed. Mostly on purpose. Kyril had hung about him for years when they were children, a clumsy, undersized boy who wanted badly to be included. The prince had taken pity on him and quickly grew to appreciate the younger child's cheerful nature and unquestioning loyalty. Since they had both come of age, Kyril had grown into a fun-loving friend, a highly competent swordsman, and an even more competent flirt. And possibly the only person at court that Ramsey trusted with his secrets, as well as his life.

But not this time. For some reason, Ramsey could not bring himself to talk, even to Kyril, about what had happened to him that day.

"Someday," he growled, "I'm going to have you locked up for insubordination. And disrespect. And anything else I can think of. Which is a lot."

Kyril just laughed, which he did often and easily. As the two of them reached the far side of the bailey and entered the castle, Kyril peeled off with a wave of his hand. "Think I'll leave you to this, Your Exaltedness." He grinned as he backed away. "Come see me later if you need a cold compress."

Ramsey almost made a rude gesture in his direction, but stopped when he spotted the cohort of his father's councilors headed in his direction down the hall. Sighing deeply, he braced himself and went back to work.

Not very much later, Ramsey was regretting not getting permanently lost in the Kingswood and refusing to come home. He sat in his father's private solar, listening to King Hollin and his first minister continue to argue over the guild situation. His father, though Ramsey loved him a great deal, was a traditionalist. And a deeply irritable one when his gout was acting up.

The king knew why the guilds were making their demands, but he disapproved wholeheartedly of their reasoning, not to mention their underhanded and disrespectful methods. Hollin was not a despot, but he believed in the benevolent authority of the monarchy. He would never sit back tamely while his authority and judgment were questioned.

While Ramsey agreed with many of his father's policies, especially in the matter of slavery, in this case he found himself more in sympathy with the first minister, who insisted that without change, they would be facing grave consequences.

"You simply can't continue to ignore the trade issue," Minister Lavan pressed on. "I've been watching reports from the larger towns, and it isn't only the guilds who are involved. Agents of some of your nobles are seeding doubts about our economic stability, even talking of shortages, and most recently spreading rumors about the incompetence of Prince Ramsey. We have to address this. I realize their methods are underhanded, but we may need to consider discussing some of their demands until we can put these ridiculous ideas to rest. Just until things settle down. You must understand, Your Majesty, there is very real danger."

"I will not pander to these ignorant fools," the king snapped, his foot propped up on a stool while his hand clenched tightly around the head of a cane he used more as a cudgel than a prop. "They would destroy this kingdom with their greed and their blundering and I refuse to be manipulated into helping them do it!"

"Father..." Ramsey tried to break in as a mollifying presence, but his parent turned on him with a vengeance.

"And I will most definitely not listen to the advice of foolish children who insist on trying to break their necks before the succession is secure." The king's neck began to turn red behind his beard as his tirade grew louder. "Is it possible that you've forgotten who will be king if anything happens to you?" He gestured furiously at the window. "You put this entire kingdom at risk with your reckless refusal to give up your reclusive habits."

Ramsey winced internally. He knew very well what his father thought of his preference for solitude.

"You're to be king, boy," the king growled fiercely. "Freedom is no part of your lot. Especially when you use it to run wild in the woods like some silly boy with no respect for the gravity of his position." Ramsey opened his mouth to protest, but his father had no intention of permitting it.

"And what's more,"—Hollin's expression narrowed even further—"my council tells me you persist in refusing to look twice at any of the ladies they've suggested as suitable brides!" His free hand slapped the table with such force that Ramsey started, trying not to trade glares with his father. "Boy, I'm considering trotting out every eligible girl in the kingdom until you stop stalling and choose one."

"I need a wife, Father, not a horse," Ramsey replied sharply, trying not to sound peevish. "So I would appreciate it if you did not speak of her as if she were a brood mare." His father's glower diminished only the tiniest bit as Ramsey continued. "And what good could it possibly do for me to choose a bride who is only using me to get to Rowan?"

King Hollin grunted, unwilling to respond to what they both knew was the truth. Oh, there were plenty of women willing to put up with Ramsey's plain and boring self in exchange for a crown. But his few, youthful forays into romance had all ended similarly: with women who feigned interest in him only until their proximity to the royal family assured them the interest of Rowan. The undeniably handsome and captivating older prince had always proven more than willing to undercut his brother when it came to romance.

Whether Rowan did so out of spite, Ramsey had chosen not to speculate, but the younger prince had yet to meet a woman who could resist Rowan when he chose to exert the charming side of his personality.

Under the circumstances, the last thing the kingdom needed was credible doubt about the paternity of its heir.

"Where is Rowan anyway?" Ramsey asked, too weary to care much for continuing a very old argument.

"Banished to the country," his father answered shortly.

Ramsey's eyebrows went up. "He's at Tremontaine House?"

"His hunting lodge," the king answered, his words oddly clipped.

"With no supervision?" Ramsey almost shuddered at the idea. "There's nothing at Ash Hollow to force him to keep up even the smallest illusion of virtue. The neighborhood won't thank you if he runs amok." His father didn't answer. Only stared towards the window. Ramsey realized something was terribly wrong. "Father?"

"I almost struck your brother today, Ramsey," the king admitted. He did not look at his younger son, but continued to gaze blindly out the window. "Your cousins..." He shook his head slowly. "They don't understand why Rowan is not a larger part of their lives." Ramsey knew only too well. And cared too much for the children to tell them the truth. "Or why they should not trust him."

A cold knot tightened in Ramsey's chest. "Father..." He couldn't even say it.

"Rowan was partying with some friends last night, late. Parry found them on the terrace, smoking their little pipes and behaving like fools."

Ramsey began to feel sick. "What was it this time?" he asked reluctantly. He had little desire to know the details of his brother's disgusting habits.

"Your brother wouldn't say." The king's expression grew fierce. "One of those treacherous weeds they use to muddle their heads. All we know is that Parry was found clutching a pipe and vomiting over the edge of the terrace while the whole miserable crew laughed their addled heads off."

Ramsey's fists clenched instinctively. Parry was only eleven. "Is he… will he…"

The king shook his head. "Boy didn't get much. Just enough to make him see monsters and put him off his food for a day or so. Healer says he's unlikely to develop a dependence after just a few puffs." Ramsey was able to breathe again.

"You don't think… Rowan didn't mean to hurt him?"

Hollin shook his head firmly. "Your brother is a manipulative, self-centered fool, but not a murderer. He claims it was nothing more than a joke."

Ramsey did not bother to hide his skepticism. "But?"

The king's answering expression was flat and empty. "Lizbet says the two of them had words yesterday morning. Less than diplomatic words. She gave him a well-earned scolding for his latest indiscretion… but she did it in a public hallway. Half the court probably heard." The king shrugged, not able or willing to continue, but Ramsey had heard enough.

Lizbet was Ramsey's aunt. His dead mother's sister. Parry was her son. As little as Ramsey wanted to believe it, Rowan may have used a child—his own cousin—to gain his revenge.

"Father, what are we going to do?" The king looked even older as he slumped in his chair and leaned his head against its back.

"I thought I made the best decision, Ramsey." The statement

might not have made sense to anyone else, but Ramsey knew exactly what his father was thinking. What decision had haunted the king for the past ten years. "I saw him using his power to gain his own ends and decided he would never be a good king. I thought it best to tell him then, so that he could grow used to it before the day came. I even thought he had accepted that the crown would never be his. That he was glad of it. But..." King Hollin looked at his younger son, his eyes red, his lips taut with emotion. "What if I was wrong? What if all he needed was my trust to develop into a decent man? What if I... created... *this*?"

"No, Father," Ramsey spoke firmly, taking care to keep his voice from betraying his own pain. Rising from his seat, he made his way swiftly around the table and knelt down to look his father in the eye. "We all loved Rowan, tried to help him, even when we saw him choosing himself over everything. You had to be a father *and* a king and you made the right decision." Ramsey's mouth quirked sadly. "And you know very well I'm not saying that because *I* wanted to be king. I cried the day you told me I was going to have to spend my life sitting in your very uncomfortable chair."

"I wanted to spare you that," his father whispered softly. Ramsey placed a strong, warm hand over his father's cold and furrowed one.

"I know, Da," he whispered back. "I know."

CHAPTER 3

*T*rystan was rather late returning home. She'd lingered at the King's Tree for far too long and nearly lost her way again in the Kingswood. By the time she found her way back to the edge of the manor, it was beginning to grow dark.

After turning Theron loose in one of the horse pastures, she sneaked in through the back of the stables and left her filthy tack in front of Theron's stall with a note of apology. By then it was too close to dinner to sneak in through the kitchen, so she was forced to climb in her window.

Leaving her without enough time to wash. Muttering self-admonitions under her breath, Trystan ripped off her rather pungent riding clothes, stashed her still-dirty boots back under the bed, and pulled on her single respectable dinner gown, a green wool crepe that was nearly two years old. It was wrinkled, her stays were too loose, and she still stank of horse, but to her dismay, Trystan's mind persisted in focusing on something other than her stepmother's disapproval.

Which was dangerous. As she wrestled a brush through her

tangled hair, Trystan tried desperately to remain in the moment. She would need to be sharp at dinner. There were sure to be questions about her day-long absence, and Trystan had no idea what Vianne's "arrangements" had been.

But her attention kept slipping away, dwelling not on thoughts of her birthday, or melancholy memories of her past, but on him. That fascinating, irritating man she would never see again.

He was not one of her stepsisters' suitors, she was sure. She would have remembered. Due to the size of her stepsisters' dowries, quite a number of eligible men had come calling, and all of them were almost excruciatingly dull.

This man had been many things, but never dull.

Their conversation had followed no rules that Trystan had ever been taught. There had been no deceptive pleasantries, no words wasted on pointless flattery. Only truths. They had both had secrets to protect, but what they shared had been honest. She had never, Trystan realized, stopped to consider whether lying would be wiser.

And why not? Even now, she could offer herself no justification. She was no starry-eyed innocent, nor so sunk in despair as to behave entirely without discretion. But when he made her laugh… no, when she realized they laughed at the same things, she could not find it in her to fear him.

At least there was no need to berate herself for being captivated by a handsome face, or an inspiring physique. The man had possessed neither. Not that he was unpleasant to look at, he simply did not conform to traditional ideas of male perfection. And yet… she'd felt drawn to him anyway.

At first he had seemed so ordinary, but then she'd begun to notice other things. Those kind, weary gray eyes. Rebellious brown hair, like a little boy who'd escaped unbrushed. Surprisingly strong, capable hands. Hands that wrapped themselves around her dirty boot as though it were a queen's slipper. And his smile... it seemed determined to trouble her peace. Not just the unexpected beauty of it, but the warmth, that crinkled the corners of his eyes and made it impossible not to smile back. Especially once she had seen behind his smile and found a battered but persistent hopefulness that echoed her own.

As Trystan hastily pinned up her hair and slid on more or less clean slippers, she wondered which disturbed her the most: that she felt like she knew him or that she knew nothing about him? That she would never see him again, or that she wanted to see him again?

With only a moment or so to spare, Trystan bolted out her door, not bothering to be quiet, only concerned that she not miss the gentle chime which signaled the beginning of the evening meal. Malisse was especially unforgiving about lateness, and it would not do to repay Vianne's generosity by failing to honor the cook's one request.

Trystan ran all the way to the dining room, a serious lapse in decorum, but it was late enough that the rest of the family would already be seated within, rather than lurking without to catch her in yet another breach of protocol.

Opening the door with as much haste as propriety permitted, Trystan remembered to cast her eyes down and mince demurely to her seat. She could feel four pairs of eyes following her progress. Three of them glanced away when the chime sounded at the very moment she took her seat and unfolded her starched linen napkin. Glancing up, Trystan happened to meet the eyes of Hoskins, the butler, just as he was beginning to pour the wine. He looked as proper as ever, but his eyes were perhaps a trifle wider than usual. Worried? Had he, too, been a part of Vianne's scheme?

"We are all so pleased that you chose to join us, Trystan."

The deceptively sweet, girlish voice interrupted Trystan's thoughts, in a tone that suggested its owner was not being precisely truthful. Trystan paused for a polite moment before replying.

"I regret having kept you waiting, Stepmother." She could not resist looking up, just then, to see the woman's lips tighten ever so slightly.

Malisse hated being called stepmother. She hated anything that might make her feel, or sound, old. At only thirty-six, Malisse Titania Colbourne was still as slender and shapely as she had been at twenty-six. Her thick, golden hair fell nearly to the floor unbound, without even a hint of silver, thanks to plucking and constant vigilance. Malisse's fine-featured face matched a stature that would barely top Trystan's shoulder, paired with a youthfully curvaceous figure and flawless porcelain skin.

It was little wonder that Lady Colbourne was considered by much of society to be a great beauty, and nearly as marriageable as her daughters. Which, Trystan knew, displeased her stepmother not at all. Malisse quite enjoyed the popularity ensured by her genteel widowhood, and seemed to have little intention of giving up either her popularity or her power by marrying again. As long as her inconvenient stepdaughter remained neatly under her dainty thumb, there was little reason for her to alter what had proven to be quite an agreeable situation.

An incontinent titter intruded on the silence from further down the table. Malisse cast an icy glance at her younger daughter, which Darya did not seem to notice. It would have taken a great deal more than a look to suppress what must surely be said lest she burst.

"I know where you were today, Stepsister!" Another giggle, followed by nudges and whispers.

"Ladies, if you cannot control yourselves, you may be forced to eat in silence." Malisse was coolly controlled as usual. Trystan did not make the mistake of assuming that her stepmother meant to prevent the discussion of her personal shortcomings. If anything, Malisse would go out of her way to make such familial unpleasantness even worse. "If you have something constructive to say," Malisse continued, "I suggest you address all of us."

Trystan rolled her eyes. Discreetly. She was not interested in a lecture on dining decorum. Though Anya and Darya could apparently have used one.

"Tryssie had to go to the healer at Evenleigh today," Darya taunted, in a sing-song voice she reserved especially for Trystan.

Anya nodded and added viciously, "For warts! On her…"

"Anya!" her mother snapped firmly. "We do not discuss embarrassing personal ailments at the table."

"But mother…" Anya was never one to give up on a juicy bit of gossip.

"I will not be disobeyed. You will find a more acceptable topic of conversation or choose to remain silent."

Trystan wasn't about to thank her stepmother for intervening. Nor was she certain whether to thank Vianne for the diversion. Warts? On her…? On her what? Probably something humiliating if Anya's expression was any indication. Trystan knew she'd find out after dinner, whenever her stepsisters could catch her alone. Anya and Darya would probably consider it a priceless sisterly moment.

Trystan picked at her food and tried again not to think about the day, without much success. Too much had happened, and the discoveries she'd made after her strange companion guided her to her destination had done even more to overset her peace. Worse, they had forced her to question long-held beliefs about her own life.

She had probably been rude, but once she finally reached the King's Tree, Trystan had desired only to recover her equilibrium. As a result she had dismissed her guide rather abruptly, reluctant to share her memories with anyone. Still less did she want a stranger to see the tears that seemed inevitable.

The first one fell when she finally sat down and opened the bag Vianne had given her that morning. Along with the usual bread, cheese, and apples, someone had neatly wrapped a napkin around a tiny cake, with pink sugar icing and a swirling letter T across the top. Exactly like the ones she'd had at her twelfth birthday. The last birthday she'd celebrated alone with her father.

By the time she finished unwrapping the precious gift, considerably more than one tear had fallen, as much for regret as for memory. How could she have missed, for so many years, that there were people in her life who cared about her?

With that thought she had remembered the tiny package Alexei had handed her early that morning, and slipped it out of her pocket. The object was tightly wrapped, hiding something small and firm. She loosened the cloth, and it fell away, to reveal what was probably the most beautiful thing Trystan had ever seen.

It was a tiny figurine, worn smooth and shiny, warm from her pocket. It was grained like wood and hard like stone, fiery chestnut in color, throwing off fierce golden sparks in the afternoon sun.

The stone was carved in the shape of a horse, featureless and

TRAITOR'S MASQUE

ancient, with a proudly arched neck, and legs outstretched to run. In style it was rough, but compelling, and appeared to have been worn to smoothness by many centuries of handling. A talisman of some sort perhaps. Meant to be carried, for identification, or for luck.

Trystan wondered where the brothers could have found it. And why they would give up such a rare and precious object.

But it was hers now. When she curled her fingers around the tiny horse, they fit so neatly that it seemed meant for her hand. A reminder that however unexpected, however undeserved, she was not without friends.

A brief, genteel clearing of throat brought Trystan's attention back to the present, and back to the table, where Malisse had apparently determined it was time to discuss whatever sensational rumors she had uncovered the night before.

"It seems, according to my sources,"—she turned slightly so that it was clear she was addressing only Anya and Darya—"there is to be a renewed push for Prince Ramsey to marry."

"Oh mother, why?" Darya whined. "It's not as if he even wants to be king."

"No," Anya chimed in huffily, "and why should he be? Prince Rowan is twice the man Ramsey is, and at least ten times better looking."

Malisse merely raised a delicate eyebrow. "Their looks are hardly your concern, girls. The point is, there may be a crown to be had, and there's no reason why you should not try for it."

"No reason," Darya replied nastily, "except not wanting to spend the rest of my life with a stodgy prig."

"I assure you," Malisse put in drily, "no matter how stodgy you find the man, there is nothing boring about a crown."

Trystan knew almost nothing of politics, except for the

67

rumors that circulated amongst her sisters' female acquaintances. The king, they said, was sick, bad-tempered and politically old-fashioned. The heir, Prince Ramsey, was ugly, uninteresting, and nearly as backward as his father. He was said to hate court and spend most of his time doing paperwork. The elder brother, Prince Rowan, was apparently the possessor of almost all the family virtues. Breathtakingly handsome, popular, engaging, and a friend to progress, he was the embodiment of perfection to legions of merchant nobility and their swooning daughters. And yet, he had been passed over in favor of his younger brother, all over a most unfair bit of family gossip that no one really remembered any more.

Trystan didn't particularly care. The kingdom seemed to function well enough, and Malisse would still be able to bully her no matter who was king. Trystan actually rather hoped one of her sisters caught the wretched Prince Ramsey. It sounded very much as though they would deserve each other. Both ugly, boring usurpers. Which was probably being unfair. Her sisters at least were regrettably attractive, as long as they kept their mouths shut.

"If," Malisse continued, "these rumors prove to be true, and *if* there is any indication that the king intends to hasten the matter of a royal wedding, we will need to be prepared."

"For what?" For a moment, everyone paused, wondering who had spoken, and no one was more surprised than Trystan to realize it had been her.

"I beg your pardon?" Malisse responded with false politeness. "Was that a real question, or were you just pretending to be provincial and ignorant? It can be so very difficult to tell."

Trystan held her breath for a slow-count of five and imagined the consequences should she actually permit her head to explode at the dinner table. It would be messy. Especially during the soup course.

"My question was a genuine one, Stepmother." Her smile was as false and saccharin as Malisse's. "I have never before been privy to the details of a royal wedding. How might one hope to be chosen for such an honor?"

Malisse laughed, a bright tinkling sound in the over-large dining room. "Well, I'm not sure I understand why you need to know, but one must be a member of the nobility to be considered, possess substantial wealth to enrich the royal coffers, and, I need not add, be blessed with such personal advantages, beauty and breeding for example, as may be sufficient to attract the notice and secure the affection of His Royal Highness. None of which," she added silkily, "need concern you in the slightest."

"Only my regrettable curiosity, Stepmother," Trystan responded in a deadly sweet voice that made even Hoskins stiffen where he stood in the corner. "I was merely wondering how likely it was that I might soon be celebrating the nuptials of one of my dear sisters."

Anya snickered.

"And I," Malisse continued in a glacial tone, "trust that you will do everything in your power to assure me that you have your sisters' best interests at heart."

"Why, Stepmother," Trystan breathed innocently, "of course!" If only she had stopped there. For some reason, her mouth just kept moving. "But I sincerely doubt they will require my assistance," she continued brightly. "After all, it sounds as if the prince is shopping for a horse, rather than a wife, and I'm quite certain they will prove convincing in the role."

A frozen silence descended, in which suffocating atmosphere

only Trystan could be heard, defiantly slurping her soup as Malisse's chest heaved in speechless fury.

"Room!" It seemed the only word Malisse was capable of uttering. She punctuated this dictum by snapping to her feet and slamming her dainty hands to the table. Trystan looked up innocently as the silver rattled with the force of the impact. Somewhere on the inside she was rather appalled at her own audacity, but not appalled enough to stop an outburst that had probably been building for years.

"Whatever do you mean, Stepmother?" She enunciated each word, clearly and precisely, looking Malisse in the eye as she did so. Trystan felt vaguely terrified, but exhilarated at the same time. Fascinated by the feeling of standing up to her tormentor, knowing full well it wouldn't last. Realizing she would regret it, but unable to care even a little.

For the second time that day, Trystan felt strangely, startlingly alive.

"NOW!" Malisse's wrath erupted in a most unladylike bellow, in response to which Trystan slowly, calmly, removed her napkin from her lap, pushed back her chair, and curtsied elegantly. A precise turn on her slippered foot left her back exposed to the full force of Malisse's wrath and her stepsisters' offended outrage, but somehow Trystan managed to mince demurely from the room, her head held high. At least until she was on the other side of the door. The footman just outside was nearly forced to catch her as her knees threatened to buckle.

She wobbled, but managed to stay upright. Lovely. Her courage *would* fail her before she could even get up the stairs. Then she happened to catch the footman's eye.

He winked.

Neither of them said a word. They stared at each other, both a little shocked, until Trystan could no longer stop herself. She grinned. And winked back.

The footman returned swiftly to his inscrutable, uniformed self, but the damage was done. She had seen him, not as a "footman" but as a person, with clear and decisive opinions of his own. Opinions that were obviously not sympathetic to Malisse.

Trystan was briefly ashamed by the few moments it took her to remember the footman's name. Farley. Some distant relation of Vianne's, hired by Lord Percival a few months before his second marriage. Farley probably remembered, as Trystan did, the comfortably informal household that had been so thoroughly overset by the new Lady Colbourne's ideas of what was due her own self-consequence. But Trystan was stunned by the fact that Farley had allowed her to see his sympathy. Was this, like Vianne's plotting, simply an acknowledgement of what Trystan had lost? Or had something changed in the household? Worse yet, was it possible that Trystan was only now beginning to see something that had been there all along?

It was an intriguing thought, but as Trystan reluctantly mounted the stairs, she found that it offered little in the way of comfort. Farley's show of support wasn't likely to make her punishment any easier to bear. The last time Trystan proved intractable, her stepmother had forbidden her to read, play or draw for a month. After four weeks of sitting silently in the drawing room listening to her sisters' insipid conversation while embroidering various useless objects, Trystan's patience had felt nearly as abused as her fingers. Her sense of ill-usage had not been improved by the fact that Malisse knew very well how deeply her stepdaughter despised the needle.

Whatever punishment Malisse chose this time, it was certain to be far worse than the last.

The next afternoon found Trystan in the midst of the gardens, gleefully contemplating her filthy hands. There was actual dirt under her nails, and the state of her clothes was simply not to be mentioned.

Malisse's wrath had indeed been terrible, her vengeance extreme. She had sentenced her recalcitrant stepdaughter to *work*, saying that if the child would speak as vulgarly as the servants, then she could work like them too. Even if it was only during those times of day when no one was likely to see her.

Trystan was not about to admit how great a relief it was to have something to *do*. Even gardening seemed like bliss after the endless days of silent decorum she was expected to suffer through inside the house.

The head gardener, Millson, was a taciturn man who grunted and pointed more than he spoke, but who seemed willing enough to trust Trystan with digging, weeding and trimming. She followed his instructions, clumsily at first, taking care to watch for the occasional surveillance of her stepmother and sisters. Trystan reasoned that if they believed her to be suffering they would continue to inflict such "punishment" and felt she could do worse than be forced to enjoy the warm spring days from the relatively uninterrupted peace of the garden. So whenever they found it necessary to promenade past the windows to check on her progress, she made certain to rub her back, look pitifully at her nails, or limp, which produced satisfied smiles on the faces of her oppressors.

In this way, life proceeded, rather peacefully for a change. Perhaps the only point of discomfort was Trystan's inability to settle what she felt were her debts, of a sort. When she approached Vianne on the topic of her excuse for Trystan's day-long absence, the dour old woman actually smiled fleetingly, before resuming her usual forbidding mien. But no matter how Trystan pressed her, the cook offered no explanation and appeared disgruntled by all expressions of appreciation.

Trystan likewise took advantage of her chance to disappear one afternoon while Malisse and the girls were out on a call, and visited the stables, where she attempted to thank the brothers for their gift. But when she asked whether they knew the history of the tiny horse and why they had chosen to give it up, both Andrei and Alexei seemed curiously devoid of expression and refused to discuss the matter.

It was frustrating, but Trystan managed to quell both her curiosity and the desire to immediately erase her indebtedness. It was strange and unsettling, that feeling of obligation, but continuing to pursue the matter could only bring trouble—for all of them—should her efforts happen to come to Malisse's attention. All she could do was wait, and hope that she could find some acceptable way to express the uncomfortable new sensation of gratitude.

∾

Trystan's next opportunity for a morning ride presented itself sooner than she expected. About a month after her punishment commenced, one of the Colbourne's neighbors, Lady Isaura Westerby, a childless widow who nonetheless managed an impressive estate, threw a party in honor of Darya's birthday.

Everyone with any pretense to importance had been invited and, like all fashionable parties, it ended very little before dawn.

Malisse and her daughters stumbled happily, and perhaps a bit tipsily, into their beds just as the sun was coming up. As soon as they were safely snoring, Trystan took her bag of lunch from a straight-faced Vianne and disappeared to the stables, not planning to be back until at least tea-time.

Trystan had no specific plan when she first cantered away from the manor. Without any real intention to do so, she found herself approaching the eaves of the Kingswood as the sun rose over the trees. A bit perturbed by this subconscious betrayal of her resolution *not* to think about her last ride, she nonetheless rode under the trees at a more sedate pace, agreeing with herself to simply enjoy the shade for a few moments before leaving. But an hour or more of enjoying passed before she realized how thoroughly she was betraying her own intentions, when Theron emerged from the trees and trotted up a steep hill. They reached the top, giving her a strangely familiar view of rolling downs, and Trystan had no choice but to laugh at whatever forces seemed to have conspired against her. It was better not to fight such forces.

With the aid of a much improved sense of direction, they cantered lazily across the fields to the now-convenient stone wall, where Trystan slid happily out of the saddle to sit on its welcoming top and soak up memories along with sunshine. Feeling oddly content, she took off her hat, unbraided her hair, and let it fall loose down her back as she sat, legs dangling into the tall grass. The sun made her feel sleepy, so, not without feeling a bit silly, she stretched out along the top of the wall, put her hat over her face, and took a nap.

She woke abruptly some time later, rested, but not quite sure what had startled her until she felt warm breath on her face.

Sitting up with a yawn, she pushed half-heartedly at the soft nose that had been snuffling curiously in her hair. Too late she realized that Theron was grazing peacefully a short distance away and that the nose she had shoved was brown, rather than gray.

Trystan turned, looked up and decided she was still dreaming when her sun-dazzled eyes finally made out the enigmatic face of her strange companion from several weeks past.

For a few moments they only stared at each other. Trystan, at least, felt oddly unsure of herself, but bizarrely relieved by the sudden thought that at least he had not been just a dream.

"I was beginning to wonder if I had only dreamed you." The man's voice startled her. Had she spoken her thought out loud? His dismount was a tired, awkward motion that made her frown, just a little. He appeared as though he had barely slept since they parted company at the Tree.

"You look awful." The words fell out of her mouth before she could stop them. Aghast, she put her face in her hands and groaned. "I didn't mean to say that out loud," she muttered into her palms.

The man only laughed, and the sound was as wonderful as her memories of it. "The truth can be a terrible thing," he agreed complacently. "I probably look even worse than that. You, however, look much the same as I remember, aside from…" He stopped, and looked a bit embarrassed. "Your hair," he said finally. "It's beautiful."

Trystan blushed in horror and jumped to her feet as she remembered her unbound hair, and hastily began to plait its reddish-brown strands back into her customary braid. "I forgot," she apologized. "I hadn't really thought I would meet anyone out here today."

"I would have come back every day, if I could," was her

companion's simple reply as he leaned back against the wall. "Unfortunately, only a very small piece of my time can be called my own. I've managed to keep this morning free each week until now, much as my keepers resist."

Trystan filed that away as a possible clue to his identity. He spoke so well, she had assumed him educated, but young noblemen rarely thought of their time as belonging to anyone but themselves. Perhaps he was not a man of leisure after all. And perhaps, if he had so little time to be alone, he might prefer her elsewhere.

"I can be getting along," she offered tentatively, "if you would prefer not to share this, um… hill." Even as the words came out she felt ridiculous. But even more ridiculous would have been the assumption that he had sought her company.

"If you find my society so distasteful," he offered with a wry smile, "I will by no means detain you. But I confess I had hoped to speak with you again, if the admission does not terrify you."

Relieved and absurdly pleased, Trystan smiled back. "I am terrified by very little," she told him, "except perhaps embroidery."

Her companion looked abashed. "I fear I must disclose a shocking truth," he said solemnly. "You see, my only true joy in life lies in embroidery." When Trystan burst out laughing, he added, "Someday, I even hope to discover whether the art has a purpose beyond drawing blood and driving young women to madness."

"I believe they tell us it improves our character, though I fear it did the opposite for mine," she admitted. "I clearly recall burying more than one sampler behind the stable and claiming pixies had taken it."

"Pixies?" The man seemed impressed. "I wish I'd thought of that when it was time for lessons. Though I fear my tutors would have been less than pleased to discover my history texts at the bottom of a midden."

He'd had tutors? That, at least, was indisputable proof that he was from at least some degree of wealth. Perhaps his father was a successful businessman.

"I'm afraid it didn't help much anyway," Trystan admitted ruefully. "As punishment I was forced to embroider handkerchiefs, which is much worse. My ste-" Trystan broke off swiftly, appalled at her conversational lapse. She'd almost revealed that she had a stepmother. And that her stepmother had been furious when Trystan convinced her father to lighten her punishment. Instead of six sets of handkerchiefs with Anya and Darya's initials, she'd completed only one, with her father's initials instead. He'd been quite pleased with them. Kept them for special occasions. Malisse had burned them when he died.

Trystan's attention was recalled abruptly to the present when Theron walked up and nudged her from behind, clearly displeased with the inactivity. Caught unprepared, Trystan staggered forward and might have fallen had her companion not caught her swiftly by the shoulders and set her gently upright.

It was terribly embarrassing. Caught between worry that she had nearly betrayed herself and humiliation at her near-accident, she realized only as she pulled back, away from her rescuer, that she had no particular objection to being close to him. Which probably indicated she was nearly as lost to propriety as her stepmother thought she was.

Trystan turned around, caught Theron's reins, and busied herself with pretending to check his bridle.

"Are you all right?" The man's tentative question did nothing for Trystan's attempt to recover her self-possession.

"Of course… thank you," she responded, in a relatively normal voice, turning and giving what she hoped was an encouraging smile.

His answering expression seemed to hold equal amounts of curiosity and worry, but he appeared to quell them both. "So whither are you bound today?" he asked lightly, leaning back against the wall. "The King's Tree again? Or somewhere more adventurous?"

"Less, I'm afraid," Trystan sighed, grateful for the change of subject. "This is as far as I go. I must be back before the revelers rise." She abruptly shut her mouth and pressed her lips together, determined to avoid any further revelatory remarks.

The man either pretended not to notice or decided not to pursue the information she revealed. "In my experience," he offered in a studiously off-handed manner, "that's rarely before tea-time. If it makes any difference in your destination."

Trystan turned to look at him dubiously. "And you offer this information because of your innate benevolence?"

He chuckled. "Decidedly not, as I have none," he responded promptly. "But there is a place I would like to show you, if time and your conscience permit."

"My conscience permits a great deal that my circumstances do not," she returned drily, "a constraint I suspect we share."

"Your suspicions may have merit," he admitted, "but today I have decided to prevent either one from interfering with my plans. Will you come?" He watched Trystan hopefully, awaiting her decision.

She knew she should refuse. It was already near mid-day, with tea time only a scant few hours away, near two of them needed for the journey home. And after all, what did she know about the man, except that he had a pleasant laugh and his hair seemed permanently rumpled? It was rather difficult to view him as a threat, but she had to consider the possibility. He had no doubt guessed that she rode in secret. If his intentions proved sinister, who would ever know what had become of her?

"What sort of place?" she asked, trying to sound more flippant than worried. "In stories, isn't that what the villain says to the heroine before he kidnaps her and drags her off to his lair?"

The man's eyes widened in evident horror, and, to Trystan's delight, his face turned rather red. "Ah, no?" He looked anxious, and a trifle apologetic. "That is, I didn't mean it like that." Her look of inquiry produced only a sheepish grin. "I suppose I've been reading all the wrong sorts of stories. I simply remembered a place in the Kingswood that I often go, and I thought you might like to see it."

"It does," Trystan allowed graciously, "sound rather less sinister when you put it like that." She grinned back at him. "Although," she added, "I've always thought it might make villainy worthwhile if one actually got to have a lair."

"Possibly," her companion admitted, "though if I had one, I promise I could think of far better things to fill it with than unwilling maidens. They would probably spend all their time complaining about the dust and the lack of variety at tea time."

"What would you fill it with?" Trystan could not help asking. "Your lair, I mean." She wondered briefly if that was too personal a question, but the man didn't even hesitate.

"Books," he replied promptly. "And horses. And perhaps a friend or two, though I suppose the idea of a 'lair' doesn't seem well suited to convivial gatherings."

Trystan chuckled. It did sound rather more like a home than a lair. What that might say about his real home was a question for later consideration.

"And you?" he prompted curiously. "What sort of place would you retreat to when the pressures of villainy grew too great?"

Caught off-guard by the question, Trystan floundered for an answer. "Ah, I... well, I don't know." What would she wish for? All she really dreamed of these days was *not* being with her family. She had never stepped beyond that dream to imagine what she might choose to do with her life.

"Just as well," the man said, saving her from having to invent an answer. "I can't imagine you would make a very convincing villain."

Trystan tried to look hurt, and failed. She couldn't imagine anyone taking her seriously either.

"So will you come?" He reminded her of his earlier invitation. "I promise there will be no embroidery, no kidnapping, and only slightly dull conversation."

She hesitated. Perhaps it would be wiser to say no. She should return home, to the company of Millson and an afternoon in the garden. But just then, she did not particularly want to be wise. She wanted a friend. The garden, while peaceful, was no substitute for human contact. There was but one condition. "If our path lies west or north, then I agree," she answered finally. "I cannot help but reveal that much, as I truly dare not be late."

She met the gray eyes next to her as she spoke. It struck her then as odd, how easily she could read what she saw there. Curiosity, of course. And a great deal of concern.

"I must ask..." he began, then stopped, and folded his arms a bit fiercely. "Do you need... Is there anything...?" He could not seem to get the words out.

Trystan was at once humiliated and warmed by his consideration. But it was not enough. She could tell him nothing that would either inform or console him. "I fear I am no more at liberty than you to divulge my secrets," she answered his unspoken question with quiet sympathy. "Our burdens, I fear, are not the sort that grow lighter with sharing."

"My obligations are not the sort that could be shared, even if I wished to," he admitted, "but how could you have guessed such a thing?"

"You've made no secret of your desire to be other than what you are," she reminded him. "And yet you return to it anyway. Your idea of rebellion is simply to be alone." She shrugged, not sure how to explain what seemed obvious to her. "It was not difficult to surmise that you shoulder your burdens because you must. Or perhaps simply because you cannot imagine forcing them on someone else."

He shook his head at her wonderingly. "Even those close to me…" he told her, "the people who know me best, seem to find my choices incomprehensible." There was pain in the admission. "But you"—he took a step forward, closing the gap between them —"I've told you so little, yet you seem to understand so much." He took another step. Trystan held her ground, heart pounding at his nearness. "How can that be?" He sounded so perplexed that Trystan looked up, into his eyes. They were fastened on hers, with an intensity that held her breathless. "Why do I feel like I know you?"

The same question Trystan had asked herself. A question she had been unable to answer, through several sleepless nights. "I feel much the same," she answered him softly, dropping her gaze, "but I suspect it is an illusion. We simply recognize ourselves when we look at one another. But we know next to nothing."

It struck her, then, the depth of her ignorance about even the people she knew best. What, after all, had she even known about her father? That he was kind? That he was handsome? That he loved her? Had she even truly known that? What would she ask him, now, if she had the chance?

She looked up again, into the man's gray eyes, and wondered. "I do not know what you love or what you fear," she told him simply. "What moves you to hatred or to envy... I might guess at what would make you laugh, but not what might make you cry. What you live for, even what you would choose to die for..." She shook her head, trying to convey something she had not really understood before that moment.

"I could not begin to imagine what things make you get up in the morning with hope instead of despair," she went on. "While it pains me that I cannot know your name, in truth, that is the least of what we hide." She had not intended to say so much, but with his eyes on hers it had not seemed possible to stop.

"And yet," he responded with growing intensity, "you see me anyway. No young woman has ever spoken to me as you do. All the polite conversation in the world cannot convey what you seem to understand without being told."

"I fear I am only beginning to see beyond myself," Trystan admitted, with a strong sense of shame. "And my life offers few opportunities to speak plainly, or at all, really. I fear you are bearing the weight of far too many words unsaid. If I have distressed you, I apologize."

Without warning he caught her hand and pressed it. "No," he said swiftly and firmly. "Not distressed. I am dismayed by your insights, but relieved, I think, by your candor. I might prefer anonymity, but to be unknown... that is not always a relief."

As he had done before, he so nearly echoed her own thoughts

that Trystan was surprised to find she had not spoken them. "But neither is it always a comfort to be known," she added thoughtfully. "Knowing can so quickly turn to hurting that it is little wonder how deeply we hide."

"I would not hurt you," the man said quietly. "Though I know you have little reason to believe it."

"I believe you would not hurt me on purpose," she answered honestly. "But I also believe we do not always get to choose who is hurt and who is not."

He looked sad and dropped her hand. "No," he said, turning away. "We do not." Catching his horse's trailing reins, he mounted and turned toward the forest. "Ride with me?" he asked. "North and west. Without burden or expectation. Just a chance to talk, of whatever would not cause you pain."

Trystan nodded, her relief and joy mingling with an equal sense of apprehension. Even more than she feared being late, she now feared how strongly she wanted to tell him everything.

≈

They rode slowly back into the Kingswood, and at Ramsey's prompting the girl managed to tell him a little of her apparently tempestuous childhood. She carefully confined her stories to her younger years, when her experiences would have been less specific, but she could not hide everything. Though she was careful not to give names, her artless telling revealed much about her origins.

Her father had clearly been wealthy, and was just as clearly long gone from her life, whether by distance or death he was unsure. Her eyes twinkled merrily as she related tricks played on a long-ago governess, apparently one of the many whose presence in the house had not lasted even so much as a month. The girl beside him was obviously educated, and probably accomplished as well, though not, Ramsey reflected with amusement, for want of attempting to avoid it.

With every word, he grew more determined to unravel the mystery he knew was better left unsolved. Who was she, and why did she hide? What drove her to sacrifice her reputation by disguising herself as a man and riding alone?

It served, at least, to distract him from his own despair.

Choose a wife, his father had said, or I will choose one for you. The guilds were insistent, his brother insouciant, and his friends sympathetic, but no one seemed to care what he wanted. The best he could hope for now was to choose a wife his own way. Even if the prospect filled him with nothing but foreboding.

If only he had more time. If only he could afford to make a choice that had less to do with his kingdom and more to do with his heart. This girl… she made him wonder what he might be missing, by entering into a marriage of state. But of all his "if-only's," the one that weighed the heaviest was Rowan. If only Ramsey was not bound to make up for all of Rowan's mistakes. Perhaps then he could consider marrying someone unexpected, someone who might not be precisely what his father and advisors had in mind.

But as his father had so recently reminded him, Ramsey was to be king. The only thing he was truly free to do was to think of his kingdom first, and a girl whose dress and behavior would be considered a scandal by the court was not what the already divided kingdom needed.

For a time, the two rode side by side, following paths that wound in more or less the right direction through the wood. But at last, when they reached an undistinguished forking, Ramsey forged briefly ahead and blocked the way, pulling his horse to a stop with a serious expression.

"There is still a place I would be pleased to show you, if your time permits. I promise it will take only a moment, and then you can be on your way."

The girl glanced up as if to see the sun, but the trees were too thick for a very clear sense of the time.

"I believe it is just after midmeal," he added, "if that aids in your decision."

"In that case, Sir Villain," she intoned gravely. "I would be most pleased to visit your lair. Lead and I will follow."

His laugh mingled with hers as she trailed behind him down the narrower path he took. It led deeper into the trees, then disappeared altogether, only to reappear behind a pile of boulders. A few moments later, he stopped, dismounted and beckoned wordlessly. After both horses were securely tethered, the girl walked silently behind him through a thicket and around an enormous oak... and into what had always seemed to Ramsey to be a different world. His private refuge. The heart of the Kingswood.

A pool lay in front of them, small but deep, ringed by moss-covered rocks and surrounded thickly by ancient trees. Ferns grew lush and green from the craggy boulders, interspersed with lupin and phlox, while pink and white water lilies bloomed from the margins of the pool. It was so still that the water lay calm and clear as glass, the lazy white clouds reflected on its mirror-bright surface mingling with the wavering shadows that lay beneath.

Ramsey stole a glance at his companion's face, feeling absurdly nervous as he watched her absorb the peaceful scene, hoping she would understand, but unable to put into words what he offered. Neither of them spoke, as though in silent agreement that words might destroy some part of the moment's perfection, but when their eyes met for a brief instant, Ramsey had his answer.

After they lingered there a few moments more, he touched her arm and led her back to where the horses were waiting.

"Why?" she asked.

There was no need to elaborate. Why had he chosen to share something so personal with a girl he barely knew? "Because," he answered helplessly, "it's all I can give you." He paused. Told himself he was a fool. Took a deep breath. "Except this." He took her hand and said, without preamble or explanation: "Donevan." And then he waited. Hoping for he hardly knew what.

"Donevan," she repeated, wide-eyed, as if testing it for fit. Unsure of her response. In silence, she untied her horse. Used a nearby rock to mount. Turned back, bit her lip, and answered.

"Embrie," she said. Then turned and rode away as if she could escape the consequences of what they had done.

But there was no taking it back now. And Ramsey would not wish it back, even if he could. He had a name, and he carried it with him as a promise that he would, no matter how unlikely, see her again. Even if the seeing could bring him nothing but heartache in the end.

CHAPTER 4

Trystan made it home before the party-goers were awake enough to demand breakfast. Or lunch. Or whatever one called the first meal of the day when it happened not long before tea-time. She was changed and grubbing industriously in the garden before a dressing-gown-clad Malisse peered out of her window with a satisfied smirk on her lovely coral lips. Trystan could not help feeling a bit gratified when her stepmother winced directly afterward, having perhaps underestimated the effect of the sun on a champagne headache.

In the past, Trystan might have occupied herself for some time with the satisfaction of having outwitted her tormentors once again, but on that day she could not seem to content herself with such a dull emotion.

She was thoroughly on edge, tense with some indefinable blend of fear and anticipation. A half-formed scream lurked in the back of her throat, borne of joy, frustration, and the urgent suspicion that she no longer fit her own life. She could remember its rhythms, its shape, and her own place within it. But even thinking about her quiet, contained existence made her itch, like clothes that were too small. She could not possibly have changed so much in a single morning, but she felt as if she had.

And she wasn't even sure how it had happened. When had she decided to trust him? She had broken nearly every rule, told him so much she had never intended to say. She had told a truth and ten more had followed and before she could stuff her tongue back behind her teeth she had told him her name.

Malisse would have her drawn and quartered if she found out. No, that was too messy. Malisse would simply follow through with the threat that had held Trystan helpless since her father died: she would be turned out of the house, accused of some crime, or saddled with the hint of a ruined reputation. The rest of her very short life would be spent either locked in prison or walking the streets, depending on how great a scandal her step-mother was willing to have associated with her own precious daughters. Though Trystan considered it unlikely that her step-mother would court scandal of any sort, she was not certain enough to ignore the possibility, and the fate of friendless young women in disgrace with society was not one she cared to experience.

Straightening from the border she was trimming to stretch her back, Trystan tried reasoning with herself. There was really no reason for Malisse to know. Trystan doubted if very many people outside the family remembered her existence, let alone her middle name, and since she never went out, she would never encounter her friend in public. It was possible, she knew, that she would never encounter him at all.

Her friend. In spite of her dour imaginings, the thought

produced an irrepressible smile. Glancing around to make sure no one had noticed, Trystan stuffed the grin back where it belonged and kept on trimming.

≈

That afternoon, Trystan was summoned to the sitting room to read improving lectures aloud while her sisters stitched and Malisse plotted. She almost fell asleep in the midst of a long passage on virtue and was jerked awake only by a pointed "Ahem!" from Anya. Before Trystan could continue there was a gentle knock on the sitting room door.

"Enter." Malisse was always stiffly formal with the servants, even when no visitors were present.

"Your Ladyship," Hoskins intoned solemnly as he entered with a single white envelope on a silver tray. The staff responded to their mistress's formality with an exaggerated degree of deference, which only Trystan seemed to realize was actually a kind of mockery.

"That will be all, Hoskins," Malisse took the envelope from his outstretched tray and nodded grandly. "You may go." He retreated silently, with a flicker of a significant glance at Trystan. Not sure what to make of it, she was looking for her place in the lecture when Malisse hissed triumphantly.

"It's true! Finally!"

Anya and Darya exchanged glances.

"Well, what is it?" Darya had always been the least patient of the two.

"There is going to be a royal wedding soon," Malisse announced. "Prince Ramsey is ready to seek a bride."

Trystan rolled her eyes, secure in the knowledge that no one would be watching her with such news afoot.

"A very odd missive, this," Malisse's triumph turned to a frown as she tapped one tiny slippered foot on the rug. "King Hollin is holding a masqued ball in one month. Prince Ramsey will, at that time, accept applications for his hand in marriage."

Trystan nearly groaned aloud. Applications? Was it to be a contest, or was Prince Ramsey really so much the reclusive clerk that he would choose a bride by her pedigree and ability to do sums? Whichever was the case, he was obviously quite certain of his appeal. It would serve him properly if he were to be stuck with a creature like Anya or Darya for a wife.

"Application?" Anya asked, confusion wrinkling her porcelain forehead. "Whatever does that mean? Are we to audition? Fill out... paperwork?" She shuddered delicately.

Malisse shook her head, appearing momentarily baffled. "This does not elaborate. I suppose we will be kept informed." Odious and vindictive she might be, but Malisse was not particularly ignorant or foolish, except as concerned the feelings of others. Trystan could see her considering schemes and plotting strategies as her silk-clad foot continued to tap the floor.

Thinking to make her escape, Trystan closed her book and rose, as unobtrusively as possible. But she did not manage to take so much as a single step towards the door.

"Trystan, my dear, I trust these past weeks of reflection and penitence have given you an appreciation for the luxuries you are permitted to share."

Trystan looked up, unable to stop her jaw from dropping just a fraction. "Of course, ah... Stepmother," she tripped over her words, having been unprepared for an attempt to sound suitably chastised. "I'm sure I will do better in the future."

"Yes." Malisse smiled without humor. "Well, I'm sure I wish I could share your optimism." She fixed her stepdaughter with a pointed stare. "I hope it's understood that there can be no further outbursts in this household. A great number of preparations are in order and I cannot afford distractions when my daughters' futures are at stake. If you cannot comport yourself with dignity and discretion then I will be forced to take measures I'm certain we will both regret."

She turned her head to one side, still watching Trystan, who thought she looked remarkably reptilian. And remarkably dishonest. Trystan could not imagine her stepmother regretting anything.

"I will, of course, respect your wishes, Stepmother," she mouthed stiffly, drawing a sharp look, but no further recriminations.

~

By the following day, life, for Trystan at least, had returned to normal. She regretted the loss of her "punishment" in the garden, and within a very short time was actually contemplating some small misbehavior in hopes of having her penance reinstated.

But she resisted the temptation, despite what proved to be no small degree of upheaval in the household. Dressmakers and seamstresses came and went, fittings and re-fittings filled the morning hours, and a steady train of excited female callers filled the afternoons. Dinners were rife with speculation on Prince Ramsey's probable tastes and possible preferences in female intellect and fashion, and bedtime became, at least for Anya and Darya, a dizzying progression of beauty routines that Trystan was endlessly thankful to escape.

Resigned to the chaos, she was busily engaged in hoping to be struck very hard on the head and so spend the next two weeks unconscious when Malisse summoned her to the salon where she dealt with whatever affairs of business she chose to care about.

When Trystan entered the room, Malisse was sitting at her writing desk. She did not bother to turn around, only held up one small white hand with a number of envelopes in it.

"Trystan," she asked sweetly, without looking up, "I need you to deliver these for me immediately."

Trystan took them, gave them a cursory glance, and looked at Malisse cautiously. "What are they?" she asked without thinking. Each envelope bore the name of one of the servants in Malisse's extravagant script. Farley, the footman. Beatrice, one of the housemaids. Hoskins. Millson. Andrei and Alexei. Only the six of them. Six people Trystan had known for years. Except for Farley, she had known them quite literally all her life.

Expecting a sharp demand that she stay out of her stepmother's business, Trystan was surprised when Malisse turned to face her, showing even white teeth in what could only be termed a predatory smile.

"Oh, it's nothing, dear, just a few servants I have decided to dismiss. I have found excellent candidates to replace them who are better able to suit my more formal way of doing things, and it will, I think, be a relief for all of us to have a bit of a fresh start, don't you agree?"

Trystan looked back, into her stepmother's ice cold eyes and felt ice cold herself. Then she felt hot. Blazing fury swept through her and left her shaking in the face of her stepmother's triumph.

Somehow, Malisse had guessed. Had realized that some of the servants had so far forgotten themselves as to reserve their loyalty for someone other than herself. Perhaps she even suspected that the stepdaughter she was determined to render powerless might have found some measure of power by accepting that loyalty.

Except that she was terribly, tragically wrong. Trystan had not until recently understood what they offered her. Had been unable to recognize their loyalty for what it was. She had certainly never dreamed she might use that loyalty for her own ends. But now it was too late, for all of them, and it was Trystan's fault.

Malisse had most likely come to the conclusion that there might be a connection between Trystan's rebellion and the people who cared for her. Lady Colbourne would do whatever was necessary to remove anything that stood between her and complete control over her domain. By ridding herself of the last of the servants Lord Percival had hired, Malisse was effectively banishing the last reminders of a time when her own will had not been law.

All that would be left was Vianne. Even Malisse would never dare fire Vianne, who had three times been offered a position at the palace itself. But the others had no such protection. Nothing to stand between them and the destruction of their livelihoods. All because they cared for a selfish, spoiled child who had never noticed. Who had only just begun to see the people around her as friends.

"No," said Trystan, her head beginning to shake, and her hands clenching uncontrollably.

"I beg your pardon?" Malisse's voice was ice and steel.

"No!" Trystan repeated, louder this time, the blood roaring in her ears. "You cannot."

Malisse sat back in her chair and smirked. "I think, dear child," she said, speaking as if to an infant, "you will find that I can."

"These people"—Trystan's voice shook with anger—"have given their lives to this place. To this family! They could have left when my father died, but they stayed and now you will turn them off to find new positions as a reward for their loyalty? Farley is young, but the rest are past their prime! They have given up chances at advancement because they trusted us! Trusted you!" Trystan was past any point of controlling her temper or her tongue. She could not have stopped if Malisse threatened her with hanging. "And all this for what? So you can have your twisted revenge on me? Why take it out on them? Don't you realize that you compromise your ability to hire loyal servants at all when you prove yourself untrustworthy? They are not fools just because they are forced to work for a living! You will end up regretting this betrayal, one way or another!"

Trystan had said far too much and she knew it, but she hovered on the brink of tears, both hurt and furious. If she stopped, the torrent would fall and she would die before she cried in front of her stepmother.

Malisse rose, regal and triumphant. "You have officially gone too far, Stepdaughter." Her voice dripped with quiet, controlled malice. "You will be confined to your room until I can determine what is to be done with you. As I cannot spare the attention from these preparations"—she waved a languid hand at the papers on her desk—"that may be for several weeks."

Trystan's chin came up. Her eyes were wide and her lips compressed to hold back tears. Her face burned with the effort, but she would not, could not let them fall. She looked past

Malisse, out the window, to the carefully manicured garden and beyond, where the green haze of the Kingswood was just visible in the distance.

A vision swam before her eyes, of a silent, hidden place that promised peace, and without another word, she turned and left the room. Malisse followed, calling after her, ordering her to…

Trystan barely heard her. She broke into a run, down the long, carpeted hallway, down the sweeping front stairs, scattering pristine white envelopes in her wake like so many dead leaves. The door seemed to open before her of its own accord and she caught a brief glance of Hoskins' face as she flashed by. It was both sad and resigned, with a note of farewell. She doubted he would still be there when she returned. If she returned.

The walk blurred by under her shoes, worn kid letting her feel the crushed rock under her feet. They stung like the tears that had begun to leak from her eyes as she ran. She reached the stables before she really understood where she was going.

Andrei looked at her in surprise. She shook her head, not really willing or able to speak, but when she met his eyes, she found that he, too, seemed to know already. Reaching out impulsively, she took his hand and pressed it, and felt his sympathy and sadness roll over her. It only made her tears fall faster. Tearing herself away with an oath, she yanked Theron's bridle off its hook and threw open his stall.

"Miss Trystan, don't!" Andrei sounded almost panicked as he followed her. "You'll break your neck. And his. Please don't!"

She was past listening, past caring. Malisse was taking away everything Trystan had only just realized she had, and the prospect of picking herself up out of the ruins of that fragile happiness held only terror and pain.

"I'm sorry, Andrei." She forced out the words between her tears as she climbed onto a trunk and threw herself onto Theron's bare back, her skirts bunching up over her knees. "Tell your brother goodbye. I don't think…" She couldn't finish, and couldn't look at her friend. Bending low over the horse's neck, she kicked him, hard, in the flanks. Theron threw up his head and bolted out of the stable at a run, throwing up clods of dirt behind them and leaving a stunned Andrei in their wake.

~

They ran for some time. Theron's back was warm and slippery with sweat, her skirts were bunched too high and her eyes were half blinded by tears, but she did not pull up until Theron's breath began to sound labored and his strides began to slow.

Even then they kept moving. It was late morning, but cloudy and gray, and the sun did not warm her as it had on her last ride. Whether she shivered with cold, with fury or with anguish she could not and did not try to determine, but simply gave rein to her misery.

Theron, tired as he was, felt something was amiss. He seemed anxious, blowing hard and widening his eyes at anything that moved as they passed finally under the trees. Trystan shortened the reins and guided him into the wood, trying to clear her eyes long enough to find the path she remembered. It took time, and it was even cooler under the trees than it had been in the open. She was wishing for her coat long before she found the tiny path.

Tying Theron to the same tree as before, she pushed through the thicket, around the tree, and let out a gasp of relief. She had, somehow, feared that the pool might not be there. Or that it would not be as she remembered it. The moss and ferns were just as green, the water-lilies still bloomed, and the silence was all that it had been. But the surface of the water seemed dull and blank, reflecting only the flat gray of the clouds, the flat gray of her future.

Even if she remained at Colbourne Manor after today, nothing would be the same. Even if she survived being locked in her room until Malisse decided to relent, everything would have changed. Just when she had finally realized that there were people who cared for her, they would be taken away. And without her fellow conspirators, her rides would be impossible. Whomever Malisse hired to take over the stables would never permit them to continue. Without that escape, without that tiny scrap of freedom, Trystan could anticipate nothing but bleak emptiness for each and every moment she remained in her childhood home.

Heedless of her already stained and rumpled skirts, she seated herself on the soft moss covering one of the rocks at the edge of the pool, drew up her knees, and wrapped her arms around them. A lump under her elbow startled her, until she remembered and reached into the pocket of her skirt to draw out the tiny horse figurine. She had kept it with her ever since she realized what it meant, but today, it seemed almost as dead as her own heart. There was no sun to strike sparks from its polished golden surface, and the friendship it symbolized would soon be gone forever. Wrapping her hand around the horse but feeling no warmth, Trystan pressed her face into her knees and let the tears fall unchecked.

She lost track of time as she sat there, shivering in misery, and was only brought back to herself when she heard footsteps approaching along the path. Her first, panicked thought was that Malisse had sent someone after her. She could not hope to untangle herself fast enough to get away, so instead she swiped viciously at her ravaged cheeks, determined to face whoever it was with what dignity was possible when your eyes were puffy and your nose was red.

When the feet finally rounded the last bend, however, she found herself looking into the startled face of Donevan. Only then did she remember that this was Firstday, a day he had mentioned was his usual period of freedom. She had, without meaning to, used the gift of his secret to trespass on his peace. The reflection was mortifying, and she tried to rise, choking on the words of her apology as she noted his sudden lack of any readable expression.

"Wait," he said, and disappeared back into the brush.

Left with little choice, Trystan dropped back down onto the rock. Her heart could sink no lower and her dignity was in shreds. How much worse could it be to lose the regard of a man she hardly knew?

Donevan returned a bare moment later, walking quickly through the brush, carrying his coat. Without a word, he approached, crouched down beside her and wrapped the garment firmly around her shaking shoulders, his gray eyes warm and questioning. She sensed his scrutiny, but could not look up for more than a brief moment. Not even to thank him for another piece of unexpected kindness.

Trystan felt, rather than saw, when he seated himself beside her on the moss, oblivious to the dampness that had already soaked through both her petticoats. Still he said nothing, only picked up a fallen twig and hurled it into the pool with surprising viciousness.

Astonished into looking at him at last, her eyes met his, and she saw a flash of anger in their gray depths. It was not, she was relieved to realize, directed at her.

"Damn secrecy," he said finally. "Is there nothing I can do?"

A brief vision arose of Donevan challenging Malisse to a duel, and a feeling of humor bubbled up in spite of everything. "I'm afraid that even your most villainous scowl would be insufficient in this case," she answered lightly, trying to brush aside his concern.

As much as Trystan longed to tell him everything, practicality still held her back. Malisse would not dare to kick her out, not even after today. With the king's masque looming so near, she would never tempt disaster with a scandal that might destroy her hopes. A disgraced sister, even one not related by blood, would taint Anya and Darya's own reputations. And if by some miracle one of them should manage to snare themselves a prince, Malisse would likewise be forced to keep her. Though she was loathe to admit it, Trystan knew that however desperate her circumstances under Malisse's thumb, they would be far worse elsewhere.

There was hope, at least for a time, until the prince married.

She glanced over at Donevan, trying to assess the effect of her words and was dismayed to see that his intensity had not wavered.

"Even if there was anything to be done, I could not ask it of you," she continued with a weary wave of her hand. "You have your own burdens, and no need of mine."

Donevan caught the waving hand, which she had forgotten was still clutched tightly around her tiny horse. "It's mine, I swear," she said, feeling an irrational stab of worry when he did not let go, fearing that he might think she had stolen such a precious thing. "It was a gift." She unclenched her hand, and his strong, warm fingers wrapped gently around hers as they unfolded to reveal her treasure. The horse lay in her palm, warmed now by her skin, still proud and inscrutable, given depth by the shadows.

Donevan's eyes widened a fraction as he gazed at the horse, turned it over, and rubbed a careful thumb across its smooth surface. "It's a chatoyant. A cat's eye," he told her. Curious now, Trystan laid it in Donevan's palm for closer inspection. "This one appears to be a talisman, carved as a symbol of a child's dedication to a particular task, or path."

Trystan had been well educated, but this was new to her. "Where did it come from?" she asked, if only to distract him from his anger. Much as it warmed her, she feared the scrutiny that accompanied it.

"There is a country north and east of Andar," he continued, still running his fingers over the smooth arched neck of the horse. "Erath. They are small, like us, and isolated, like us, and do not readily accept outsiders. The Erathi believe that everyone is called to some particular gift. They also believe that these gifts are, well, magic."

Fascinated in spite of herself, Trystan hoped he would tell her more, wondering anew how her friends had come to possess the horse, and what might have motivated them to give it to her. "Is it true? About the magic? And have you seen it?"

"I don't know," Donevan admitted. "I have never seen evidence of magic, only know that they believe in it. In truth I'd never seen one of these myself, only the drawings of travelers who claimed to have visited Erath, before…" He trailed off, sadness mingling with curiosity in his expression.

"Before?"

He handed the horse back to her, obviously unwilling to answer.

"They're gone," he said finally. "At least most of them. We aren't sure exactly when, but near twenty-five years ago, Erath was overrun by Caelan, and they have enslaved most of the Erathi people. According to the information we have, the Caelani take their talismans and destroy them." He gestured at the horse in her hand. "This one gives me hope that perhaps a few Erathi escaped with their lives and remain free. The talismans are considered symbols of a person's magic, of their heritage, and they rarely give them up, especially to outsiders."

Trystan was momentarily without words. Where had Andrei and Alexei come by such a thing? Unless they were Erathi themselves. They had always been uncannily good with horses, though Trystan had never seen anything she would have cared to call magic.

"I have read," Donevan added, "that they might be surrendered as a token of pledge, either of fealty or betrothal, but that is little more than rumor." He hesitated. "You said it was a gift?"

Shocked and strangely uncomfortable, Trystan was unsure how to answer. If what Donevan said was true, why would her friends do such a thing? Offer such a gesture to her, who might never understand the significance of their sacrifice? "Yes," she said finally. "From a friend." She wanted to explain, and yet she didn't. Probably couldn't.

"Whoever gave you that gift cares for you." Donevan's tone seemed strangely reluctant. "Believes in you. Probably," he continued gently, "would be grieved to see you in so much pain."

Tears sprang into Trystan's eyes without warning. "I cannot think why." Her voice betrayed her with a quaver. "I have brought them nothing but ruin and grief. It seems everyone I care about must suffer for my mistakes and I am powerless to change it."

~

Prince Ramsey was experiencing quite a number of unexpected emotions. He had ridden out, daring to hope that Embrie had understood his hint and would meet him this Firstday morning. When she had not appeared at the wall, he had ridden to the pool, admitting the foolishness of his optimism, but unwilling to relinquish it.

At the sight of Theron, his heart had given a strange leap, and then fallen almost as abruptly when he noticed that the gray gelding was lathered and without saddle. The worst of his misgivings had been realized when he found a miserable, shivering Embrie by the pool.

Absurdly disappointed by her surprise at his appearance, he had offered what comfort he could, despite his own growing anger at her situation. Though she was clearly still unwilling to reveal the truth, her fear and distress were obvious. And then, he had been surprised by jealousy when she showed him the talisman. A gift that spoke of deep affection and loyalty. The sort of gift a man might give to a woman he intended to marry.

There was, of course, no indication it had come from a man. And, Ramsey did his best to rationalize, if there was a man in her life who cared so much for her, why was she out here crying and shaking with cold in the middle of the wood?

A rush of shame followed as Ramsey realized he was desperately hoping there was no such person.

There seemed no words that he could offer in the face of her despair. Without knowing of her past, anything he might say could be little other than trite and patronizing. He knew what it was to feel powerless, to realize that others were suffering for his mistakes, but dared not tell her so.

What he needed was to clear his head, to find that sense of calm patience that served him so well at court, but that seemed to be impossible with Embrie sitting so close. All he wanted at that moment was to pull her into his arms and hold her until she stopped shaking, but, whether it made him a coward or a saint, he dared not. He had no right to offer hope where there could be none. Which brought into question his motives for riding out today at all.

Desperate to say something, anything, to break the bleak mood, Ramsey settled for an attempt at distraction. "Your, ah, riding attire is a bit unconventional today." It was underhanded, of course, but probably the best that either of them could hope for.

Embrie glanced down at herself, wiped her cheeks with an already sodden sleeve, and smiled. It was a bit rueful and rather damp, but a smile. "I was not really doing very much thinking when I left," she said, brushing ineffectually at her skirts. "I was more concerned with just leaving." She shrugged. "Not terribly intelligent, I admit... especially since my lack of foresight seems to have deprived you of your coat." She made as if to remove it, but he stopped her, and settled the garment firmly back around her shoulders.

"I assure you, I don't need it." He would have given the same answer if it were snowing. "Was feeling rather foolish for having brought the silly thing. I should thank you," he added absurdly, "for renewing my faith in my own foresight." She laughed at him weakly, as of course he had meant for her to do. It was truly ridiculous how happy it made him to hear her laugh.

"I wish I didn't have to go home." Her sudden admission threatened to tear his heart into teeny tiny shreds.

"Then don't." His answer burst out before he could stop it.

"For a while," he amended hastily. "Stay this afternoon, and I will tell you as many horrifying tales of my childhood as I can think of to distract you."

~

Trystan knew she was unlikely to ever see him again. That when her occasional rides ended, so would this improbable friendship. And if that were true, she wanted to take as much of him with her as she could.

"Thank you," she said, "I would like that."

And so, as the sky gradually cleared, Donevan leaned back against the mossy boulder, folded his hands behind his head, and began to spin fantastic tales of a curious little boy who lived in an enormous house with an adventurous older brother. He meant, perhaps, to hide as much as he told, but Trystan could begin to glimpse some of what he dared not tell. His firm sense of duty. His love for his family. And his enormously self-deprecating sense of humor.

It was far past tea-time when she finally gathered her courage and pushed to her feet, interrupting a companionable silence. "I should get back before dark." Which was ridiculous, when she thought about it. What difference did dark or not dark make?

Donevan wrinkled his forehead as if trying to decide something. "I could escort you. Just part way," he added, "enough to know you're safe."

Trystan shook her head adamantly. "I cannot risk being seen with you, nor, I suspect, can you risk being seen with me."

He stood up next to her with a mulish expression.

"Don't argue!" she begged. "You know that I'm right." She took off his coat and tried to hand it back.

Donevan folded his arms and glared.

"You must," she insisted, badly as she wanted to keep something to remind her of this friendship. "I am warm enough now, and I cannot be found with this. There would be too many questions."

He took it back, obviously unhappy, and followed her to where the horses waited, half-asleep under the trees. Trystan untied Theron and looked around for her makeshift mounting block, but he was too fast for her. As he had that first afternoon, Donevan knelt and offered her his cupped hands. She could barely see for the sudden tears, but managed the process somehow, once again tossed onto Theron's back as if she weighed nothing at all. She opened her mouth to say goodbye, but nothing came out.

How did you say goodbye to someone who was most likely leaving your life forever? Was that why she had run away? So she would not have to say goodbye to people she would never see again? Confused and miserable, she would have just turned and left, but Donevan caught her rein and then her hand.

"Embrie," he said, then stopped, obviously struggling to know what to say. "Promise me you won't despair." He sounded somehow both fierce and desperate. "Whatever you may feel, there is always hope. Do not let them win."

She nodded blindly. He pressed her hand tightly, then stepped back. She turned to go, looked back to where he stood, a watery blur. Still, no words came. Trystan wheeled and rode away before her courage failed her entirely.

~

Behind her, a solitary figure clenched his fists to hold back the sting of tears he could not afford to shed. He never should have come. He never should have let himself care, but it was far too late for that now. Ramsey cursed himself for a fool even as he watched her go, and it took everything he had to simply stand there and do nothing. After she finally disappeared into the shadows, he closed his eyes and raised a hand in an unwilling and unseen farewell.

CHAPTER 5

*W*hen Trystan dismounted outside the stable, the inside was dark, as she had known it would be. She cared for Theron herself, walking him until he was cool, brushing him thoroughly and giving him his evening ration of grain. She checked to see that the other horses were well watered, cleaned Theron's bridle, polished the bit, and then admitted to herself that she was stalling. The unpleasantness would not be less for putting it off.

Her steps slow and heavy, she went to the house, her courage not quite up to using the front door. Instead, she cut through the kitchen garden and went in through the scullery. The usual after-dinner chaos was not as chaotic as usual. The same tasks were being done, but there was an eerie quiet, which diminished to near silence when someone caught sight of Trystan.

Whispers sprang up, then died down again as Vianne appeared from somewhere. With a single look, she sent everyone in the kitchen back to their assorted tasks, grasped Trystan's arm and with uncharacteristic haste, bustled her into the storeroom.

"Sit!" Vianne pointed to a stack of empty wooden bins. Trystan sat. Her legs were unlikely to hold her up much longer in any case. She tried looking at the cook, but the woman's gimlet gaze was too pointed for her to hold for long. "Why, child?" An unexpected note of exasperation crept into Vianne's voice as she folded her arms and addressed her former employer's daughter.

Trystan did not really have an answer, though she tried, her eyes fixed on the toes of her ruined shoes. "She was sending them away! With nothing! I couldn't just pretend it didn't matter…"

Vianne cut her off impatiently. "I know, child! We all knew! It was only a matter of time."

Trystan looked up, confused. "Then why did they stay? They could have had new positions, looked for better pay. If they knew, why didn't they leave before it was too late?"

"Tush, child, are you blind?" Vianne's tone was harsh. "They cared about you! They stayed to watch you and make sure you would be all right."

Trystan only felt worse. "Then this is all my fault…"

Vianne leaned forward, seized her chin and forced it up. "Stop that this instant. I will not listen to you snivel!"

Trystan sniveled. Then looked for a handkerchief she knew she didn't have. Vianne produced one and waited while Trystan blew her nose and wiped her eyes.

"Everyone who was dismissed today has had a plan ever since your father passed," Vianne stated flatly. "We all planned to stay as long as we could, but none of us expected it to be even this long. That woman was going to assert herself sooner or later." Her vexation grew considerably more apparent. "All you accomplished today was to worry us half to death and make certain anyone who cared about you in the least would be forced to leave without getting to say goodbye!"

"I know." Trystan had no defense for her actions, but wanted Vianne to know she was honest enough to acknowledge her reasons for running. "I think... I think I left because I was afraid of saying goodbye, because then I would have to admit how much I cared." She looked down at her filthy hands, twisted in her lap. "I have never been an easy person to care about, I know." Her mouth twisted a little with self-loathing. "It took me far too long to realize that I still had friends, and I think I could not forgive myself that I never told them..." She could not really continue, but Vianne was wise enough to see it.

"They loved you, child." Her words cut through Trystan's misery. "Not because they expected you to give them something in return, but because you were as much ours as your father's. Whether you saw it or not."

The moment Vianne said it, Trystan knew it was true. Her father had been a very present influence in her life, and she had never doubted his love, but it had been the servants who had raised her in many ways. It should have made her more miserable, but oddly, it did not. There was a comfort in knowing you were loved, even when you could no longer acknowledge it.

"She is going to lock me up," Trystan admitted in a small voice. "Until after the prince's masqued ball. I... I don't know what else."

Vianne snorted. "Trystan, child." She forced Trystan's chin up once more. "You can bear it, whatever it is. You will not be alone. She thinks she has beaten you, but Her Ladyship does not know how strong you are, or how many allies you have."

Trystan forced herself to meet Vianne's eyes and found that they appeared less granite than usual. The cook's expression was grim, but her eyes looked almost... Wet? Never. Trystan knew she was mistaken. She could no more imagine Vianne crying than Malisse being kind.

And she knew Vianne was right. As if Vianne had ever been anything else. Trystan smiled through her pain, stood up, and hugged the woman who had restored the faintest spark of hope. She didn't much care whether Vianne wanted a hug or not.

Stiff with surprise, the older woman returned the hug briefly, then set her back. "Get on with you, child. You need to get it over with."

Trystan nodded, wiped her eyes, returned Vianne's handkerchief, and left the kitchen to face her stepmother's retribution.

∾

After seven days, Trystan was not feeling nearly so brave. The preparations for the masque went on, even as she spent each day staring at the same four walls. The door was kept locked, only opened for meals and the emptying of the chamber pot. Even the window was secured. Malisse was taking no chances.

It could, in truth, have been worse. The maids who brought food had smuggled in books. Her sketch pad had come in with the bathtub. Even the hated embroidery had kept her hands from beating on the walls for a few more hours. But as the days till the masque grew shorter, time itself seemed to stretch. Eight more days, and who knew how many after?

There were a few distractions in the midst of Trystan's boredom. The callers had grown ever more numerous as the days wore on, and the sounds from beyond her door more varied, and indeed more shrill. Sometimes Trystan would stretch out on the floor and watch the strip of light under her door to see who passed and guess where they were going. It was pathetic, but she was not yet ready to resign the fight.

That afternoon, Trystan was awakened from a nap by an unexpected visitor.

Malisse. She stood in the doorway looking both angry and perplexed. "Get up," she ordered without ceremony. "And change your dress. That one looks ridiculous."

"Why?" Trystan asked sleepily. "I'm the only one who sees me and this one is comfortable."

"Do as you're told!" Malisse snapped. "Then come downstairs. And see that you're presentable." Her face twisted as though she had eaten something that disagreed with her. "You have a caller."

A caller? Trystan couldn't quite believe the words. She had never been allowed callers, even when she wasn't doing "penance." Who could have bullied her stepmother into letting her out of her room?

Could it be... No! She quelled that thought as soon as it rose up. She would not think of Donevan. Not ever.

Trying not to speculate, Trystan did as Malisse had requested. Her green crepe came out again, and her best slippers. She twisted her hair up into a reasonable knot, and washed her face. That was as far as she would go for her stepmother's reputation.

As she descended the stairs and approached the sitting room, she could hear voices. One was Malisse. The other was similar, both feminine and decisive. It sounded familiar. Trystan opened the door and curtsied... to their neighbor, Lady Isaura Westerby, who rose from the settee and returned the curtsey.

"Trystan, my dear, how very lovely to see you!" she said, coming forward to grasp Trystan's hand in her elegantly gloved one. "It has been a very long time indeed." She smiled, and it actually looked genuine.

Trystan knew she was doing a poor job of keeping confusion from showing on her face, but it was all a bit too much to sort out so soon after waking. Lady Isaura had not spoken to her since Lord Percival's death, nor had she shown much real interest even then.

"Now then," Lady Isaura continued, "I was most distressed not to have the pleasure of your company at the party I gave for Miss Darya's birthday. Your lovely mama indicated you had been unwell, and I do hope that it was not too serious."

Trystan blinked, thought some rather disrespectful things about her stepmother, and replied as politely as confusion would allow. "Of course not, Lady Westerby." She smiled as naturally as possible under the circumstances. "I have since made a full recovery…" Trystan paused, trying desperately to think of some genteel inquiry she could make that would not strain the bounds of propriety. As it turned out, she could remember little about Lady Westerby save that she was fond of parties and that her husband had been in the wool trade. Neither of which made for thrilling conversation. She was saved by Lady Isaura's next comment.

"You know, Trystan, you do put me so much in mind of your father. He had very much the same eyes, I believe, and the same chin."

Well, this was going too far, even for the sake of politeness. Lord Percival's eyes had been green, and his chin decidedly square. Trystan's chin was nothing if not a bit pointed.

"Thank you, Lady Westerby," was the only safe thing to say. "I've often missed him, these three years. It is a comfort to know he has not been forgotten by all his friends."

Lady Isaura inclined her head in a gracious nod. "Not at all! In fact," she added, turning to Trystan's stepmother, "it would please me greatly, Malisse, if you would permit Trystan to come and have tea with me. Perhaps tomorrow? I should very much like to spend some time reminiscing about those days, when my dear Osric was alive and the neighborhood was more lively."

It was the first time in Trystan's memory that Malisse had *not* been in charge of a conversation. Lady Isaura had very neatly outmaneuvered her neighbor, and even offered her a thinly veiled insult, all in such a way as to make it impossible for Malisse to refuse her what she wanted. Trystan was notably impressed.

"I'm sure Trystan will be delighted, Lady Westerby." Malisse managed to get the words out between frozen lips, though her eyes promised painful questions for later.

The usual pleasantries were exchanged and polite farewells were uttered, polite mostly on the part of Lady Westerby. Malisse was obviously feeling thwarted and Trystan was too preoccupied to do much more than curtsey perfunctorily.

She was honest enough to admit her lack of attention to social intricacies, but her instincts insisted that Lady Isaura's invitation stank of intrigue. Even if the point was only to annoy Malisse. Which, if Trystan's memories were accurate, seemed a bit too petty for Lady Isaura.

Lord Percival had always seemed to respect the Westerbys as business associates and had bored a younger Trystan to near tears over several dinners with rather heated discussions of the economy and politics, discussions in which both Westerbys had figured as prominent and vocal participants. Trystan doubted Lady Isaura was now stooping to petty annoyances, especially not so soon after she had gone to great lengths to court Malisse's goodwill by throwing a rather elaborate birthday party for her youngest daughter. No, Trystan would have to watch where and when and how she stepped. If she survived Malisse's retribution.

No sooner had Sanderl, the excessively pompous new butler, closed the front door behind Lady Westerby, than Malisse pinched Trystan's ear and forced her back into a seat, expression wavering between fury and speculation.

"What"—her tone could have frozen a teakettle—"is the meaning of this outrageous display of... of misplaced distinction?"

True, the invitation excluded Anya and Darya, but Trystan knew Malisse had no legitimate excuse for her ire. Society dictated that if anyone was to be singled out for attention, the eldest was given precedence. And Trystan's acquaintance with Lady Westerby had existed far longer even than Malisse's. Still, there was no sense in ruffling Malisse's feathers any further than necessary.

"I'm sure I have no idea, Stepmother." Trystan shrugged, her tone as bland as she could make it. "I have not spoken to Lady Westerby since the funeral." The word still burned her a little. "She was friends with Father, but she has never shown much interest in me personally." Let her stepmother believe it was really about Lord Percival. "I'm sure it's as she said, that she wishes to speak of the past."

Malisse harrumphed loudly, an unladylike sound of disbelief. "*You* may be sure, but I will want a full report of what is discussed." She hissed in frustration. "And if you set so much as a toe out of line, or dare to mention the slightest hint of our private affairs..." She had no need to elaborate.

Trystan rose, bobbed another respectful curtsey, and began to leave.

"Wait." Malisse looked as though she had eaten something

sour. "Much as it pains me to waste my resources on a thankless dowd..." Her sigh was as theatrical as she could make it, conveying worlds of heart-rending regret. "You cannot go to Lady Westerby's in that"—she shuddered in horror—"dress, I suppose you call it."

Trystan glanced down at her green crepe. They were both well aware of who had refused to have any new dresses made for the last two years. She raised her amber eyes to Malisse's blue ones and met them coolly. "Then I suppose you will have to arrange for it, Stepmother. It would be rather difficult for me to procure a new wardrobe from the confines of my room."

Malisse's eyes narrowed, but for the moment, at least, her nails were clipped and she knew it. "The modiste will be in to see you this afternoon. Perhaps we can make over something to fit you." That, however, was the end of her grudgingly bestowed largesse. "Until then," Malisse continued sweetly, with a predatory smile, "you will return to your penance."

Trystan did not deign to respond, only left the hall and retreated to her chamber to consider the possibilities.

Trystan was agreeably surprised by the gown that appeared that afternoon in the hands of a highly affronted modiste. It was one of Anya's, only slightly outmoded, in a shade of blue that was not entirely unflattering. Apparently, Malisse was not willing to risk critique for any perceived failure in matters of fashion. The modiste, conscious of what she considered a slight to her dignity, muttered under her breath for the entire hour that it took to adjust and pin the dress appropriately. While Anya and Trystan were of a similar height, Trystan's stepsister's build was decidedly more curvaceous than her own willowy figure.

The rest of her day she filled up by embroidering and practicing dance steps with a ghostly partner who she very carefully did not imagine with Donevan's face. At least, not more than once or twice. She slept soundly, for a change, and woke pathetically eager for tea time to arrive. Even dangerous and unknown intrigue would be an improvement on imprisonment and ennui.

Shortly after Trystan finished an uninspiring luncheon of cold meats and leftover pudding, Malisse appeared with the altered gown and a frustrated temper to give her final instructions. There were to be no vulgar outbursts. No discussion of private family business. And absolutely no disclosure of the details of Trystan's "penance."

"You are not to breath a word about it. No matter how shameless you may be, I will not be exposed to censure because of the measures I must take to control your disgraceful behavior!"

Trystan waited patiently as Malisse finished. Emboldened a trifle by the imminent adventure, she employed her sweetest voice in retaliation. "No, Stepmother, of course not. I would never want anyone to discover the truth of your inability to govern one poor, fatherless girl."

Malisse stiffened. Her face, to Trystan's surprise and satisfaction, turned an alarming shade of red, right before Malisse slapped her with startling violence. "Hold your tongue, you wicked, selfish girl." Malisse's voice was hard and wintery cold, overflowing with long-suppressed bitterness. "You have *no* idea what I put up with while your father was alive. From the very moment I entered this house I was forced to take second place to a spoiled, self-centered child. Percy permitted you an unseemly degree of latitude, even over-ruling my express wishes in favor of your petulant demands. I became mistress of this house for the first time when your father died, and I will never," she said, hissing the word with virulent force, "*never* permit you to rule me again."

Stunned into immobility by the depth of her stepmother's long-held grudge, Trystan could only sit silently while Malisse recovered her equilibrium.

"Be ready in half an hour," was her last curt command as she unclenched her hands, smoothed her dress and stalked out of the room.

Trystan wasn't entirely sure she would be able to move by then. She felt a bit ashamed that she had never truly considered the source of her stepmother's hatred. It did nothing to change her feelings toward the woman, but it did, loathe though she was to admit it, cause her to question her memories of her father. She was aware that Lord Colbourne had been over-indulgent, and perhaps less than strict in her upbringing. Until very lately, she had always assumed it was because he loved her.

The terms of his will had made her question the depth of his love to a point. Knowing that his second wife despised his daughter, he had still failed to leave Trystan with any means of independence. She knew he had not expected to die so young, but it was still an enormous oversight for a man whose business dealings were usually both punctual and precise. Over time, she had forgiven him, excusing his thoughtlessness so she could go on believing him a paragon.

But these new revelations, even if Malisse meant them only to corrupt Trystan's image of Percival Colbourne as a faultless parent, had all the bitterness of truth, blended with the sting of reproach. Love, Trystan thought with a pang, was not the same as latitude, especially not when it proved the means of fracturing what might otherwise have become a family.

Trystan's thoughts were still thus unpleasantly engaged when she was summoned downstairs to make her brief journey to Westhaven. Her mind was blessedly re-directed almost at once by the sight of the unfamiliar, rather florid man who drove the coach. Loyalty to her friends may have colored her assessment of him as a lazy-looking villain who had not bothered to brush the team properly before putting them in harness, but as a driver he seemed competent enough. He pulled up smartly before the front door of Westhaven at a fashionable five minutes till tea time.

Trystan was shown into an elegantly appointed sitting room by a uniformed footman who wore more polish than expression. The atmosphere felt... carefully selected. Trystan wondered whether she, too, had been carefully selected and for what.

Lady Isaura rose from her seat and greeted Trystan warmly, with a rather too-familiar peck on each cheek. As usual, the dignified, dark-haired, dark-eyed widow showed little sign of either age or care, remaining much the same at fifty as she had at thirty. At least to Trystan's eye. Perhaps it was some age-defying secret she shared with Malisse, worth a small kingdom or two if it could be reproduced.

"Trystan, dear, so delighted you could come!" This was followed by further inanities, to which Trystan replied with growing impatience. The tea was of the finest quality, and the cakes unparalleled, but Trystan had not paced her room for hours over a matter of victuals. Fortunately, Lady Isaura came to the point of her invitation before her guest came to the point of desperation.

"Trystan, it has come to my attention, through channels that need not concern you, that your situation"—Lady Isaura invested the word with a great deal of weight—"at home, is not, perhaps, all that could be desired for a girl of your station and upbringing."

Trystan translated mentally, wanting very much to know about those "channels" she was not to be concerned with. In her experience, when someone said not to be concerned, it usually meant you should be. And she was not nearly certain enough of Lady Isaura's intentions to pay her the compliment of answering honestly.

"I am not certain what you mean, Lady Westerby." She widened her eyes innocently and put her head to one side. She had seen Darya do it often enough to know that it made one look like an imbecile.

"Trystan," Lady Isaura sighed as though in reproof, "do an old lady the favor of dispensing with pretense. I know very well that your father would not have approved of your treatment these past few years."

Trystan's first thought was a bitter reflection that her father must have approved or he would have taken steps to prevent it. Her second was to wonder why Lady Isaura would care, but she was careful to voice neither of these. "Lady Westerby, I confess I do not quite understand the reason for your disclosure. You must know that I am hardly at liberty to discuss these matters with you, or anyone else."

"In my home," Lady Isaura said firmly, "anything you say will be held sacred. You have my word that no hint of our conversation will be repeated to interested parties."

In light of Lady Isaura's earlier reference to "channels," Trystan felt very comfortable *not* accepting this assurance of secrecy. "Even if what you say is true, I'm afraid I still cannot see the purpose of your interest in my circumstances," Trystan responded warily. "My situation is unlikely to be affected by considerations of public disapproval. Any accusations will simply be denied, with no evidence to the contrary." It was a tacit admission of the truth of Lady Isaura's statements, but that could not be helped.

"You are, of course, quite right." Lady Isaura looked pleased at Trystan's response, as though her guest was a favorite dog who had learned to fetch. "Which is why I would never attempt such a thing." The older woman fell silent. Pretended to consider.

"Trystan," she began again, "you are, I am sure, aware that I have taken over the management of these estates since my dear Osric's death." Trystan nodded, not quite sure where this was going. "You are also aware that I was a close friend and confidant of your father's, and that he shared with Lord Westerby and myself his hopes for your future." Trystan was aware of no such thing, but held her tongue. "Hopes that cannot ever be realized now that Lord Colbourne has passed on." Well, that was true enough. "What I doubt you have realized under your present constraints is the dire situation in which our kingdom finds itself."

Aha! Perhaps *now* she meant to make her point.

"I am not a political creature, Trystan, I am only a woman of business, but even I can see that our kingdom will suffer without a certain number of necessary steps towards securing our future. Steps that will assure us our rightful place in the world, assure the welfare of future generations. Generations that I, sadly,"—she looked away in what appeared to be genuine regret—"will never contribute to. But that does not," she continued firmly, "mean that I would be justified in turning my back on my kingdom's concerns. We are living in truly exciting times." Her eyes brightened as she warmed to her subject. "There are opportunities at hand, should we have the courage to grasp them. But..." She sobered abruptly. "There exists yet a lack of determined leadership in charting the best course through the upheavals we are now experiencing. Uncertainty is a terrible thing for a kingdom, especially in those persons"—the barest pause—"who, it must be acknowledged, may have for too long occupied unassailable positions of authority."

Silence. Trystan was hard-pressed to control her eyebrows, which were trying to climb into her hairline. She would have liked to assert that she was no fool, but sadly that would be a lie. She had been many kinds of fool in her life, and was daily discovering more. But not fool enough, she realized, to fail to recognize the import of what Lady Isaura seemed to be approaching in a bewilderingly indirect fashion. This, Trystan decided, was about Politics.

"Lady Westerby," she said, stalling for time, "I apologize for being obtuse, but I'm afraid I don't understand. I have never been very fond of politics, nor they of me, and I cannot imagine what this might have to do with my situation."

Lady Isaura smiled indulgently, and enlightened her. "I have come, dear, to a realization. Our kingdom is in need of aid, which I cannot give it. My situation as a widow, and a woman of advanced years, renders me unable to do what is necessary. I, and indeed a number of other concerned members of the nobility, have agreed that we require the services of someone rather younger than ourselves. Someone," she said, with a pointed look at Trystan, "unconnected with the ongoing political conversation."

This much Trystan could acknowledge to be true. One could not possibly be less connected than she was. But what could that possibly have to do with anything? "Again, I apologize,

Lady Westerby. What is it you are suggesting I could aid you with?"

"Not aid *me*, Trystan," the older woman admonished gently, "aid our kingdom. In this present crisis, nearly all of the noble families have already firmly entrenched themselves on one side or another. Our positions are well known, and any common ground that may exist between us is swiftly disappearing. Even at court, these days, the atmosphere can be... quite tense. What is needed now"—she gestured at Trystan—"is someone without prejudice or established associations. Someone who has both the means and the courage to bridge the gap between the estranged parties." Lady Isaura contrived to look sadly hopeful. "And, if that person can be found, perhaps they may somehow bring about the reconciliation, the unity, that our kingdom so desperately needs."

Oh, Trystan thought. Oh! The thought was capitalized, ornate, and covered in curlicues. A very interesting world of speculation had blossomed. This was about the succession! Anya and Darya's friends had let fall enough gossip for her to know there was some disagreement amongst both the nobility and the merchant class as to the wisdom of the king's choice. Lady Isaura obviously belonged to the group who disapproved of Prince Ramsey. Why they should disapprove did not really concern or interest Trystan. Nor did the issue of who should or should not be king. Whichever backside warmed the throne, her own life was unlikely to change one whit. What did interest her was the dissenters' unlikely choice of agent.

"I find that I am curious, Lady Westerby," Trystan asked carefully. "What exactly is the nature of the aid my kingdom requires and why is it that I am best suited to offer it?"

Lady Isaura leaned back in her seat and regarded her guest. "A reasonable question, Trystan. I do not wish to be unpleasant, but the running of a kingdom sometimes requires unpleasant realities to be faced. Occasionally, information comes to light which is of vital importance to those in a position to make wise judgments, to aid them in determining how best to proceed. This type of information," she pointed out, "often cannot be communicated in the usual ways. There would be far too many opportunities for misunderstanding. Those of us who are concerned about the kingdom's future would like to request your aid in ensuring that this communication takes place. By doing so, you would ensure that those with the greatest regard and care for the future of our kingdom are best equipped to make the necessary decisions for the good of Andar."

Trystan was now more confused than ever. "I am not sure how you expect me to communicate with any of these 'concerned citizens,'" she responded, with a rather pointed edge. "You have most likely noticed that I rarely move amongst exalted company."

"No need to be snide," Lady Isaura said drily. "We are of course aware of your restrictions. Which is why we have a more formal proposal to lay before you, a way that perhaps we may all benefit from the situation in which we find ourselves." She eyed Trystan deliberately before continuing.

"We would like you to attend the masque."

Trystan opened her mouth. She closed her mouth. She leaned back in her seat. Then sat up again, entirely unequal to the task of concealing her surprise. The masque? Where the much-maligned Prince Ramsey intended to hold auditions for his future wife?

"Lady Westerby," she said, and stopped, unsure how to express her misgivings, both with the idea and the motivation behind it. And with her own ability to fulfill the request. While she technically possessed the training to move in the highest circles of society, she had next to no practice in doing so. Nor was she certain she cared to change that.

"Lady Westerby, I find myself unsure of your intentions. I should assert"—Trystan met Lady Isaura's eye with firm conviction—"that I have no desire to attend a masque. None. At all. If you assumed I would be overwhelmed by the offer of an opportunity to wear a lovely gown and dance with a prince I should inform you that the assumption is in error. The prospect, I assure you, sounds very much like torture."

Lady Isaura did not appear in the least surprised. "I have known you for some time, my dear, and did not for a moment assume otherwise."

"Then I'm afraid I still don't understand," Trystan repeated. "Why would you single me out for a task I have no desire to perform?"

A thoughtful look appeared on Lady Isaura's face. "In other words," she translated, narrowing her dark eyes sharply, "what's in this for you?"

Trystan inclined her head modestly, willing to play along with the supposition. "My father did teach me to protect my interests, Lady Westerby," she said apologetically, "even if I have not always proven successful in the past."

Lady Isaura nodded slowly, then appeared relieved. "I must say, Trystan, I did not expect you to grasp the situation quite so clearly. I have been pleasantly surprised in you." Was that a compliment? "I am, as I have said, a woman of business, and not a charitable institution."

Trystan was somewhat relieved that the older woman had abandoned her pretense of solicitude. Mercenary motivations were far easier to understand.

"Under the circumstances, I am prepared to offer you value

for value." Lady Isaura had clearly thought through this possibility beforehand. "As you may have grasped, our desire is for Prince Rowan to succeed his father. We feel that the stability and safety of our kingdom, both now and for future generations, depend upon it. If you agree to do as we ask and are successful in your task, we are prepared to offer you your independence."

Her independence... Was that even possible? Trystan had been expecting something more on the level of a pony. Momentarily shocked into silent immobility, she mentally reviewed what she thought she had heard. Her freedom. From Malisse. Forever.

Lady Isaura went on. "As you know, I am childless, and both my dear Osric and I were without siblings. There is, at present, no suitable heir to the Westerby properties. I propose that in the event you succeed in your assigned task, I will immediately sign one of my larger properties over to you." She watched Trystan closely. "It would be sufficient to secure your financial independence and provide for a lifestyle in keeping with your status. The only condition is that you attend the masque, where you will be expected to retrieve an important message without being detected."

Lady Westerby fell silent for a few moments as Trystan's thoughts churned violently. The sordid truth was finally made clear: Lady Isaura had just asked her to become a spy. Was she expecting an answer?

"We understand, of course, that you will require time to make a decision." Trystan's hostess spoke graciously, as though conferring a favor. "I would caution you, however, to be prompt. This offer is not a perpetual one." She fixed Trystan with her gaze. "Should you fail to respond in a timely manner, we will be forced to proceed to the next most appropriate candidate."

Trystan nodded in what she hoped looked like grateful understanding, without much inclination to answer aloud. There was far too much speculation raging through her mind to leave room for further pleasantries. Fortunately, Lady Westerby knew very well what she had wrought, and rang the bell for her footman.

"I believe I may have overwhelmed you, dear. Of course you would like to go home and consider in peace. Barnaby will show you out." She rose, once again all elegant poise and politeness.

Trystan curtsied, not bothering to murmur any polite words of thanks or farewell. As she was about to exit the room, Lady Isaura's voice rose once more behind her.

"I suppose I need not remind you that the subject of our discussion ought not be aired at Colbourne." A warning. And an unnecessary one.

"Of course, Lady Westerby. I quite understand."

The remainder of Trystan's exit was swift and without ceremony. The coach awaited her as if by magic and delivered her to the front door of Colbourne Manor long before Trystan was ready to face anyone, let alone Malisse.

Her stepmother was, of course, waiting in the front hall, and dragged her into the sitting room without permission or preamble. "Well," Malisse asked sharply, "what did she want?"

For the second time that day, Trystan's mouth opened and no sound came out. She shut it and tried again. "As you suspected, Stepmother," she said, laying aside the fact that it was Trystan, and not Malisse, who had suggested the possible reason for the invitation. "She wished to reminisce over past associations. Share her memories." Trystan improvised the possibility that Lady Isaura had a heart. "After all, she has no children. She seems more sad than I recall. Perhaps she regrets that she leaves no one behind to remember her."

The invention seemed to satisfy Malisse. It even made her

look thoughtful. "I suppose so," she allowed. "If that is the case, perhaps we should encourage her visits. One never knows where such attachments might lead."

Trystan was too tired to bother rolling her eyes. Her stepmother's mercenary turn of thoughts might not surprise her, but it did disgust her.

"I am terribly weary after my outing, Stepmother." She blinked owlishly to demonstrate. "Perhaps I should go lie down before fatigue brings on a headache."

Malisse looked at her sharply, but relented. "And see that you stay there," she reminded Trystan. "Your penance is not ended simply because Lady Westerby has conceived an affection for you." She sniffed irritably, but allowed Trystan to leave.

~

As soon as she closed her door safely behind her, Trystan removed her made-over dress and fell gratefully onto the bed, with very little intention of getting up again. Even the idea of dinner held little appeal. She had far too much to think about.

The life of a gently-born lady was, as Anya and Darya gave ample proof, not much given to deep thinking. They were expected to be accomplished, ornamental, and amiable, but certainly not introspective. Trystan was beginning to perceive the vast discrepancy between her ability to see the world clearly and her present need for clarity.

Up until a relatively short time ago, she had confined her interest and understanding to very little except herself. This private universe had once included her father, but only as an orbital object, and after his death, it had contracted down to a seething stew of her own anger and misery. It was only lately that

Trystan had begun to learn that it was necessary to look beyond her own grief. To see others and consider them for their own sake, rather than for the ways that they affected her. But Trystan's world, despite its growth, was still a small one. The world Lady Westerby inhabited was much larger and had bigger teeth.

It was not a world Trystan knew how to navigate. This was about Politics and Business and other words with capital letters. She had little hope of understanding exactly what Lady Isaura hoped to gain from this undertaking. Most likely it was about Money. Lord Percival and his associates had been perpetually concerned with making more of it. But Lady Isaura's concern for the kingdom had sounded genuine, her actual goal a simple and easily comprehended one. Exchange one prince for another. Why should that matter so much? Why should Lady Isaura care so deeply that she would offer a great deal of money to a fatherless girl in exchange for one simple message? And why choose Trystan? She understood why Lady Isaura could not do it herself, but was there no one else?

Trystan had no desire to be used. Especially not in the service of some plan she had no part in, for purposes she could not understand. But she also had no desire to remain under Malisse's thumb forever. Trystan faced the very real prospect of spending the rest of her life subject to her stepmother's whims.

And once Anya and Darya were well married, what then? Would there be anything to prevent her stepmother from carrying out her threats to throw Trystan into the street to fend for herself? Surely one evening of suffering and suspense could not be so terrible in comparison to either of those fates.

And there were other considerations. As she had told Lady Westerby, her father had indeed taught her to protect what was hers. Trystan had come to the conclusion that her father had failed miserably to follow through on his own precepts. He had, perhaps, developed too narrow an understanding of what was his.

A surprising number of people had been looking out for Trystan's welfare for years, and had been punished for it. No matter what Vianne said, Trystan needed to do something to set that right. Farley, Beatrice, Hoskins, and the others had been turned out into the streets without warning, and in some cases without much hope. With the exception of Andrei and Alexei, they would not have an easy time finding new positions. If Trystan had her own household, she could offer them a home. Stability. Hope for the future.

In the end, it was this that convinced Trystan to ignore her concerns about Lady Isaura's motives. The political end of the affair was unlikely to materially affect the lives of those Trystan was closest to, and therefore could not figure in her calculations. The only way to protect herself and those she cared about was to put herself beyond Malisse's control, and this was the only chance she'd been offered to do so. Likely the only chance she would ever have.

Trystan decided to take it. It was only one evening. One message. A few words from one person to another. Even if this mysterious message proved upsetting to the succession, as Lady Isaura seemed to hope, Trystan was unwilling to believe that her contribution would make so great a difference. Prevailing opinion seemed so heavily in favor of the paragon Prince Rowan, that it surely was only a matter of time before the irksome and unwelcome Prince Ramsey abdicated out of sheer embarrassment anyway. Her services would be merely an afterthought in an expensive dress.

Content with her reasoning, Trystan took considerable time

penning a message to Lady Westerby, ostensibly thanking her for the invitation to tea, but also conveying her acceptance of the kindly tendered offer. It was worded so as to escape either detection or censure should Malisse be rude enough to read the letter before sending it, which Trystan had no doubt she would.

The remainder of the afternoon was spent in agreeable reflection on the many things she would do when she was mistress of her own fate. She was aware that such reflections were perhaps a bit premature, but was enjoying herself far too much to rein in her imagination. There would be time later for considering irksome details, such as complications and consequences. To name only a few.

CHAPTER 6

*P*rince Ramsey was knee-deep in both complications and consequences, mostly not of his own making. After several long nights with his father, numerous advisors, countless councilors and a few well-meaning relatives, he had resentfully agreed to satisfy the growing demands of the court that he marry. There had been ominous hints of increased unrest should he fail to provide the stability of an heir, little better than threats if one read them cynically.

Ramsey had always known he would have to marry someone. And that his position most likely meant he would be lucky to find a woman he could love. Until lately, however, he had managed to hang on to a tiny bit of hope, even if that hope had become a vague desire to marry someone who liked him better than they liked his brother.

Now he just wanted to get it over with.

Prince Ramsey was fairly certain he had met all of the eligible daughters the kingdom had to throw at him. Not a one of them had impressed him, though to be fair, the balls and parties arranged for the purpose of bringing eligible young people together rarely gave opportunity for honest conversation. It was possible that an intelligent, sympathetic and slightly blind young lady who would not swoon at the sight of Prince Rowan was still out there somewhere. Which was why Ramsey had convinced his father to hold the masque before the elder prince's period of exile had expired.

It was not a perfect plan, but at least Ramsey would be spared the aggravation of looking over his shoulder the whole night. And if he had the chance to impress a girl with his wit, intelligence, and humor before she could be overwhelmed by his brother's angelic good looks, smoothly flattering manners, graceful dancing and... Oh, who was he kidding? The only motivation a girl could have for marrying Ramsey was his crown. Not, historically, a boon to lasting marital affections. Of course, it would also help to meet a girl who could see through his brother's charming facade to the self-absorbed manipulator underneath, but Ramsey had yet to find one.

Except for his Aunt Lizbet.

The second part of his plan to find marital bliss (or perhaps simply to avoid marital catastrophe) had been Aunt Lizbet's idea. She was his mother's sister, nearly twin in appearance, and married to one of his father's councilors. Usually a quiet and reserved person who was fiercely protective of her family, Lizbet was also one of the few who had always thought Rowan would look better wearing chains and a prison uniform. After the incident with Parry, she had apparently threatened him with bodily harm should he ever approach one of her children again. Ramsey had seen her with a sword once and would have recommended that his brother find himself a new continent rather than face her.

When Lizbet had first proposed her idea for the masque Ramsey had been a bit disgusted, but once she had explained, it made at least as much sense as picking a wife because she was an excellent dancer and looked good in a dress.

"It makes me sound like an insufferably conceited clerk!" he had complained.

"In case you haven't noticed," his aunt retorted dryly, "that's what most of them already believe you to be."

Which was, regrettably, true. While his older brother had been busy charming the masses, Ramsey had been working, learning to run a kingdom and cleaning up after Rowan's many indiscretions. On the occasions when Ramsey had been forced to mingle with people his own age, it was typically in company with his brother, who had always made Ramsey feel clumsy, tongue-tied and inadequate. Rather than compete, Ramsey had chosen to stay in the shadows, publicly cast by Rowan in the role of disapproving chaperone. It was little wonder girls considered him a "stodgy prig," as he had once overheard at a crowded party. He was beginning to agree with their assessment himself.

And so, the invitations had gone out to every family in the nobility that could reasonably be supposed to have daughters. Those missives had cryptically stated that he would be accepting applications for his hand in marriage, but had carefully *not* detailed what those applications would entail. Lizbet had laughed a bit evilly as she painted for him a vivid picture of the turmoil those invitations would create in the minds of scheming mothers and mercenary daughters across the kingdom.

"But what's the point?" he asked, sitting in his aunt's rooms one rainy afternoon. "What do I gain with this embarrassing charade?"

"Hopefully," she answered, "a little honesty. Perhaps even a girl who can learn to love you, as I know you deserve to be loved." She smiled and ruffled his hair as she said it, much the way his mother would have. "Although," she continued, her gray eyes thoughtfully piercing his own, "I would have said recently that perhaps you had already found such a one, if the idea were not so absurd."

Ramsey dropped his eyes and fell to fiddling with one of his cousin Prisca's toys, a carved wooden horse that suddenly made him think of another horse and so he was forced to set it down before he threw it across the room in frustration.

"Or perhaps not so absurd?" his aunt added gently.

Ramsey glanced across the room to where Parry and Prisca were bent over books and slates, the day's lessons nearly completed, not wanting them to hear what his aunt suggested.

"Aunt Lizbet," he began, but stopped, feeling unequal to an explanation, to even thinking about what he wished he could explain. "Whatever you think, whatever you know, promise me you'll forget?" he begged, hoping she would hear what he could not say. "I assure you there's nothing in it but pain, for everyone. Even if you were right"—and at these words her eyes darkened in understanding—"it's impossible, and no one... *no one* will be better off by pretending it could be otherwise."

The compassion in her eyes was almost too much for him. Lizbet was only ten years his senior, but she had been the closest thing he had to a mother since his own died when he was five. And she had always known, somehow, when something was hurting him. Always been able to draw him out, even when he was no longer a little boy hiding in his brother's shadow. Now she obviously sensed his pain and echoed it back to him quietly with her sigh.

"I am very sorry, Donnie." She squeezed his hand in sympathy. "I wish that your life had permitted you to sit in a different chair."

It was one of their morbid family jokes, but today it was even darker than usual to Ramsey. If his brother were not what he was, Ramsey would be free, and this travesty of a marriage would be unnecessary. He could marry when and where he chose, even if he happened to choose a strange young woman who wore men's clothes and rode alone through the Kingswood and didn't bother with diplomacy when she spoke. Which was a foolish and pointless thought, as she might not have him even if he were free and there was that nameless good-for-nothing who had given her the horse to consider, and after all he didn't even know where she lived or worse yet, what she was hiding from and who had hurt her, though if he ever found out he would go looking for the torture chamber that proper castles were supposed to have so that he could break every bone in that unfortunate person's body one by one by one... Ramsey realized suddenly that his face was scowling without his permission and tried to retrieve the situation by smiling at his aunt, who was not remotely fooled.

"I wish you could tell me about her," she said wistfully as her nephew rose to leave.

He looked back and surprised himself by answering. "So do I." Then he dropped a kiss on Prisca's hair and left, before he was tempted to unburden himself and tell his aunt everything.

∾

Two days after the fateful tea at Westhaven, Lady Westerby herself appeared once again in the Colbourne sitting room with the most marvelous suggestion. As Malisse was no doubt worn down by the distressing number of details involved in preparing her daughters for the upcoming masque, perhaps it would be a relief to her sensibilities if she knew her eldest, and most emotionally fragile, was distracted by the diversions of a pleasant stay at Westhaven.

It would be, Lady Westerby assured Malisse, a great favor. Lady Isaura's distant cousin by marriage, a provincial young woman from the north of Andar, had sent a letter indicating her intention to visit Evenleigh as a distraction from personal disappointments. Lady Isaura had little experience with entertaining young persons, especially the socially unpolished sort she expected her cousin to be, and would be vastly comforted by the knowledge that the girl would have someone of her own age to contribute to her entertainment. Trystan would then have no opportunity to become distraught by her own inability to bear the pressures of attending the masque herself, and Lady Westerby would be able to enjoy the benefits of female company in her large, lonely household.

It was a masterfully worded invitation, and it caught Malisse in a trap of her own making. After cutting Trystan out of the social world with precisely such nonsense about her emotional state, Malisse could hardly gainsay her own lies. There was no benefit to be gained from suggesting Anya or Darya as a more appropriate companion for some backwards, countrified young debutante, and Malisse could hardly claim that Lady Isaura's cousin might prove to be a negative influence on a child she already portrayed as a social disaster.

Trystan could go, though not without Malisse warning Lady Westerby of what dangers she could expect, for herself and her no doubt impressionable young relative, should Trystan become emotionally overset. The poor child was clearly still not well and needed a firm hand if she was ever to be able to rejoin polite society.

Lady Westerby made the appropriate noises of sympathy until she and Trystan and Trystan's bags were inextricably ensconced in the Westerby carriage, at which point she favored her young protégée with her own personal estimation of Malisse's many deficiencies. Trystan did not feel it would be quite proper for her to publicly agree, but as Lady Westerby did not seem to expect a reply, she was able to listen in comfort to the diatribe until they pulled up at the door to Westhaven.

Though Trystan had, inevitably, a few misgivings, she could not help but look forward to her sojourn at any place which did not also contain her family. For the first time in six years she was free of her stepmother's judgments and complaints and she was determined to enjoy it.

Lady Westerby, however, had other ideas. No sooner had Trystan's things been settled in a guest room than she was summoned to the drawing room to begin her education.

Trystan had admitted to Lady Isaura that her knowledge of society and her experience in navigating it were both rather lacking. While she had enjoyed the benefit of the usual education available to gently born young ladies, her execution had, demonstrably, lacked application. Lady Isaura seemed determined to make up for Trystan's lack of experience in a bare five days.

"Please, sit down my dear," she said to Trystan, when they were both finally seated in the drawing room. "We have very little time to prepare for the masque, so we must make what we can of it. As you may have guessed, I have established a name and an identity for you, and made arrangements for my 'cousin' to receive an invitation to the masque. It is imperative that your attendance seem entirely natural."

Trystan was surprised. She had not expected that such elaborate preparations would be required, and said so.

"Trystan, we live in a very small kingdom." Lady Isaura spoke in a tone of reprimand. "If you expected to appear as a mystery girl and leave without being identified then you have been reading too many stories. Should you arrive at the masque without a name and a reason for attending, there are fifty people who will make it their business to find out why, and you do not, believe me, want that kind of scrutiny."

Trystan could see the wisdom in that.

"Your name," Lady Isaura continued, "is now Elaine Westover, and you are my late husband's very distant relation from the northern borderlands."

"Is there such a person?" Trystan asked curiously.

Lady Isaura laughed. "Not likely," she answered with a shrug, "though I suppose I cannot be sure. Osric did have a great-uncle who moved his family out there many years ago. I will vouch for your identity and your bloodlines, and plan to spread a great deal of gossip about the reasons for your visit with those women I know I can rely on to spread the story rapidly." She smiled slyly at Trystan. "You should know that you are here because your parents betrothed you while still a child to a suitable young man who recently ran away to sea rather than marry you. I judged it best to work with what we have rather than attempt to confine your naturally vibrant personality."

Trystan raised an eyebrow at her potential benefactress.

"I am a realist, Trystan, and you should learn to be. You are a very direct young woman, and while I cannot fully appreciate your ungoverned style, I feel we may be able to use it to our advantage in this case."

Trystan held her tongue. She knew only too well that her

temper was not as fully under rein as it should be, but was not sure she appreciated the aspersions on her "style." She could hardly have survived her past three years had she not learned to govern herself to a point, and if by "governed" Lady Isaura meant the insipid manner affected by Anya and Darya's friends, then Trystan would prefer to be herself, thank you. And as for her fictional fiancé, she would like him to know that at least one young man had not seemed to mind her straightforward ways. But she was, of course, not going to think about that. Or him. So she focused intently on Lady Isaura's continuing instructions.

"Your parents are, of course, dead—your father only a short time ago—but prior to his passing your father made a small fortune from his lumber mill. Large enough to be eligible, but too small to attract significant notice. You have no siblings, so you expect to make at least a decent match on the strength of your inheritance. Your father wanted you to marry someone closer to home, so your future husband could assume responsibility for the mill, but you are determined to get away and enjoy your freedom, taste the delights of the court. You are considering selling out of the family business if you find you prefer the city. Are you getting all this?" Lady Isaura asked, with a sharp glance at Trystan, whose eyes had begun to glaze over just a bit.

"Yes, of course," she answered brightly, not really understanding why she needed quite so much backstory. When her fictional history had been sufficiently explored, Lady Isaura began to tell her exhaustively of the influential families whose acquaintance she would naturally be expected to make as a young noblewoman on her first visit to court.

By dinnertime, Trystan's head was stuffed and aching with the names and relationships and rivalries that most other young women had been drilled in since birth as a matter of etiquette.

Even the minor detail of having never been to Evenleigh before would not excuse her from the necessity of being conversant with social politics.

After dinner, they repaired again to the drawing room to discuss Trystan's repertoire of dances, a slender thing indeed, for the remedy of which Lady Isaura had hired a very discreet dancing master who would arrive the next day. She had also arranged for her own modiste to see to Trystan's costume for the masque, a necessity considering the need for secrecy. Trystan retired that evening with a pounding headache and the beginnings of misgivings about her role in this charade.

The following days proved too full for her to dwell on any possible feelings of regret. She needed to practice speaking with the more clipped accents common in the northern part of the kingdom. Then there were the dancing lessons, instructions on etiquette, tests of her memory for names and relationships, and more than a few little sermons on the importance of secrecy and the implications of both success and failure. These, Trystan largely ignored. She could not really imagine failing to retrieve a message. Her goal was the freedom to choose her own life, not the alteration of the political and economic destiny of a kingdom, as Lady Isaura so eloquently rendered the aims of her interference. The sentiments were stirring, and no doubt noble, but not really of much concern to her protégée.

The day before the auspicious event, Trystan's costume was unveiled, a beautiful mahogany silk gown, embroidered in gold with climbing vines. Trystan's masque had been made using the same silk, cut in a butterfly pattern. Though her mouth was left bare, the fabric covered most of her face, allaying most of her concerns about being recognized. The rest were easily dismissed when Lady Isaura explained the dark brown dye that would be disguising Trystan's decidedly reddish locks. Even Anya and Darya, Trystan thought with satisfaction, would stand little chance of finding their despised stepsister under all of her finery.

That same day, Lady Isaura summoned Trystan to discuss yet another point of concern: the application for Prince Ramsey's hand.

"We have still received no clarification on that point, which is just like the man I must say. So I cannot really advise you on how to handle the process once we arrive."

Trystan frowned. "I assume it would be preferable for me to at least participate in whatever it is. For a provincial girl with aspirations, it would seem very odd to refuse a chance at marriage to the man who might be king."

Lady Isaura nodded her agreement. "Of course. You would not want to seem backward, and it would certainly do us no harm for you to be seen conversing with Prince Ramsey. He has no opinions that matter, but if he can be seen to approve of you then you will likely be free from suspicions of involvement in anything untoward."

Trystan politely expressed her disbelief in this possibility. "I very much doubt the prince will have opportunity to make small talk with every woman in the room, and I am certainly not interested in putting myself forward. Would it not be more to the point for me to pass unnoticed?"

Lady Isaura did not seem to appreciate Trystan's reasoning. "Your success is dependent upon your ability to fill your role as naturally as possible," she rejoined sternly. "There is not a young noblewoman in the kingdom who would fail to pursue the notice of the man intended to wear the crown. I suggest you spend less time arguing and more time studying."

But Trystan was not yet ready to capitulate. "I really don't see…" she began, only to be firmly interrupted.

"What you don't see, Miss Trystan, is precisely the point," Lady Isaura said coldly. "If given the chance, you *will* cultivate a conversation with the prince, if only to make everyone else wonder what he sees in you. If you wish to be successful in your task then I suggest you allow yourself to be guided by those with a keener understanding of exactly what is at stake. As you have no political knowledge or ambitions of your own, your success, and indeed I may say your future, depend on your willingness to submit to those wiser than yourself. Your responsibility is to do as you are told, not to have opinions. I trust there will be no need to remind you of this in the future?"

Trystan agreed, in humbled accents, but not without feeling a bit of a chill. It had finally occurred to her that she was but a minor player in a game that was deadly serious, for reasons that were still a mystery. Why would Lady Isaura and her friends care so very much who was to be king? Her sisters cared, but that had more to do with the princes' physical attributes than their political policies. Despite her desperate desire to gain her freedom, Trystan was beginning to feel uneasy about her position. She knew what was in it for her. Was it time to ask these shadowy "others" what was in it for them?

～

The day of the masque dawned warm and cheerful, much to Prince Ramsey's private dismay, as he was feeling neither. He attempted to see to his usual duties, only to be driven off with cheers and mocking commentary to prepare himself for the upcoming ordeal. He would much rather have kept busy.

Just after mid-day, while he was in the training yard attempting to thrash a grinning Kyril, his father sent for him. Ramsey aimed one last kick at Kyril's unrepentant backside, wiped the sweat from his face and went to his father's rooms.

He wasn't looking forward to it. He loved his father deeply, but knew he was about to hear a sermon on the duties of a son of the royal house. What kind of woman he was supposed to marry, what kind of dowry she needed to have, how short of an engagement was necessary, what would be expected of him after the wedding... He was not at all in the mood to hear his father tell him about his duty to produce sons.

When Ramsey arrived at his father's apartments, King Hollin was standing by the window, leaning heavily on a cane and looking unusually pensive. His gout had been even worse than usual of late, and, since winter, he had granted fewer audiences than ever.

"Father?" Ramsey asked tentatively. "You asked to see me?"

For a few moments the king did not turn, but continued to stare at the landscape as though he had not heard. Ramsey knew he had. His father was gouty and grouchy and probably rheumatic, but not even slightly deaf.

"I am sorry, you know," the king said without preamble. "I know that you know, but I needed to say it before tonight."

"Sorry, Father? For the idiotic mobs of people throwing tantrums, for choosing me over my brother, or for all the fools too blind to see through him? They're all an equal part of this insanity and none of them are really your fault."

Ramsey's tone was weary rather than sharp. Whatever he believed about the economic unrest that was forcing his hand, he mostly agreed with his father's policies that had sparked them. This was about so much more than his future or his children. If he had to marry to stop the kingdom from falling into violence then he would do it, and try his damnedest to ensure that it was a palatable arrangement for him and his future wife.

But that did not stop him from wishing he could beat some sense into the many parties responsible for his misery. If the guilds would stop whining and stirring up discord, if his brother were a decent human being… Of course, all of it would be easier to accept *if* Ramsey could discover the existence of a suitable young woman who would not make his domestic life miserable. But, if, in the course of twenty-five years, he had yet to meet even one acceptable female who inspired him to the smallest speculation of compatibility, it would take a special kind of insanity to believe that he could find one in a single night at a masqued ball.

"I loved your mother," the king said without preamble.

Ramsey had been told, though not by his father, that his parents' marriage had been a happy one, but his mother had died so long ago that he had little memory of it.

"We knew each other for years before we married," King Hollin continued. "I once beheaded one of her dolls and she filled my bed with spiders in retaliation. She knew I couldn't stand them." A small smile twisted the king's lips as he continued to stare out the window. "I think even while I was busy screaming my head off, I knew she was the one I wanted." A short, strangled laugh. "She told me on our wedding night that she had been dreading our marriage for most of her life. But she said it with a smile, and I believe she loved our life together as much as I did." Finally, the king turned and faced his son, tears burning trails down his cheeks and soaking his beard.

"We wanted that for you. Both of you. Everything in life—

even the terrible, painful things—becomes easier when you stand next to someone who truly knows you and cares for you anyway." His lips trembled with long-suppressed emotion. "Son, I want you to choose someone you can love. I know your advisors will tell you many things, about dowry, property, even *fertility*… may the gods spare you from that discussion! But I hope you will put those things aside. Outside of your heart, only the law matters. As long as you choose a woman of good reputation, who is a legitimate daughter of landed parents, the law, your councilors, even your critics must be content."

Ramsey was surprised and nearly moved to tears of his own. His father had been the most aggravating proponent of his marriage for the past five years. He would never have thought to look there for support in his search for a kindred mind and heart.

Acting solely on impulse, Ramsey did what he had not dared since he was a very small boy: crossed the room and wrapped his arms around his father's shoulders. The hand that was not grasping a cane came to rest on Ramsey's arm, and when he finally broke the embrace, Ramsey felt oddly comforted knowing that the king would be his ally when he made his choice. They could force him to get married, but perhaps he could still find it in him to hope that no one could force him into a life of misery.

~

A few hours later, as the sun was setting, a nervous and grim-looking Prince Ramsey emerged from his rooms to oversee the final preparations for the evening's entertainment.

He did not doubt the ability of the palace staff to follow their instructions. Lizbet had been his proxy for most of the arrangements and she was almost dazzlingly competent, especially when it came to the details that most people would overlook. But sitting in his rooms fiddling with his clothes was beginning to make him contemplate throwing himself off a balcony, so he left in search of someone to order around. Of course, he ran directly into Kyril, who was loitering in the hall waiting for him.

"Just shut up," Ramsey growled warningly at the impeccably decked out younger man, whose insouciant grin promised at the very least a lengthy assessment of Ramsey's personal style. "One word out of your mouth and I'll go find an oubliette just so I can lock you up in it."

Kyril threw a companionable arm around his friend's shoulders. "I'm crushed," he intoned mournfully. "I've sacrificed my entire evening just to support my dearest friend in his quest for matrimonial bliss and all he can do is threaten me with torture. I wasn't even going to tell him that his black formal coat looks entirely too grim for the occasion. Or that he forgot to comb his hair."

Ramsey put him in a headlock.

"All right, all right," Kyril yelped in indignation. "I promise not to flirt any more than usual. And to say nice things about you at every opportunity!"

Ramsey snorted and let him go. "I've never asked you to lie for me, Kyril."

"I've never offered," his friend retorted. "Seriously, brother," Kyril said in a far more sober tone, "you know I'm here for you. Whatever you need, say the word. I'll even offer to distract interfering potential mothers-in-law so you can whisk their starry-eyed daughters into quiet corners for romantic kisses."

Ramsey rolled his eyes, but with more relief than rancor. He could always count on Kyril to lighten the mood. It was probably why they were such good friends. One of them was too serious, the other never serious enough.

"Your job is simple, my friend," said Ramsey with a heartfelt sigh. "If you see a smart one, don't let her get away."

Kyril favored him with a mock-salute. "Anything else, Your Highness?"

"If you see Rowan, stuff him in the moat," Ramsey suggested.

Kyril grinned. "You don't have a moat."

"Dig one then."

Kyril bowed deferentially. "Of course, Your Gracefulness. I'll go get my shovel, shall I?"

Even Ramsey could spare a smile for the appealing thought of Rowan soaked and spluttering. Even if one of the main points of the evening was that the elder prince not be there at all.

"You know, Kyril," Ramsey suggested, in a deceptively off-handed tone, "I see no reason why you shouldn't keep your own eyes open, just as long as marriage is in the air."

Kyril's eyes narrowed suspiciously.

"Every eligible woman in the kingdom is going to be parading through the palace tonight," Ramsey continued, "and you might as well take advantage of the opportunity to find one for yourself."

"Hah." Kyril barked a sharp laugh. "I'm no such fool. My father is too busy to push me into matrimony. And besides"—he glanced sideways at Ramsey—"we wouldn't want any confusion. If both of us eminently eligible young fellows fell for the same girl, she would probably go into a decline for fear of making the wrong choice."

Ramsey raised an eyebrow. "I'm sorry, but I don't see the problem."

"Your crown or my dashing good looks and winning personality," Kyril supplied helpfully. "Do you really want to put some poor girl through that sort of dilemma?"

"The only dilemma I see," Ramsey grumbled, "is whether you deserve thumbscrews or the rack."

Kyril showed no indication that he took the threat seriously. "You wouldn't put me on the rack," he asserted cheerfully, "it would spoil my perfectly pleasing physical proportions."

"Precisely," Ramsey shot back, his heart noticeably lightened. As he knew Kyril had intended. "Thank you, brother," he added, more seriously, as they neared the bustling corridors around the hall where the masque was to take place. "You know I—"

Kyril cuffed him lightly on the back of the head.

"Yes," he said quietly. "I know."

～

Not so very far away, Trystan stood silent and still in front of the mirror that graced the front hall of Westhaven. In the reflection, her dress and hair perfect, her masque in place, the slender dark-haired girl appeared fully prepared for her court debut.

The mirror lied.

Trystan barely recognized herself. It wasn't just the silk dress or the expensive jewelry, or even the unfamiliar sight of dark brown hair. Even less familiar were the knots of tension that snarled in her stomach, ached between her eyes and made her hands shake in their constricting elbow-length gloves. She was used to being angry, sad, or even just plain afraid. There had never been much opportunity to experience nerves.

Lady Isaura had grown increasingly petulant and difficult to please as their preparations had drawn to a close. She was never quite happy with Trystan's progress, and certainly seemed displeased whenever Trystan expressed an interest or opinion about the more political aspects of her undertaking. Any questions about the message she was to retrieve were met with stony silence, until Trystan felt as trapped in her assumed role as she did in her incredibly tight dress.

Endless instructions chased each other around her head. Her memory was beginning to fail her on key persons and associations. She needed air and a drink, but she suspected that any attempt to breathe or imbibe would cause her stays to explode.

And the hour of doom had arrived in spite of her. A uniformed footman approached, bearing a long, hooded cloak which he placed carefully about her shoulders. As Trystan adjusted the fit, Lady Isaura descended the stairs, looking regal, impeccable and implacable in a deep purple gown and black masque to indicate her widowhood. Trystan managed to hold her breath while she was examined from head to toe.

"You look well, but I hope you intend to stop shaking," Lady Isaura noted disapprovingly. "Confidence is absolutely essential."

"Yes, Lady Westerby," was all the reply Trystan could trust herself to make. Any more and she might have to breathe. Far too soon, the coach was at the door. They were assisted into it by a pair of footmen and the door closed behind them with a very final-sounding thud.

Trystan tried not to think about the consequences of what she was about to do. She was beautifully dressed, on her way to a royal ball to dance with a prince. It could be enormously entertaining. If only she hadn't begun to wonder whether it might also be betrayal.

CHAPTER 7

*L*ady Isaura had not wanted to be early. It wouldn't do to seem eager, she said. So they arrived at the castle just after full dark, in the midst of a vast press of coaches, sedan chairs and horse-drawn vehicles of every description. Lady Isaura's footman handed them down with punctilious formality into a sea of silks and satins that reflected the wavering light from what seemed to Trystan to be thousands of torches. The final stretch of road to the castle had been lined with them, the gate and the bailey were apparently ringed with flames, and the great hall where they entered seemed to flicker with shadows. Fire shot through the gems on dresses and masques, and made each pair of eyes seem somehow threatening.

Trystan walked a little behind Lady Isaura as they passed under the arch and inside the castle, hoping not to be crushed by the press of others arriving at the same time. Trystan was not, by nature, a retiring person, but she had learned caution, and had no desire to put herself forward until she had an opportunity to observe the behavior of others. It would not do to assume that everyone else in the room would be as foolish as her stepsisters. A bit of observation would help her find her feet... but a fierce pinch under her arm interrupted these sober plans.

"You are supposed to be a provincial heiress looking for excitement, not a country miss cowering behind her chaperone's skirts," hissed Lady Isaura in her ear. "If you cannot strive for presence, we might as well go home!"

Trystan swallowed an ill-judged retort and concentrated on breathing instead.

"Once we get inside the Grand Ballroom I will be introducing you to some of my friends. I trust you plan to appear more as though you're looking forward to the evening and less as if you expect to be murdered." Lady Isaura paused for a moment. "And remember, your contact will find you. Your task is to behave naturally and ensure that the message is not discovered."

Trystan nodded, trying to focus on her true purpose and, to a point, failing.

She was a bit disappointed in herself. Even Malisse had never made her feel this way—pressed, crushed, and utterly bewildered by the sounds and sensations of being surrounded by people. She needed courage. A friendly face would have been her first choice, but she was all too aware there would be none of those this evening. As her second choice, she slipped her hand into the pocket beneath her voluminous skirt and closed her fingers around the tiny horse. It was warm, and as she clutched it, she could almost believe it was truly a talisman. Almost believe there was something to Donevan's tale of magic. The shape of it beneath her fingers reminded her fiercely of Andrei and Alexei, of Hoskins and Beatrice and Farley. Of all the people she could help and protect if she was successful tonight. This was no longer just about her, but about the people she claimed as her own. Her friends.

A few short moments later, Elaine Westover took her place at the side of Lady Isaura Westerby as they moved through the grand doorway and handed their invitation to the Master of Ceremonies. Elaine's artfully dressed brown ringlets bobbed in excitement as she chatted blithely with her companion, the always dignified widow Westerby. Elaine was young, pretty, and rich, and enormously pleased to be standing in the heart of Evenburg Castle awaiting her debut on this propitious evening. No one needed to know that Trystan Embrie Colbourne was hovering worriedly inside her head, wishing the night were already over.

～

The Grand Ballroom was indeed looking grand for the occasion. Lamps and chandeliers were ablaze, and dark green velvet draperies artfully concealed the cold stone walls, while a profusion of flowers and potted trees offered the illusion of an indoor garden. A chamber orchestra played peaceful accompaniment from a cunningly concealed loft, soft music that enhanced conversation rather than obscuring it. Elaine gazed around her with unfeigned admiration. The space had been quite adeptly arranged, with plenty of room for dancing, tables and chairs tucked neatly around the edges, all warmly lit and easily accessible. The high stone ceilings had been made to feel shorter and cozier, permitting a more festive atmosphere, despite the presence of numerous green-coated guardsmen standing about as unobtrusively as possible. The effect was very attractive, and Trystan offered mental applause to whoever had been responsible. They had done their work well, judging by the unconstrained conversation already rising around her in a persistent buzz.

There was a dais on one end of the room, directly under the musicians' loft, but for the moment it was empty. Apparently the prince had not yet seen fit to arrive at his own ball. Well, Trystan could hardly blame him. Under the circumstances, she could easily have forgiven him for running away entirely.

Through a doorway on the other end of the ballroom appeared to be a porch, or balcony, an absolute necessity when there was to be a great deal of dancing in a crowded room. For fresh air, of course, not for clandestine meetings or romantic assignations, though Trystan had read enough novels to be amused by the sight.

Before she was quite finished getting her first, admiring look at the inside of the castle, Lady Isaura found one of her "dearest" acquaintances, and introduced Elaine to Lord and Lady Fellton, a jolly-looking round-cheeked couple with a jolly-looking round-cheeked daughter wearing puce satin and a feathered masque. Elaine was delighted to meet them and eager to discuss the forth-coming entertainment. Trystan couldn't help wondering if the rotund pair were amongst the mysterious "they" who were spon-soring her presence at the masque.

She was doomed not to find out. Lady Isaura's chief aim in the introduction had been to pair her with the garrulous, puce-gowned Larissa Fellton, who apparently boasted an acquaintance as large as her store of harmless prattle, which had not stopped since their introduction. The giggling debutante needed very little encouragement to put her arm through Elaine's and bear her off in the direction of refreshment and friends.

They were halted on the way by a knot of lazy-looking young men wearing half-masks, all of whom seemed vaguely amused by

Larissa and not at all amused by Elaine. Several of them straightened up and tugged their cravats when she was introduced, and one of them was so forward as to kiss her hand and wink. Larissa teased them good-naturedly, but did not seem even slightly put out by their obvious admiration of her companion.

Trystan realized belatedly that Elaine was one of the very few people in the room who would not be well aware of everyone's identity, despite their masques. What could be the point in pretending to hide when none of your fellows were fooled?

"Why, Larissa," one of the young men simpered, which Trystan had not realized young men could do, "wherever did you find such a"—the fellow looked her up and down in a suggestive and insulting manner—"delightful new friend? I thought I was *familiar* with all the pretty girls in town."

To Trystan's horror, Elaine giggled flirtatiously and lowered her lashes. "But I've just arrived, Lord Tavender, and don't really know anyone at all," Elaine reminded him coyly. "Miss Fellton has promised to introduce me to everyone who matters."

Two of the young men swelled visibly, but Lord Tavender only smirked in self-satisfaction. "Then I believe she must be finished with the introductions for the evening, aren't you, Larissa?"

That damsel only giggled and patted his arm, still smiling, but obviously a bit confused.

At this point, Trystan decided she was done with the pretense, and regained control of her own mouth. "Actually," she responded brightly, "we were on our way to acquire some refreshments, while we're waiting." She lowered her voice conspiratorially. "I've been reliably informed that most of the *best* families aren't even arrived yet." Taking Larissa's arm before any more words could escape, Trystan steered the other girl inexorably towards the food, leaving Lord Tavender to the disbelieving laughter of his companions.

So she had made her first enemy. Larissa was still not speaking, only staring at her in something like awe. Curiously, both circumstances made Trystan feel much better.

"Miss Westover, I don't think anyone has ever talked to Wilfurd like that." Larissa's eyebrows were scrunched into a worried expression. "He won't like it at all. Girls always flirt with him, on account of his being quite a catch, except for the ones who are too rich to even look at someone who hasn't an estate of his own. His parents have a lot of money, even though he's only the second son, and he knows he's nice to look at."

Was she concerned for Elaine or for herself? Trystan was considering an apology when Larissa giggled, her worry apparently short-lived.

"But I don't really like him, even if I do flirt with him," she confided. "I don't know anyone who does. Like him, I mean." Larissa leaned in and spoke in a loud whisper. "His friends will probably cut you something awful, you know. Partly because they do what he tells them and partly because they're not very happy about any of this. The masque, you know." Another giggle.

Trystan wasn't sure how many more she could stand.

"Now you never heard this from me," Larissa told her, trying to look conspiratorial, "but I've heard of at least three betrothals that have been called off since the invitations went out."

Trystan turned to look at her companion in surprise. It seemed a foolish presumption, to throw away a certain attachment to pursue something as uncertain as royal caprice.

"I know it looks awful," Larissa hastened to reassure her, "but we all have to do our best, you know, for our families, and Prince Ramsey is really our only chance at a crown."

It was uttered entirely without rancor and with every evidence of conviction. Trystan was quietly appalled.

"Although," Larissa added, as though parroting something she'd heard too many times to disbelieve, "it really is a shame. Everyone knows Prince Rowan would be a better king."

Trystan focused on that last comment, spoken without bothering to glance around to see who might be listening. Obviously it was no secret amongst the nobility that Ramsey was not everyone's first choice for the throne. If giggling, oblivious Larissa knew it, why bother with all the intrigue? Surely the king was aware that his nobles preferred his eldest son.

The two girls finally managed to acquire small plates of insipid edibles and small cups with what Trystan very much hoped was more than punch. They seated themselves with a few of Larissa's other friends, three young debutantes who did not seem very interested in a country girl making her debut. Trystan was just beginning to feel comfortable being ignored when she caught sight of one of the many things she had hoped very much *not* to see during the course of the evening: her family. As if she could have avoided it—they were impossible to miss. Anya and Darya somehow managed to look smug even while wearing masques. Malisse, of course, looked stunning, in red satin with a tiny black masque that only accentuated her fair coloring. Trystan's stepsisters wore blue dresses that matched their eyes, Anya in a gold-and-topaz masque and Darya in white, studded with tiny diamonds. Perfectly coiffed and smiling. Trystan tried not to grind her teeth.

Whatever their faults, she was honest enough to admit that the girls were beautiful. And with their impressive dowries, both enhanced by funds that should have been Trystan's, either one of them would make a fabulous prize. Even for a prince. As much as

Trystan hated to acknowledge it, Malisse was very well placed to get what she wanted out of the evening. If Trystan's stepsisters would cooperate.

The contre dances began shortly after Malisse's perfectly timed arrival. As neither Elaine nor Larissa was in demand as a partner, Trystan spent the first few dances passing around the margins of the room, moving from group to group in the wake of her perpetually giggling new confidante.

At first Trystan had questioned Lady Isaura's wisdom in selecting the Fellton heiress as her companion for the evening. As time wore on, however, Trystan began to feel rather in awe of Lady Westerby's foresight. Larissa was friends with everyone and taken seriously by no one, and her light-hearted progress through the gathered guests encompassed nearly all the families Lady Isaura had insisted were important.

Trystan chatted inanely with their daughters and flirted duti-fully with their sons, all while asking wide-eyed questions about court and the royal family that escaped comment only because of her status as a slightly rustic outsider. Those she interrogated may have dismissed her as a hopeless provincial, but Trystan did not particularly care about their opinion. She would not, after all, have reason to see them again, and there was a part of her that was not quite satisfied by Lady Westerby's explanation of the political situation.

While Trystan was really only concerned with winning her freedom, she was curious enough to wonder whether things were really as simple as her benefactress had made them out to be. Long before their circuit of the grand ballroom was complete, she was finding odd contradictions between Lady Isaura's impas-sioned speeches and the common gossip.

While Lady Isaura, and indeed many others, seemed

convinced that Rowan would figure as Andar's salvation, his general reputation was much harder to pin down. Of the scandal that had precipitated his fall from grace, Trystan learned nothing. When that was spoken of at all, it was obliquely, with shrugs and significant sidelong glances. Older women seemed disapproving, but resigned. Younger women seemed scandalized but fascinated. Among the men, only a few let fall any information of value, but Trystan formed the general impression that Rowan was little more than a charming and charismatic wastrel, oblivious to the attention of his father's discontented nobles, preferring to involve himself in personal scandals rather than politics.

If that was true, it explained the disapproval of the matrons and the infatuation of girls like her sisters, but it only complicated the political question. According to both Anya and Larissa, "everyone" knew Rowan would make a better king. What, exactly, did "everyone" know that made it so obvious? Trystan had heard Prince Ramsey accused of little worse than being boring and backwards. Was dullness more to be feared in a king than dissipation?

The question continued to nag at her throughout the early hours of the evening, even as she and Larissa finally reached what seemed the end of their tour through most of the upper echelons of Andari society. Trystan's brain was staggering beneath the weight of remembering not only her own identity, but the names and titles of everyone she had been introduced to.

She was not without her own admirers within their number, which was gratifying, despite Larissa's warning that she would not be asked to dance until everyone had a chance to gossip thoroughly about her family and fortune. Trystan had obligingly chatted at great length about her fabricated history to anyone who would listen. By the time she rejoined Lady Isaura just before supper, Trystan had succeeded, even to that exacting woman's standards, in establishing Elaine as a pleasant, if provincial, young woman with a small fortune, in search of entertainment after a romantic disappointment. Though pleased by her progress, Lady Isaura was still filled with instructions.

"The royal family and their intimates most likely won't appear until after supper," she explained, low-voiced and insistent. "That is when you will need to be more forward in conversation. Be sure you do your best to gain an introduction to the prince, or those close to him."

Trystan avoided rolling her eyes only by calling on long practice, and by reminding herself that she would not be forced to endure instructions during dinner. Lady Isaura had insisted it would be unwise for them to be seen much together, given her known political associations. It seemed silly to Trystan, but she had learned the futility of objection, and so applied herself to remembering her table manners.

She ate little at supper, unsure of the wisdom of filling herself with rich foods before a potentially strenuous evening. If she were to be asked to dance at all, it would be better not to mix food with nerves. Practicing with Lady Isaura's dancing master was a far different experience than navigating a crowded ballroom while wearing tight shoes and a corset. Trystan was aware that avoiding collision was typically the task of the man, but having observed the vast quantities of wine being nearly inhaled by many of her potential partners, it seemed politic to be ready for anything.

About the time it appeared that supper had been fully consumed, but before the guests had any opportunity to grow bored, the music started up once more, but this time it was not dancing music. The strident tones were quite unmistakably a summons. After only a short burst of sound, the atmosphere throughout the room was entirely altered. Eyes glittered, chatter turned nervous, chairs were pushed back hastily and dinner partners forgotten. A steady stream of people poured from the dining rooms back into the Grand Ballroom, where it was immediately obvious that the dais was now occupied. Though not by anyone Trystan had expected.

A slender, ordinary-looking woman stood there, her brown hair neatly rather than elaborately coiffed, her dress plain but flattering. She appeared to be about Malisse's age, and completely unperturbed by the turmoil that had overrun the rest of the room. With no more than a raised hand, she spread ripples of quiet across the crowded ballroom, until only occasional murmurs could be heard echoing over the distant clinking of supper being cleared away.

"Thank you." Her voice was clear and firm, and seemed a bit amused. "For those of you new to our court here at Evenburg, I am Countess Norelle. We are pleased that each of you has accepted your invitation and chosen to be present for this momentous event." She paused, looking over the crowd as though noting who was present and who was absent. As if anyone was.

"Tonight the Royal House of Tremontaine seeks the benefit of her subjects through royal marriage." Her tone grew more forceful, as though to impress upon her listeners the gravity of her words. "His Royal Highness, Prince Ramsey Tremontaine, heir to the Throne of Andar by the grace of His Majesty King Hollin Tremontaine, has determined to solicit a wife from amongst the esteemed families of our kingdom, thus strengthening his ties to the land and her people."

The countess paused again, as if in consideration of what she was about to say. "Prince Ramsey's many duties have demanded that his time be spent in the council chamber, rather than amongst his people. As a result, and to his regret, His Highness finds that he has formed no lasting attachments that might be considered a basis for a royal marriage. Nevertheless, His Highness is committed to a marital union that will prove not only of benefit to the kingdom, but of lasting benefit to the health and prosperity of both participants."

The murmuring swelled and buzzed. No one seemed quite sure what to make of this speech.

"To this end," the countess continued, a bit louder to be heard over the susurration, "we have chosen to accept applications from those ladies whose eligibility is certain, whose character is above reproach, and whose desire is to serve their kingdom through marriage to her prince. Should you choose to apply, ladies, you should be aware that your prince is seeking an alliance not only of name but of mind."

Even Trystan knew that this was an odd thing to say. Royal marriages were about pedigree and behavior, money and fashion. And if this Prince Ramsey was so dull as her sisters claimed, what kind of girl did he expect to get in a marriage of the mind?

"I believe," the countess finished with a warning note in her voice, "the wisest course I can advise is that of honesty."

Trystan nearly laughed aloud. She wondered if any honest words had been exchanged that evening. Certainly not on her part. The thought made her unexpectedly weary, and in that unguarded moment she thought of Donevan. Wondered what he would say if he were present. He had not seemed to her the sort of man who would be expected to attend an event such as this. Or who would have come even if he were invited. It struck her that if he had come, she could have told him what she was thinking and he would have understood. Would have laughed with her. She would not have felt so alone in the midst of so many.

Pointless and distracting speculation, Trystan reminded herself firmly. She had a job to do and moping did nothing for her chances of success. Besides, the countess was speaking again.

"I would ask those of you who intend to apply to step into the antechamber behind the dais. Applicants only, please. There you will receive instructions on how to proceed for the remainder of the evening."

Trystan tried not to give rein to a rather evil grin. She could appreciate the humor in the situation, and perhaps even the strategy: separate the girls from their mothers, keep them off-balance, then watch to see how everyone reacts. She suddenly wondered whether Prince Ramsey was even now watching the whole affair. It was lucky she didn't care one whit how the whole thing turned out, because part of her was beginning to like this unknown prince.

One by one, the girls filed through a door that opened in the wall behind the throne. As they disappeared, the whispers in the Grand Ballroom rose to a roar, abruptly cut off as the door closed behind them. About fifty young women found themselves in what appeared to be a modest audience chamber. It was lined with tables, each of which bore a number of inkpots and a selection of quills. At the head of the room sat a desk. At the desk sat a somber looking man in a wig and a green velvet coat, who eyed the roomful of twitching debutantes over his spectacles as he straightened a stack of paper. Trystan raised an eyebrow in interest.

"Ladies, please approach the desk one at a time. You will receive an application and take it to one of the tables provided to complete the questions. You will at no time speak to one another or discuss your answers. When you are finished, please bring the completed application to me and wait near the door. When everyone is finished, you will receive further instructions."

By now, every girl in the room was about to burst with nerves and uncertainty. Questions? Were they hard? Did the prince expect them to know anything about history or commerce? Know how to do sums? Trystan summoned a satisfying image of Anya and Darya biting their perfect nails.

The girls were apprehensive enough that there was no mad rush for the desk. Trystan took her time, and was near the last to reach the green-coated man, who handed her a single sheet of paper. Trystan took it to a table, took up a quill, and glanced at the questions. There were only three. First, the paper requested her name. Elaine Westover. Second, the paper asked very simply: Do you wish to marry Prince Ramsey Tremontaine? Third: Why?

Trystan almost chuckled in unrestrained amusement. The audacious fellow was actually asking fifty girls why they wanted to marry him. As if he expected them to be honest. It was, she thought, with a brief inner shrug, better than simply choosing a girl for her dowry or her dancing.

Thinking for only a brief moment, she scribbled her answers with a smile. If they wanted honesty, they would get it. Nine words later, she folded her application and handed it back to the man behind the desk, who raised surprised brows at her, then favored her with a brief lifting of the corners of his mouth.

Trystan returned to the door to wait and watch as the other girls stared at the ceiling in thought, scribbled furiously, or looked around suspiciously as they tried to hide their answers from everyone else. On the opposite side of the room, Anya and Darya appeared to be more occupied with glaring at each other than actually writing anything down. It was quite a while before anyone else finished, an eternity before the last application was handed back. Shortly afterward, the Countess appeared again, picked up the stack of applications, and addressed the room.

"Ladies, we thank you for your time and consideration. At this time, His Highness Prince Ramsey would like to address you."

As a door in the back of the room opened, the girls sank instantly into deep court curtseys. With her head properly inclined, Trystan wondered what he would look like, this boring prig of a man who wanted an honest wife. Short, bald and bespectacled? Mustached and inclined to fat? Or tall, thin and dry, with a voice like chalk on a slate? She raised her head in unison with the rest of the room, as a well-built young man of medium height seated himself informally on the front of the desk and looked dispiritedly around the room.

Trystan had been prepared for many possibilities, and had formed few expectations. She was even inclined to be entertained by the spectacle. But every scrap of her cheerful indifference vanished into nothing as she looked up—at the tired, sardonic expression on the face of her friend Donevan.

The boring prig.

The threat to his kingdom's security.

The man she had been asked to betray.

Suddenly all of these men had a face, *the* face that had haunted her since her eighteenth birthday. His Royal Highness, Prince Ramsey Donevan Tremontaine.

Of all the hearts in that room, Trystan's was probably the only one that truly skipped a beat when the prince spoke. Her head was spinning so hard and her mind was so very blank that she almost missed his actual words.

"Thank you for coming this evening." His voice was soft; his tone conveyed both confidence and courtesy. "I hope you all understand that I regret the necessity of haste as much as, no doubt, do you. I'm sure no one desires to enter into something so solemn as marriage in haste."

Trystan felt quite sure, watching him, that he did not desire to enter into matrimony at all. That this was one of the burdens she had seen in his eyes.

"And yet," he went on, "for the sake of our beloved Andar, it cannot be helped. It has become essential that the House of Tremontaine take a bride. In the midst of my regret, I am none-theless committed to finding a woman who will, one day, be a queen that Andar will remember with both fondness and pride. It is to this end I have accepted your applications, and to this end that I chose to hold a masque." He looked at the floor for what seemed a long pause.

Trystan could see him searching for the right words. Wanting to be open, knowing he would be mocked for it.

"I hope to convey to all present that I do not seek to marry a girl with only a charming face, or a splendid dowry, or even an impeccable pedigree. I wish to know what is in your minds and hearts, not in your jewel boxes. Please accept my apologies for speaking plainly, but I think it best that you know, now, what I am seeking. If you find yourself unable to enter into this under-taking with honesty, then I hope you will accept that a marriage between us could only prove painful to both parties." He stood then, and addressed them more firmly, looking at each in turn.

Trystan tried desperately to hide behind a taller girl in front of her.

"You were invited for tonight so that you could answer my questions and enjoy the evening. Over the next few hours the dancing will, of course, continue and I hope you will enjoy the opportunity to meet each other. I regret that I will only be able to dance with a few of you before the evening is concluded. Tomorrow, however I hope to rectify that. Your applications will be reviewed before morning. A smaller number of you, that I wish to speak to more privately, will be invited back, with your families, for an informal luncheon tomorrow. As I said, I wish to convey that I am choosing a wife, not an ornament. If there are any questions, they will be taken by the Countess Norelle. Please accept my apologies if we do not have a chance to speak later in the evening."

With that he bowed formally and left the room.

~

How Trystan made it out of that room she was never quite sure. She found herself standing in the Grand Ballroom, arm-in-arm with a nervously chattering Larissa.

"… And I didn't have any idea what Mother would have wanted me to write, it's not like she's prepared me for writing things. What do you suppose he wanted me to say? Talk about my father's business? Or whether we support the crown?"

Trystan stopped listening when she saw Lady Isaura beckoning her from across the room. They had agreed not to speak to each other where Malisse might see or overhear, but as Trystan's stepmother was whispering furiously to her daughters in the opposite corner, there seemed little danger of that.

"What did they say?" hissed Lady Isaura impatiently, after Trystan managed to evade Larissa. "Did you see the application? What was it like? Did you see the prince?"

Trystan could only look back at her in uncomprehending

silence. Her tongue was frozen and her mind was still stuttering.

"Yes," she managed.

"Yes, what? Really, Elaine, if you cannot do any better than that, we may as well leave now. I cannot imagine why I thought you were capable of this task!"

Her blustering didn't really seem important. Trystan looked blankly at Lady Westerby, trying to remember her questions. She just needed time to *think*!

"Yes," she repeated eventually. "There was an application. It had"—Trystan counted carefully on her fingers—"three questions. We all answered them and the green man said a few of us would be invited back tomorrow. Now we dance." She stopped. That was all the information that seemed pertinent.

"Well, what were the questions?" Lady Isaura was not going to let her go that easily.

"Did we want to marry the prince and why."

The older woman's brows shot up, then drew together in frustration. "That's ridiculous. What did you say?"

Trystan shook her head muzzily. "I don't remember. I need a drink." She was done talking. No matter what Lady Isaura thought or threatened, she didn't have any more words in her.

Trystan turned and walked away, through a crowd of milling people, mostly parents conversing in frustrated tones with their complaining daughters. When she reached the opposite side of the room, she ducked around some potted trees, pulled aside one of the green velvet curtains and walked between it and the wall until she reached the end of the ballroom closest to the balcony. Glancing behind her for pursuit and seeing none, Trystan slipped outside, strangling a groan of relief at the relative coolness and quiet. She could still hear the sounds of the ball, but they seemed muted by the dark, and not as threatening.

There were benches on the balcony, mostly unoccupied at the moment due to the furor inside, and Trystan appropriated the one farthest from the open ballroom doors. She plopped down defiantly in the middle of it, hoping to warn off any unwary persons who chose to interpret her solitude as an invitation. If anyone approached her she would probably punch them.

So he was here after all. Donevan. Prince Ramsey. The heir to the throne. The man she had called a prat, who had held her filthy boot in his hand, who had given her his coat and sworn she was not alone... this was the man who would one day be king. Well, unless Lady Isaura had anything to say about it.

Trystan could blame herself for not having guessed, but she would rather blame her stepsisters and their friends. Either they were blind or they were all prodigious liars. Donevan was neither boring nor remotely ugly. It seemed exceedingly odd to Trystan that no one managed to describe him accurately.

It was not, however, odd enough to distract her from the miserable irony of her situation. Her secret friend, a man she had grown to like and respect, had turned out to be the prince. And she was here, at his masqued ball, a mysterious stranger wearing a beautiful dress. If this had been a story, she would simply walk inside, dance one dance, fall in love, marry her prince and be happy forever. Except, of course, this was not a story, and she had not gone to the ball to marry the prince but to betray him.

It was an ugly word, betrayal, but Trystan could no longer deny that it fit. Nor could she truly deny that she had known it all along. But now, the object of her betrayal had not just a name but a face—a familiar face that forced her to confront the depth of her own foolishness.

She had convinced herself that her task that night would be simple. Even meaningless. Whatever was going to happen would happen anyway, with or without her, and no one need ever know of her part in it. No one would be hurt; well, no one who mattered, and certainly no one Trystan knew. It had seemed such a small price to pay for her independence.

It had been too great a temptation, and in her frantic haste to grasp that impossible prize, Trystan had refused to face her own doubts. She had recognized that the task was too simple and the rewards too great and then chosen to ignore her own warnings. She had foreseen the possibility that Lady Isaura might be using her and decided not to care. In the end, the people Trystan cared about would be safe. The people who might be hurt were not her problem.

But that was no longer true. How could she pretend even for a moment that it didn't matter if she hurt Donevan? How could she blithely betray a man who had shown her only warmth and courtesy when she was nothing to him but a nameless acquaintance? And if she could not betray him, could not go through with her purpose for being there, what in all the hells *was* she going to do?

Trystan did not really even know where to start. She sat on her bench in the dark feeling shattered, crushed, and bewildered, listening with only half an ear to the dancing music that continued to play, and the inane chatter of the other guests that filtered out into the night. For everyone else, nothing had changed. The ball went on, dancing and flirting went on. Several couples, oblivious to the presence of anyone else, strolled about the balcony or leaned on the balustrade, each pair content with the company and conversation of one another. Trystan watched them, jealous of their closeness. Coveting the certainty of someone she could trust with her whole miserable, foolish story, someone who would then hug her and laugh and tell her what to do.

She was in desperate need of advice. More than anything else, she wanted to ask Donevan... no, Ramsey, to give her that advice. She knew he would be honest, that she could trust him to tell her the truth about anything. Which was, of course, the problem.

The truth, in this case, was that she had done something unforgivable, and if he ever found out, he would hate her. Even the thought twisted like a knife in Trystan's chest. Better that she never speak to him again, never even see him again, than to have him look at her with loathing in his eyes.

But neither could she go to him and not tell him any of it. Pretend she had been Embrie all along. That Elaine was simply a game she was playing. Even if he never found out what she had promised to do, it would look as though she had pretended to be someone she was not in order to attract his attention. In order to become a more fitting bride for a prince who could not afford a scandal.

And, of course, he would learn the truth eventually, whether the truth about her attempted betrayal, or the truth about herself: Trystan Embrie Colbourne, a fatherless, dowerless, social outcast. If Trystan did not tell him, Malisse would be sure to do so, including whatever details she thought would serve to separate her stepdaughter from any hope of happiness.

No, her friendship with Donevan was over, and it hurt, that recognition, in a way that nothing, not even her father's death, had hurt her before. Trystan acknowledged the hurt even as she shied away from the reason for it, even as she forced her heart to accept that whatever was between them had been doomed from the start. And if it hadn't been, she had destroyed it with her own hand the moment she agreed to Lady Isaura's plan.

Eyes burning suddenly behind her masque, Trystan rose from the bench and walked the edge of the balcony, staring fixedly into the dark, willing the tears not to fall. She could admit now to a hope, one so secret she had barely admitted it to herself, that there might be something between her and Donevan beyond friendship. That once she was her own mistress, with a home and a respectable dowry, she might seek him out. But that was before she had known who he was. Now she knew that it would have been too late. He would be married. To one of those girls in there who would never stop comparing him to his brother.

Which, really, was the problem at the heart of this entire unspeakable disaster. Everyone seemed to want to compare the two princes, and Ramsey was always the one who suffered for it. What was it about Ramsey's mysterious brother that caused so many people to overlook the scandals and ignore the fact that the elder prince seemed to care even less about politics than he did his own reputation?

Everyone in Trystan's life wanted to claim that Ramsey would make a poor king. But the man she knew cared about his people. He cared about his duties, even the boring ones, and yes, probably even the paperwork. And what, Trystan now wanted to know, was so wrong with that? More importantly, what was so wrong with it that half the kingdom would prefer to be ruled by his irresponsible older brother?

Trystan realized that she no longer just *wanted* to know the answers to her questions, she *needed* to know. She could not continue to charge forward blindly without some guide beyond vague, secondhand impressions. Personal ambition was no longer enough. She had to make certain of Lady Isaura's motivations. If the older woman's observations and fears were accurate, Trystan needed to understand why they didn't match her own.

And if they were not accurate, if Lady Isaura had lied, Trystan realized with a chill that there could be far more riding on her own actions than she had assumed possible. Not to mention there had proven to be far more to lose than she had ever stood to gain.

~

At about that same time, in the warm, fire-lit sitting room of Lady Lizbet Norelle, a handful of people sat poring over fifty hand-written sheets of paper. Lizbet sat next to her husband, Count Caspar Norelle, an older man who had been one of the king's most trusted and valuable advisors over the years. Together, they boasted a formidable knowledge of the kingdom and its most influential people, and Ramsey trusted them implicitly.

Brawley, looking ill-at-ease, sat across from them. In addition to his keen ability to judge the political climate, as an armsman, Brawley was often ignored by people who considered his station beneath them. He had been standing in corners unseen for years and probably knew as much unpleasant gossip as a chambermaid.

Next to Brawley sat Kyril, serious for once. As a youthful member of the nobility and a notable flirt, Kyril was acquainted with nearly all of the girls downstairs to a degree that Ramsey could not hope to better. And while he might flirt outrageously, Kyril had proven a shrewd judge of people and their motives. Between the five of them, Ramsey hoped to single out five to ten candidates that might not drive him to insanity within a year of their marriage.

Lizbet had already rejected a number of girls based on her

own information. There were four who had broken engagements when they learned of the masque. Three whose scandalous relationships with various unsuitable persons had been a matter of gossip for years.

Brawley offered a list of young women whose parents were vocal and possibly seditious supporters of the movement to place Rowan on the throne, and though Ramsey thought it might not be entirely fair to reject a girl for her parents' politics, he accepted Brawley's recommendations.

Kyril was, perhaps, the most useful. He knew better than any of them what sort of girl his friend needed, and was able to disqualify quite a number of them on the basis of character and personality.

When they had finished this initial sorting, only about twenty applications were left. These they settled in to read, not without an occasional strangled laugh from Kyril.

"Well, brother, you can take heart," he noted cheerfully. "There's fifty girls downstairs and they've all accepted your proposal. Can't find a single one who says she doesn't want to marry you!"

"Actually," Lizbet broke in, "I did find an odd one here who isn't sure. Kyril, what do you know about an Elaine Westover?"

Kyril's brow furrowed in thought. "I'm not sure I've ever met her. Is she new?"

Lizbet nodded, looking pensive. "My sources say she's from the northern border. Father made his money in timber. Her parents are dead, so she's guesting with Lady Westerby."

Brawley looked up. "Throw that one out, Your Highness. Isaura Westerby is up to her neck in something. We've never been able to pin it down, but she's definitely someone you don't want to mess with."

Surprisingly, Lizbet spoke up in disagreement. "Actually, Donnie, you might want to consider this one. She's never been to court before, that I am aware of, and doesn't seem to be acquainted with Lady Westerby at all beyond a distant relationship with the deceased Lord Westerby. I believe he was a cousin of her father's. From what I've heard, Miss Westover came to Evenleigh for a diversion, after being jilted by her betrothed."

Kyril raised a skeptical brow. "And we're considering this recently-jilted distant relation of a known dissenter why?"

Lizbet held up an application and smiled at her nephew. "Because she at least has the virtue of originality. Look at this! Nine words, including her name. Her answer to the first question is 'I don't know.'"

Ramsey was interested in spite of himself and took the paper from his aunt's hand. "Elaine Westover" was written at the top in a neat, rather than flowing script. Elaine said she didn't know if she wanted to marry him because: "We've never been introduced."

Kyril laughed when Ramsey showed him the paper, but didn't seem much impressed. "Lady Norelle, I hate to be snide, but this might be a simple case of witlessness, rather than originality. If she was jilted, perhaps there was a reason."

Lizbet shrugged, but did not discard the paper. "I think you should at least try to find out," she encouraged Ramsey. "If she's new, she won't have any of the political connections a lot of the other girls bring with them, good or bad. You wouldn't be giving either side a chance to feel slighted by your choice."

Ramsey nodded slowly, not quite willing to agree, but seeing the virtues of his aunt's argument. "All right, we'll consider it. Who else?"

"I think you should invite a few girls you are not actually

considering," Count Norelle put in unexpectedly. "Pick a few from families across the political spectrum, to keep speculation open about whether you are trying to court favor by your choice."

Kyril agreed. "It's a good idea, Ramsey. And it'll keep everyone guessing what you're actually looking for. You know they didn't really believe a word you told them tonight."

Kyril was right, of course, much as it galled him.

"Any suggestions?"

"Larissa Fellton," said his aunt without hesitation.

"Really?" Kyril grimaced. "She's so... silly."

Lizbet nodded an affirmative. "Yes. And I'm fairly certain she's harmless. She's also friends with everyone who's anyone, if only because no one can bring themselves to rebuff her. It would be like kicking a particularly friendly puppy. And her parents are dangerous seditionists with ties to a lot of other dangerous seditionists."

Kyril growled under his breath, but agreed. "As long as you promise not to make me dance with her. She's not as harmless as you think. That girl could smother you with nothing but meaningless conversation."

Still muttering, he sorted through the pile of discarded applications until he found the one he was looking for. "Here you are. Beautiful. Rich. Apolitical family. Absolutely not to be considered."

"Are you going to give us a name?" Ramsey asked sarcastically, not really in the mood for humor.

"Anya Colbourne."

Ramsey thought for a moment. He couldn't remember meeting any Colbournes.

"Blonde, blue-eyed, nice complexion." Kyril supplied helpfully.

"She's cold-blooded, childish, and has the brains of a cabbage. Comes complete with a predatory mother and an identical younger sister."

Ramsey winced. "Do I have to?"

Kyril grinned at him, not without sympathy. "You don't have to marry her, just dance with her and ask her to dinner. Not necessarily in that order."

"Ick." Ramsey was already tired. "All right, who else?"

Over the next hour, they sorted and discussed until they agreed on a group of ten. Five who seemed less objectionable than the others, and the best potentials for an actual proposal. Five more to throw the gossip-mongers off balance. It was not a very encouraging process.

Lizbet seemed hopeful about the first five. She knew four of the girls and their families and felt there was at least some chance for common ground between them and her favorite nephew. Brawley didn't appear very hopeful about any of them, which did not surprise Ramsey at all. Brawley considered it his job to be suspicious, and especially suspicious of anyone who was about to get close to his prince.

Kyril favored the whole process with a characteristic shrug. He had probably already judged the available damsels as being unworthy of his best friend, and seemed no better than resigned to the idea of Ramsey's marrying any of them. His own part in this evening's program was coming up, and he would no doubt do it well.

As Lizbet cleared away the papers, Kyril looked over at Ramsey, who felt he would have preferred throwing himself out the window to what they had to do next.

"Are you ready, brother?"

Ramsey really couldn't do anything except nod. They were

expected to join the party at some point. To single out a few young ladies for attentions that would set tongues wagging until tomorrow. After straightening each other's cravats and brushing off their formal coats, they left Lizbet's rooms and headed back downstairs. But before they could get very far, Kyril looked both ways down the hall, grabbed Ramsey by the arm and dragged him forcefully through a nearby door, into... a linen closet? Pushing the prince up against a row of shelves covered in neatly folded sheets and towels, Kyril folded his arms and glared at him grimly.

"All right, Ramsey. Right here, right now, it's time you tell me the truth. Before we go down there and ruin your life forever, you're going to tell me about her and why you can't ask her to marry you."

Ramsey's brain froze in shock. "Kyril, I don't have any idea what you're talking—"

"Enough!" Kyril kicked a shelf in evident frustration. "Don't lie to me, Ramsey. It's stupid and it hurts."

Ramsey flinched from the pain in his best friend's voice. It wasn't that he didn't trust him. It wasn't that at all.

"I know you met someone," Kyril continued, "and I think you love her, if you've ever loved anyone. Or at least you think you could. But you've decided you can't have her or maybe that she won't have you. And I want to know why." He glared at his friend fiercely. Daring him to lie again.

Ramsey wilted under the accusation in Kyril's eyes. Put his face in his hands and groaned. "How did you..." He stopped. That didn't really matter. Lizbet had seen it too. Maybe he had smiled too much, gotten lost in thought too often. What mattered was that Kyril be made to understand he had not lost Ramsey's trust.

"Kyril, this isn't about whether I trust you. Yes, I met someone. And yes, I care, more than I thought I could possibly care about a girl I've only seen three times. I barely know her name. But I do know that she's not here tonight. I'm not 'permitted' to consider her as anything but a momentary folly! "

He tugged at his hair in frustration and exasperation.

"Yes, I think she could be perfect. She's everything and she's nothing and she's hurt and she's sad and I can't help her! I have to pretend she doesn't exist because I have this damned kingdom and its damned expectations hanging around my neck!"

Kyril stared at him, his mouth slightly open, looking vaguely ashamed. "I'm sorry," he said slowly. "I should have—"

Ramsey stopped him abruptly. "No, Kyril," he admitted tiredly. "*I* should have. Should have at least trusted you with that much. But…" He held up his hands, resigned and discouraged. "I didn't even know what to tell you. You're my brother in every way that matters, but I couldn't think how to explain what it feels like, how wonderful and horrible at the same time."

He couldn't really go on. Embrie's face was already going to haunt him. He would be seeing her behind every girl he would be forced to dance with, her smiling eyes instead of their mocking ones, her tears instead of their masqued and painted cheeks.

"When this is over, will you tell me about her?" Kyril's question brought him back and took him by surprise. "I want to know who you could have fallen in love with, if you were just Ramsey, and she were just…"

"Embrie," Ramsey offered, surprising himself and Kyril. "Her name is Embrie."

Kyril reached up and gripped his shoulder in sympathy. Ramsey, oddly, felt better for having been dragged into a linen closet and forced into a confession. Shared pain was not lessened, but it was far easier to bear.

CHAPTER 8

Trystan forced herself to return to the ballroom. Her shoulders were tense, her head ached, and her fingers could not seem to stop clenching around fistfuls of her already crumpled skirt. The evening was probably not even half over and she was tired. Tired of thinking, tired of feeling ignorant, foolish and confused.

And she wanted to go home. If she even had one, after tonight. Where was home? It should be a place where she could put her head under a pillow and make the world go away. Especially this world filled with light and music and tight dresses and shoes that pinched before she'd danced a single step.

Trystan wiggled her toes irritably, or tried to. If she was forced to waltz in those ridiculous slippers, she might never be able to walk again.

But she could not put her head under that mythical pillow just yet. If her fledgling search for the truth about their Royal Highnesses was going to get anywhere, she would have to work quickly. She certainly could not ask Lady Isaura, any more than she could ask Donevan, whom she was still having a difficult time thinking of as Prince Ramsey.

Her misgivings could hardly be discussed with Malisse, either. Trystan was beginning to doubt whether anyone in that glittering crowd had more to offer than common gossip. Even if they did, pointed questions in the middle of a masque would sound highly suspicious.

Who could she find that might answer her inquiries without worrying about her motivation?

Trystan went to look for Larissa.

By that time, the contre dances had given way to couples. A rather strenuous mazurka was being performed by several dozen pairings, one of which, Trystan noted, contained a polite but stiff-looking Prince Ramsey. She was, at least for the moment, safe from his notice.

Larissa was standing next to her mother, watching the dancers wistfully, and appeared pathetically relieved at Trystan's approach.

"Elaine, there you are!" She grabbed Trystan's arm with something like frantic haste. "I need a drink. Do you need a drink? I'm sure you do, it's so hot in here! Come on." Fanning herself and tugging at Trystan's arm, Larissa towed her inexorably towards the refreshment table, while her mother stared after them with lowered brows.

"Oh gad, Elaine, you have no idea how horrid my mother is being about this whole thing. She thinks my chances are ruined and wants me to remember every word I wrote and of course I can't on account of being so nervous when I have to write anything and now she's probably going to sit around all evening glaring at Prince Ramsey unless he asks me to dance, which he won't, and if he does she'll just glare at me again and ask me to repeat everything we talked about the whole time and I won't be able to remember because I'll be so nervous about remembering where to put my feet, and if I forget and trip or step on his feet she'll never forgive me and I'll have to run away from home…"

Trystan listened in growing amusement as Larissa cut off her hair, ran away to sea, and married one of her father's ship captains, whom she liked but wasn't allowed to speak to because he was beneath her. By the time they acquired two glasses of punch, Larissa's three darling little boys had become pirates and her parents had died in shame.

"But then," Larissa added, "I suppose maybe I won't step on his feet after all. I have been practicing nearly forever!"

Despite her own worries, Trystan couldn't stop a peal of delighted laughter. "Larissa, you'll be fine. And if not," she added mischievously, "I'm sure you'd make an excellent sailor." She paused. "I didn't know your father was in shipping."

"Oh yes," Larissa waved one gloved hand dramatically through the air as she sipped her punch with the other. "He has ever so many ships. He used to take me to see them, until Mother caught me telling sailor stories to my dolls. I don't know why she minded so much, but Mother said they were scandalous and not at all the thing for a young lady to know. That probably just meant they weren't boring, like the books she makes me read. And Captain Masterson, when he would come to visit, used to tell me all about the exotic places he's sailed to, like Thalassa, Fren, Caelan…" Larissa was forced to break off by the sight of her father bearing down on them, his face no longer looking very jolly.

"Larissa, my dear, I think you've had enough punch. Come back over here by the dance floor where you can be seen."

Larissa pouted, but did as she was told, leaving Trystan to

stare after her thoughtfully. What was so very wrong with Larissa talking about sailing stories?

Setting down her empty cup, Trystan made a face at it. Punch was actually an appalling beverage. Did they serve water at balls? Turning to eye the refreshment table in a spirit of curiosity, she caught sight of Lady Isaura, walking towards her in the company of a large gentleman in a wig. She looked entirely too pleased with herself.

The bewigged fellow turned out to be the ceremonial steward, who begged leave to introduce a young man who most particularly wished to make her acquaintance. The two older people performed the necessary formalities, making Elaine Westover known to Lord Kyril Seagrave.

Lady Isaura had included a treatise on Lord Seagrave in Trystan's brief but harrowing education at Westhaven, and by the time Trystan took his arm for the next dance, she had managed to remember the pertinent details. Younger son of an earl. Permanent fixture at court. Popular with the ladies. Principal confidant of His Royal Highness.

Trystan was not at all sure what she ought to do in this situation. It was probably an honor to be singled out by such a dashing figure, but she was hardly a practiced flirt. If he expected her to understand the intricacies of coquetry, he would likely be both disappointed and bored.

Before they could push through the crowd to the dance floor, Lady Isaura stopped her. "Elaine, my dear, I hope you will forgive me for deserting you, but I'm feeling rather poorly." She seemed to have developed a sudden headache of some severity, from the grimace on her painted lips.

"Of course, Lady Westerby, allow me to get my things and we will go at once." Trystan was well aware that this was the expected reply, and that Lady Westerby had no actual intention of permitting her to leave the ball.

"Why, Elaine, I wouldn't dream of taking you away so soon, before you've even had a chance to meet anyone." She place a reassuring hand on Trystan's arm. "I've arranged it with Lord and Lady Fellton. They will offer you a ride home in their carriage when you are ready."

Trystan thought this odd, but did not presume to question it, merely offered her condolences and promised to be mindful of Lady Fellton's direction. As Lady Isaura moved delicately towards the exit, Trystan's partner, Lord Seagrave, who had listened with silent politeness to the exchange, placed a hand over the one resting on his arm and turned towards the dance.

Trystan darted a covert glance in his direction. Lord Seagrave was shorter than average height and stocky, not fat, with wavy blond hair and charming blue eyes—eyes that were watching her with a gleam of both intelligence and curiosity from behind a green leather masque.

So he was probably not just a flirt. It occurred to her abruptly that any friend of Donevan's was likely to be more than *just* anything. This was going to require caution.

"Miss Westover, may I be the next in what is, no doubt, a long line of admirers to welcome you to our court at Evenburg." His glib flattery was delivered in obviously overstated accents. Was he hoping she would laugh or that she wouldn't notice? "I hope," he continued, "that you have been as enraptured by the entertainment as I have been to discover such an exotic creature amongst our number this evening."

Though he kissed her hand as he said it, the barely leashed amusement in his tone needled Trystan into responding. She craned her head and scanned the room in apparent confusion.

"I'm sorry, did you lose something?" her partner inquired curiously.

"Possibly," she responded. "I was hoping for a camel. I've heard they're very unusual. Or perhaps a peacock. The pictures I've seen are exquisite."

Lord Seagrave appeared quite politely confused.

"Well I may be an uncivilized child of the north, but I hardly qualify as exotic," Trystan explained, letting more than a hint of sarcasm color her tone.

Her partner narrowed his eyes at her briefly, then flashed a grin that was both devilish and unrepentant. "Our waltz, Miss Westover?"

Trystan nodded, swept up her train and was swept in turn into the small sea of twirling couples. Lord Seagrave was, she was relieved to note, at least as accomplished at dancing as he was at flirting. He guided her effortlessly around the floor, leaving her free to respond to his conversational sallies.

"Since you are unamused by my flattery, Miss Westover, I hope you will permit me to express my condolences on your recent disappointment, if it is not too forward to mention the circumstances that bring you to Evenleigh."

Trystan raised a surprised eyebrow under her mask. Gossip did move fast. Apparently, Lord Seagrave had already been apprised of her reluctant suitor's flight and preference for maritime pursuits. And was pushing for information that she did not intend to give him.

"I suspect, Lord Seagrave, that your conversation is almost entirely composed of forward remarks. If I were to forbid them we might run the risk of dancing in silence." She quirked a smile at her partner. "Since that is almost as great a solecism as daring to mention a lady's disappointments in love, I believe I must allow it." She had intended to divert him from his purpose, not to make him laugh. But he did so, with a great deal of enjoyment.

"Miss Westover, you seem to have taken my measure quite accurately, which leaves me at something of a disadvantage."

"Lord Seagrave, I doubt you have experienced many social disadvantages lately. I've been advised that you are considered something of a sensation by the unattached ladies at court… and something of a menace by their parents."

Lord Seagrave looked pained. "I wish, Miss Westover, that you would tell me who has been spreading such tales. I assure you my reputation for wrongdoing is mostly fabricated and entirely exaggerated, though"—Trystan detected a sharp curiosity in his voice—"Lady Westerby no doubt considers it her responsibility to safeguard your character by warning you away from fellows like me."

Trystan reminded herself to be careful. This could be a perfect opportunity to gain information, but it wouldn't do at all to give away more than she got. "Lady Westerby has been very kind," Trystan agreed, "but we scarcely know each other. My father was a very distant relative of Lord Westerby, so this is, I believe, the first time we've met. I'm very grateful for the invitation, but I don't presume to ask her for social advice. Her station is far above mine."

It wouldn't hurt to convince the prince's best friend that she was a nobody, and a provincial one at that. His disapproval of her court manners would ensure that she did not merit Prince Ramsey's attention, which might dismay Lady Westerby, but would greatly relieve Trystan's fears of being recognized.

"If it's social advice you need, Miss Westover, look no farther," Lord Seagrave answered with a disarming smile. "I am considered a leading authority on most topics of social interest."

Trystan decided to take the bait. After all, who better to help her unravel the mysteries surrounding the royal brothers than someone who knew them both?

"Well," she said, trying to sound as innocent as possible, "there is one thing you could help me with." Her partner nodded encouragingly as Trystan looked directly into his blue eyes. "You could tell me why no one will talk about Prince Rowan."

~

Kyril Seagrave was having a very interesting evening. His task was to get to know the five young women who were still considered serious contenders for Ramsey's hand. Four of them he had met before.

His first dance that evening had been with Miss Hester Ulworth, a staid young woman from a pedestrian, shop-keeping family which had nonetheless managed to build a comfortable fortune and purchase a respectable estate. Miss Ulworth was undeniably well-educated, but dull and almost painfully dutiful. Her parents could probably have guided her right off a cliff, and most certainly into a loveless political marriage. In her favor, Kyril thought she would be unlikely to make his friend's life miserable with tantrums or whimsy, or to throw herself wantonly at Ramsey's brother once they were married. In short, boring but safe.

This girl, Elaine Westover, was not at all boring and almost certainly not safe. In fact, Kyril was finding himself hard-pressed to label her at all. She seemed attractive enough, from what he could see, and well-spoken, possessing a dry sense of humor that appealed to him. Flattery seemed to make no impression, and she was canny enough to avoid the most pointed of his questions.

Then, of course, she had looked at him innocently with those enormous amber eyes and asked bluntly about Rowan. Not where he was, or why he wasn't looking for a bride, the usual questions girls wanted to ask about Ramsey's chiseled blond bastard of a brother.

Well, not bastard in the parental sense. The elder prince's parentage was, regrettably, not in dispute.

No, Miss Westover seemed to be inquiring about scandals, or at least wanting to know if there was any truth to them. Unless she really was that naive, which he very much doubted.

"Don't tell me our Evenleigh gossip hasn't made it all the way to the wild northlands yet." Kyril wasn't sure how to answer even if he'd wanted to. The breadth of opinion about Rowan made it difficult to determine what, if anything, anyone knew about him and to what degree his public figure failed to match up with his private one.

"I'm afraid I'm acquainted with very little news of court," Miss Westover admitted, lowering her lashes, "though not for want of trying. My mother believed in keeping me unsullied by the world." A corner of her mouth twitched, as if her words were a private joke.

"Am I to believe you ask such a thing in innocence?"

"Believe what you will, Lord Seagrave," the girl answered without embarrassment. "I am new to society and woefully behindhand in matters many girls consider commonplace. I would like to understand this world, which is very different from my own." A smile briefly crossed her lips. "It would seem wiser not to make myself an outcast for no better reason than ignorance. If this disgusts you, I understand, although"—her brief look held more challenge than discomfiture—"I fear I will not apologize."

Kyril was fascinated despite himself. Elaine Westover was making no attempt to impress him, and seemed on the brink of actively trying to discourage his interest. If he were any other dandy of the court, she probably would have succeeded. Her straightforward confidence of manner would be seen as both provincial and provoking, though her dancing left nothing to be desired and her behavior was otherwise decorous. It was her conversation that unnerved him: intelligent, educated, and utterly unpredictable.

"What *does* one hear of Prince Rowan in the Northlands?" He covered his surprise with an open-ended question.

"Nothing, for the most part," Elaine tilted her head as if considering. "No one really talks *of* him, they talk around him."

Her assessment was interesting. And alarmingly perceptive. Most people did, indeed, tend to talk around Rowan, at least when he or anyone else likely to be unsympathetic was present.

"Perhaps there's a very good reason," Kyril tried to deflect her, but the words fell flat as soon as they left his mouth. He could see her scorn even behind her masque.

"And now you sound very much like my nurse. You know," his partner said thoughtfully, "I'm beginning to wonder if he's not actually a person, but more like a malevolent spirit who haunts you if you say his name three times."

Kyril gaped at her, not at all equal to the task of maintaining his own decorum in the face of her audacity. "You do know," he said, unable to stifle a grin, "that it's considered unwise to speak ill of royalty?"

A corner of Elaine's mouth quirked in humor. "Prince Rowan, Prince Rowan, Prince Rowan?"

Kyril knew he shouldn't encourage the girl, but her perfectly timed response, and the casting of Rowan as some sort of evil imp, nearly brought him to his knees with laughter. He almost lost his balance and had to pull the insufferable girl out of the dance for a moment.

He decided later that her jest had been an act of providence. It meant he was better able to keep both his feet and his head when the dancing faltered and silence spread across the ballroom.

The locus of the disturbance seemed to be the moonlit balcony, and the tall, stylish figure that detached itself from the shadows. It moved forward, out of the night and dawned into the already brightly lit ballroom like a new and glorious sun.

Prince Rowan had arrived at the ball.

CHAPTER 9

Trystan was slightly appalled by her own temerity. She hadn't meant to stir up trouble, only ask a provoking question to see if she could get a response. Lord Seagrave actually seemed a likable, even kindred soul, with a daring sense of humor. Even so, Trystan was entirely unprepared for the hilarity unleashed by her unguarded commentary on the elder prince. The hitherto self-possessed Kyril actually had to stop dancing for a moment in order to regain his composure, causing Trystan to wonder whether she had unwittingly hit rather too near the mark.

It was as they stood there, outside the dance, her partner trying very hard to contain his laughter, that it happened. Ripples, through the crowd, as from a rock thrown into a pond. A very large, shiny rock, Trystan realized. The ripples were moving outward from a man who had appeared as if by magic on the balcony. A tall, beautiful, golden man who appeared unsurprised by the effect he was having on the assembled company.

Lord Seagrave saw him and froze, every muscle tense, his

teasing good humor replaced by disbelief, anger, and palpable dislike. He also made an almost imperceptible move to push Trystan behind him. She was peering over his shoulder at the crowd when he looked back at her with a question in his eyes.

"You called, Miss Westover?" He raised an eloquent brow. "A malevolent spirit indeed."

Trystan could only return his look, numb with surprise. "Perhaps what you meant to say," she answered, when she finally found her voice, "is 'be careful what you wish for.'"

Lord Seagrave only grimaced in agreement. Trystan found it interesting, if not surprising, to discover such hostility between the heir's friend and his brother. She found it much more than interesting that Kyril's first instinct had been to put himself between her and Rowan. As if to shield her from something. Something he didn't wish her to see, or something he didn't wish to see her?

~

Everyone in the room was conscious of the exact moment the royal brothers became aware of each other. Prince Ramsey stopped dancing to look at the prodigal with an unreadable expression, while his partner hung on his arm with obvious dismay, looking from one face to the other. Rowan, on the other hand, advanced into the room like the tide, smiling and holding out his arms to his much shorter brother, who now looked nothing if not drab by comparison.

"Ramsey, what is this?" Rowan appeared genuinely surprised. "Seems a bit too lively for one of your parties!" He turned to gaze admiringly about the room. "Most of Evenleigh is here! There's even music, and dancing! Have you finally learned to enjoy life, while I've been away? I've come to expect your entertainments to feature more books than beautiful women!" He paused a moment to laugh at his own wit, prompting a few sickly sounding chuckles from the otherwise silent onlookers. "It seems that my invitation to these festivities has gone astray. Perhaps it missed me as I travelled back from the country, eh?" He clasped Ramsey's shoulders in good-humored camaraderie. "No harm done, though, brother! I seem to have arrived in time for the best part." He released Ramsey, who had grown noticeably stiff and silent, and bowed to the crowd. "And if the young ladies will forgive my riding dress and muddy boots, I would like nothing better than to join the celebration without delay!"

Rowan looked back at his brother. "I do understand correctly that this is a celebration? Of your upcoming wedding?" His smile grew even more angelic. "Then I will be sure not to distract you from the vitally important task of choosing a bride! Go on then! Don't let my humble presence disturb you." He gestured to the musicians in the gallery, waved commandingly at the couples who had been standing like stones since his arrival, and, within the space of only a few moments, both took command and made himself at home in the midst of his brother's ball.

Trystan watched this little drama from the sidelines, still tucked behind Lord Kyril's shoulder, with a mixture of revulsion and admiration. It had been a masterful performance. Rowan had taken advantage of his surprising entrance, superior height and polished address to completely overwhelm the room with very little effort. Even Trystan could note that all eyes now tracked his movements, rather than Ramsey's. The dancing may have continued, but it was half-hearted. Everyone's attention was divided. Some, Trystan saw, were watching after the elder prince with hard, angry expressions. Prince Ramsey was not, then, entirely without partisans. Others looked calculating; still others, voracious. No one knew what was about to happen, and no one wanted to be left out of whatever it was.

Trystan risked a look at her partner. "You know," she whispered under her breath, "if you continue to wear that expression, the guards will be forced to arrest you for attempted murder."

Lord Seagrave started, and glanced at her as though he had forgotten she existed. He probably had. His answering smile was both apology and dismissal. "I regret, Miss Westover, that our conversation and our waltz have been spoiled in such a spectacular fashion." He lifted her gloved hand and kissed it gallantly. "But I'm afraid I must beg your indulgence and offer my sincere hopes that fate will permit us to make another attempt at a later time."

Trystan did not feel inclined to cavil. "I thank you, Lord Seagrave, for the honor and the pleasure." She curtsied with grave propriety and left the floor, feeling that her partner's distraction was entirely understandable.

And quite welcome, as it permitted her to turn her thoughts in other directions. First, why had Lady Isaura left the ball? Her timing had been bizarre and her behavior inexplicable. After keeping such a close eye on Trystan all evening, why would she simply abandon her before the most important part of the evening? Lady Isaura did not seem the sort of person to be overwhelmed by a simple headache. Unless, perhaps, something had gone wrong with the plan.

Had they been discovered and Trystan left behind to take the fall? Or had Lady Isaura managed to obtain the message after all without needing Trystan's help? It would certainly be convenient, but seemed unlikely. Apparently, Trystan thought bitterly, the mysteries she presently had to contend with were not enough.

And just as apparently, she was going to have to muddle through them on her own.

Lady Fellton seemed to have completely disappeared, showing few signs of being concerned with the possibility that her new charge might be inclined to behave scandalously. Larissa? Trystan searched the refreshment tables, the walls, everywhere, and eventually spotted her dancing—with none other than Prince Ramsey. He must have changed partners when Rowan took it upon himself to re-start the music.

Trystan smiled to herself at the sight. Larissa did not appear to be stepping on anyone's feet, despite her voluble misgivings, though her eyes did roll a bit wildly at every turn about the room. Hopefully Larissa would be able to remember what Prince Ramsey talked about, as Trystan was certain Lady Fellton would be demanding a full report.

She did not have time to notice much more. The steward applied to her for another introduction, after which point the honor of dancing with her grew to be quite a popular one. She was passed from partner to partner, all of whom were interested to a varying degree in what she had talked about with Lord Seagrave. No one seemed interested in speculating about the motives behind Prince Rowan's spectacular entrance. Frustrated by the failure of her own attempts to discover anything meaningful, Trystan subjected her partners to meandering answers to their queries, leaving most of them with the impression that she and Lord Seagrave had spent their waltz discussing camels.

After nearly an hour, Trystan could no longer manage to feel much of anything beyond disappointment and fatigue. She wished the ball would simply end. There was no way to know when Lady Isaura's shadowy contact might slip her the message, but surely they did not expect her to wait until dawn. It was already past her bedtime.

Trystan retreated again to the balcony, where she found an empty bench and claimed it with a yawn. Her feet hurt, her ribs hurt, even her face hurt from the chafing of the mask. One of those, at least, she could remedy.

Under the concealing volume of her skirts, she used her toes to remove both shoes and stretched out those offended digits with a groan. If all dancing shoes were that tight, it was a wonder any of the other girls still had feet.

She had one shoe back on and was searching for the other with her foot when a tall, masculine figure approached her bench. Trystan meant to warn him off and insist that she was resting, not looking for company, but the words died in her mouth as she looked up and saw that the figure bearing down on her was none other than a warmly smiling Prince Rowan.

Who apparently even looked good in the moonlight.

"Your Highness," she managed to say, and tried to rise so she could curtsey properly, but found she was standing on her skirts and still missing a shoe. She tripped, and would have fallen, had the prince not caught her arm and lowered her back onto the bench with a look of solicitude.

"Please, do not concern yourself with courtesies," he said quickly. "Are you injured?"

Trystan laughed in spite of herself.

"No, Your Highness, I assure you, it's only that I seem to have… um… misplaced my shoe."

An expressive face turned towards her and brightened in a burst of infectious laughter.

He really was beautiful, Trystan realized. His eyes, his hair, his teeth—all perfect. His voice was like butter and his laugh was like sunshine. A peerless golden prince, sitting next to her, offering sympathy with a smile. It was no wonder people were starting riots in his defense. He was positively overwhelming in person.

"Please," he offered, "allow me to help."

Trystan tried half-heartedly to protest, but he managed to shift her flowing skirts to one side long enough to locate the offending dancing slipper. Kneeling in front of the bench while holding it out, he obviously intended to put it back on her foot himself. It was extremely forward, highly improper, and Trystan knew very well she ought to say no. Somehow the gleam in his eye over-ruled her and she began to put her foot out, but before she could, one of his hands slipped beneath the trailing edges of her skirt and found it himself. Shocked, Trystan could only stare at him as he used the other hand to gently replace her slipper, lingering a bit as he did so, never taking his gleaming eyes from hers.

It was a mesmerizing performance. So mesmerizing that Trystan had risen and accepted his arm, as well as his invitation to dance, before she realized that her shoe now contained something besides her foot.

∾

The dance was a simple one and thankfully did not require much concentration, as Trystan had none to give it. She was twirling about the room in the arms of the enigmatic Prince Rowan, a strange and scandalous creature who might be Lady Isaura's mysterious contact. She could feel the pressure of jealous regard from nearly every girl in the room. She wondered too about another set of eyes, and whether they were watching. What Donevan might be thinking about his brother's choice.

Rowan was watching her closely as they danced, with a concentrated attention that might have confused onlookers into believing it was romantic interest. Trystan could see his eyes. They were now more calculating than warm.

"Your Highness," she managed, "I find myself surprised that a newcomer to your court would merit your attention."

Rowan's expression did not change. "Then you know little of court, Miss Westover, first that you call it mine, and second that you are surprised."

"Oh, I think I have its measure well enough," Trystan responded, surprising even herself. "It is yours that seems to elude me." Despite her uneasiness, she found she was unwilling to be intimidated.

"And by what standard would you measure me, Miss Westover?" The prince raised one elegant eyebrow, even as he spun her through a flawless turn. "I confess I frequently find myself confused by the scope of my own reputation."

"How very strange!" Trystan allowed her eyes to widen expressively behind her masque. "It seems we have something in common."

Rowan's steps seemed to quicken a trifle, though his face betrayed nothing. "How tragic for both of us, then," he said blandly, "that it is my brother's reputation in question this evening, and not my own."

Trystan managed to meet his eyes levelly. "As you have said, I know little of court," she replied, "but I have a strong impression that you may be mistaken." Taking another step out on the limb, she continued: "This evening seems to have everything to do with your reputation."

Rowan's hand tightened almost imperceptibly around hers, and his arm around her waist seemed made of steel as it drew her closer. "What a clever little mouse my lady has sent me!" His mocking voice sent shivers down Trystan's back. "But not too clever."

"How would you know that, Your Highness?" Trystan was too curious not to take the bait.

He leaned even closer, dancing as though entranced by her nearness, and breathed his answer into her ear. "You are dancing with me."

Trystan drew back as far as his arm would permit, her body tense with a sudden premonition of danger. Was he trying to warn her? Or perhaps just frighten her enough that she would stop asking questions? Could she have put herself at risk by allowing him to single her out so publicly? Or did he simply enjoy being annoyingly mysterious? She would have pulled her hand from his in the middle of the dance, had he not grasped her even tighter.

"Oh, no, little mouse. We have a dance to finish. You seem curiously concerned with my reputation, so I will give you the opportunity to enhance my mystique." He smiled again, good humor seemingly restored in an instant. "And by the end of this dance, if you are very lucky, no one will know what to make of you either."

"Am I expected to be grateful?" Some asperity leaked into her voice, however hard she tried to hide it.

The song and the dance ended as she spoke, and her companion swept her a graceful bow. Carrying her hand to his lips for a kiss, he whispered for her ears alone. "Go now, little mouse, and you will find *me* grateful."

Releasing her, he swept away into the crowd, leaving Trystan feeling curiously bereft and deflated. But relieved. Being near Prince Rowan, she decided, was like dancing on the edge of a cliff. Exhilarating and frightening.

She had no idea what, if anything, he meant for her to gain from their conversation. One minute threatening, the next cajoling. Changeable and beguiling. Trystan could see both the confusion and the appeal. What she still could not see was what this had to do with the throne.

How had such a creature convinced anyone to hand him a crown?

And what in all the hells had he put in her shoe?

Loathe as she was to admit it, he had been right about one thing. She needed to leave, and soon. But how could she? Until Lord and Lady Fellton were prepared to leave, she would be forced to remain. With a piece of paper burning a hole in an already very uncomfortable shoe.

It was not hard to find Larissa and her parents. They were engaged in yet another animated discussion about Larissa's surprising dance with Prince Ramsey. The look of delighted awe on Larissa's face suggested that she had not, in fact, stepped on his toes and would therefore have no need to turn pirate. Trystan congratulated her as warmly as possible and tentatively broached the subject of departure.

"Why, my dear, whatever are you thinking?" Lady Fellton seemed sincerely shocked. "The ball will be continuing for several hours yet. Perhaps if you had some punch, and a rest, even some fresh air... I'm sure you cannot wish to leave so soon."

Cringing inside at the thought of remaining for hours, Trystan was forced to agree and go off with Larissa in search of Lady Fellton's prescription of punch, rest, and air. One thing was certain: as long as she was in Larissa's company, there was no need to go looking for air.

"He was actually very polite," that damsel was saying, as they took their punch and retreated to a corner table. "And he didn't treat me at all like other boys do, like I'm just some silly thing they flirt with until the pretty girls show up. He asked about my family and how I was enjoying the ball and whether I would like living in the city and what I liked best about where I live now. And he seemed very surprised when I told him I liked the ocean and my father's ships and all the stories about the strange places they visit, which my father doesn't like me to talk about, but I'm sure Prince Ramsey knows about them already. Although, he didn't seem to know very much about Caelan, which is strange, I mean because they are our closest neighbor, but he kept asking me what stories I knew about it and whether I knew anyone who had gone there."

As inane as they sounded, Trystan could sense there was significance in those questions. It seemed she was not the only one who had realized the usefulness of poor Larissa's inability to stop talking.

If only she could find somewhere quiet to think about all that had happened. There had to be an answer somewhere in the muddle of her thoughts, something that could help her decide what to do next.

At this point she would have little choice but to deliver the message hidden in her shoe. But after that? Leave things to take their course? Or choose to reveal the truth, thereby involving herself in a scandal that could send an entire kingdom into turmoil?

She did not feel substantially better prepared to make that decision than she had a few hours before, and could think of no one she could ask for help. Vianne, perhaps, would be willing to listen, but she seemed so far away, and Trystan was not sure when she would be returning to Colbourne Manor.

Again, she found herself wanting to talk to Donevan. Again she felt the sting of regret when she remembered that she could not. That she had to do everything in her power to avoid him. Which should, in retrospect, have warned her that he would be standing right behind her, waiting to ask her to dance.

She froze at the sound of his voice. For a moment she could not even force herself to turn around. But she did, eventually, and lifted her eyes to his with a composure she did not feel.

Donevan—no, Prince Ramsey—looked weary and dispirited, and Trystan had to catch herself before she reached out to him in reaction.

"Miss Westover?" he repeated, and Trystan realized he was waiting for her response.

"Ah... of course." To her chagrin she stuttered over her answer. When he looked askance at her, Trystan cringed inwardly, pleading with providence that he would be too tired and distracted to recognize her voice. She had remembered to use her adopted Northern accent, and hoped it would be enough to hide any similarities.

Trystan followed Prince Ramsey through the crowd and into the dance like a sleepwalker, trying not to feel the warmth of his arm through her glove, trying not to tremble with the dread of being identified. Perhaps if she could redirect his attention somehow. Ensure that he was focusing on something other than face and voice. She did not have to look very far for a distracting topic.

"Are you as good a dancer as your brother, Your Highness?"

~

As Ramsey watched his latest partner gather her train for the redowa, he was trying desperately to focus on the moment. With his future happiness at stake, he should probably make a point of not permitting his mind to wander. Especially in the company of this particular girl.

He had begun the latter part of the evening with an uneasiness that had blossomed into full-blown suspicion of Miss Elaine Westover. Arrived under the wing of Lady Isaura Westerby. Befriended by Larissa Fellton. Made an object of peculiar gallantry by Rowan.

Only the glowing report of an impressed and equally amused Kyril had kept Ramsey from rejecting Miss Westover as a possibility. His friend had reported that Miss Westover possessed both intelligence and wit, and a disconcertingly straightforward mode of conversation. It had piqued Ramsey's interest enough that he brought himself to seek her out, despite being exhausted and utterly infuriated by his brother's deliberate sabotage.

The evening was fairly well ruined. Though perhaps he should be thankful. Watching three of his potential brides making eyes at Rowan had pretty well soured him on the notion of proposing. It seemed that if he expected anything like fidelity from his future wife, he was down to two: a Miss Hester Ulworth, and Miss Westover.

Kyril's description of Miss Ulworth had been uninspiring, if not frightening. She would, at least, probably not embarrass him. Miss Westover, on the other hand, was nothing if not a bit of a conundrum. And a sharp-tongued one at that.

"You tell me." Ramsey let irritation color his answer to her rather impertinent question, not really wanting to think about, talk about, or even look at his brother at that moment.

Miss Westover was silent as the dance began. Her silence

lasted through one complete turn about the room until she broke it quite suddenly.

"Yes," she said.

Ramsey was startled. "What's that?"

"Yes, you are as good a dancer as your brother," she answered patiently. "Your style is certainly different, but I find it infinitely more restful."

Ramsey felt his mouth open in surprise. Kyril had said she was straightforward, but even so… "Should I be flattered?" he ventured curiously. "Or insulted? Or perhaps waiting to catch you in case you suddenly fall asleep in the middle of the floor?"

His partner smiled slightly, despite his caustic tone. It was an oddly familiar smile. Very strange in a girl he had never met before.

"Well, it *is* past my bedtime, but I believe I can promise that I will not fall asleep in your ballroom," Miss Westover answered with gracious condescension.

Ramsey's eyebrow twitched. What young woman of fashion admitted to having a bedtime? "Beware, Miss Westover," he cautioned her with mock seriousness. "You betray your origins with such words. The true aristocrat never admits to fatigue at a party."

His partner nodded, matching his pretense of gravity. "You are right, of course. I do apologize. It would be much more fashionable to adopt a languid air and complain of unbearable ennui. I hope you have not been made to regret your invitation of such a shocking provincial."

Ramsey looked at his partner more sharply. For a moment there she had even sounded familiar. But that was impossible. Miss Westover had never been to Evenleigh before, according to his aunt's usually accurate sources of gossip. It was probably her rather alarming candor, which reminded him very much of Kyril, and of… but he had promised himself he wouldn't think about Embrie. That was probably who Elaine reminded him of. She was about the same height and build, same light brown eyes. Aside from the hair and the odd northern accent, they could have been sisters.

"Do you have any sisters, Miss Westover?" Ramsey cursed his tiredness and his tongue the moment that comment slipped out. He hadn't meant it to. It made him sound peevish and rude and terribly un-princely. Not that he felt much like prince of anything at that moment.

"Regrettably, no," Elaine answered, with no apparent petulance at his slip. "Though if I had, I would be happy to allow you to compare our dancing in retaliation."

Ramsey couldn't help smiling. "I assure you, I meant no such thing. It's only that you…" He stumbled over what could not help but be an awkward explanation. "I suppose you reminded me of someone I met recently and I was overtaken by a sudden idea that you could be related. It was foolish and rather absent-minded, and I'm afraid I will have to beg your forgiveness."

There. Hopefully the sharp-tongued Miss Westover would accept his apology. He felt her stiffen in his arms, followed by silence. It did not seem likely that he had avoided giving some kind of insult. Which was just his luck. He was down to two possibilities and he'd managed to offend one of them. Perhaps it was a blessing. He would be saved from having to make a choice by his own abominable manners.

~

Trystan was not offended, she simply found herself incapable of uttering a word.

Up until that point her mouth had been functioning independently of her brain, managing to sound clever and unintimidated and far too much like Trystan Embrie Colbourne for her peace of mind.

It was Donevan, she realized. Being that close to him, speaking to him as an equal, seeing him for who he truly was… it had somehow overset her common sense.

The worst part was, she wanted to be there. Wanted to whirl the evening away in his arms, talking and laughing endlessly about the whole world and everything in it, whether it was their shared opinion of embroidery or their penchant for running away from their own lives. Or the potential horrors of having siblings.

She was trapped between two desires—the yearning for him to know her and the dread of him finding her out. She wanted to stay and she wanted to run. And she wondered how she had ever thought Rowan was beautiful.

No, that was not quite it. Rowan *was* beautiful. But Ramsey Donevan Tremontaine made her want to smile when she looked at him. He made her fingers itch to smooth his ordinary brown hair. He made her wish she could provoke his tired gray eyes to warmth with shared laughter.

And most of all he made her regret that she had ever made a promise to Lady Isaura, ever agreed to come to the ball, or ever heard the name of Elaine Westover. At that moment, Trystan knew she would rather go home, back to Malisse, back to being invisible, because nothing could be more painful than waltzing across the floor in his arms with the knowledge that she might be about to betray him.

It was little wonder she could barely think, with all that seething beneath her skin and a piece of paper burning a hole in her foot. And Donevan believing he recognized her...

"Are you all right, Miss Westover?" Donevan's voice broke in on her thoughts.

"Just thinking," she responded, without thinking, trying to avoid his eyes.

"About how much you wish this dance would be over?" her partner asked, lips twisted in self-mockery. "Or how much you would rather be dancing it with someone else?"

"Stop belittling yourself, Your Highness." Trystan answered far more sharply than she'd meant to. "Not everyone in this room is under your brother's spell."

Prince Ramsey's breath caught. Trystan cursed inwardly and damned her unruly tongue. She was not supposed to be trying to make him feel better. She was supposed to be ensuring that he would dismiss her as utterly forgettable.

On the other hand, he might be about to dismiss her as utterly impertinent.

"That was very near insolence, Miss Westover. I cannot allow Prince Rowan to be spoken of in such a way without reminding you that he is your prince and therefore demands your respect."

She made the mistake of looking up at him, into his eyes. Donevan's eyes. At least they no longer looked weary, flat and dull, but were kindled with something between interest and anger. When gray met amber, a spark flashed between them before she could look away.

"Forgive me, Your Highness," Trystan said in a small voice, shocked into remembering that she was not addressing a friend, but the heir to the throne. "I will try to remember my courtly manners." She could feel him watching her but kept her eyes down. Silence reigned between them for a time that seemed interminable.

"Please." The prince finally broke the silence, sounding exasperated. "Stop trying to look penitent. I know perfectly well you're not sorry and you ought to know that I'm not going to eat you for telling the truth."

With those words he became Donevan again and Trystan barely caught herself before she gave in to the overwhelming temptation to smile at him.

She had thought her waltz with Rowan was like dancing on the edge of a cliff. This was far worse. Like dancing on the edge of a knife. She was tired, she was confused, and she needed to go home.

Too deep in thought, too far from the demands of the moment, Trystan put a foot—the foot that presently concealed the proof of her betrayal—wrong, and stumbled in the middle of the dance. Her ankle wrenched painfully and she would have fallen if Donevan had not caught her.

"What is it? What's wrong?" His arm was around her waist, strong and sure, his voice in her ear, far too close. Her mind flew to everything that was wrong, and at that moment, it was a lot. Truth, lies, politics and her heart rose up to choke her, along with the painful and troubling matter of an aching foot in an overcrowded shoe.

He was standing there, holding her up, waiting for an answer and all she could think to say was: "My foot." And then wished she hadn't. The last thing she wanted was for anyone to look more closely at her shoe. But it was far too late to retract her traitorous words.

Prince Ramsey was already helping her make her slow and painful way off the floor. When they reached the edge of the dance, he lowered her into the first available seat, a cushioned bench under a potted palm. Dropping to a knee in front of her and looking desperately concerned, he held out a hand. "We should make certain you have not sprained it."

Competing images rose up and stole Trystan's ability to move or speak.

Prince Rowan, kneeling before her, holding out her silken dancing shoe with the gleam of confidence in his eyes.

Donevan, on one knee in the wet grass, holding her stained and filthy riding boot as he lifted her effortlessly into Theron's saddle.

"No!" She spoke more forcefully than she intended. "Please, don't concern yourself. I'm sure it will be fine with a few moments' rest."

Prince Ramsey looked skeptical. "Miss Westover, you can barely walk. Perhaps I should call for my father's physician."

"I assure you, that won't be necessary." It was not at all difficult to sound a bit embarrassed. "It would be rather humiliating to have to admit to tripping over my own feet, and I'm sure I'll be all right shortly. If not, I can beg Lord and Lady Fellton to provide me an escort home."

Ramsey still looked doubtful.

"Please, Your Highness, I have no wish to spoil your evening with my clumsiness. I would feel much better if you continued to enjoy your ball."

Ramsey stood up slowly, looking unconvinced, but nodded in acquiescence. "If you insist, Miss Westover. Please accept my condolences and my personal wishes for a speedy recovery." There was weary humor in his voice, and Trystan could not help but look up as she replied.

"Your Highness, I feel certain that your royal condolences will do a great deal to hasten my convalescence." Her response drew a laugh, even as Ramsey bowed in farewell, kissed her hand, and disappeared into the crowd.

He was gone.

Trystan's breath left her in a sigh of relief that was very nearly a sob, while her eyes blinked rapidly against the sting of tears that had nothing to do with her injury.

It took only a few moments for Lady Fellton to appear at Trystan's side, having witnessed her accident from across the room. "Miss Westover, are you badly hurt?" Lady Fellton sounded more peeved than concerned. Any serious condition on the part of Elaine would, by necessity, cut her own enjoyment short.

"Not too badly, Lady Fellton, though it does ache a great deal."

Lady Fellton frowned. "I suppose we shall have to take you home, though it does seem a shame to leave the ball so early."

She was angling for an alternative and Trystan was only too happy to give her one. "Lady Fellton, I beg you not to trouble yourself. If I could only have the loan of your carriage, I am sure it could take me home and be back before the ball is over."

Lady Fellton seemed pleased, but demurred. "You know Lady Westerby would never allow it, Miss Westover, and I promised her I would see that you were properly chaperoned at all times."

Trystan smiled up at her as winsomely as possible. "It would only be for the ride home, not truly improper at all. And there really would be no reason for Lady Westerby to know, would there?"

Lady Fellton appeared to consider the proposal. As if there were really any doubt of her accepting it. "Well, I suppose... there wouldn't be a great deal of harm in it. Our coachman could take you to your door and there would be no need for anyone to see that you were alone." Her face was pathetically hopeful. "Are you sure, Elaine, dear? You know we would be happy to escort you if there was need."

Trystan knew very well that Lady Fellton would not be happy, but merely protested that there was not the slightest need and that she would do very well alone. Lady Fellton bustled off to order her coach, and to order Larissa to help Miss Westover to the door. Larissa was exceedingly sorry to see her go, and to find her injured, and expressed it by engaging in a greatly detailed description of her own conquests of the evening. This recitation lasted all the way from Trystan's bench until the carriage door closed behind her. With great effort, Trystan managed to feign both interest and regret until the coach jerked into motion.

Quickly, while the coach was still moving through the torchlit bailey, she scrabbled under her skirts and ripped off the offending shoe, breathing a sigh of relief for her pinched toes even as she hastily retrieved the mysterious paper. It was small and rectangular, warm and rather rank from too much time spent in a very hot shoe.

After a swift glance out the door, Trystan felt her hands begin to shake as she unfolded the note. She knew Lady Isaura would be furious to find she had read it, and had probably never intended to leave her in a situation where she would have the opportunity. But Trystan needed to know what the message contained. Now that the paper was in her possession, Prince Rowan would know if she failed to make the delivery. The only choice left to her was whether or not to reveal its contents to someone who could stop the conspiracy.

The coach moved slowly through the gate and down the sloping road. The way was still lined with torches, but the light was thin and wavering, so Trystan moved closer to the window.

Glanced at one side of the paper, then the other. She held it nearer the window and scrutinized it closely, from corner to corner. It had nothing to offer but further confusion.

There was no doubt, even in the poor light—the paper was blank.

CHAPTER 10

*H*er mind spinning, Trystan managed to refold the paper along the same lines and reinsert it in her shoe, wincing painfully as she once again crammed her foot into the torturous slipper. As the coach continued to rattle and jostle on its way across the cobblestones of Evenleigh, she pressed her foot firmly against the floor, trying to ensure that the paper would appear appropriately flattened for having spent an entire evening being waltzed upon. It seemed more important than ever that Lady Isaura never know she had read it.

Despite her fatigue, Trystan was now forced to consider an entirely new set of questions. Why had Lady Isaura sent her to the ball to intercept a fake message? Why had Prince Rowan put a blank paper in her shoe? It made no sense no matter how she looked at it. Unless… perhaps the message had been a decoy. But why? If no one knew she would be there and no one would be watching her, why bother with the deception?

Trystan's mind grew more and more tangled with uncertainties and possibilities, but none of her conjectures seemed very likely. Perhaps Lady Westerby's response once she arrived home would give her some clues.

For the moment, however, she should be enjoying the fact that it was over. No one had recognized her. She had completed her task. There would be plenty of time later to dwell on her regrets and misgivings, which now seemed likely to come to naught.

There was little she could do about a plot that seemed no more complicated than a blank piece of paper. Even if she wanted to tell someone, there was really nothing to tell.

"Oh, by the way, Prince Ramsey, your brother put a blank piece of paper in my shoe!"

It sounded ridiculous, even to her. She had no proof of malicious intent except her conversation with Lady Westerby, which no one could corroborate. If there was a serious conspiracy, she could neither confirm nor expose it.

Which left her with one small, nagging question: why would they propose to give her an independent fortune for performing a meaningless task?

Only a few lamps were still lit when the coach pulled up at the front door of Westhaven. Despite the lateness of the hour, it was too much to hope that she would escape Lady Isaura altogether. The lady of the house would have sent the servants to bed and be waiting up to snatch the offending paper.

Slipping out of the carriage door without waiting for the footman, Trystan limped hastily up the walk. Above all, she needed to avoid any scrutiny of the interior of the carriage. Lady Isaura must not know that she had arrived alone, with a chance to read the potentially incriminating note.

The door opened at her approach, even as the coach rolled away down the drive. The entry was lit by a single sconce, and, true to Trystan's prediction, Lady Isaura stood in the open door to the drawing room, robed in her dressing gown, her hair curling across her shoulders. Her face and the set of her shoulders indicated a state of nervous impatience.

Trystan was impressed in spite of herself. Either the older woman's acting was without peer or she truly did not know what awaited her in the bottom of that dank and sweaty slipper.

Beckoning quickly, Lady Isaura ushered her young protégée into the dimly lit drawing room, glancing both ways down the hall before she shut the door behind them.

"Report." Her tone was clipped, anxious. Had she actually had a headache, Trystan wondered, or had Lady Isaura found another reason to be absent for the latter half of the evening?

Trystan removed her cloak, slowly and deliberately, folded it and laid it over the back of the settee. Moving around to the front, she spread her skirts and seated herself, reached for her shoe, and stopped. "Do you want the message or the report first?" she asked, striving to sound both anxious and innocent.

Lady Isaura huffed impatiently and sat down across from her. "Both, immediately." She obviously felt Trystan was being obtuse. Which was no less than the truth. "Stop behaving like an imbecile. This is not a game, child!"

Trystan nodded obediently and pried off her shoe. She removed the paper and handed it over with a curious glance at both sides. "I suppose this is the message. At any rate, it's the only one I was given." She cocked her head to one side. "Though you might have told me whom to expect, you know. Prince Rowan nearly gave me heart palpitations!"

Lady Isaura snatched the paper from Trystan's fingers, but did not unfold it. "Everything went well, I take it? No one asked any questions? Did you speak to the prince?"

Trystan nodded, but without much enthusiasm. "Yes. We danced, actually. He was a bit distant. Preoccupied. I don't think he paid me much attention."

"Good." Lady Isaura looked thoroughly satisfied. "Did anyone indicate what other arrangements have been made? How Prince Ramsey will eventually choose his bride?"

Trystan shrugged nonchalantly. "I believe it was said that they will be inviting back a select few, and that Prince Ramsey will pursue a closer acquaintance with them and their families. Tomorrow sometime." She yawned and stretched. "Though I'm certain he was not impressed enough to invite me back."

Lady Isaura looked thoughtful, but nodded. "Very well." She stood in dismissal. "You have completed your task admirably, child. I'm sure you are tired. On the morrow we will discuss remuneration as promised. Until then, I am sure you could use your rest."

Trystan rose to her feet, wobbled a bit for effect, and agreed. "I confess, I am fatigued. I had no idea a ball could be so exhausting!" She walked slowly towards the door, her ankle still throbbing, but likely not seriously damaged.

"Good night, child." Lady Isaura inclined her head graciously as Trystan walked past her. "You have done your kingdom a brave service today. Few people may ever know, but those who do will have great cause for gratitude."

Trystan waved a gloved hand and yawned again. "Happy to have been of service, Lady Westerby." Another yawn. "Good night."

Despite her unfeigned yawns, Trystan did not immediately find sleep. While still convinced that there was little she could do, her doubts and suspicions refused to die. What had she really done and did it matter? Who were the villains and why? What did they want and how far would they go to get it?

If nothing else, Trystan knew that at some point during the evening, the question of the succession had become greatly important to her. Should she support Rowan, the polished, calculating plotter? Or Ramsey, who was tired, dutiful and sincere? Lady Isaura thought Rowan was the man to lead the kingdom into the future. What future? What did she think Rowan could accomplish that Ramsey could not? Or perhaps *would* not?

After her brief time in his presence, Trystan felt comfortable with the assertion that Rowan possessed few scruples. Despite her complete lack of experience in political matters, Trystan rather doubted that this was a good thing in a future monarch. The king of Andar held a great deal of power, and though in her memory it had never been abused, that was no guarantee that it could not be.

Whatever King Hollin's faults, he had never been accused of being a despot, only of being overly traditional. Lady Isaura believed that Ramsey would follow in his father's footsteps and prove likewise traditional with regard to policy. As Trystan knew Donevan to be neither ignorant nor incompetent, she had to assume that the conspirators' complaints must be in regard to something her friend would not permit. Something that perhaps the unscrupulous Rowan would.

The harder Trystan looked at the situation, the more clearly she realized that her actions had the potential to affect far more than which man wore the crown. This wasn't just about Donevan anymore. Whatever was going on, whether or not she decided to further involve herself, the outcome would not affect just one person, but many.

How could she possibly decide?

Despite the endless litany of her doubts and questions, Trystan eventually fell asleep.

~

It felt like five minutes later when the pounding commenced. Befuddled by drowsiness and confused by dreams, it took Trystan a moment to remember where she was and why it sounded like the house was falling down around her. Someone, or an army of someones by the sound of it, was determined to beat her door in.

"Trystan!" Lady Isaura's strident tones made her exasperation clear, even through the heavy wooden door. "You must get up this instant! Answer me! Trystan!" A bit of muttering, still audible. "Ridiculous child. Why she never said… This is a disaster!" Louder. "Trystan!"

Trystan cracked an eye and wished she hadn't. The light pouring in from the window suggested it was late morning. It also triggered a sharp pain in her head that suggested she may have had more to drink than was good for her. Which was ridiculous, as all she'd had was punch. What did they put in that stuff?

She finally managed to croak out a response. "What is it, Lady Westerby?"

"Open the door! It's late and we have no time to prepare!"

"Wha'?" Trystan mumbled to herself sleepily and managed to get out of bed, noting as she did so that her ankle was still a trifle swollen. It had not bruised, but she would obviously not be dancing on it again anytime soon. Shuffling over to the door, she opened it to admit a wrathful and harried Lady Isaura, who was waving a large, official-looking piece of paper in one hand and what looked like a dress in the other.

She stopped abruptly and looked at Trystan with an appalled expression. "You look dreadful," she pronounced, sounding unnecessarily irritated by the fact. "How I'm supposed to make you presentable inside of four hours I'm sure I don't know."

Trystan still felt groggy. Why did she need to be presentable? "Is Malisse coming?" she asked. "To take me home?"

Lady Isaura's frown suggested that Trystan had suddenly become a simpleton.

"Of course not! Don't be a dullard, we haven't the time." She waved the paper in front of Trystan's nose.

Trystan took it and tried to read it, but her eyes crossed. Which hurt. "What is it?" She would put up with being called a dullard as long as she didn't have to focus on anything. Her head wasn't quite up to the task.

"Your invitation! Apparently, Miss Colbourne, you are far too socially inexperienced to know when you have caught a man's attention."

Lady Isaura's astringent tone made her opinion of Trystan's romantic ineptitude clear. Unfortunately, her scorn was wasted on the now-gaping Trystan, who was firmly in the grip of panic.

"What? I can't be... No, that's not right... it's a mistake, I swear it. There's no possible way!" Wide-eyed and gabbling, Trystan sat down heavily on her bed, under the bemused eye of her hostess.

"I assure you," Lady Isaura replied sarcastically, "it's no mistake. This was delivered by a royal courier only a few moments ago. It clearly has your name on it." She favored Trystan with a look of suspicious inquiry. "Is there anything you have not yet seen fit to tell me? Anything that might explain this?"

"No!" Trystan's temper flared sharply. "I told you what happened! We danced, he seemed distracted. I hurt my ankle, he left." She groaned and flopped back onto her pillow. "This is terrible! I can't go back! What are we going to do?"

Lady Isaura appeared shocked. "Whatever are you talking about? Of course you can go back. You must!"

Trystan shook her head. "I can't! Without my masque, Don…" She barely stopped herself in time. "Someone might recognize me. Anya or Darya could be there with Malisse!"

Lady Isaura frowned at her, but thoughtfully. "Well, what do you suggest? You can hardly refuse such an exclusive invitation without seeming suspicious."

Trystan stood up and paced the room, limping a bit as she cast about wildly for an excuse. "My ankle!" she said suddenly. "I was dancing with Prince Ramsey when I injured it."

Lady Isaura nodded, pursing her lips.

"Surely," Trystan continued, "he would not expect me to come to a party if I am abed with a dreadfully swollen ankle." She sank theatrically onto the bed and assumed a pitiful expression. "He need not know that I am still able to walk."

"Perhaps it would be for the best," the older woman admitted, though she seemed reluctant to do so. "But…" She paused, tapped her foot, and was silent for a brief period. "Very well." She sighed and picked up the letter of invitation from where Trystan had let it fall. "I suppose that will have to do. I will send a note with your extreme regrets."

Trystan leaned back into her pillows, trying to hide the depths of her relief. "After all," she offered lightly, "it's not as though we could go through with it, even if he wanted to marry me. It would surely prove awkward when he discovered that Elaine Westover does not actually exist."

Lady Isaura stopped and glanced back sharply as she was leaving. "Do not imagine, child, that such a trifling matter could not be dealt with. If it is possible that he would propose."

Trystan scoffed aloud, but inwardly quailed. Could Elaine's resemblance to Embrie have influenced Ramsey more than she, or even he, had realized?

"As I had no inkling of his interest, I cannot suppose it likely," she asserted. "I presume he invited me to be polite, as I am from out of town. Or perhaps to express his condolences over my injury last night." She grimaced. "In any case, it hardly matters, as I cannot go."

Lady Isaura's mouth twisted oddly. "Of course, you are right," she allowed. "You should stay in bed, in that case. I will send someone up with your breakfast.

"Perhaps," she added, "you should compose your own note to Prince Ramsey, expressing your dismay and desolation at being unable to accept his invitation."

Slightly worried by the new tone of calculation in Lady Isaura's suggestion, Trystan nonetheless agreed, anxious for the conversation to be over. It could do no harm to write a brief message. She would be as bland as possible, and leave Prince Ramsey to his remaining candidates. Leave Donevan to another woman who very likely would not love him.

Trystan closed her eyes and her heart. She would not think of that. Their paths should never have crossed and she must go on as if they never had.

Prince Ramsey awakened that morning from unpleasant dreams. Only to realize that they had been vastly more pleasant than his reality. Rolling over, he pulled his pillow over his head and groaned.

His calves and his feet ached like the devil. He had forgotten how much he hated dancing and drinking until dawn, though he hadn't really done much drinking. His head thought he had, and was pounding insistently even in the relative darkness under his pillow. It was probably still morning. He had hoped not to awaken until well after midmeal, having not been permitted to fall asleep until the sun was already on its way up.

The whole travesty of an evening crashed in on him then, reminding him forcefully of why he needed to be awake.

Rowan was in residence. He had come back in defiance of their father's orders. There was going to be a lot of shouting.

Wincing, Ramsey made his way out from under the pillow, noting the advanced hour from the light coming from behind his curtains. Not advanced enough, but he shouldn't have slept this late as it was. Hells, maybe he shouldn't have bothered sleeping at all.

Getting out of bed required a few more theatrical groans as his much-abused feet hit the floor. It was little wonder poor Miss Westover had hurt her ankle last night. Even with the benefit of being allowed boots instead of those ridiculous little satin slippers young women were expected to wear, his own feet were suffering. Shuffling painfully, Ramsey managed to ring the bell for his valet. The tone had scarcely sounded when a quiet knock came at his bedchamber door. Ramsey pulled it open, impressed.

"Your timing is…" He trailed off. It was not his valet. His Aunt Lizbet stood there, her mouth ajar, a bit wide-eyed at his disheveled state. "Er, Aunt Lizbet?" He remembered suddenly his state of near undress and bolted for his dressing gown, which lay in a crumpled heap on the floor.

"I just rang… thought it was Foster," he called over his shoulder, a bit embarrassed. "What are you doing here this early?" A touch more presentable, he tied the sash and turned around to look quizzically at his aunt, who still stood in the door. Her expression… something was wrong. Lizbet's face was still and careful, her eyes shadowed.

"Donnie," she said carefully, "you need to come with me. Your father…" Ramsey crossed the room in a few quick strides and grasped her arm.

"He's not…" he couldn't even say the words. "Aunt Lizzie, tell me!"

She looked him in the eye and he could see her fear. She did not even call him out for using the name that had so annoyed her when he was a boy. "No, Ramsey, he's alive. For now. But he is not well. We've called for more healers. Emersen can make nothing of it. It's like…" She trailed off hopelessly.

"Like what?"

"I don't even want to say it," she admitted, "but I feel as though something terrible is happening and I cannot stop it."

He could see tears in her eyes. His indomitable Aunt Lizbet was crying.

"I hate feeling helpless, Donnie. It was so sudden. So strange. He was fine last night!"

Without another word, Ramsey wrapped his arms around her, offering comfort to one who had comforted him more times than he could remember. "Don't worry, Aunt Lizzie." This time, she glared at him through her tears. "We'll find someone who can help. Da is not a weak man, nor is he so old that he'll go without a fight." He tried out a small smile. "Besides, he's gone to so much trouble to see me married, he's no doubt stubborn enough to live until it happens."

His aunt nodded, clearly unconvinced, but desperately needing the hope in his light-hearted dismissal.

Foster arrived a few moments later. When he was finally dressed respectably, Ramsey joined his aunt, who had been waiting in his sitting room. She stopped him before they left.

"You should know that I found your brother in my office this morning."

Ramsey grimaced, instantly suspicious even if he had no idea of what. "What could he have been doing? Do you keep anything important there?"

Lizbet bit her lip and looked a bit ashamed. "Ramsey, I fear I may have. I think he may have been trying to uncover information about the guest list. For today."

Ramsey considered. It was certainly possible. Though to what end he could not imagine. "Do you think he found it?"

Lizbet sighed. "I'm almost certain he did. Last night was so late, Prisca was having trouble sleeping, and at the time I was thinking of it as a marriage, not an affair of state. I dropped my notes on top of my desk and left them."

Ramsey hastened to reassure his aunt. "Aunt Lizbet, you're not to blame for anything. Rowan could find a way to make trouble out of nothing, and you had no reason to suppose he would be looking." He paused. "What did he say when you caught him?"

Lizbet snorted indelicately, sounding much more her usual self. "He had the audacity to claim he had come to apologize. About Parry."

"What did you tell him?" Ramsey asked.

His aunt glanced sideways at him. "Something intemperate

I'm afraid. I believe I was rather loud. Threatened him with bodily harm if he ever approaches Parry again. The usual."

Ramsey reached out and ruffled her hair. She slapped his hand away, but with a tiny smile. Her first that morning.

"Auntie Lizbet, I can always count on you to make my day better. The thought of Rowan suffering bodily harm is almost enough to make me glad I got up." She rolled her eyes, but with obvious relief.

There was one responsibility dealt with, thought Ramsey wearily. His aunt did not need to carry the burden of so many things all at once. She had her family to think of. He, on the other hand, had nothing but his own wedding to consider. A seriously ill father and a conniving brother would be just the thing to take his mind off of marriage.

～

A few painful and interminable hours later, Ramsey, Lizbet, Count Norelle, Brawley and Kyril sat together in Ramsey's apartments, where they could be certain they would not be overheard.

Ramsey had spent the remainder of the morning questioning Emersen, seeking answers, and lingering by his father's bed. The king had grown delirious, suffering from fevers and chills and even spasms that shook his body. A few healers had suggested malaria, complications from gout, even old age. None of them had managed to convince Ramsey.

"What now?" he asked wearily of the assembled company. "We can't go through with this party, while my father is ill. It will seem… disrespectful. Heartless." Frustration leaked into his voice. "Anyway, there's no way I can focus on women I don't even like while my father might be dying!"

Surprisingly, it was Count Norelle who answered him. "Your Highness, you must," he said gently. "This only makes it more imperative that you marry, and quickly. If, heavens forfend, anything should happen to His Majesty, you must have an heir as quickly as possible."

Ramsey scowled.

"Besides, we are allowing no word to get out of the severity of your father's condition. Our official word is that he is suffering from a mild spring fever, nothing to cause alarm."

"How long will that last?" Kyril asked skeptically. "The moment one of those healers gets loose it will be all over the kingdom. 'King Hollin's mysterious illness!'"

"Your Highness," Brawley offered hesitantly, "have you considered the possibility that His Majesty's condition may not be illness?"

The room went dead. Everyone looked uncertainly at everyone else until Ramsey gave voice to their skepticism.

"Why should we? Brawley, I've never even heard *rumors* of anyone being poisoned in Evenleigh. Are you sure it's even possible to buy poison in Andar?" He meant it as a weak joke, but Brawley looked at him as though he'd taken leave of his senses.

"Your Highness, any apothecary or simple seller of herbs can make a poison. I could make a poison."

Ramsey raised an astonished eyebrow.

"Don't pretend to be shocked, Your Highness. A man in my position has to know things he might wish he didn't."

"But," Ramsey insisted, "that doesn't address the question of why. Who would kill my father? They may disagree with him, but why kill him? All they get is, well, me!"

"I'm sure you can think of a few reasons," Brawley answered impatiently. "There's no shortage of folks who wish the king ill.

Most of them would stop short of murder, but I can't swear to you they all would. Make enough people unhappy and eventually you make some bad enemies. Enemies who won't stop at complaining to the court. Enemies who know how to make a death look natural."

Ramsey knew Brawley's job was to see a threat behind every curtain and every bush. The man had made a profession out of paranoia. But poison the king? It seemed so excessive. So dramatic. So pointless!

"Whether it was poison or not," Lizbet broke in, "Caspar is correct. The party must go forward. As we are only allowing it to be known that the king has a mild illness, it would seem very odd if you cancelled such an important event."

"The invitations have gone out?" Ramsey queried.

Lizbet nodded, then looked chagrined. "I'm sorry, Donnie. In all the excitement I forgot to tell you that we have received a note of regret. From Elaine Westover."

Everyone looked startled.

"Why?" Kyril was clearly frustrated. "We only have two candidates left and one of them is begging off? Who throws away a chance to marry a prince?"

Ramsey eyed him sideways.

"Well, perhaps I should say," Kyril amended, "who wouldn't want to marry your dazzling intellect and dashing good looks?"

Ramsey aimed a kick at his shin.

"Boys!" Lizbet glared at both of them. "Apparently the young lady in question was injured last night. Her ankle is now too painful to permit her attendance."

Ramsey rubbed his head and swore. "It's true," he admitted ruefully. "She twisted her ankle while we were dancing and then refused to have it seen to. I left her sitting on a bench, a few hours after midnight."

Kyril's jaw dropped. "You left an injured lady to her own devices? Might I say, Your Highness, how very unchivalrous of you?"

"In my defense, there was rather a lot going on in my life at the time." The biting tone of his reply was only partially in jest. Ramsey had probably had worse days, but he couldn't remember any.

"Speaking of which," Kyril said curiously, "I'd give my left arm... well, a couple of fingers... to find out who tipped off Rowan about the ball. If he was stuck at Ash Hollow, how did he know when to show up?"

Lizbet sighed and rested both elbows on her desk. "Lord Seagrave, you need to pay more attention to the people around you. Even Ash Hollow is full of servants. Servants have to leave the house to do their jobs. They go to market, they meet other servants. Servants talk. It's not malicious, just common gossip. Rowan probably knew about the masque as soon as the invitations were sent."

Ramsey had to agree. "However he got here, now we have to deal with him. He's finally chosen to disobey a direct order from Father, and I certainly can't control him. Any ideas how to proceed?"

Blank looks all around.

"As planned," Lizbet answered with a sigh. "The garden party this afternoon will go forward. Ramsey, you will need to be at your best, and make certain you reassure everyone about the state of your father's health. Rowan will probably be underfoot, but you will have to ignore him. We can try to sort it all out afterward, but right now we simply don't have enough time for a new plan of action."

There were nods from everyone in the room. Except for Brawley.

"Your Highness…" He hesitated.

"What now?" Ramsey tried not to sound impatient. He knew Brawley's only concern was his safety, but he didn't have the luxury of indulging groundless suspicions.

"I still think you should consider poison. And if it was, we have to consider that whoever did it has nothing to gain unless they kill you too." The words came out in a rush, as if Brawley knew how they would be received.

Lizbet sat back and folded her arms, brow wrinkled in thought.

Ramsey just looked at him. "Brawley, you always think someone wants to kill me. How is this any different?"

Brawley scowled, clearly frustrated with his stubborn charge. "Maybe not kill you, but get you out of the way. So there will be no choice but to put Rowan on the throne. I've been telling you and His Majesty, there are a lot of powerful folks who say he would be the better king. What if they decided to do something about it?"

"Look," Lizbet interrupted, before Ramsey could offer a response he might regret, "Brawley could be right. We can look into it. I will question some of the healers, discreetly, and find out what I can. In the meantime, we must remain calm. Stop barking at each other!" It was her mother-voice, which permitted no questions and promised grave consequences for disobedience. Even Brawley looked chastised. "Caspar and I will be meeting with the king's council shortly to discuss urgent matters of business. The garden party will be starting in a few hours, and there are still preparations to be made." She glared individually at each man in the room. "This will no doubt be a hellish day but we have to get through it."

Ramsey spotted Caspar Norelle gazing at his wife in obvious admiration. Twelve years of marriage and the man was still utterly besotted. Many noblemen Ramsey knew would have been embarrassed by such a commanding performance, but Count Norelle had never been one of them. He had married Ramsey's aunt as much for her fiery, opinionated nature as her quieter, domestic side, and supported her fully as she accepted growing amounts of responsibility for the inner workings of the court.

It was, Ramsey thought wistfully, the sort of marriage he wished for so desperately. The sort he was becoming increasingly certain he would never have.

The meeting broke up quietly. Before Ramsey could leave, his aunt stopped him and handed him a small, neatly folded paper that smelled of perfume.

"The note," she explained briefly. "From Miss Westover. It was addressed to you, so I thought you'd want to read it yourself."

Lizbet's expression was odd, but he could not place it, so he thanked her and left to check on his father and ensure the preparations for his guests were complete. As he walked, his thoughts grew increasingly gloomy. Miss Westover wasn't coming. Eight of his guests were either impossibly unsuitable or firmly in Rowan's pocket. Was Miss Ulworth really his last option? When had his search for a woman to spend the rest of his life with become such a farce? Probably the day he was born. The day Rowan was born. Why couldn't he just give up and accept the inevitable?

CHAPTER 11

Ramsey hated all parties, but he especially hated garden parties. He never knew what to do with his hands, other than hold tiny glass cups of some insipid beverage or other while munching endless little sandwiches. In the end, he could only stomach so much punch, and would no doubt be reduced to stuffing his hands in his pockets in a most un-princely manner. If he had pockets, which his embroidered green dress coat did not. Probably because Lizbet knew he would use them.

And that was his attitude on a good day, which today was most emphatically not. His father might be dying. His brother was likely even now hatching a plan to disrupt the proceedings, and he, Ramsey, was probably about to propose to some woman he wasn't even sure he liked, let alone loved. And in the midst of it all, he was expected to behave with his utmost royal decorum and pretend he wanted to be exactly where he was, doing what he was doing and with whom.

Ramsey's personal dramatic skills had never been equal to such a challenge.

He was aware that the weather was lovely, and the gardens superb. His guests had only told him so eight or ten times. Each.

Ramsey had been doing his princely best to pay attention to their conversation. He had thought himself succeeding until he caught Kyril's frown from across the lawn and realized he had been scanning the crowd for his brother, rather than attending to Miss Colbourne's highly educational conversation on the subject of herself.

She was, he could admit, fully as beautiful as Kyril had suggested: blonde and blue-eyed, with a flawlessly pale complexion and perfect teeth that she displayed rather more frequently than necessary. Her smile terrified him. It was fixed, predatory, and about as warm as a stone floor in the winter. And her eyes, like his, seemed to be wandering, looking for something that wasn't there.

Rowan's absence was not necessarily a hopeful sign. If Ramsey knew his brother, Rowan would be waiting for the perfect moment to make his entrance, and would arrange his timing so as to create an optimum degree of chaos. The older prince would be irresistibly charming, impossibly charismatic, and irritatingly condescending. He had put on that particular performance so many times before that Ramsey could predict his movements with depressing precision.

Fortunately, Kyril had assured him that there would be one bastion against Rowan's all-conquering personal charms: Miss Hester Ulworth, potential future bride. Perhaps the only potential. Staid, unimaginative, biddable to a fault, and undoubtedly advised by her stern parents of the importance of at least attempting to secure a royal proposal. And she was not remotely Rowan's type.

The older prince tended to prefer women who were both

decorative and witless, not quiet girls with years of experience in the particulars of managing the family business in dry goods. Ramsey's brother would have a difficult time trifling with the affections of Miss Ulworth even should he be desperate enough to try.

Now that Ramsey thought about it, where *was* Miss Ulworth? He had greeted her family when they arrived and exchanged pleasantries with her father over his first cup of whatever it was they were drinking—Ramsey thought it tasted like cucumber juice—but that had been well over an hour ago. One young woman couldn't be too hard to find in a group of only about five-and-thirty people.

Ramsey scanned the crowd again even as he nodded politely in response to one of Miss Colbourne's witticisms. There were several small knots of chattering females strung across the lawn and wandering amongst the shrubberies, plus a few family groups clustered around the tea tables. Under the green baize awning were a pair of dowagers sheltering from the sun and a stout young woman fanning herself vigorously with what looked like her sandwich plate. He almost smiled, but caught the edges of his companion's conversation just in time to assume a more sympathetic expression.

"... And then of course I fainted. What else was I to do? It was simply horrid! I could have died, you know." Painfully aware that he had no idea what sort of perils Miss Colbourne had just finished describing in lurid detail, Ramsey decided to extricate himself with as much delicacy as possible.

"Miss Colbourne, your continued health is a source of great relief to me, I assure you." Ramsey kept his face scrupulously straight. Possibly even solicitous. And hoped Kyril wasn't watching. "Even the memory of such trials must be a great burden and I beg you will avail yourself of some refreshment before you are again overcome." Perhaps that was laying it on a bit too thick, but he was fairly certain his secret was safe with Miss Colbourne. She flashed her predatory teeth at him again and they parted, probably in mutual dislike.

Tugging surreptitiously at his cravat, Ramsey looked around again for Miss Ulworth as he walked across the lawn to Kyril, who took his leave of his own companion when he saw the look on Ramsey's face.

"My condolences, brother," the younger man said under his breath, with a cheeky grin. "I trust you appreciate my taste in unsuitable brides."

Ramsey's expression promised volumes of retribution to be exacted at an unspecified time and place. "Lord Seagrave, I assure you, your services to the crown will not go unrewarded."

Kyril just clapped him bracingly on the shoulder. "Buck up, my liege. Just think how much worse it would have been if she were smart enough to notice you were ignoring her."

Ramsey had to give him that. But there were more pressing matters at the moment than exploring the myriad deficiencies of Anya Colbourne's character.

"Kyril, I've been looking for Miss Ulworth. I should probably at least make an effort to get to know her, but I can't even seem to find her. I'm starting to suspect she's avoiding me."

Kyril looked around, scanning the lawn, the shrubberies, and the tea tables to no avail. "Devil take it," he muttered. "I know she was here not that long ago. Do you see her parents?"

They simultaneously spotted the elder Ulworths, engaged in what appeared to be animated conversation with Lord and Lady Fellton, though Ramsey was hard-pressed to determine whether it was animation or animosity. From what he knew of the two families, it was likely fortunate that weapons were not permitted at a garden party, or more might have been flying than just words.

After requesting that Kyril conduct a more thorough search, Ramsey approached the foursome as cautiously as possible. Lord Fellton spotted him first and broke off in the middle of a sentence.

"Your Highness!" How the man managed to go from apoplectic to jovial in the space of a heartbeat Ramsey had no idea. "May I say, what a fabulous afternoon for this little gathering. And how thrilled our Larissa was to be invited!"

His wife put her hand on his arm as though to shush him, but Lord Fellton was not the sort of man to be shushed. He droned on for a few moments while Mr. Ulworth scowled darkly and Mrs. Ulworth looked on in prim disapproval. She looked so very like her daughter that Ramsey found himself beset by a horrifying vision of Hester, gazing at him with that exact expression, for the rest of his life. It might have unnerved him, had it not been far too late to succumb to such squeamishness, or give rein to the vagaries of his imagination. Which was not usually so wildly overactive. Perhaps he could blame the cucumbers.

"Lord and Lady Fellton, Mr. and Mrs. Ulworth, may I say again how pleased I am that you could join me today." Polite nods all around. "Mr. Ulworth, may I request a moment of your time?"

The stocky, bearded Mr. Ulworth looked grudgingly gratified and consented, leaving his wife to the tender mercies of Lady Fellton with nothing more bracing than a vague pat on the arm.

Ramsey decided to approach the conversation as straightforwardly as possible. "Mr. Ulworth, I'm sure you are aware of the implications of your daughter's invitation today."

The older man nodded cautiously as they moved off together

down one of the neatly shorn garden paths. "Of course, Your Highness. My daughter's been taught what her duties and obligations are and I'm sure you will find her—"

Ramsey interrupted, trying hard not to shudder. Duties and obligations indeed. What a lovely way to begin a marriage.

"Mr. Ulworth, at the moment I find myself more concerned with your own opinions on the matter. Have you any questions for me? Any potential objections to the idea of your daughter entering into a marriage of state?"

Poor Hester's father looked utterly perplexed. His lips actually moved as he tried to wrap his mind around Ramsey's words. "Why the devil… er, pardon me, Your Highness…"

"No, please, Mr. Ulworth," Ramsey offered politely. "I beg you will feel free to speak plainly."

"I don't see what there could be to object about." Mr. Ulworth was at least refreshingly candid, though apparently lacking in compassion. "You're the heir to the crown. My Hester would make you a compliant wife and I'm sure you'd see to it she's kept comfortable." There was an awkwardly long pause.

"Ah, yes," Ramsey managed finally. "I'm sure I would. And you, Mr. Ulworth?" He glanced at his companion, as if to assure himself the fellow was real. "How might you feel about the possibility of linking your family name so closely with the crown?"

Mr. Ulworth appeared unsurprised by the question. Unsympathetic he might be, but a man did not make a fortune keeping a shop without a bit of native shrewdness. "I think I take your meaning, Your Highness, and I can assure you my wife and I have always been loyal to His Majesty. We'd be honored to link our humble house with the House of Tremontaine and that's a fact." Mr. Ulworth seemed uncomfortable for a moment, but forged ahead. "And may I add, Your Highness, our best wishes for His Majesty's health and recovery."

Ramsey accepted, startled for a moment by the reminder. His father. Who could be near death at that very moment. Shaking off the weight of melancholy, he asked one final question. "Thank you, Mr. Ulworth, for your time. I've been hoping to have the opportunity to speak with your daughter this afternoon, but unfortunately I seem to have, ah… lost her. Perhaps you could assist me?"

Hester's father appeared momentarily nonplussed, but grunted assent and turned back the way they had come. "I've no doubt she's talking with one of the other young ladies, or perhaps gone for a bit of a walk through the garden."

He began to look about as they walked, obviously expecting to see her at any moment. When they arrived back at the lawn, however, with no sign of the missing Hester, he grew more agitated. "Well, I can't think where she might have got to… perhaps the, er…" The now rather red-faced Mr. Ulworth evidently intended to imply that she had gone in search of the necessary.

"In fact, sir," Ramsey informed him, "I have been looking for her for some time without success. I doubt she would have remained inside so long." He continued to gaze hopefully at his quarry's parent.

"I… well, perhaps I should ask Mrs. Ulworth." Patently relieved by this thought and clearly beginning to be concerned by his daughter's apparent absence, Mr. Ulworth scurried off in his wife's direction.

Ramsey watched him go, frowning, until he became aware of a stir behind him—the familiar sound of murmuring voices, rising in a wave of admiration, anger and probably awe. He didn't even need to turn around to know what he would see, but he turned around anyway. Someday he would be smart enough or bold enough to just walk away, but this, alas, was not that day. He had guests. So he turned, nearly running into his brother in the process.

Rowan wore black and an ominous expression and he bore in one hand a folded piece of paper. A note. It was small, square, and smelled of perfume.

Oh, not this, Ramsey thought wearily. Not again.

The entire assembly held its breath as Ramsey reluctantly accepted his brother's offering, trying not to glare at the offending messenger.

"The young lady begged me to deliver this to you, brother." Rowan's voice was politely low, but of course, not low enough. He wanted every ear on this conversation, every eye on Ramsey's reaction. Which meant Ramsey would be a fool to fall for it.

"Thank you, Rowan." Ramsey began to tuck the note inside his jacket with every appearance of unconcern. "I'll be sure to attend to it later, after I have seen to our guests."

Rowan put out a forestalling hand as Ramsey began to walk away. "No, brother."

Ramsey's arm clenched under his brother's grip. It took every bit of self-control he possessed not to rip himself away. Ramsey had such a tentative hold on his temper that he did not dare look at Rowan's face to see the sorrowful expression of sympathy he was certain it was wearing.

"Please, Ramsey, you should know. Before you go any further."

Ramsey looked up then. Up the several inches necessary to meet the shining blue eyes of his taller sibling. Eyes that wore only a veneer of sorrow over a deep well of mocking triumph.

237

Triumph over what the note contained? Or triumph over having forced Ramsey's hand? Ramsey would look nothing but churlish now if he refused Rowan's request to read the note here and now. It was an old game they played, and Ramsey had never mastered it.

Mentally cursing himself, Ramsey pulled the note from his jacket, painfully aware of the weight of so many pairs of eyes. Behind him, abruptly raised voices seemed incongruously loud in the midst of such ominous silence.

Mr. and Mrs. Ulworth. Still unable to locate Hester. And then he knew. He looked again at Rowan and saw confirmation. Unable to stop himself, Ramsey unfolded the note.

The hand was unexpectedly florid, a bit untidy, and obviously hurried.

To His Exalted Highness, Prince Ramsey Tremontaine, Regrets.

Forgive me. I have done that which will shame me in the eyes of yourself, my parents, and indeed the world, but I could not do otherwise. My affections have long been given, though we dared not request my father's approval, and could not once he became aware of the opportunity to bestow me more eligibly. We have long despaired, having no means to establish ourselves without our parents' consent. It was only this morning that we suddenly found hope for our future together, and have had no choice but to grasp it. I know not how such an exalted person came to know of our plight, I only thank providence for the blessed and timely intervention of His Highness, Prince Rowan, who offered us the means to escape from the bleak fate that has so long confronted us. Forgive me, Your Highness, if I have offended you, or caused you embarrassment. I never sought your attention, though in duty to my father I have presented myself to your notice and for that

deception I am deeply sorry. While I honor you as my Lord and my
Prince, and consider myself your loyal subject, I cannot pretend that a
marriage between us would not be repugnant to me. I beg you would
convey the contents of this message to my honored parents and accept
my eternal gratitude for the services of the House of Tremontaine in
securing my happiness. I remain,

Your Loyal Subject,
   Mrs. Hester Ulworth Arthur

Ramsey felt a fool. A blind, heartless fool.

There was blame aplenty to go around. Rowan for purpose-fully handling this in the most scandalous way possible. Mr. Ulworth for using his daughter for his own purposes. Kyril, for assessing her character without knowing her heart. And himself, Ramsey, for daring to presume that his own needs were the only ones that mattered.

Deep down, he had let himself believe that all he needed to do was choose. Not that his choice would love him, but that she would take him. Would he have asked, if they had met, what her choice would be? Or would he have gratefully accepted Kyril's off-hand assurance that Hester would do whatever her father told her, as though she were something to be sold in his shop?

Ramsey mentally raised a glass in toast to the not-so-dull or dutiful Miss Hester Ulworth. A braver and better person than he by far. She had complicated his day beyond all measure, leaving a mess that would require weeks to sort out, but he wished her well. More than well. Whoever the lucky Mr. Arthur was, Ramsey hoped they would be deliriously happy.

He was hoping much more violent things for his brother. Being eaten by rats would be ideal. If it had not been for the pressing necessity of appearing nonchalant in front of his guests, Ramsey could have gone on fantasizing about large, hungry rodents for some time.

Instead, he used up several weeks worth of self-control and smiled at Rowan. What Rowan had accomplished may not have been villainous, but neither his methods nor his motives were much concerned with anyone's agenda but his own. An agenda that could not help but appear suspicious, even if Ramsey had neither the time nor the opportunity to explore the issue.

"My thanks, brother. You may be sure I will see to it without delay."

Ramsey was grimly delighted to find that Rowan's own game could be used against the smug bastard, who had no choice but to step back graciously and be dismissed.

Now for the hard part. Well, harder. The party would have to be dismissed and the news conveyed to Hester's parents. They would likely wish to pursue her, as she could not have been gone over an hour, though Ramsey would be very much surprised if Rowan had not managed the business well enough to prevent pursuit.

Under every watching eye, Ramsey beckoned to Kyril and stepped aside with him for a moment, speaking as quietly as possible. "We've the devil's own stew here and not much time. I need your help." Kyril nodded. No questions, no doubts, just waited for his instructions. Ramsey wondered if he had ever appreciated such friendship as deeply as it deserved.

"I'm going to court a great deal of displeasure and announce that the party must be hastily dismissed, due to my father's worsening health." Kyril blanched. "No, it's not, but I have to get them gone. I need you to delay the Ulworths. Ask them to step inside. Do what you must to avoid a scene."

"Done." Kyril probably had questions, but knew better than to ask them. "Anything else?"

Ramsey shook his head minutely. "Not now. But later I may ask you to find me some rats."

～

In the end there were token protests, shocked gasps, discontented pouts, and calculating glances, but the remaining guests were eventually dispersed with disappointed certainty that Ramsey's choice had been made. He had no desire to dispel their misconceptions. Gossip was light on its feet, and they would all learn the truth soon enough.

By the time his obligations as host were discharged and Ramsey finally managed to locate Kyril in one of the castle's receiving rooms, Mr. Ulworth was midway between chafing and frothing and his face was anything but friendly. Ramsey took the precaution of stationing two guards at the door before he went into the room. Where Kyril had wisely stationed another guard.

"Mr. and Mrs. Ulworth, I thank you for waiting."

Mr. Ulworth bristled. His patience was quite clearly gone. To be fair, Ramsey couldn't blame him. His daughter was still missing, and Kyril hadn't been able to answer any of his questions.

"Your Highness,"—it sounded as though Mr. Ulworth would rather have dispensed with the honorific—"I would be happy to know what has been done with my daughter." The poor man's dignity, and his manners, were hanging by a thread.

Ramsey bowed slightly. "I assure you, Mr. Ulworth, nothing has been 'done' with your daughter. It appears she had some, let us say, objections, to your hopes of a royal marriage and has made her own arrangements to avoid it." He handed the note to her father before the man could protest Ramsey's choice of words. They were mild compared to the ones he would have liked to use. Damned diplomacy.

Mr. Ulworth had not come this far by completely failing to control his temper. He took the note, his hand shaking visibly, and read it. His mouth began to fall open, slowly, by degrees, until at a predictable point in his daughter's explanation it began to flap in an unmistakably fish-like manner. His eyes widened, and his cheeks grew pink. All the while, his wife watched, a curious expression on her face that was most notably *not* one of surprise.

"This is *his* fault!" Mr. Ulworth finally hissed when he finished and threw the note to the floor in disgust.

Well, thought Ramsey, he could at least place as much blame on his own child as on the poor Mr. Arthur. It sounded very much as though it had not been Mr. Arthur's idea in the first place.

"That... That monster!" He rounded on Ramsey with a vengeance. "Your brother has stolen my daughter and he will answer for it!"

Now it was Ramsey's turn to look a bit fish-like. He had fully expected the need to shield Rowan from a piece of the blame, but all of it? Seemed a bit excessive, though it felt decidedly odd to be defending his brother, even inside his own head. Perhaps if he thought of it as defending the crown from the consequences of his brother's idiocy. *That*, he had been doing for years.

"Mr. Ulworth, may I suggest that you moderate your language?" Ramsey did his best to sound stern and in control of the situation. "I understand your concern, and will render what aid is necessary to recover your daughter, but I must insist that you speak with more respect for His Highness, Prince Rowan." The search for a diplomatic turn of phrase necessitated a pause. "Your prince may not have acted with sufficient courtesy to your feelings as a parent, but he has acted to preserve your daughter's happiness and to protect the dignity of the crown, should this prior attachment have remained hidden until it was too late."

Perhaps it was time to impress upon Mr. Ulworth how impolitic his deception had been. "I asked for honesty, Mr. Ulworth. Your daughter was under no compulsion from me when she stated, in her own hand, that she wished to marry me. I find it difficult to believe, under the circumstances, that she did this of her own free will."

Ramsey did not ask the question, merely dangled it in front of Hester's father, hoping he would bite. The poor man probably would have. He was not much given to subtlety or discretion, which made Ramsey feel a bit of a beast for baiting him, as necessary as it was to shift the blame away from Rowan. To his relief, absolution was granted to all, from an unexpected source.

"Francis, stop." Mrs. Ulworth had small, bright spots of color on her cheeks, but she did not look otherwise disturbed, only determined. Ramsey found himself thinking incongruously that he had never met a man who looked less like a Francis.

Mr. Ulworth rounded on his wife, opened his mouth once, but subsided at her expression. Interesting.

Mrs. Ulworth turned to Ramsey. "Your Highness," she said firmly, "Hester has indeed been secretly engaged to Mr. Arthur for nearly a year."

Francis, predictably, exploded, though thankfully not in Ramsey's direction. "Secretly what?" he roared impressively.

"That boy hasn't the brains or the nerve to place an order in person! How could they be engaged?"

Mrs. Ulworth regarded him with weary complacency, seeming, if anything, a bit relieved to be having this tiff. Ramsey was relegated to the highly preferable role of observer.

"Hester is a woman, Francis, not a fool. She knew precisely what you would say to Hensley on the subject of their relationship and preferred to keep it a secret. If she never told you, you couldn't forbid it."

"Forbid it? Of course I forbid it!"

This was going to be a long argument. And Ramsey didn't really have time to wait for them to finish. "Mrs. Ulworth?" he interrupted. "I wish to render assistance if it is necessary, but perhaps, in light of these revelations, I should inquire... Do you wish to pursue your daughter?"

Both parents were silent for a moment. Francis began to speak, but it was short lived. His wife, for the moment at least, had the upper hand, by virtue of being in possession of both herself and all the facts.

"No." Her voice was soft and firm, and her face showed regretful certainty.

Ramsey recalled his earlier assessment of her as prim and disapproving. Perhaps he had been as wrong about the mother as he had been about the daughter. He held her gaze for a moment, wanting to be sure, but she never wavered, so Ramsey nodded in assent. "Accept my condolences, and those of my House," he said formally, before Mr. Ulworth could recover and start bellowing again. "The steward will show you out and send for your carriage whenever you are ready."

Mrs. Ulworth acknowledged him with a formal curtsey and a

sad curve of a smile. "My thanks, Your Highness, and our regrets."

Ramsey nodded and left. Whatever conversation came next, it would not be one that required an audience.

∼

Ramsey spent the next hour or so going through the motions of attending to his duties. He dictated a note of apology to his disappointed guests, approved a crown gift of dowry to Mrs. Hensley Arthur (it seemed appropriate, considering that Rowan had, essentially, given away the bride), and met with one of the healers attending his father.

At least that report was somewhat encouraging. The king was improving, his color seemed better, and he had been able to swallow his gout medicine without choking.

Mostly, Ramsey was avoiding anyone who would ask for an explanation of what had occurred that afternoon. Or who might expect him to know what he intended to do next. He really had no idea what there was to be done.

He still needed to marry, that much was certain, but what were his options now? Anya Colbourne? He would rather throw himself into the nonexistent moat.

Perhaps he should pretend this was nothing more than a treaty negotiation. Ask his advisors to suggest the most suitable bride according to her family's wealth and her father's politics. Not even bother to meet her until they stood up together for the ceremony.

Feeling something alarmingly close to despair, Ramsey needed space to think. Or not to think. To put aside his anger at his brother, his fear for his father and his vexation with himself long enough to make a decision that had a chance of not being a huge mistake. For once he did not want to ask Lizbet, or Kyril, or anyone else. This was his, and his alone. Lingering wistfully on the idea of running away to his forest haunt, Ramsey's steps turned instead to the tower.

It was the most pretentious bit of architecture in an otherwise quite practical castle. Used for very little, the tower's sole purpose seemed to be adding consequence to the building's profile. Ramsey had discovered as a small, easily embarrassed child that its seclusion, reached only by climbing far too many steps, offered a retreat from the often humiliating voices of his peers.

Fortunately, it was a warm enough day that the unadorned stone floor was more hospitable than usual. The sun slanted in cooperatively through tall glass windows as Ramsey sat, closed his eyes against the afternoon light, and leaned back against the wall.

A crackling issued from the front of his jacket as he did so, and he remembered suddenly that he had tucked Miss Westover's note there for later perusal. So much for peaceful reflection. Remembering Lizbet's odd expression when she handed it to him, Ramsey reached into his jacket, pulled out the offending paper and unfolded it. The contents were unlikely to prove more distressing than those of the previous note he had received.

This one was written on plain, white paper, in the same neat script he remembered from the application. Though he noted that the mysterious Miss Westover was marginally more verbose on this occasion.

To His Highness, Prince Ramsey Tremontaine,

Please be so kind as to accept my regrets in the matter of your very flattering invitation to the festivities this afternoon. I fear that my own embarrassment at my ineptitude during the dancing last evening led to an undoubtedly foolish rejection of aid that has rendered me unable to walk without difficulty this morning. Though, in an effort to salvage what I may of my own pride, I have decided to place a great deal of the blame on my shoes. I suspect a dungeon somewhere is missing two of their finest devices of torture. Please likewise accept my humblest wishes that my own failures will not in any way disrupt your plans. I was most grateful for the honor of an invitation to Evenburg last evening and feel that it greatly aided my social education. To thank you for the honor of your notice, I am entirely without resource. Though I must say, if I had known that impudence and ineptitude are acceptable methods of securing a man's attention, I might have attempted it sooner. I remain,

Your Obedient Subject,
  Miss Elaine Westover

It was impossible to read without laughing. Even tired, confused, afraid, and out of options, Ramsey sat on the stone floor in the sun and permitted himself an uninterrupted moment to appreciate Miss Westover's rather audacious humor. So different from what he had come to expect from young women courting a man's favor.

Coming from anyone else, he might have suspected they were *trying* to offend him. From the strange young woman of last night, he really couldn't be sure. But sitting there, alone, pressed on every side, Ramsey was suddenly very sure of one thing. He wanted to see her again.

His party had been a disaster and his plans were in shambles.

If he still had to marry, and he did, he wanted one more chance to find out what sort of girl Miss Westover was. No secrets, no masques. There had been enough of those, and this last secret had nearly proven disastrous.

Brawley had suggested that her ties were suspicious. Well, he would ask her. Show her that she was not the only one capable of straightforward conversation.

Ramsey was not fool enough to suppose that she would not lie to him, but still... He could feel his mood lightening noticeably with the realization that he had not quite reached a dead end. If he did not at least make this attempt, he knew he would always wonder whether Miss Westover might not have been a better choice. Better, at least, than whomever his advisors could come up with. Not best.

For some reason he could not explain, even to himself, best would always be a girl he had only met three times and could never hope to marry. If he was honest, he would even admit that the only reason he wanted to meet Elaine again was that she reminded him of Embrie.

CHAPTER 12

Trystan lay in bed the next morning, trying not to feel. Sore, lonely, bored, worried, relieved, confused—if she pretended not to feel any of it, perhaps she could pretend that the ordeal was truly over. If she was very lucky, she might even fool herself into believing that everything was going to be fine, that all of her problems were solved, and that being wealthy, independent and alone was the pinnacle of her dreams.

She wasn't nearly so lucky. In fact, she didn't even feel very triumphant. It was rather difficult to believe she'd accomplished anything when she was celebrating her victory by hiding in her room with a sore ankle.

To be fair, it was larger than her bedroom at home, with an unlocked window, a convenient ivy trellis, and all the comforts she could ask for, but it did seem a bit ironic that after gaining her impossible prize, she was in much the same position as when Lady Isaura found her in the first place. And felt even more fully a prisoner.

Trystan wondered when there would be news from the palace

of an impending engagement. She thought about who it might be. Lady Isaura had not said who else had been invited to the garden party the previous day, though Trystan had no doubt she knew. Probably a lot of girls that Trystan had never met, and wouldn't care to meet.

She wondered when the wedding would be, and who would be invited, and whether her stepmother would be there, trying to trip the bride. Unless the bride was Anya. Trystan very carefully stomped on that thought, ground it to teeny tiny bits and brushed it to the back of her mind. Where it would probably itch until she found a way to learn whom Donevan... no, Prince Ramsey, had chosen.

Lady Isaura had spent much of the previous day in meetings. She had gone out for several hours, returned, and passed the evening closeted in her study. Trystan would rather have gotten the business of her payment for services rendered out of the way as soon as possible. Not that she suspected Lady Isaura meant to rescind her offer. As long as the older woman was still pretending that the note was meaningful, it made perfect sense for her to reward her protégée for completing a dangerous and difficult task.

But time could be running out. Malisse had to be wondering why her recalcitrant stepdaughter had not yet been sent home, and Lady Isaura could hardly tell her that Trystan had sprained her ankle dancing at a ball. Despite the fact that the ankle seemed almost entirely recovered, Lady Isaura had insisted that Trystan maintain the fiction of her injury for a while longer, as it kept her away from any possible scrutiny. The last thing they wanted was for the curious to come to the house in search of "Elaine," and find only the neighborhood madwoman. In a day or two, Lady Isaura would put about that her cousin had departed suddenly for home, and then Trystan would be free.

Trystan was just beginning to feel restless enough to countermand her orders when she heard voices in the hall. Polite voices, though with an edge. Lady Isaura had a visitor, and she was bringing them to see Trystan. That could really only mean one thing: her dear stepmother had come to make sure she was suffering sufficiently.

At least, Trystan thought with a grimace, she had remembered to wash the dye out of her hair the day before. She might have had a difficult time explaining its sudden change of color.

Unsure what Lady Isaura had already told Malisse, Trystan sat up in bed, smoothed her hair as if to reassure herself, and tried to look... What would Malisse hope she would be feeling? Chastised? Bored? Jealous? She settled for bored. With a hint of dyspeptic.

Lady Isaura knocked gently.

"Come in." Trystan turned towards the visitors, assuming an expression of alarmed surprise when she saw her stepmother.

"Trystan," Lady Isaura prompted in her kind, elderly lady voice, "your mother is here to see how you do. I sent her a note about your accident, on the stairs, and she was worried enough to enquire after your recovery."

Ah. So now clumsy was to be added to Trystan's list of faults.

"Though I must say I am not surprised," Malisse interrupted, sternly. "I hope you have not been troubling my dear friend with any of your distempers, Trystan. It was too good of her to take you off my hands and I would very much dislike hearing that she has had any cause to be disappointed in your behavior."

Lady Isaura saved Trystan the trouble of responding, probably hoping to avoid any real confrontation. "Of course not," she replied soothingly, patting Trystan's head with brightly smiling condescension. Trystan managed, barely, not to glare. "She has been a great consolation to me these past days. It is often so quiet and lonely that I have found myself quite diverted by her conversation." As though Trystan were some sort of amusing pet.

"And then, of course," Lady Isaura added, "she has been quite helpful in the matter of entertaining my cousin, whose visit has been such a delightful surprise."

Malisse was obviously unconvinced, but seemed anxious to turn the conversation to other matters. "My dear Lady Westerby, as she is still recovering, and the two... no, three of you seem to be getting on so well together, I wonder if I might beg a favor."

"But of course, Lady Colbourne, you need only ask." The sugared insincerity was so thick, Trystan wished she had a spoon. She could have eaten it with cream and called it dessert.

"I was hoping it might be possible for you to keep her here for a few more days. Perhaps she could continue to be company for your guest?" Malisse looked insufferably smug about something, and was obviously begging for someone to ask her what it was. Lady Isaura sacrificed herself, probably aware that Trystan would rather have cut out her own tongue.

"Why, Malisse, is anything the matter?"

Trystan's stepmother smiled coyly, tilted her head, and waved a languid hand. "Oh no, I assure you, nothing the matter. It is only the news, you see, from the palace..." she paused for effect.

"News? Malisse, what have you heard?" Trystan had not realized that Lady Isaura could gush. And so effectively too.

"Why, Lady Westerby, you mean to say you didn't know? About the party yesterday? I take it your cousin was not invited?"

Lady Isaura dismissed the idea in no uncertain terms. "Malisse, my cousin is an unrefined, and frankly rather ungoverned, child. She could hardly have been of interest to a man of Prince Ramsey's stature. And anyway, she is shortly to return to the north. I believe she misses her home."

Malisse smiled beatifically, obviously sensing no threat from a girl so retiring that she had no visitors and failed to greet guests. Lady Isaura had known her neighbor long enough to guess aright that she would trouble herself no further over the matter of the unknown cousin.

"Well," Malisse confided, "you wouldn't know then that only nine girls were invited yesterday for an exclusive meeting with His Highness... Anya, was, of course, among them." She said this as though it were impossible for it to have been otherwise, but was patently hoping for congratulations, which Lady Isaura was wise enough to offer.

"How wonderful for you, Malisse. I know it is what you have always hoped for."

Malisse nodded, all grace and benevolence. "Yes, though we had for a time despaired." Her voice lowered conspiratorially. "It seemed all but certain that the prince had chosen, though I, for one, cannot imagine it was ever so. Hester Ulworth? Such an embarrassing family! Very common, if I may say so."

Lady Isaura made all the necessary noises of agreement.

"But now, this morning?" Malisse went on, too taken by her own story to notice interruptions. "The truth has come out and the chit's parents must be beside themselves. They say Hester fled, rather than marry Prince Ramsey! That she has eloped with a tailor's son and no one knows where they have gone!"

Malisse spoke with vicious glee, and Trystan could see why. It would have been an intolerable insult had poor Hester been chosen over the rich, beautiful Anya Colbourne. This turn of events ensured not only that Anya was still in the running, but that Hester's presumptuous family would suffer all the mortification that Malisse believed they deserved for daring to consider themselves the equals of their more gently born rivals.

Of course, Malisse also wished to flaunt Anya's success in front of Trystan, as revenge for her injudicious commentary at dinner some weeks previously.

"Well!" Lady Isaura's look of shocked affront appeared quite genuine. "I hope His Highness has not been too embarrassed. What an insult to the crown!"

Malisse shook her head, obviously not finished with her tale. "He seemed only too glad to let her go, and who would not be? The truth is, he's distracted. Have you not heard? The king is taken suddenly ill! Some say he lies near death. It could be that Prince Ramsey will not be a prince much longer."

Trystan felt these last words knife their way coldly into her heart. She did not hear her stepmother's next words at all, and the rest of the world seemed dim and colorless. The king? Donevan's father? Her friend's life was already beset by difficulties and sadness. How could he lose his father? After being so cruelly disappointed by the woman he had chosen to marry!

Her distress and dismay felt like a physical wound. Distantly she noticed both Malisse and Lady Isaura looking at her oddly, but could not escape from this pain that had nothing to do with her.

She had never met the king, and could feel no sorrow at his illness, but she guessed that his son would be grieving. That grief had somehow reached out and included her, for no better reason than friendship.

The thought stunned her. She had not known until that moment what it was to feel another's pain. She had not realized that she could.

"… Never seen her like this. Trystan? I say, Trystan, are you ill?" Malisse's strident tones finally broke through the fog of Trystan's misery.

She looked up dully, no longer very interested in what Malisse had come to say. "No, Stepmother. Not ill. That is, I feel a bit odd, but I'm sure if I lie down for a little longer it will pass."

Malisse harrumphed as loudly as decorum would permit. "Well. I trust I will have no reason to be concerned for her health." This to Lady Isaura as that lady gently ushered her visitor out, though not without a searching look at Trystan. "I had believed these fits of hers were well and done, but perhaps I was mistaken. If you wish I could call for…" The voices trailed off down the hall as the door closed behind the two women.

Trystan sank back onto the bed and was immediately forced to turn her head into the pillow to hide the tears she could no longer stop. She rarely cried, but somehow it seemed to ease the ache. If she was wise, she would not permit herself the luxury for long. Lady Isaura would be back, and Trystan could offer no explanation for a wet pillow and swollen eyes. At least, nothing that would satisfy that woman's sharp looks and pointed questions.

Scrubbing her face with an already rumpled handkerchief, Trystan sat up, turned over her pillow and tried to compose herself. Tried to think about Anya's face, when she first learned she had been rejected in favor of a shopkeeper's daughter. Tried not to think about Anya's face when she learned that the shopkeeper's daughter had eloped with someone else.

And then, because she could not help herself, she wondered what Donevan… Prince Ramsey, was doing. Was he truly grieving? Did he love his father so much that he couldn't bear the thought of life without him? Or did he hate his life so much that he questioned the love of the father who had forced him to live it?

As Trystan had begun to question her own. In that moment, she was finally able to admit to herself that she didn't believe her father had loved her.

If he had loved her, wouldn't he have married someone who would share that love? And wouldn't he have tried to make them a family, instead of driving them farther apart by his indifference?

But he hadn't. He had known his wife despised his daughter, and had done nothing to protect her.

Because he hadn't loved her enough, or because he hadn't loved her at all?

And if he hadn't, if what they had shared was not love, had she, Trystan, ever truly loved anyone?

Trystan was standing at the window, still lost in miserable contemplation, when she saw the Colbourne carriage rattling back down the drive and heard the knock on the door.

"Yes." She wasn't really ready to see Lady Isaura, but couldn't exactly tell her to go away. The door opened and closed quietly. Trystan did not turn around.

"I think that perhaps," Lady Isaura began carefully, "you have not told me the whole truth, Trystan."

Trystan turned to face her hostess as nonchalantly as possible. "I'm not sure what you mean, Lady Isaura. Did my stepmother tell you I'm likely to have fits, because it's not true. I haven't had a fit in ages."

Lady Isaura frowned. "Not about that, Trystan, about the ball."

Trystan's eyes widened fractionally in response, but she said nothing.

"I think you were not entirely honest about your feelings

towards someone. I saw your face when Malisse mentioned the king." Trystan tried not to hold her breath as Lady Isaura stared at her. "Is it possible that you have conceived an... an attachment?" Her voice lowered to almost a whisper. "For Prince Ramsey?"

Trystan's usual glibness failed her utterly. "I... I don't see how," she protested. "We danced. Once. That was all." It sounded like a lie, even to her.

Lady Isaura's face brightened with the discovery. "It's true!" she breathed, as if in awe. "You love him!"

Trystan shook her head vehemently in denial. "No, no I don't! Perhaps I found him attractive. Maybe even interesting. But I don't love him!"

The other woman did not seem to hear her. "Then that explains it!" Lady Isaura glared fiercely, but seemed exhilarated rather than upset. "Wait here." She left the room in a great hurry, leaving Trystan staring after her in consternation.

Damn her feelings anyway. How could she have failed so badly at hiding them? When Lady Isaura returned a moment later she held a note in her hand.

"This came, this morning, and I had not bothered to read it as I thought I knew what it contained, but now I suspect..." She handed the note to Trystan, who knew as soon as it entered her hand both who it was from and that Lady Isaura had lied. She had most certainly read it and knew exactly what it contained.

Trystan opened it, trying not to let her hands shake. Hoping it wasn't what she thought it was.

To Miss Elaine Westover, Greetings,

I suspect that you will, by now, have become privy to the details of the events of yesterday. While rumors do not express the whole truth of the matter, suffice it to say that I am still rather embarrassingly in need of a bride. Due to other recent developments, it has become clear that, much as I deplore it, haste is now more important than ever. Miss Westover, I wish to be honest with you. My situation is such that I do not have the luxury of marrying for mutual affection. All I can look for now is to find someone who might, someday, learn to care for me and I for them. A kindred mind, if you will. I hope you will not find me forward, but I felt, inasmuch as such things are possible after a meeting of only a few moments, that yours might be such a one. I have even dared to believe that perhaps, given a chance, you might not find me entirely repugnant. If I am in error, then I apologize, and beg that you honor me only with your reply. If, however, you feel that there exists even the smallest possibility for mutual respect between us, please honor me instead with your presence, at a private meeting tomorrow. By your acceptance, you would be implying nothing more than your willingness to discuss the matter. I will await your reply.

Respectfully,

    Ramsey Donevan Tremontaine

It was not what she thought. It was worse. Donevan had seen through her, somehow. He wanted to meet her, without the masque, all of her secrets laid bare. To find out if he could love her. It was at once profoundly satisfying and deeply horrifying. He had seen through her disguise. Even without seeing her face, he had known her. And all she had to offer him was pain.

How could she tell him what she had done? She didn't even know what she had done, except that it had been wrong, utterly wrong.

Too late, she noticed a motion from Lady Isaura, who

snatched the note from her hands and pretended to read it. There was a light in the older woman's eyes, something disturbing, but Trystan could not name it, she could only think frantically of what excuse she might offer this time.

Lady Isaura took the decision out of her hands. "My dear Trystan, this is wonderful! You must be so happy! He cares for you! Not for that Ulworth girl after all!" She took Trystan's face in her hands and beamed. "I'm sure you are much too excited to reply so I will do it for you... no, don't trouble yourself, I will see to everything! And don't worry about your stepmother, dear child. I'm certain I can invent an explanation that will satisfy her. And besides, once you are engaged to Prince Ramsey, even Malisse won't dare interfere."

And then she was gone, hastening away before Trystan could protest or call after her. Trystan knew there would be nothing she could have said. Lady Isaura was convinced of Trystan's feelings and no protest would have swayed her from her intentions.

The question was now no longer whether she would tell Prince Ramsey. It was a matter of *what* she would tell him. And how.

~

Trystan was numb with misery all that long afternoon, as Lady Isaura hummed and chatted and primped and planned. She had accepted the invitation on Trystan's behalf, and after an exchange of missives via royal courier, the meeting was set for the following day, at dusk.

Trystan briefly contemplated running away. If she disappeared, it was unlikely any concerted effort would be made to find her. Lady Isaura would simply say that her cousin had returned to the north, and Malisse was more likely to offer up prayers of thanks than send anyone after her.

It was, perhaps, only her newfound sense of empathy that made her stay. She simply could not do such a thing to Donevan. One girl had already fled rather than marry him. It would crush him if she did the same. Though she did not know whether the truth she had to tell him would be much easier to bear.

And which truth would it be? She could tell him she was Embrie and that she had lied in order to go to the ball. Pour out the sordid story of her family and hope he was sympathetic. She could even claim that she pretended to be Lady Isaura's cousin because Malisse would not allow her to leave the house. And then what? Wait for Rowan to denounce her? Wait for the mysterious conspiracy to reveal itself?

What if she chose to tell Prince Ramsey everything? She still had nothing better to offer him than the information that his brother was plotting against him. If she told him the whole truth would he even believe her? Or would he order her imprisoned for impertinence?

Her misery seemed to increase in direct proportion to Lady Isaura's excitement. Shortly after supper, in exasperation with what she chose to term Trystan's "nerves," Lady Isaura ordered her to go back to her room and clear her head. Trystan went, paced, cried, stomped, pulled her hair, then summoned a servant to tell Lady Isaura that she was going to bed. In case someone chose to check on her, Trystan arranged a few pillows and a nightgown until she was satisfied that it would be convincing. Then she dug into her closet and donned her boots, thanking providence she had thought to bring them. The window presented little difficulty, though it squeaked as if it had not often been opened. Before she could think better of it, she was out, down the trellis, and walking away across the lawn into the gathering dark.

Part of her longed to go home, to find Vianne, pour out her story and hope the cook's wisdom could get her out of this mess, as she had done so many times before. The wiser Trystan knew she would never make it so far on a slightly sore ankle in the dark. She simply needed to walk and think. And hope that silence and solitude and the cool night air would aid her in finding an answer.

~

She walked for a very long time. Then she sat, then walked again. Trystan had no idea how late it was when she at last returned to the house, weary, and still without answers. She approached her window at first, then noticed that most of the lights were out. Lady Isaura could be in her room, which was very near Trystan's. The last thing she needed was for the squeaky window to alert her hostess to her nighttime wanderings. Disgruntled, Trystan went in search of another window. Fortunately, she found one of the front sitting room windows that a maid had forgotten to close. It was low enough that she was easily able to climb through and break her fall on a nice soft settee. Very convenient. Almost as if someone knew she was out and about. Trystan grinned at her luck, in spite of everything, and crept out of the room, glancing down the hall. The lamps were extinguished, and everything seemed quiet. Apparently everyone had gone to bed. How long had she been gone?

Stealing silently down the darkened hall towards the stair,

Trystan caught a glimpse of light, coming from under the not-quite-closed door to Lady Isaura's study. A few steps closer and she could hear voices. Someone was still up! It was late enough that all the servants would be in bed, and Trystan could not imagine who else Lady Isaura could be talking to at this hour. The oddity of it piqued Trystan's curiosity enough that she inched forward until she drew even with the door. Trying not to breathe, she leaned in and placed her eye to the crack.

Inside, a single lamp burned. Lady Isaura was pacing feverishly from one side of her desk to the other, while a second person sat in the chair in front of it, his back to Trystan. Definitely male, short, and balding... he looked familiar even from behind. It did not take long for her to realize that the nocturnal visitor was Lord Fellton! Was this some sort of romantic assignation? Probably not in the study.

"Don't you understand, this solves everything!" Lady Isaura's voice crackled with excitement. "If he marries her we will have no need to go through with it."

Trystan froze. Definitely not a romantic assignation. Were they talking about her? They had to be. Unless Lady Isaura was making a habit out of arranging marriages.

Lord Fellton's voice sounded more skeptical. "Don't be a fool, Isaura. How is his marrying your *cousin* going to help us?"

Lady Isaura's soft voice was both exultant and threatening as she answered. "Because I know who her mother was."

Trystan felt a strange shiver down her spine. How could Lady Isaura know that? Her father had never allowed anyone to speak of her mother. Even Vianne had refused to answer Trystan's questions, but Trystan had always attributed their silence to grief.

"And," Lady Isaura continued in that same voice of long-awaited triumph, "I also know that she was not married to Lord Percival."

What?

Not married.

That meant.

Trystan was illegitimate. If she married Prince Ramsey, he would no longer be eligible to rule. Rowan would be king. This was their new plan!

Wait. New plan? What had the old one been? Despite the roaring in her ears, despite her shock and distress at the revelation of what seemed yet another disheartening fact about the man she called Father, Trystan kept listening. She had to hear more.

"I still think it would be simpler to get him out of the way permanently. Tie everything up neatly. Why risk being discovered? Just… give him whatever you gave Hollin! That seems to be working well enough."

Lord Fellton sounded both petulant and impatient. One would never have guessed he had just implied that the king had been… poisoned? Trystan clapped a hand over her mouth to keep from gagging in horror. Had he really said that? Had her neighbor, her hostess, the woman who had eaten at her father's table, really given poison to Donevan's father? But how? And more importantly, why?

"Because, fool, it's too soon!" Lady Isaura was no longer the pleasant, genteel widow Trystan knew. She was a commanding woman who apparently possessed both the means and intention to kill. "Rowan says we must act now! Besides, the boy has no desire to wear the crown! Take it away from him legally and he will simply fade into the background. But for now, he still has too many supporters. If he died, so soon after his father, there would be nothing but suspicion and outrage. This is far simpler, and, more to the point, faster."

Lord Fellton made a grumbling sound. "The girl will do it?" He sounded doubtful. "Do you think she suspects?"

"Victor, you must think me an imbecile! Of course she will do it! Do you think I would risk everything we have worked for on a girl I was not sure of?" Trystan could hear a snort of disbelief. "She loves him, for some idiotic reason. Even if she suspected, she would do nothing." Lady Isaura sounded utterly confident. "She has no hope of marrying him if she does not go along with our plan. Can you imagine a young woman in love, willing to give up a prince over a small matter of principle?"

Trystan went cold. Was that what Lady Isaura thought of her? Even worse, could it be true?

"And His Highness agrees with this course of action?" Ramsey's brother was a part of this whole diabolical scheme?

Lady Isaura appeared to indicate that he was and he did.

"And who will be getting rid of the evidence?"

The evidence? Of what? Of the king's poisoning?

"His Highness has suggested it would be a simple matter to hire someone to deal with her."

Who, Trystan wondered frantically, was "her"? Surely not herself. Surely Lady Isaura would not... This conversation had rapidly spiraled beyond anything she had imagined, but she had no time to think. Lady Isaura was still talking.

"I have taken the liberty of dismissing her servants already, and closing the house."

Trystan would have sighed in relief on her own behalf if she'd had the time. It could not be her.

Lady Isaura went on. "They have been told that their mistress is moving to Evenleigh with no intention to return, and she has no other acquaintance that is likely to travel this far. Once she is disposed of, I see no reason Trystan cannot become Elaine permanently. At least until after the wedding, when we will expose the truth of her parentage."

Her eye glued to the crack, Trystan felt her relief drain away. The moment extended out into eternity as she watched a perfectly ordinary woman speak words of unimaginable horror.

Lady Isaura had lied. About so many things. But most importantly to Trystan, she had lied about Elaine.

Elaine was real. She had a home, servants, a life. And she was about to lose it all so that Trystan could become the tool they needed to make a monster into a king.

~

Trystan could barely breathe. Her heart seemed louder than Lady Isaura's voice. She had to get back to her room. Now. Quietly. If they heard her, she was dead. Literally. Trystan did not for a moment imagine that Lady Isaura possessed any fondness for her as a person that would outlive her discovery in that hallway.

Lifting her skirts, Trystan moved backwards, ever so slowly, one foot at a time, until she was outside that brutal sliver of light. Still silent, still hardly daring to think lest she be heard, she turned and crept at an agonizing pace until she reached the stairs. She let herself go more quickly then, still holding up her skirts so there was no chance of tripping. Up, up, up, soundlessly down the hall, counting the doors till she found her own. She twisted the knob, eking out her patience for a few moments more until finally, finally she was inside her room and could close the door behind her.

Some of the terror began to ebb, some of her breath began to return, but not until she was in her nightgown and under the blankets did she eventually let go her furious tears and allow herself time to mourn her own innocence.

Well, she had wanted to know. Trystan still could not imagine why they wanted Rowan to be king, but it no longer really mattered. All she cared about now was the means, and they had used her, Trystan, because she was fool enough to let herself be used. She had done no murder and brewed no poison but her choices had made it possible. If she had not said yes, never agreed to this plan, Elaine Westover would not now be in danger. The king, she believed, would not now lie dying.

The note, she could see now, was a ploy, meant solely for her! Lady Isaura had used her to gain entrance to the castle, on a night when everyone would be looking the other way. That was why she had left the ball early, not to go home with a headache, but to work her mischief above stairs. And now, because of Trystan's unlooked-for success, they were determined to take another young woman's life so that Trystan could go on living it.

She could not. Would not. She hoped it would always have been so. But the question she did not have the courage to answer for herself was this: had she not met Donevan in the Kingswood that day, had she been a stranger to him, so that no danger could be found in the baring of her face, would she have said the same? Would she have refused to steal for herself the life she desired? Or would she, as Lady Isaura had seemed so certain, have traded her principles for her prince?

There was nothing she could do to change what had passed. Her guilt was not a thing that could be hidden, or made reparation for. But she could act. Change what was yet to come. The future was not yet so certain as Lady Isaura believed.

Trystan would meet with Ramsey, tomorrow, at dusk, as promised. She would tell him everything, and then accept her punishment. Her true punishment, she knew, would be his eyes. Donevan's eyes, when he realized she had betrayed him. That would haunt her long past any other punishment they could devise.

Reaching over to the table beside her bed, Trystan found her little golden horse and clutched it to her chest. A token of fealty, Donevan had said. A gift given in faith. And she had proven faithless. To everyone who had ever trusted her. She could no longer help Andrei and Alexei, or Hoskins, or Beatrice, or any of her friends. Those hopes were gone. But she would have one last chance to prove herself not entirely unworthy of their gift. One chance to make everything right. To prevent even more people from suffering for her decisions.

Silently, tears sliding down her face onto her pillow, Trystan began to apologize. To an entire life's worth of people. To her father, for worshipping him instead of loving him. To Vianne, for never really listening. To Andrei, Alexei, Hoskins, and the others, for not being able to help them. For not letting them say good-bye. For not seeing how much they cared until it was too late. To King Hollin, for bringing Lady Isaura to the ball. To Elaine, for stealing her name and her life. And to Donevan. For everything.

Long before she ran out of apologies, Trystan fell asleep.

CHAPTER 13

*E*venburg Castle was waiting. Above and below stairs, from the bailey to the garderobe, every breath was tense, every step fraught with questions. The king, contrary to expectations, did not improve. In fact, he seemed worse. And yet, despite the physicians' inability to identify what troubled him, despite his age and unsettled constitution, he seemed too tenacious to die. Ramsey had tentatively begun to believe in his own prediction: that his father would prove unwilling to depart this life until he had seen his son safely married. It was a tiny, flimsy thing to cling to, but he could scarcely grudge himself the deception. Today, for the first time in weeks, he felt hopeful.

Elaine had agreed to meet with him.

He tried not to let it distract him. Pretended that he hadn't re-read her original note three times already that morning and that it was not currently lodged in his jacket pocket as he went about his tasks. But he had and it was and in truth Ramsey felt a bit ridiculous about it.

He had barely spoken to the girl. At best, all she knew about him was that he was grumpy, but a passable dancer. No… a better dancer than Rowan. Or so she had said. He was much too old to be succumbing to the peculiar feeling of satisfaction that gave him. But it seemed worthwhile to remember that he had been very nearly at his worst when he danced with Elaine three nights ago, and she had still agreed to see him again. He had been a poor enough partner that she had sprained her ankle, and yet she had decided to give him another chance.

It was with an uncharacteristic spring in his step that Ramsey entered his aunt's office. He suspected there would be a great deal of unpleasantness to deal with that day. Despite Mrs. Ulworth's assertion that they did not wish to pursue the newly minted Mr. and Mrs. Arthur, Mr. Ulworth had initiated a quickly widening search. Andar was a small enough kingdom that they could hardly avoid detection forever, but without Rowan's assistance in the matter, Ramsey doubted they would be found soon.

Predictably, the older prince had disappeared before he could be questioned. Despite the pointlessness of recriminations, Mr. Ulworth's missives were growing increasingly acrimonious, and not only towards Rowan. He seemed ready to blame his daughter's precipitate actions on just about anyone or anything other than himself and his own overbearing nature.

In addition, there was quite a bit of business that the king usually dealt with, waiting for someone with enough authority to take it in hand. Complaints from the guilds, a border dispute in the south, and reports of a Caelani ship lurking off the coast, which seemed ominous considering the recent trade discussions. All told, it was more than enough to fill up his day until the appointed meeting at dusk.

Lizbet glanced up from her papers as he entered, greeting him with a wan smile and a look of concern. Ramsey kissed her cheek and smiled back more naturally, perfectly willing to offer the confirmation she sought—that he was not quite ready to run mad.

"You look… happy." Lizbet sounded worried, and Ramsey didn't blame her. He didn't fully understand his own lightness of mood.

"Not really." He shrugged, trying to convey his own inability to explain his frame of mind. "Just feeling hopeful." His eyes met hers over a desk full of problems that didn't seem quite as big as they had yesterday. "Like nothing is quite as bad as it seems. I can't understand it myself, but I need it, so I'm choosing to believe in my own foolishness."

"Hope," said Lizbet gently, "is rarely foolish. But Donnie,"— she bit her lip and looked away—"I do not want to see you disappointed. I'm afraid, both for your father, and for this meeting of yours tonight. Things may not be what they appear." Her appeal was so painful that Ramsey longed to comfort her.

"I promise I have not completely taken leave of my senses, Aunt Lizzie. I can probably think of as many ways this could go wrong as you can. And I don't feel like I'm being blindly optimistic. But"—he touched her hand where it rested on a pile of correspondence—"that's why I have you, you know. And Caspar, and Kyril and Brawley. To keep me sensible and responsible."

Lizbet favored him with a look of deepest sarcasm. "Ramsey Donevan Tremontaine, you have always been more sensible and responsible than is good for you. I swear, I used to want to rub dirt on you and throw you in a pond just to see what would happen."

"Aunt Lizbet, you wouldn't have!" Ramsey's jaw dropped a

little at the idea of his practical aunt trying to get him into trouble.

"Maybe I should have," she argued. "You were always far too old for your years." There was a smile on her lips, but her eyes said she was in earnest. "There has been a weight of expectation on you since you were the age where most boys are falling into ponds on purpose! But not you, Ramsey."

She was right. He had always been careful to stay out of trouble, sensing very young the need to balance Rowan's wildness, despite how much he had loved his elder brother.

"You have spent so much of your life trying to be what your brother isn't," Lizbet went on thoughtfully, "I wonder if you really know who you are, apart from him. What path you might have chosen had he not always shared it with you."

Lizbet's words gave Ramsey no pain he had not felt before, no bitterness that had not already cost him sleep. But what alternative had he been given? Who had the luxury of making decisions with only themselves in mind? Only someone like Rowan.

"Aunt Lizzie, how could I even begin to guess? How could anyone? What would you be without Caspar in your life?" Her answering grimace suggested it was not something she cared to contemplate.

"Without Rowan," Ramsey admitted, "perhaps I would be less than I am now. Have failed to learn or see the things I need in order to be what I must. I am no shining example of anything but foolishness, but I can, on occasion, be brought to see that foolishness." He needed his aunt to see why she should not pity him, no matter whether he sometimes pitied himself. "Rowan has taught me how greatly I should fear myself," Ramsey went on. "That I could become the greatest danger this kingdom faces. For that alone, I should thank him"—he shook his head grimly—"much as it galls me to think of it."

Lizbet had a peculiar expression on her face as he finished. "You're wise to see it, Donnie, and I would not change you. Not even the teeniest, tiniest bit of you. Except, perhaps, to see you smile more often." Her eyes shone with unshed tears. "But think on it anyway," she added gently. "If we spend our whole lives reacting to something, it can be difficult to know what to do when the time comes simply to act."

Ramsey really could not imagine a time when Rowan would not be the axis about which they all turned. When his every decision did not have to take Rowan into account. But his aunt was rarely wrong, so he promised to consider her advice before turning the conversation to other matters.

∾

They worked for hours, barely pausing for lunch. Advisors came and went, Parry and Prisca played under their mother's desk for a time, and several of the healers stopped in to make their reports. Ramsey had decided to close the court for a few days, until his father's illness took a turn either for the better or the worse. They had a system in place for handling emergencies, and he simply didn't have the time or energy for dealing with the face-to-face business his father conducted every single day. There was a reason Ramsey had gained a reputation for being fond of paperwork: he infinitely preferred it to most people.

It was nearly mid-afternoon when they paused to stretch and get a breath of air. Ramsey had poured a cup of cider and was standing at the window, drinking thoughtfully, when the door burst open without much warning. Expecting Parry, or Prisca, who often lacked enough forethought to knock, Ramsey turned with the beginnings of a fond smile, only to be confronted by Brawley, his expression cold, grim, and determined.

"Countess Norelle, apologies. Your Highness, you need to come with me." This was not the resigned and apologetic Brawley Ramsey spoke with most days. This was the Brawley who felt the weight of responsibility for his prince's life, and would let nothing, not even the king, stand in the way if he felt there was a threat. Immediately alert, Ramsey motioned for his guard captain to come in.

"Shut the door, Brawley. Tell me what's going on."

"I don't know, Your Highness, but until I do I want someone with you and armed at all times." His face said this was not an option, but an order.

"Slow down, Brawley." Ramsey tried to sound as calm as possible. The captain did have a tendency to jump straight into over-protective mode. "Something has obviously happened and I need to know what."

Brawley would not look him in the eye. It was bad, then. His captain clearly didn't want to be the one to tell it, but somehow found the words.

"Two of our men just returned from a trip north. They were on their way back, two days ago, when they were caught out near nightfall. Spotted a house, back off the road and went to ask for shelter for the night. There was no answer, but something seemed off, so they went looking around. Ended up being attacked by a couple of mercs who obviously held no respect for the king's colors."

"Were they harmed?" Ramsey found he had enough remaining

energy to feel outraged. No one waylaid the king's men. The green coats had been a guarantee of safe passage for many more years than he had been alive.

"Nothing serious," Brawley told him impatiently. "They searched the house. It seemed rundown, barely lived in, except for one of the upstairs bedrooms." Ramsey waited patiently as his guard paused, his lips thinning as he pressed them together, still not quite wanting to say what he had come for.

"Brawley…"

His man looked up at him, eyes hard, but regretful. Sad in the midst of terrible anger. "There was a girl, Your Highness. She'd been kidnapped, held hostage there for some time."

Ramsey was stunned. Kidnappings were rare and usually for money. He'd heard nothing of a missing girl, or any ransom demands.

"Is she hurt? Has she been returned to her family?"

Brawley shook his head. "She's frightened, but whole. She has no family."

Ramsey gestured impatiently, hoping Brawley meant to come to the point. There was obviously more to this than a kidnapped girl, odd as the circumstance was.

"Your Highness, she says her name is Elaine Westover."

It was the longest day of Trystan's life. The day her father died, the day he told her he would marry again, even the horror of his funeral paled in comparison to this interminable dread that seemed heavier with every moment that passed. Each hour seemed more surreal than the one before. She could barely eat her breakfast, watching the woman who had plotted someone's death spread jelly on her muffin with sublime unconcern. Trystan's nausea had nearly overwhelmed her at luncheon as Lady Isaura spoke of how happy Trystan would be, married to the man she loved. It took every scrap of self-control learned under Malisse's tutelage to pretend that everything was fine. That she was overjoyed. That this day was not going to end in tragedy.

Trystan went to her room to dress as afternoon wore on towards evening. Lady Isaura had provided her with yet another gown, a green satin that was, of course, meant to replicate the king's own color. Trystan did not wear it. Instead, she reached into the back of her closet and pulled out the green wool crepe. The one dress she had brought from home. She doubted she would be returning to Westhaven and would feel more comfortable wearing her own clothes. Underneath the dress she put on her boots, the most sensible shoes she owned. And best for running, she was practical enough to admit. Over it all she put on a cloak. The cloak was not hers, but it was necessary. Long and dark, with a deep hood, it covered her dress completely, and hopefully would hide her identity until she told Donevan what he needed to know. She did not bother re-dyeing her hair, merely braided and pinned it up tightly. Into her pocket she slid the hard warmth of her little horse, gripping it for comfort and courage as she stood, fully dressed and ready, before the window.

Lady Isaura would not be accompanying her this time, preferring, as Trystan now understood, to distance her "cousin" from her own political preferences. Her cause would hardly be aided if Ramsey should see the two of them together.

Standing motionless at her window, thoughts and limbs frozen, Trystan watched as the sun dropped towards the trees. It was so very nearly over. However hard she tried, she could not quite banish the questions that assailed her as the shadows in her room began to lengthen. What would she do if Prince Ramsey chose not to imprison her for treason? She supposed she would run. As far and as fast as she could. Any other choice might mean death. The shadowy conspiracy that had plotted the murder of a king would hardly cavil at taking their revenge on the friendless girl who had betrayed them. On second thought, Trystan's lips twisted at the idea, perhaps she should beg for imprisonment. It might be the only way to keep her life. If that sort of life were truly preferable to death.

At last it was time. Trystan waited to descend the stairs until she was verging on lateness. She did not want to be stopped in the hall for an inspection, or be forced to endure any words of either wisdom or congratulation from Lady Isaura.

True to her hopes, her hostess only shooed her frantically through the door and into the waiting coach, smiling like a proud parent as she shut the door and waved Trystan off down the drive. Even in her dread and despondency, Trystan spared herself a hopeless giggle that sounded more like a sob. Riding off into the sunset to meet her true love, like some dreadful novel gone wrong.

The journey was not long enough. It was perhaps some eight miles from Westhaven to Evenleigh, but it seemed like two. Even the cobblestones were louder than Trystan remembered, and the castle seemed larger. Everything loomed. When the coach stopped inside the Evenburg bailey, she almost shouted for the driver to keep going. Back home? Back to Westhaven? Were there really any choices anymore?

The footman opened the door for her, expressionless as

always. Was that a test, she wondered, if one had aspirations to be a footman? Or were they all merely carved from granite to be animated when needed?

"We'll be waiting, Miss, till called for." The coachman's unnecessary words intruded on Trystan's frantically incongruous thoughts. Of course they would be waiting. Even if she had no intention of calling for them. She wondered if they would wait all night, or if they had instructions to return after a certain time. What did coachmen do if they had no instructions? Her thoughts both fractious and petulant, Trystan barely managed the wave of dismissal that left her standing, insignificant and alone, in front of the wide entry doors. There were a handful of guards stationed about the bailey, but they did not seem quite human enough to count as company.

Full dusk had fallen, she realized, and even without the rings of torches that had brightened every corner on the night of the ball, the bailey seemed as crowded as she remembered it. Not with the clatter of wheels, the shouts of greeting, or the murmur of massed voices, but with shadows and silence. They pressed tightly against her already trembling hands, made it difficult to even draw a breath. And into that awful quiet came the gentle sound of hinges. The massive doors were opening.

A gray-haired and blank-faced steward bowed politely and ushered her into the entry hall, as oddly empty as the bailey.

"Lady, if you would be so good as to follow me?" The steward addressed her with formal courtesy. "His Highness has requested that you wait for him on the balcony." Trystan was surprised, but a bit relieved, she realized. The balcony would serve her purposes well. It was wide and dark, and there were stairs, as she recalled, leading off into the garden. Perhaps having an escape route would give her enough courage to say what was needed. And the darkness would hide them both. Her task would be that much easier if she could pretend it was Ramsey, not Donevan, to whom she spoke.

The steward led her through the gloomy depths of the great hall, which was largely unlit and echoed eerily with their footsteps, to the edge of the unoccupied balcony. Its dimness was brightened only by the distant gleam of lamps from the garden paths below. How romantic, was Trystan's first, hysterical thought. How horribly, tragically, romantic.

"His Highness will be with you shortly." The steward vanished back into the hall so thoroughly that Trystan could not even hear the sounds of his retreat.

She looked around frantically, hoping to occupy her mind, slow her thoughts, gain control of herself before he arrived. Should she sit? Should she stand? Place herself as close to escape as possible? Her eye fell on the bench, but it was the same bench she had occupied only a few nights before when... her thoughts shied away from that memory. Lost in fruitless argument with herself, Trystan was still standing at the balustrade when the last light of the sun died and she realized she was no longer alone.

⁓

She was waiting for him by the railing, frozen in a state of watchful stillness Ramsey could recognize, even in the dark, as fear. Her hand was clenched on the stone; her breath came fast and uneven. A dark cloak with a deep hood covered everything but those hands—pale, ungloved and trembling. Ramsey had expected to find her calm, possibly flirtatious, or even triumphant. She could not know that he had found her out, could not have realized that the real Elaine had finally shivered herself to sleep only a few hours before in his aunt's apartments. She should have displayed some portion of that self-possession which had so impressed him at the ball. But she did not. Whoever she was, this nameless woman who had played him so skillfully and plotted the death of a harmless child was now quite obviously terrified.

Good.

"Take off your hood." His voice grated harshly in the silence. He wanted to look at her, even in the dark. Wanted her to be brave enough to face him.

"No." Her answer shocked them both. They stared at each other warily. "I came only to speak to you." Her voice was tremulous, uncertain. "There are things that must be said. I did not come to discuss marriage, but... there seemed no other way to reach you. I have to tell you, before it's too late." Her voice broke off, as if she searched for words. "Please, this is not for me, but for the good of the kingdom. I only ask that you hear me, and then I will go, unless you command otherwise."

Ramsey's mouth twisted in revulsion. He had intended to draw her out, bait her into confessing, but the day had worn him past endurance. His anger and contempt were past being contained. "Really? The good of the kingdom?" Sarcasm fueled every furious word. "By all means, 'Elaine,' tell me of the good of my kingdom! Tell me of your glorious plans for me and my court! Dazzle me with your lies if you still think you can!"

The girl's breath caught. Her body went rigid.

"Oh yes, Elaine." He spat the word with revulsion and scorn. "We found her. Your poor terrified twin. How far did you think you would get on a stolen life? How great a fool did you think me?"

She started to answer, growing frantic with denial, but he was not quite ready to hear her excuses. He stalked across the balcony until there were only a few paces between them and she shrank back, away from his rage.

"No, Elaine, don't answer that." His voice dropped to a threatening tone just above a whisper. "I know exactly how great a fool my kingdom thinks me to be, and now I can only agree with them." He regarded her coldly, arms tightly folded as if to hold himself back. "After all, if it had not been for a lucky accident, I might have married you. And spent the rest of my worthless life shackled to a scheming, treacherous fraud!"

He saw her flinch. Almost it made him question his judgment. She should not have cared what he thought, but his words had wounded her.

"She is alive? Unharmed?" Her question shook with something repressed. Nerves? Pain? Ramsey did not care. Promised himself that his rage was justified.

"Harmed beyond days of helpless terror? You dare even ask?"

"Please!"

Her raw plea shook him. Forced him to see her. Holding her ground in the face of his uncharacteristically brutal temper.

"Tell me if she is well!" The girl was neither smug nor unconcerned, but instead seemed fiercely determined. Ramsey was silent for a moment. Took a step back, both mentally and physically. Was she a brilliant actress, or was there more going on here than any of them had yet guessed?

"She will be." His reply was succinct but sufficient, a bridge between them that he was loathe to offer. He wanted nothing more than to give vent to his anger at whoever was responsible for this contemptible plot, a plot that had nearly ensnared him. But the woman's response had been nothing like what he imagined. If she had truly not known the fate of the real Elaine, what *had* she done? And, more importantly, why? If she was nothing but a mercenary schemer, why had her shoulders slumped in relief at his answer? Was it genuine consolation or a consummate performance?

"Thank you," she murmured. Almost too quietly to hear. "I am glad."

∽

It was something like peace that settled over Trystan as she heard that Elaine was unharmed. That the girl would live. Recover from her ordeal. It gave Trystan enough courage to say what she had almost decided not to. As terrifying as it had been to think of confronting Donevan when she believed the truth would hurt him, the reality was infinitely worse. He had come already convinced of her perfidy. Her story would now, at best, only sound like a frantic attempt to clear herself of guilt by casting the blame on some shadowy conspiracy. With the burden of suspicion already resting squarely on Trystan, it would be difficult indeed to convince Ramsey of the need to investigate others. Especially when she possessed nothing resembling proof. Only a few words overheard by chance, words that no one could or would confirm, that sounded too horrific to be true, even to Trystan.

But in the end, no matter how Ramsey chose to respond, what other course could she choose? This particular plot may have been thwarted. Ramsey would be safe for now. But they would try again, and again. Rowan, she believed, would not stop until he had gained the crown. But how did one already under suspicion of attempted murder go about convincing a man that his brother wished him dead?

"Yes, I'm sure you're glad." Ramsey's icy sneer interrupted her thoughts. "Glad that your little plot has failed. What I wish you would tell me is this: what could you possibly hope to gain? A crown? A kingdom? I cannot believe you blind enough to think that no one would ever find out. That you could go on forever living a lie."

At that moment, Trystan felt she could not bear to hear more. The part of her that had ridden through the Kingswood in blissful innocence was already dying, shattered and grieved by the harsh words from a man she had so very nearly loved. With almost her last breath, that girl grasped for comfort, reaching into her pocket to grip the golden talisman hidden there and remember his hands, Donevan's hands, curled warmly around hers.

But her fingers stopped before they reached their goal. There was another part of Trystan that refused to give in. Refused to be crushed by disdain. The girl who had borne her stepmother's caustic and crushing commentary for years without being utterly defeated. Who rose up now to confront her prince with every bit of pride, every scathing word she had buried rather than said.

"Do you truly wish to know?" Trystan squared her shoulders, released the railing and took a step in Ramsey's direction. "Or have you already decided what to think? I will answer your questions, Your Highness, but it will do you no good if you have chosen not to hear me!"

She could see him shift backwards, surprised that she attacked when he expected her to retreat. Perhaps she had a chance. If she could keep him off balance long enough to tell him the truth.

~

Ramsey was indeed startled. He had confronted the girl with her crime, flung it in her face, surprising even himself with the strength of his anger. The sight of the real Elaine, trembling, pale and terrified, had affected him more than he realized. He expected at the least that the impostor would be cowed into admitting guilt. Perhaps make a tearful attempt to win favor by offering to name her confederates. Instead, she flung it back at him with defiance. A fine show of spirit, if not wisdom.

"Why should I trust you?" The way he said it, it was more an accusation than a question.

She did not falter at his coldness. "Because there is no one else to trust." The ice in her voice matched his own. "Unless you prefer to ask your brother."

His breath caught in shock. She dared to accuse Rowan? To involve him in her guilt? "That is a gross breach of courtesy as well as sense," he snarled, taking another threatening step towards her. "I will not permit you to—"

The girl did not even wait for him to finish. "Do not play games with me!" Her anger left him stunned and silent. "Either you want the truth or you do not! Evil does not stop where we wish it to! Not for me and certainly not for you. You know your brother's character better than I, but if you cannot bear to hear someone else recognize him for what he is then say so and I will stop before your delicate humors are disturbed."

Ramsey wanted to lash out. To silence her. To pretend he did not know what she meant. But he could not. Because even as she offended on every possible level, she offered what every instinct screamed was the truth. The guilty were not always liars. And he did indeed know Rowan's character. Or thought he did. So he said nothing as she tore his world to shreds.

"I do not attempt to deny my guilt," she began more calmly, "only to say that I am not guilty of what you think. I knew nothing of Elaine until last night."

That was almost preposterous enough to be true, Ramsey thought. Only an idiot would have tried to convince him of it. But there was more.

"I chanced to overhear a conversation between Lady Isaura Westerby and her confederate, Lord Victor Fellton. They confirmed a number of things, but the most important are these: they have attempted to poison the king, they intended to murder Elaine, and they planned to disqualify you from ruling by tricking you into marrying me." She paused. "They also appeared to believe that their actions enjoyed the full knowledge and support of Prince Rowan, whom they are determined to see crowned in your place."

Trystan sounded much calmer than she felt. She still shook with the effort of standing this close to Donevan, bearing the weight of his anger. But even so, she was relieved, by the knowledge that she had passed the responsibility for her information on to him. Knowing full well that he would probably never believe her, she watched Ramsey's face. It was still and emotionless now, watching her in the near dark.

"Tell me then," he said finally, with deadly calm. "What guilt *will* you claim? You say that these others have plotted against me without your knowledge. Very well. Of what am I allowed to accuse you? Attempting to trick me into marrying you?"

It was the worst question he could have asked. But Trystan was ready for it. She had already answered it for herself. "I am guilty of not caring enough," she answered quietly. "Of being blind to needs that were not my own. Of saying yes when I should have said no. They offered me the prize I desired above all others and I shut my eyes to the consequences. No..." She held up a hand to silence him when he would have begun to speak. "It was not a crown I sought. I had no thought of marriage when I came here three nights ago." She drew a deep breath.

"They offered me my freedom. And I was so anxious to grasp it, that I chose to be blind to all else." Her voice broke a little with regret. "They did not tell me what they intended. Or why they chose me. I had not the smallest idea there were lives at stake. Not His Majesty's, not Elaine's. I did not know there *was* an Elaine. But I was pleased to be ignorant, so that I could tell myself my actions did not matter, and for that, I consider myself guilty." There was silence. Long and tense.

"And now?" Ramsey asked, his voice rough with some suppressed emotion. "Do you know why they used you?"

Trystan's reply was heavy with self-loathing. "Because I was unknown and unwise. They told me they wished me to carry a message. Because I would not be suspected. And because I cared nothing for society or politics. Even the message was a lie. The paper your brother gave me was blank. A ruse, to gain access to the palace, so they could poison your father."

"And the marriage?"

"Again, they knew what I did not." Though how they had known when Malisse had not she could scarcely imagine. "My father was never married to my mother. It seems," she added bitterly, "I am twice the bastard."

"Well," said a coldly mocking voice, "at least on one point we are agreed."

⁓

Ramsey could have sworn for a moment that the voice was Rowan's. They were certainly Rowan's words. He was appalled and ashamed when he realized a moment later that the voice, and the words, had been his own.

He wanted so desperately to punish her. To make her bear a part of his pain at hearing the truth she had offered. But he was forced at last to silence by his own traitorous logic. So many little things, words, accidents, and coincidences, etched in his memory, began to fall into place. His brother's conspicuous absences. The growing complaints by the guilds. The Caelani ship off the coast. Larissa Fellton's artless disclosure of her father's involvement in illegal trade. And now Victor Fellton's name again, in conjunction with treason and his father's suspicious "illness." As the picture grew more ominous with each moment it also pointed to one other unavoidable fact—the girl was probably innocent. Oh, not entirely. But Ramsey was astonished by the discovery that he was beginning to believe her. His memory turned traitor and reminded him of the night of the ball. Of her behavior, towards him and towards Kyril. Entirely at odds with the scheming opportunist he so badly wanted her to be. She had been nothing if not honest, that evening. Even tried to avoid his invitation the next day. She could not have counted on being asked to return.

It galled him, but if it was true, he had no time to waste in considering her further. Whatever her petty crimes, they paled beside what he now faced. His brother was not simply the charming, infuriating wastrel they had assumed, but a willing party to the death of his own father. It seemed obvious in hindsight that Rowan had not been the cheerfully unwilling object of the support and admiration of the guilds, but an active participant. He had the loyalty of much of the merchant nobility. Could he have gained the loyalty of others as well? Of the servants? Of the guards?

He looked back at the girl who had come to warn him. She was watching him, he could tell, from under her deep hood. She looked smaller now, her anger spent. Defeated. Awaiting judgment. But she waited, and for that he felt a rush of grudging admiration. He utterly ignored the voice that suggested he might owe her an apology.

"I will not thank you," he told her, compelled by her courage to give her that much. "I cannot begin to be certain of either your innocence or your honesty. But I find myself, against my better judgment, inclined to believe you." He closed his eyes against the pain. "And because I believe you, I have no time to decide what to do with you." His lips twisted. "My captain would insist on death or the dungeon. But I've no wish to deal out death, and our dungeon, it seems, may soon be filled with much worse than you. It would appear I have little choice but to let you go."

She made not a sound, either of thanks or protest, only bowed her head and turned towards the steps in retreat.

"Wait!" he called after her in spite of himself. She stopped, but barely, standing poised on the top stair, still facing away from him. "Give me a name. You owe me that much."

Her shoulders bowed as she turned towards him a fraction. "Please," she begged, her voice trembling and hoarse. "Don't ask me that. I beg you, not that."

"Why not? I have pledged to let you go. You are free, and believe me when I say that I have no wish to see you again. But I need a name, if you expect me to convince anyone of your story."

She was crying, he realized. Shaking her head. Her small, white hands fisted at her sides.

"No," she cried out, anguished. "I cannot." And, like a frightened deer, she fled into the dark. Within moments, the night had swallowed her up as though she had never been.

CHAPTER 14

*T*rystan ran. How she found her way out of the garden, away from Evenburg, and through the streets of town with tears blurring her vision she would never know. By the time she reached the far edge of Evenleigh, every breath was painful and her feet were already sore. She dropped to a faltering walk as the lights of town fell behind. Even in the dark, the road would take her... Where? Colbourne? If she wanted it to. She could hardly return to Westhaven. What she wanted, what she needed, was comfort and familiarity. A haven from guilt and memories. Which Colbourne Manor could never be, not while Malisse was still there and still herself. What Trystan truly longed for was home, and she found as she stumbled down the uneven road, her feet blistered by the unfamiliar chafing of boots unsuited for the task, that she still had no idea where that was.

It was past midnight when the road finally led her to the head of Colbourne Manor's long drive. Most of the lights were out. The house would be asleep, even the butler and the footmen. She could wake them, but Trystan had realized several miles ago that she had no desire to play the penitent, returning to beg forgiveness and a pallet in the kitchen. Nor could she assume that her own window would have been unbarred since her precipitous departure to Westhaven.

Instead, her steps turned away and continued down the road another mile, to the village. She had never once visited anyone there. Neither her father nor Malisse would have permitted it, though they knew nearly all the inhabitants by name. But despite their strictures, Trystan knew who lived in the quiet thatched house at the end of a lane, easily found by the light of a rising moon.

It was too late to be assured of welcome, but she was very sure of a scolding if she simply sat on the doorstep and waited for dawn. So she knocked. Quietly. No one would thank her for waking the neighbors. A few moments passed in silence, so Trystan knocked again, hugging herself nervously as she waited. Finally she heard stirring and muttering from inside, and through the window saw the sudden flare of a lit candle. Someone fumbled with the latch and swung the door open.

Trystan had known her since infancy, and she was certain she had never seen Vianne's face change expression quite so swiftly. It went from scowling irritation to surprised relief to disapproval and back again in the time it took Trystan to whisper a hesitant greeting. Vianne said nothing, only looked back up the lane, grabbed Trystan's arm and nearly yanked her inside. Only once the door had been closed and firmly latched did the older woman turn to consider Trystan, her face returned to its usual bland expression.

Silence ruled for a considerable period. About the time Trystan had begun to wonder whether she had made a mistake in coming, Vianne spoke.

"Do I even want to know, child?"

Trystan thought about the question. About what Vianne was really asking. About how swiftly her life had become so very complicated. Starting, she realized, the day of her eighteenth birthday. In the end, the answer was a simple one.

"No." And then, of course, because she was exhausted, overwhelmed, and crushed by regret, she did the last thing in the world she would have chosen to do in front of Vianne. Trystan began to cry.

She might have been surprised by Vianne's response if she had not been so busy trying to stifle the sobs that seemed to shake her entire body. The older woman quietly removed her cloak and drew her into a chair, pulled off her abused and soiled boots and began to build up the fire. By the time Trystan's tears began to ebb, she had been given both a handkerchief and a cup of hot tea, but no further words had passed between them. Until Vianne spoke again.

"Do you need to tell me anyway?"

Trystan started to shake her head. She had hoped fervently that no one would ever find out how foolish she had been. But this was Vianne. Who had been, Trystan now realized, far more of a mother to her than Malisse had ever even attempted to be. There was a very large part of her that wanted to tell the cook everything. But first...

"Vianne, how long have you known? About my parents?"

"What about them, child?" Vianne looked wary.

"That they weren't married."

Vianne's expression sharpened momentarily. "Who told you that?" Her tone was level but harsh.

"Lady Westerby," Trystan admitted. "She said she's always known. But if she knew, then Malisse must have known. And if she has been convinced all these years that I am a bastard, why has she never rubbed my face in it?"

Vianne froze. Thoughtfully. Her eyes narrowed. "And why did Lady Westerby seem to think the subject of your parentage was a fit one for conversation?"

Trystan squirmed in her chair. "I may have overheard her talking about it. With someone else."

Vianne's expression grew even more stern. "I hardly know which disturbs me more: that you were so lost to propriety as to eavesdrop or that Lady Westerby was discussing your mother with a stranger."

"My mother?" Trystan's brow furrowed in confusion. "Vianne, they didn't say anything about my mother except that she wasn't married to my father." It was Trystan's turn to look suspicious. "Vianne, if you know something, why won't you tell me?"

Vianne had the grace to look a trifle uncomfortable. "Your father was very firm on that subject, child. No one was allowed to speak of it."

"My father is dead, Vianne." Trystan was no longer concerned with avoiding that fact. "And I'm becoming convinced that he was hiding a great deal from me." Vianne said nothing.

"Vianne, I know he didn't love me. At least, not enough." The older woman looked at her in surprise. "If you are afraid that I might not have the strength to face the truth, let me assure you that I have lately faced a number of uncomfortable truths." She tried a watery smile. "And I'm neither dead nor run mad, so please don't hold back on my account."

Vianne shook her head, an odd sort of pain in her eyes. "I'm not certain I should, child. There's so much…" She did not go on.

Trystan huffed in frustration. This was a useless conversation. And not the one she had come here to have.

"Vianne," she said suddenly, "can I stay here? With you?"

Vianne's eyebrows shot up. "I do not have guests, child," she answered, clearly surprised, "and I believe you have a home. Besides, I'm fairly certain your stepmother will be upset when she realizes you are no longer at Westhaven."

"Er, yes," Trystan muttered. "About that…"

It seemed to suddenly occur to Vianne to question her appearance. "Trystan, child, did you walk here all the way from Westhaven?" She sounded rather shocked. When Trystan didn't answer, she tried again. "Does Lady Westerby know where you are?"

Trystan thought for a moment, but shook her head. "I doubt," she answered slowly, "that Lady Westerby will be very concerned with my whereabouts after tonight."

After another period of silence, Vianne seated herself firmly in the only other chair in the room. "Well, child? Are we going to be here all night or are you going to explain yourself?"

Heaving a rather uncomfortable sigh, Trystan leaned back in her chair and looked at Vianne. And for some reason thought of Larissa Felton. Who would have no trouble at all explaining even a story as crazy as Trystan's…

"Would you believe that I went to the masqued ball as Lady Westerby's cousin Elaine because Lady Westerby asked me to carry a message in exchange for a house of my own? But really she just meant me to be a spy, because she wanted me to betray Prince Ramsey, but when I got there I found out that I knew him." Vianne very loudly said nothing. "He didn't recognize me with my masque on, and I had to fill out that silly application and pretend I wanted to marry him like all the other girls, and we danced once, only I sprained my ankle so I couldn't go to the garden party, and when he asked me back to talk about marriage,

I overheard Lady Westerby talking to Lord Fellton about how they poisoned the king and meant to murder her cousin so that I could marry Prince Ramsey because I'm illegitimate and then Prince Rowan could be king instead." Vianne's silence grew more ominous. "And then I went to the castle to meet with Prince Ramsey so I could tell him everything even if it meant I had to live with Malisse forever but they had already found Elaine and he thought I meant for her to be murdered so I could marry him and now everyone thinks I'm a traitor and a murderess and he will never speak to me again. At least, he wouldn't, but he didn't see my face so he doesn't know who he's not speaking to." A pause. "And Lady Westerby is probably going to be arrested for treason."

Trystan let out a long breath as she finished, completely perplexed as to how Larissa managed to talk like that *all the time*! It was useful though. All of those painful events had been relayed without any further blubbering. It was a relief, to have said it all out loud. To feel as though she was no longer the only one carrying around so many dreadful secrets.

She glanced at Vianne, who was looking a bit as though she'd been struck over the head with one of her own frying pans.

"I'm sorry, child, but…"

Trystan nodded encouragingly. No doubt more than one point in that recitation had proved confusing.

"Did you say you knew Prince Ramsey?"

It was Trystan's turn to look surprised. Out of that entire convoluted mess, the one thing Vianne had fixated on was her relationship with the prince?

"Ah, yes," she answered, blushing slightly. "I didn't realize it was him until the night of the ball. We met several times, while I was riding."

Vianne looked scandalized. "Little wonder he didn't recognize you, the way you dress those mornings. Did you ever… talk to him?"

Again feeling a bit awkward, Trystan nodded. "I didn't mean to, but we kept running into each other. The last time…" She squirmed. "That time may have been on purpose."

Vianne fixed her with an odd stare. "Then there was something between you?"

Trystan groaned and put her face in her hands. "No! Yes… it doesn't matter!" She glared at Vianne, not really ready to revisit this yet. "Even if it were possible for a prince to have feelings for a girl who rides around the woods alone looking like a stablehand, he never knew who I was. I only told him my name is Embrie. He doesn't know the girl he met while riding is the same one who betrayed him, and he must never find out, which he will if he ever sees me again!"

Vianne was silent again for a long time.

"You may stay," she answered eventually. "For tonight. After that, your stepmother will need to be informed of your whereabouts." Trystan jumped up to thank her, but Vianne fended her off. "Don't thank me yet, child." The look she turned on Trystan was rather grave. "We will speak tomorrow of this story of yours. And of other things."

Sobered, Trystan nodded. There would no doubt be more than a few "other things" to talk about.

Vianne led her to a tiny room just off the kitchen, which, not surprisingly, looked unused. There was a narrow bed, a washstand, and a chest tucked into the corner. The cook rummaged in the chest for a moment and came up holding a nightdress, which actually looked very near Trystan's size. She also produced a blue blouse and faded brown overdress, which likewise appeared very much smaller than anything Vianne had ever worn. Trystan accepted them with thanks.

"Vianne, whose were these?" Her question was merely curious but Vianne slammed the lid of the chest with a frown.

"We will talk tomorrow, child."

Feeling chastised, Trystan bid her a good night.

After Vianne shut the door and returned to her own bed, Trystan realized once again how utterly exhausted she was. Her feet ached, her head ached, and she could think of nothing better than burrowing under the blankets and letting it all go away. But as she began to remove her dress, she suddenly remembered that she had carried her horse with her when she left Lady Isaura's that evening.

Perpetually afraid of losing her keepsake either to careless-ness or washing day, Trystan reached into her pocket to retrieve it. Withdrew her hand, empty. Reached into the other pocket. By now feeling a bit frantic, Trystan turned both pockets inside out, only to discover a sizeable rent in one. The horse must have fallen out shortly after she put it in. Which meant... it was probably sitting on the floor of her room at Westhaven.

Trystan tried to be practical. She knew very well the possible consequences of returning to Westhaven, now or ever. But she found the loss of that tiny bit of stone to be inexplicably devastat-ing, to the point that she almost felt like crying again, which was ridiculous. There could not possibly be any tears left in her body. She rather hoped to reach the decrepit age of thirty before weeping that copiously ever again.

But she simply could not face another loss. It was as though her friends had been taken from her a second time. And those memories of Donevan... She slammed the door on that thought as hard as she could. Perhaps someday she would remember that moment without pain, but she doubted it.

As silently as possible, Trystan dressed once more, but this time in the outfit provided by Vianne. It fit her reasonably well and had the added benefit of being clean. Afterwards, she sat on her bed, and waited until she was reasonably certain Vianne would be asleep. Then she crept into the kitchen. Rummaging around with a silent apology to her hostess, she eventually found a worn bit of paper with a recipe on one side. Turning it over, she fetched a bit of charcoal from the hearth and wrote Vianne a hasty note, telling her where she had gone, in case she woke before Trystan returned. Then, not without a groan for her blistered feet, she put her boots back on, fetched her cloak and slipped out the door. With luck, she would be back before dawn.

~

For some time after she left him there, Ramsey could not bring himself to leave the balcony. He had no desire to face what he had learned. It was not what he had learned about his people, or even his brother, that distressed him the most, although they waited close at hand.

He could not bear to face what he had learned about himself. That he could be every bit as cruel and cold as Rowan. There was no shortage of excuses for his behavior. What the girl had done was terrible, even if he believed her story. There was the strain of realizing his brother was a murderer. The pain of knowing that his father was dying. Righteous anger at what had been done to Elaine. He had been deceived, it was true. His reasoning had even been sound. But none of it could excuse his behavior. None of it would wipe from his memory the moment that he had heard his brother's voice, his brother's cruel words, coming from his own lips.

What he had told Lizbet had become prophetic. He was capable of horrors as great as any Rowan could imagine. It was, perhaps, only a lifetime of his own scars that had kept him from inflicting them on others. Until tonight.

He stood there, begging the darkness for absolution, but it gave him nothing. No forgiveness, no answers, no courage. Only the memory of a voice, telling him that he would not always get to choose who would be hurt and who would not. It had been true, for so many. For his father and for Elaine. Even for Hester, whose estrangement from her parents might have been prevented. All for the sake of what was, in the end, a rather ugly hat. And a not very comfortable chair.

But there was one person that he, Ramsey, had chosen to hurt. Whether she deserved it or not, he had deliberately inflicted pain and he would never be able to remember it without despising himself. Perhaps his punishment would be just. Without her name, he would never be able to find her. Never be able to apologize. Never be forgiven. By her, or by himself.

In that moment, he was almost tempted to abdicate. Turn the crown over to Rowan, put a stop to the madness by giving way to their demands. He would not be forced to deal with any of the ugliness waiting for him the moment he left that balcony. He could walk away, find Embrie, and live happily ever after in a cottage somewhere far, far away from court and all of its sordid complications. In his head, he heard Lizbet, urging him to make his own choices, for his own reasons, not because of who his brother had forced him to be. Sober, responsible, reliable. What would he do, what would he choose, if there was no Rowan? If the kingdom was safe? If his father was well? What life would he want, if he could change his destiny?

To his surprise, Ramsey realized almost in that same moment that he wouldn't change a thing. Whatever forces had shaped him, whatever regrets he may have had, they no longer mattered.

He was a prince, destined to be king, with all of the wearisome burdens that entailed. And for the first time in his life, he accepted them. Welcomed them. Gave himself fully to the demands of his life, not because they had been thrust upon him unwilling, but because he chose them for himself. He could be a capable king, if not always a wise one. But only if he stopped whining and sat in his father's chair like a man who belonged there.

Lizbet had been right about one thing: he had spent years thinking of himself as no better than a usurper. Second choice. It was time to act like something more. To shoulder the responsibilities of his birth and his office. To leave no doubt in the minds of his court that he would be king, and that he would protect what was his. His crown, his kingdom, and his people.

~

When he entered Lizbet's office a few moments later, he interrupted a meeting. Lizbet, Caspar, Brawley, Kyril, and Mortimer, his father's steward, were engaged in a tense and heated discussion. Ramsey burst in on them without warning or preamble. He did not give them time for questions.

"Lizbet, I need you to summon every healer, every physician you can find. Get them to my father's apartments, tell them I will meet with them shortly. Caspar, I need everything you know about Isaura Westerby and Victor Fellton. Location, habits, friends and confederates." He barely even paused for breath. "Brawley, I need men. Everyone you can spare, without stinting the usual guard, armed and ready to go when needed. It may be tomorrow or the next day, so they should be prepared to stay on alert." He turned to Mortimer. "The castle stays empty. No visitors until I personally give the word. Any servants you cannot personally vouch for need to be given temporary leave." The gray-haired man floundered a bit with the enormity of his instructions, but nodded. "Kyril." Ramsey paused. Met his friend's eyes. "Stay with me for now. I need to explain. Before I send you."

The room exploded with motion. Ramsey was grimly pleased that no one questioned him, or argued, despite the answers they were probably burning to know. What had taken place on that balcony? What had he learned? What would he do now? They would find out soon enough, and like him, wish they had not.

When the room was empty, but for him and Kyril, Ramsey found himself looking for words.

Kyril came to his rescue. "Whatever it is, Ramsey, you know I'll do it."

Ramsey gripped his friend's... no, in truth, his brother's shoulder. "I never doubted it," he answered seriously. "But you may be gone the longest, so I wanted you to know the truth." He bowed his head, then looked up, hoping Kyril would be willing to believe him. "Rowan is plotting to take the throne."

He expected something. Shock, outrage, disbelief.

Kyril only raised one eyebrow. "This is hardly news, Ramsey. He's been trying to get it back since he came of age."

Ramsey gaped at him. "You knew? Of the plot?"

Kyril shook his head. "Not specifically. But yes, generally we knew." He looked speculatively at Ramsey. "We tried to tell your father, but he preferred to believe Rowan was simply selfish and misguided. Never listened when we suggested he might be dangerous."

Ramsey was left floundering. "You never told me."

Kyril smiled sadly. "Would you have listened? I know how much you used to love him, despite everything. How much you wanted him to be different. Without proof, could you have brought yourself to believe your big brother was a monster?"

Ramsey wanted him to be wrong, but knew he would be lying to himself. He would not have believed it. Not until tonight.

"Kyril, he poisoned my father."

It was Kyril's turn to be shocked. To look like he'd been punched in the gut. "No. Ramsey, not even Rowan would…" He broke off, eyes wide, looking for a way that it might not be true.

"Not directly, no. But he encouraged it. Approved it. Enabled it. He meant to kill Father and disqualify me."

Kyril turned away from Ramsey and walked across the room. Slammed his fist against the wall in furious grief. When he looked back, his eyes were haunted.

"Why?" It was not really a question, but a plea. For Ramsey to unsay it.

But Ramsey had no comfort to offer. "I can't begin to pretend to know what he was thinking. But I do know he had help."

Kyril's fists clenched. "Who?"

"Westerby and Fellton for sure. I'm certain there were others, but those are the only names…"

Kyril was looking at him speculatively, able to read his friend's face better even than Lizbet could. "You believe her." It was not a question.

"Yes. Heavens help me, I do." Ramsey shrugged helplessly, not sure he could find the words to explain why. Even if he'd had the time. "I wouldn't have, but it all began to make sense. All the complaints from the guilds involved in the luxuries markets. All the pressure on Father to change his trade policies. Rowan's absences. This morning, Lizbet told me there has been a Caelani ship lurking off the coast for several weeks. I believe it's all connected. I'm only guessing, but Rowan may have made promises. All of his known supporters are among those agitating for trade with Caelan. Fellton is already doing it illegally, according to his daughter. What if Rowan promised them a contract? In exchange for making him king?"

Kyril's eyes narrowed thoughtfully. He folded his arms. Paced across the room. Nodded. "It would explain a lot." He glanced up, clearly confused on one point. "But even if they succeeded in"— he winced—"poisoning your father, you would still be in the way. What were they going to do with you?"

Ramsey laughed softly, without humor. "Oh, that was the best part. They hadn't even planned it, but I fell into it anyway. Elaine, the fake Elaine, was only an excuse to allow Westerby access to the palace. But then they realized I was interested. Rowan must have lifted the guest list, and my choices, from Lizbet's desk. By getting Hester out of the way, they ensured I would turn to their little pretender. Who, as fate would have it, is illegitimate."

Kyril whistled softly at the neatness of it all. "You don't think she was in on it?"

Ramsey shook his head. "No. I did, at first. I was... not kind, in expressing my feelings about her actions. I wanted her to be responsible for all of it, so I didn't have to look any farther. But," he admitted, "the more I thought about it, the more it didn't make sense. Everything she said, everything she did, didn't add up to the calculating impostor I wanted her to be." Ramsey scrubbed his hands through his hair in resignation. "She's not entirely innocent, but near enough. They used her. Played her like a flute, but she's not the real villain."

"Who is she?" Kyril asked curiously.

Ramsey closed his eyes, still feeling the sting of that denial. "I don't know," he answered quietly. "I don't think I'll ever know."

"Ramsey," Kyril asked seriously, "what would you have me do?"

"Find Rowan," Ramsey said. "I need to know where he has gone and what he is planning. It can't be good. We may have uncovered part of his plan, but I very much doubt he is without other resources. Other... avenues, of accomplishing his goal. I know it's asking a great deal. But I need Brawley here, and there's really no one else I would trust with this."

Kyril seemed grimly pleased with the assignment. "Any place I should start?"

Ramsey thought about it. "Close," he decided. "I doubt he's gone far. He needs to be here in person if he plans to grasp this opportunity. I would start with Evenleigh. Ask around. Report back to me before you leave town."

Kyril agreed and headed for the door, already anxious to be gone, but Ramsey stopped him.

"Kyril?" The younger man turned back, waiting. "Be careful."

Kyril offered back a mocking parody of his most courtly bow. "Of course, my liege. You know I'm always careful. But then, nobody wants my job badly enough to kill me for it."

Ramsey's lips twisted humorlessly as the two men parted and his own steps turned towards the king's apartments.

His next task? A new and terrifying fight for his father's life.

∾

Fortunately for Trystan, it was not far to Westhaven from the village. Less than a mile across the fields. As she drew nearer the house, though, she began to feel cold and clammy with nerves. If Ramsey believed her story, he may already have sent men to arrest Lady Westerby. Or he could simply have set someone to watch the estate. Trystan had no desire whatsoever to be caught by a royal guard while trying to sneak into Lady Westerby's house. On the other hand, what if Lady Isaura was still waiting up for Trystan to return?

Trystan really couldn't decide which one would be worse. Caught by a suspicious prince who had barely let her go the last time or by an angry, murderous traitor bent on revenge?

Deciding there was wisdom in caution, Trystan concealed herself in some brush for a while and watched the house. The lights were out, and nothing seemed to be moving. The place might have been empty, but Trystan doubted it. If anyone had been sent from Evenburg, they would almost certainly have passed her on the road towards home, and she had encountered no one. She decided to be optimistic and assume that everything was quiet because everyone was asleep.

As she snuck around the corner of the house, Trystan performed a cursory search of the front walk, in case she had lost her talisman between the front door and the carriage. Finding nothing, she circled the building until she came to the trellis beside her window. Closing her eyes and breathing carefully, she pulled herself up and began the ascent.

Her window was as she had left it. Wincing as she remembered the squeal, Trystan gave it a quick, hard shove. Better one unexplained noise than many. With a single sharp protest, the window gave and Trystan tumbled swiftly into the room. She froze there for a few moments, listening. When it seemed that no one had marked her entry, she dropped her gaze to the floor. The moon gave a little light, but it was still dim enough that she was forced to find her way by feel.

In the end, the room was large, but not that large. After less than half an hour of searching, even crawling under the bed, Trystan became uncomfortably certain that her treasure was not there. She must have lost it after she left the room. On her way down the stairs perhaps? Stifling a groan, she realized that she would have to search the rest of the house unless she wanted this whole uncomfortable business to be for nothing.

Still sitting on the floor, muttering barely-audible curses, Trystan scooted towards the door. When she was almost there, she stopped and listened again. Still nothing.

It should have been a simple matter to stand up, open the door and sneak downstairs. She had been doing it in her own house for years. But even the fear of being caught by Malisse had never been so strong as the strange, creeping dread that held her there, not quite willing to open the door. Her hands should have obeyed her, but they were clutching her skirts.

Disgusted with their insubordination, Trystan shut her eyes, breathed deeply, told herself that no one was awake, and got to her feet. Planting herself firmly to still the tremors, she reached out with tentative fingers for the door handle.

Just before she touched it, the door, soundless and slow, drifted open on a chill breeze from the dark of the hall.

Standing silently in the shadows just outside was the white-robed form of Lady Westerby.

Her dark hair fell down her back unbound, and her dark eyes were pools in her pale face. Her hands were empty. She did not move, only stood in the doorway and watched. Trystan swallowed reflexively. She wanted to glance at the window, thinking to escape that way, but could not bring herself to move. Not with those eyes on her.

"You could have had everything." The voice was dull, flat and lifeless and it shocked Trystan. It barely sounded like the same woman who had waved goodbye to her so cheerfully earlier that evening.

"Lady Westerby." She tried to hold her voice steady, but the apparition in the hall unnerved her badly. "You lied to me about Elaine." Trystan threw out the first accusation that came to her, in an effort to gain some confidence.

Lady Isaura's expression did not change. "I would have lied about my own mother to gain my revenge, little girl. And Elaine was a spineless fool with no one to mourn her."

Now Trystan felt sick. She clenched her teeth and swallowed the impulse to vomit. "Revenge?" she bit out angrily. "You told me this was about the kingdom! About doing what was best for everyone! Now it's about you and your revenge?"

Finally, Lady Isaura's response carried a bit of emotion. "It was always about revenge! I told you what you needed to hear. I care nothing for politics or trade like that poor fool Fellton and his ridiculous friends. They were always doomed to disappointment."

Confused and still very nervous, Trystan crossed her arms and took a step back. Nearer the window. "Well, you were right about one thing," she shot back defiantly. "I would never have helped you if you had told the truth. I might not care about politics, but I never agreed to murder."

"But you agreed to betrayal, little fool. There is not, after all, so much road between them."

Trystan felt a flush of shame. "Yes," she admitted, "I was a fool, but I'd like to think I learned something. And"—she lifted her chin—"that I chose rather better in the end than I did in the beginning."

Lady Isaura's pale face turned slightly to stare at her, eyes glittering in the dark. "And yet you could have had all you ever dreamed of." Her voice was bereft of everything but cold, frozen hatred. "I had done it all. Laid down a path for you that would have secured your happiness. And you," she sneered, almost without expression, "were such a witless dupe that you refused to take it. You threw it away."

"I could never have lived with the knowledge that my happiness had been purchased by death!" Trystan snapped back, by now nearly as angry as she was frightened.

"But you loved him!" The flat voice suddenly changed to a hiss. "If you really loved him, you would have done anything, *anything*, to be with him!"

The heady combination of terror and fury gave Trystan a sort of courage. "I think you know nothing of love, Lady Westerby. Nothing!" Her own eyes sparked with passion. "Love that kills and destroys to protect itself is not love at all."

No longer detached, Lady Isaura advanced into the room until she stood only a few steps in front of Trystan. "Nothing of love? I?" Her eyes spat fire and her hands curled into claws. "I know more of love than a pitiful, self-centered child like you could ever dream! My Osric was the only thing that ever mattered to me. More than my fortune, more than my own life." She turned slightly, approached the room's empty dressing table and stared into the mirror. "They stole him from me. With their pride and their power, they murdered him as surely as if they had knifed him in the back."

Trystan could barely recall Lord Osric's death. She had been perhaps eight or nine, and had barely known her father's fashionable friends. She could remember that he had been ill for several weeks before he died. It had not seemed to her at the time that Lady Isaura's grief had overwhelmed her, but Trystan knew herself well enough now to suspect that she had viewed the scene through the passionate self-interest of youth.

"Who is 'they,' Lady Westerby?"

The widow whirled on Trystan abruptly. "Who? Who else? Your sterling prince and his pathetic father! The ones who decreed in their infinite wisdom that we could not lawfully trade with Caelan. A foolish cavil over slaves! They made it a crime to bring goods across the border. And my Osric died for it!"

Trystan blinked. Tried to make sense of it. Gave up. "I'm sorry, but what…"

"He had mountain fever." Trystan had never heard of it before, but Lady Isaura seemed to expect this. She turned away and paced over to the window. "It's rarely seen, and does not pass from person to person." She seemed impatient, scornful. "Our healers could do little more than diagnose him. There is only one known cure and it can be found in only one place."

Trystan thought she understood. "And so you poisoned the king? Because you blamed him for Lord Osric's death?"

Lady Isaura turned to face her again, drawing herself up with dreadful conviction. "If he had not refused to open the borders, the medicine would have been available. We sent a trader to Caelan, but it took time to avoid the patrols, and the journey was too long. My Osric was dead before he could return."

Trystan actually felt a pang of sympathy. To watch someone you loved die because the cure could not reach you in time—she could not imagine the torment.

"I'm sorry," she offered haltingly, "but—"

"I wanted them to feel what I felt," Lady Isaura interrupted in a low and terrible voice. "To know the terrifying helplessness of watching someone die. The guilt of believing you could have done something different, better, faster…" She broke off with a furious-sounding oath. "That fool Ramsey will be just like his father. To rid this kingdom of them both seemed the most valuable service I could perform before I died. And I so nearly succeeded." Lady Isaura turned the full force of her gaze on Trystan. "Except for you."

Trystan froze. The naked hatred in the older woman's eyes pinned her where she stood. She suddenly knew what it felt like to be hunted.

Her heartbeats were loud enough to count. Five, she had marked, when the figure in white moved, striking, all claws and cold fury. Trystan had endured too much terror, in too short a time. Her thoughts were slow, sticky, and muddled. Her body moved for her.

Like a wild creature, she bolted for the door, looking for any way of escape. Panic lent her speed, but it was dark, and the house was not her own. For an instant, she turned the wrong way, thinking of her own room, her own hall, her own stairs. The delay was not long, but it was enough.

She had just reached the top step when her head flew backwards and her feet abruptly lost purchase. Her body whiplashed sharply and struck the floor without warning, the tearing pain in her head her only clue. Lady Isaura had a handful of her hair and seemed prepared to rip it out.

Screaming involuntarily, Trystan shielded her eyes as she caught a glimpse of nails, striking for her face. She wriggled and twisted frantically, ignoring a sharp pain from her ribs in her need to get off the floor. Striking out with elbows, feet, anything she could still move, Trystan landed a surprisingly hard blow to her assailant's face. She heard a strangled shriek from Lady Isaura, followed by warm, wet drops, indicating she had probably broken something.

The grip on her hair eased and Trystan took advantage of it to scramble to her feet, only to be knocked into the wall, the bannister pressing hard and cold into the small of her back. She tried to find her feet again, only to realize that she was half on, half off of the stairs and there was an implacable grip around her throat. Lady Isaura's pale face came suddenly into view, blood now smeared in a dark pattern across her skin and dripping down the icy white of her gown.

"I'm sorry, Trystan." A harsh whisper emerged from that bloodstained mouth. "But I do not like to lose."

Her grasp tightened. Trystan's vision blurred.

In a desperate panic, she kicked out as hard as her borrowed skirts would allow. The worn material ripped, an incongruous sound in the midst of their now silent struggle. Trystan kicked again, harder, this time connecting solidly with Lady Isaura's knee.

It gave. The grip on Trystan's throat did not.

Overbalanced, Lady Isaura fell backwards, momentarily taking Trystan with her. In one last, flailing effort, Trystan's hand caught the bannister behind her. And held on.

The sudden jolt tore the vise from around her neck, letting her draw one gasping, shuddering breath. For the space of that breath, Lady Isaura balanced, between lunging and falling, her face wavering between hatred and terror. Until, with one surprisingly forlorn wail, she lost her fight with gravity and toppled backwards.

The staircase had never seemed so long to Trystan. She watched, helpless, one hand on her bruised neck, while the white-clad form of Lady Westerby tumbled endlessly towards the bottom, going limp before it finally ended its descent.

Hysteria took a fresh hold on Trystan's throat, wringing a few helpless whimpers from somewhere deep and uncomprehending. She waited for Lady Isaura to move. Waited for her to speak. Waited for someone else to speak. Surely someone had heard the sounds of their struggle and would come. No one did. Trystan was shaking almost too badly to move. She did not trust her legs. She could only inch down the stairs, clinging to the bannister, believing with each breath that the pale, blood-spattered body at their foot would at any moment rise up and renew the assault. Almost hoping that it would. Desperate for proof that she was not alone in the house with empty darkness and a dead woman.

By the time she reached the base of the stairs, Trystan knew her father's friend was gone. Her limbs were too far askew, her head at too unnatural an angle, for there to be any doubt. But she approached the body anyway, reached out a shaking hand, needing to see the face of a woman she had known since childhood if she was to believe completely in her death.

Shuddering in revulsion, she touched Lady Isaura's shoulder and rolled her slightly, till her hair fell back. Her dark eyes were wide and staring, an unblinking accusation even in the dark. Which was not, Trystan belatedly realized, as dark as it should have been. Moonlight streaked the floor with long, deep shadows, moonlight that was entering through the wide-open front door. The door that had not been open when Trystan sneaked across the walk. She glanced back at the body, but body it was and would remain. She could accomplish nothing by staying.

Throttling back the urge to scream, whether in horror or frustration she wasn't sure, she rose from the floor and began to limp hastily away.

Or at least, she tried. Trystan let out a shriek of terror when her progress was impeded by a warm, solid wall.

The tall, dark figure laughed in a very un-wall-like way as he twisted her round and clasped her wrists together behind her back with one, remorseless hand. "Hello, little mouse." The silken whisper sent tremors down her spine and raised bumps on every inch of her skin. "I'm so very glad you've come."

CHAPTER 15

*K*yril Seagrave was not a man much given to anger. Curiosity and irreverence were his besetting sins, and though they frequently infuriated other people, he rarely suffered such strong emotions himself. But that night, as he strode swiftly towards the outer bailey and his waiting horse, Kyril was cold with rage and did not bother to hide it.

He had known the brothers Tremontaine for most of his life. As a child, Kyril's natural disadvantages had made him a perfect butt for Rowan and his friends, and it was only Kyril's determination never to return to his own home that had kept him at court. Well, that and his eventual friendship with his tormentor's brother.

The younger prince had idolized the elder, and despite his anger and frustration at Rowan's lack of compassion or discretion, Ramsey had never really stopped believing that Rowan would one day come back to him. Perhaps tell him that all those years of cruelty had been nothing but a joke.

Unfortunately, King Hollin shared that blindness where his

elder son was concerned. Frequently incensed or despairing at his erstwhile heir's behavior, he had never quite been able to bring himself to believe in the depths of Rowan's depravity. And now? That blind love was about to prove deadly. And to more than just the king.

Elaine, the real Elaine, had nearly paid with her life as well. A pale, shivering creature, the girl had managed to stutter her way through her story, which had told them very little they had not already known. She had seen no one, knew nothing, and only wanted to go home. At least it had answered the question of why Lady Westerby had bothered with an imposter. The real Elaine was so timid she had nearly fainted when Kyril spoke to her. She would never have survived the ball, let alone a political conspiracy.

And Rowan had stolen her life. Wrenched one girl from the midst of her quiet, retired existence and used another as a dupe. He had driven a wedge between a woman and her family, stirred up violent unrest and attempted to murder his own father.

Kyril did not really care why. All he felt was a grim sort of pleasure at the task his friend had set him: find the bastard before he could hurt anyone else.

It was already growing late by the time he left Evenburg. The streets of town were lit and all but the wealthy or bored had retreated to their own homes for the night. For several hours, he drifted, between taverns and the newly fashionable clubs, buying drinks and listening. Little of note was being said, but there was an undercurrent of tension. Threads of uneasiness ran through the gilded and carpeted parlors of every exclusive establishment he visited. It seemed uncomfortably like waiting, even if no one knew for what.

Dawn was approaching when Kyril officially gave up and

sought his horse. No one was talking, about Rowan or anything else of import. He needed a new source, and it did not take long for his brain to suggest one. He knew Ramsey planned to set someone to watch the homes of each of the suspected conspirators. Wait for them to move. See who their friends were. But he needed to find Rowan sooner than that. Though he had not dared admit it to Ramsey, Kyril still clung to hope. The king seemed too tenacious to die, and if they could find out what poison had been used, perhaps there was a chance that Hollin could yet recover.

Kyril did not return to the castle to ask for permission, nor did he pause to consider whether Ramsey would approve. Instead he turned his horse towards the outskirts of town and, within minutes, left it far behind. The sun would be rising soon to light the road and Lady Westerby's estate was less than ten miles distant. With luck, he would be back before anyone thought to wonder where he had gone.

～

Vianne awakened early that morning feeling uncomfortably queasy. She did not for a moment suppose she was ill. In all her years at Colbourne, she had never taken a day off for sickness. Nor for any other reason. And that had been nearly forty years.

She'd had opportunities elsewhere, but had chosen to stay, not for the pay or the prestige, but the location, close to her family. Over the years, she'd had many opportunities to regret that choice. And many reasons to rejoice in it.

One of those reasons was Trystan—the wild, impossible child who had last night appeared out of the dark and demanded the truth. Truth that Vianne had promised she would never share with a living soul. And yet, the man to whom she had made that promise was dead, and he had taken his threats with him.

Trystan was very much alive and had been made to suffer, horribly, for the sake of one man's pride. For the sake of the child she loved, Vianne knew she would have to break her promises, and possibly even lose her job. The story she had heard, so breathlessly related in front of her own fire, demanded nothing less.

Trystan had never lied to her. And the girl was far too intelligent to invent a lie so utterly preposterous as that tale she had told last night. No, Vianne believed her, and that belief was going to bring her a bushel's worth of trouble. Once she managed to get out of bed and quell the sensation of dread that had tied her stomach in knots.

Grumbling under her breath, Vianne eased her aching joints out from under the blankets and dressed in her usual uniform. It was early yet, and today was her half-day, so there would be enough time to rouse Trystan and have their conversation before she would need to return to the manor.

Entering the main room of her house, however, Vianne's gaze was instantly drawn to the paper left on the tiny table. It was one of her recipes, turned over and scribbled on with a bit of charcoal that rolled off onto the floor when she picked up the note.

Vianne,

(it read, in a nearly indecipherable scrawl)

Please forgive me, but I did not want to wake you. I have lost something important and realized that it must be at Westhaven. Have gone back for it. Whether I find it or not, I should be back before dawn. Hoping all my previous experience in sneaking will finally be of use.

Trystan

Dread indeed. Vianne's gaze caught on the fallen piece of charcoal where it had rolled into a puddle of early morning sunlight. It was long past dawn, and there was no sign of the child.

Old she might be, but her thoughts could still move swiftly. A few snippets of Trystan's tale chased each other through her head, followed closely by both determination and a plan. It was not much as plans went. A few ingredients without any clear directions. But Vianne had been improvising recipes for years, and people, to her mind, were not that much different than food. Both were highly predictable if you paid attention.

First, Vianne returned to her bedroom and removed a small, flat, cloth bag from beneath her mattress. Then she tied a clean apron over her dress and left the house, locking the door behind her and taking the same road she always took, if a bit more briskly than was normal. She entered the kitchen at Colbourne Manor with her usual brusque appraisal and went straight into the storeroom that served as her office.

"Grita," she coolly addressed the young kitchen maid who brought her morning tea, "I wish to speak with all of you. It appears we have a situation with which I require your assistance."

The girl's expression very carefully remained unchanged as she bobbed a curtsey and left. A few moments later, she returned, followed by the other four kitchen maids, the two girls from the scullery, and Umbersley, who kept the kitchen garden. To Vianne's surprise, both footmen crowded in after them, as well as the parlor maids, the girls from upstairs, and Malisse's personal dresser. It was a tight squeeze.

No one spoke as she regarded the crowd rather skeptically. "I am forced to suppose that none of you know why you are here."

A murmur worked its way around the group, but it was Grita who answered. "Ma'am, you said you wants help. You never ask help with nothing, so we know you mean to do something. About the Mistress. And we all wants to be in on it when you do."

Vianne looked around her with what she had to admit was surprise. She had not expected... but perhaps she should have. Everyone knew what had happened to Hoskins, Millson, Farley, and Beatrice. Sanderl was not popular, and Vianne suspected that even without her influence this group might have been brought to mutiny by his introduction to the household alone.

Very well. Her plans might prove simpler than she had anticipated.

"I have no intentions of harming anyone, or gaining revenge, so if those are your thoughts I suggest you leave now," she began. "I also suggest that you become aware of the possibility that we could all leave here today without a position." As one, the group began to look exceedingly mulish and unlikely to budge. "That said, it seems I have a need of assistance."

Vianne hesitated. She could scarcely believe she was about to say this. "I need to retrieve something from Her Ladyship's office."

There was silence for a long, pregnant moment. It was broken by one of the parlor maids. "From her desk or from the safe?"

Vianne looked up in surprise. "Do you mean to say you know where she keeps her valuables? Her papers?"

The little maid grinned shyly. "It's my job to dust, Mistress Vianne, so I see pretty near everything. Her Ladyship keeps her papers in a locked box behind the portrait of Lord Percival. I found it because it was the only thing in the room that was never dusty."

Vianne's mouth dropped open in spite of her. "I don't suppose you know how to get into it?"

She was answered by the tall, sour-faced woman who had come in last and least expected: Malisse's personal dresser. "She carries the keys around her neck. Most nights she sleeps with them."

Vianne frowned in disappointment. She didn't want anyone to lose their job over this. How could they get those keys and put them back without the wretched woman noticing? Deep in thought, she almost didn't notice the thin-lipped smile on the dresser's face.

"Of course, there is one time she takes them off," the woman offered helpfully.

"Yes?" Vianne asked, trying not to hope for too much. The maids started giggling before the dresser had a chance to answer, but the sinister smile on her face was all Vianne really needed.

This might not be so very difficult after all.

Lady Colbourne was having a very trying day. Her dresser had gone missing at precisely the wrong moment, Darya had woken up with spots on her face, and no one had been able to find out anything about a royal wedding. It was as though the palace had ceased to exist. No gossip had come out of there since reports of the by-now infamous flight of Hester Ulworth.

Malisse was being forced to commit a great deal of effort to remaining hopeful on behalf of her beloved Anya. Her only consolation was that if she had received no news, neither had anyone else. At worst, Prince Ramsey had decided to put off marrying for a while longer. Not ideal, but better than having lost him altogether.

She was still musing on a possible course of action when there came a gentle knock at the door of her study. Malisse was not expecting anyone, so she frowned. Not too deeply. That sort of thing put lines in one's forehead. "Who is it?" she queried sharply. It never hurt to let the servants know you were displeased. They tended to put more effort into ensuring that your displeasure was not directed at *them*.

"Deirdre, Your Ladyship."

Ah. One of the parlor maids. Whatever could she want? The room was clean and it was too warm for a fire. Her Ladyship's frown grew more ominous, and less concerned with appearances. "I did not call for you," she said loudly and firmly. "Go and find Sanderl if there is a problem." Silence answered her. Nodding briefly to herself, Malisse had only just turned her thoughts back to her personal difficulties when the quiet knock was repeated.

"What now?" This time she was perhaps more strident than sharp. A lady could only tolerate so many interruptions.

"Deirdre, Your Ladyship."

Malisse's bosom swelled in aggravation. What ailed the girl? She should know better than to bring her petty problems to the mistress. And if she didn't, she was about to learn.

"Enter."

The little maid opened the door as silently as only a servant could and stood, head bowed, just inside the room, her shaking hands clasped in front of her as if in supplication.

Malisse rose from her chair with awful dignity. "Deirdre?"

The girl nodded without glancing up. "Yes, Mistress… I mean, Your Ladyship."

One sculpted eyebrow shot up, and the coral-painted lips thinned a trifle.

Well. Malisse could see this child needed taking in hand. Where the devil was that butler? It was part of his task to see to it that the staff adhered to her wishes in matters of decorum.

"I believe I instructed you to leave. I therefore fail to understand what could have possessed you to intrude upon my solitude a second time."

The girl raised one shaking hand in appeal. "But, Mistress… oh please, I'm sorry, Your Ladyship…"

"Silence!" Strident gave way to what could only be termed a bellow. "When I want you to speak I will command you and as I have no desire to hear your mewling complaints you will have no occasion to do so, is that clear?" Malisse had thus far had no reason to complain of Sanderl's competence. He had proven quite exacting in matters of propriety and precedence, and provided swift punishment without any need for prompting. But the fact that this upstart parlor maid felt it appropriate to approach her mistress without proper attention to the priority of rank spoke poorly of his superintendence. What could the wretched man possibly be doing?

"Now, Deirdre, you will tell me at once why you have failed to attend my orders and given me ample reason to consider your immediate dismissal." The girl wrung her hands pitifully and bit her lower lip. "Well?"

"It's Sir, Your Ladyship."

Malisse was beginning to feel rather put upon. Why should she be expected to listen to the incomprehensible babbling of this undereducated and dull-witted child? If she wanted to oversee the staff herself, she would hardly be wasting her money employing a butler. "Must you behave like a simpleton? Who is Sir and why can you not manage to answer my questions?"

The maid's voice dropped to a whisper and she glanced over her shoulder nervously. "Sanderl…" She glanced beseechingly at Her Ladyship. "He says we must call him 'Sir.'"

Malisse nodded in understanding. Of course. It was very proper in him to expect such deference. Though she found it rather unsettling that the chit seemed more afraid of her butler than her mistress. No one ought to command more respect than she did.

Preoccupied with these thoughts, it took her a moment to notice that the girl had fallen silent again. No wonder her butler seemed so perpetually peevish, with lackwits like this child to work with.

"Oh, for pity's sake, what ails you? Where is Sanderl?"

"Begging your pardon, Your Ladyship, but that's the thing. We can't find him."

Malisse threw up her hands and stalked across the room. Of all the times for him to disappear! So many things on her mind and a visit planned this afternoon to some friends of Anya's from Evenleigh. Butlers simply didn't vanish! They counted silver and called for the coach. It was unthinkable!

Seething in frustration, Malisse left her study to look for him, quite forgetting the parlor maid, whose indiscretions paled in significance next to the need to find Sanderl. On her way down the hall, Malisse questioned Darya's maid and one of the footmen, who both claimed neither sight nor knowledge of the man since very early that morning.

She checked the library and the spare bedrooms without success, then continued downstairs. The dining room, the silver

closet, the linen pantry, the sitting room, the drawing room...
still nothing. By the time she reached the back of the house,
Malisse had encountered nearly every member of her staff and
none of them seemed to have seen anything, let alone a portly
and self-important butler.

Malisse paused before she crossed over the threshold of the
kitchen. She would not have cared to admit it even to herself, but
her cook was perhaps the only person she knew who had the
capacity to intimidate her. In her own mind, Malisse had
convinced herself that ladies did not enter the kitchen and had
no need to communicate with such persons as cooks and scullery
maids. In truth, the kitchen felt like someone else's territory and
for a woman accustomed to mastery, it was an unpleasant sensation she had never intended to repeat. Alas for unfortunate
necessity.

Steeling herself against the vexation in store, Malisse stepped
through the door, expecting to find it bustling with activity. She
was not disappointed.

Her ears were immediately assaulted with undignified
screams. The kitchen, she saw at a glance, was filled, not only
with chaos, but with smoke! At once terrified and outraged,
Malisse shouted for Sanderl before she remembered he was still
missing, and certainly nowhere to be seen in the midst of the
panicked kitchen maids. Even the cook was nowhere in evidence.

Beginning to feel just a trifle panicked herself, Malisse was
momentarily frozen in indecision when one of the maids spotted
her and screamed even louder.

"Fire, Mistress! Quickly! This way!"

The smoke and the confusion were too much for Malisse's
gently bred sensibilities and she did not, for once in her life, hesitate to follow the maid's instructions. She followed her in the

direction of the nearest exit, which happened to be the scullery. It could not, of course, have been blamed on the kitchen maid that they attempted to pass through the door at the exact same time that one of the scullery maids was attempting to do so, in the opposite direction. And it could not really be the scullery maid's fault that she was hastening to put out the source of the smoke with a very large pail of washing water. The resulting collision ended rather badly for Malisse. And for her silk morning dress.

It was, of course, rather difficult for a lady to know what to do in such a circumstance. Torn between the need to escape the smoke, bemoan her ruined dress, berate the clumsiness of her underlings, and shriek incoherently at the feeling of dirty wash water running down her neck, Malisse found herself quite speechless for several endless moments.

The kitchen maid seemed incapable of doing anything but stare, her hands pressed to her cheeks in horror. The scullery maid had fallen to her knees, and was now sobbing in terror. The tableau remained frozen, except for the steady drip of water from once carefully coiffed golden hair, now sodden and featuring what was unmistakably a bit of potato peel.

It might have been the worse for the scullery maid had this interesting scene not been overrun by the sounds of an approaching stampede from the kitchen. There was little for Malisse to do but either run with them or be run down. She staggered gracelessly out the door, into the kitchen garden, suffering the first pangs of what would no doubt have been strong hysterics, had she not stumbled into the approaching form of Umbersley.

The poor man had, quite properly, been hastening to assist with the crisis. In fact, he had arrived so hastily that he had not stopped to put down his large basket of compost, only just fetched from the stable midden. Umbersley was a tall man, and impressively strong, capable of supporting a very large, very full basket on one broad shoulder. He could not, it must be noted, have foreseen that her ladyship would be coming out of the scullery, let alone with such indecorous haste, and nearly throw herself in his path. And he was, as must be expected in the lower classes, a rather clumsy man, who had been about to set down his burden when he was almost overbalanced by the collision. Rather than commit the ghastly error of permitting Her Ladyship's person to fall into the mud of the garden, he had dropped his basket and caught his mistress. It was only an unfortunate accident that the basket upended itself on the way down. And it was no doubt coincidental that it did so directly over Her Ladyship's head. Compost met wash water and their union was the source of indescribable delight to the eyes of what suddenly seemed like every menial in the house.

It was not one of Colbourne Manor's finer moments. Unless of course you were to consult the servants, in which case you might find that it was considered, beyond all doubt, the most beautiful thing any of them had ever been privileged to experience. No one ever really did determine what happened afterward. The fire, if there had been one, was put out. The smoke cleared. The probable culprits seemed to disappear as a stunned and incoherent Malisse was led solicitously led away by her sympathetic dresser and a fluttering upstairs maid.

After such a morning, the chaos would have to sort itself out. The mistress could not really be expected to be herself under such conditions. Recriminations and investigations would have to wait. Her Ladyship was in very great need of a bath.

∾

When Kyril finally rode up the drive at Westhaven, the sun was pouring over the trees. The grass was drenched with dew, but showed no tracks, indicating that no one had been there for a few hours at least. In fact, no one seemed to be about at all. If Ramsey had sent anyone to observe the house they remained well concealed.

Musing on the probability that he would be severely chastised for this escapade, Kyril urged his horse briskly up the front walk and dismounted in front of the door. Normally, by this time, an outraged butler would have appeared, begging him to wait until someone could be found to take his horse. Of course, normally, the front door would not be standing open on a silent front hall.

Suddenly aware of all the ways in which this might have been incredibly stupid, Kyril put one hand on the dagger under his tunic as he moved to investigate, leaving his horse munching unconcernedly on the shrubs. He could plead for clemency later, if that turned out to be necessary. Which, he knew within moments of cautiously peering through the doorway, it would not be.

The sound of his boots echoed eerily down the silent hall as he stepped in and made his way to the foot of the staircase. Lady Isaura Westerby was not likely to be very worried about her shrubs, now or ever again.

He should have felt something, Kyril thought, as he gazed at the body of the woman who had tried to murder her king. Her neck was obviously broken, probably from falling down her own stairs. Or perhaps she'd had help? There was blood, staining her white gown and crusted on her still, white face. Someone had hit her very hard in the nose. A friend and fellow traitor, perhaps? Whoever they were, Kyril doubted they had remained in the house. Even the servants seemed to have deserted their mistress, and who could blame them?

Leaving the body where it lay, Kyril moved off to search the premises. Lady Westerby might be dead, but she may have left clues as to the identities of her compatriots. Even more importantly, he might find a clue as to the nature of the poison.

The first few rooms offered nothing much of interest. The sitting room and parlor seemed cold and sterile, empty of anything that might give them personality. The dining room was dark and seemed largely unused, so too the library. But when he entered what he thought had probably been the late Lord Westerby's study, the story changed drastically.

The space was obviously in use. Lady Westerby had likely adopted it for her own work in the absence of her husband, but it remained a masculine room, down to the high, dark wooden beams of the ceiling. From one of those beams hung what was unmistakably a noose. The lady had perhaps planned a different death for herself than what she had suffered.

Crossing to the desk, Kyril was unsurprised to find on top of it a single paper, folded and sealed, addressed to Prince Ramsey Tremontaine.

Normally, Kyril would have been appalled by the idea of reading a note meant for someone else. But with the king near death and a body in the hall, he felt not even a twinge of guilt as he broke the seal and perused the text of the message, hoping to find some clue that would aid him in his search. A detailed recipe for an antidote, perhaps? Or maybe even a map. With Rowan's location marked by a giant red "X."

The note contained neither of those things, but as Kyril waded through the final words of a traitor and murderess, he began to gain a clearer picture of what had occurred. And why.

Lady Westerby had been little more than a catspaw. The other members of her conspiracy had used the tragic death of her husband to goad her into action, into doing a deed they had no stomach for. Politics had been a secondary matter, at least for her. All she wanted was revenge, on the people she considered responsible for her grief.

It was fortunate indeed, Kyril mused grimly, that she was not only vengeful, but paranoid. Feeling betrayed, she had listed each of her confederates by name, with a brief but florid account of his or her transgressions. Elaine Westover's name was conspicuously absent, as was Rowan's. Even so, the list would no doubt prove to be fascinating reading for someone back at Evenleigh. Brawley, perhaps?

Kyril was briefly disappointed that of the three women listed, none were young enough to be the mysterious imposter who had warned them of the plot. For whatever reason, Lady Westerby had not seen fit to include her name, perhaps concluding that Ramsey would have already dealt with her perfidy sufficiently.

But in the end, there was nothing much to help him in his present situation. She made it very clear that she hoped the king would suffer, and that his loved ones would suffer with him, from the agony of unfounded hopes. Kyril was going to have to look elsewhere for answers and hope she'd been careless.

Tucking the note inside his jacket, he continued the search, opening doors, tapping on walls for secret panels, looking in drawers and rifling through books. Nothing he uncovered seemed odd or even remotely worth his scrutiny. From the study he moved to the kitchen, then upstairs, not without a grimace as he stepped over the body. Perhaps he should cover it.

Most of the bedrooms proved empty. Towards the end of the hall, there was one that seemed to have been occupied. The window stood open to the morning breeze, and the closet contained several dresses, one of which he instantly recognized as the russet silk that the false "Elaine" had worn to the ball. He paused for a moment to reflect on their brief acquaintance and contemplate her identity. She had seemed so wry and unaffected. Well-bred and well-educated, but utterly lacking what usually passed for social polish. And it was unlikely, considering the outcome of her attempt at intrigue, that she had been hired for her experience in deception. An amateur, playing a game that had quickly taken her out of her depth.

Or had it? Whoever she was, she seemed to have fled. Possibly ridding herself of witnesses on the way? It roused a flicker of anger in Kyril, anger with himself and with her.

He had liked her. Been utterly taken in by her combination of biting wit and innocent observation. Even if what Ramsey said was true and she was largely a pawn, he was not yet ready to forgive her for deceiving him.

Two bedrooms left, and precious little evidence of anything untoward had presented itself so far. The bedroom next to Elaine's had probably belonged to Lord Westerby, and looked unoccupied. Its connected twin, however, did not. Lady Isaura's bedroom was largely as uncluttered as the rest of her house, though very expensive in its simplicity. The bed was neat, the linens undisturbed, and there were no discarded garments to be seen.

When he came to the bureau, however, Kyril knew he had found what he was looking for. The dark, polished top was swept clean of any ornamentation, save for one incongruous object in the exact center. A vial. Stoppered glass. With only the tiniest drop of liquid in the bottom. Kyril knew it instantly for what it was.

A taunt. It may or may not have contained the poison Lady Westerby had used on King Hollin. But she knew very well that they would not take any chances, or leave any avenue of possibility unexplored. They would be forced to assume it might be important, and go to any lengths to determine its origins. It would be especially sweet if all their efforts proved to be in vain.

Cursing the traitor's thoroughness, Kyril pocketed the vial and decided his search was finished. He would return to report his findings to Ramsey, so they could decide together what should be done next. There seemed no evidence that Rowan had been there, and little reason for him to return. Kyril would continue the search elsewhere. He might even ask for Ramsey's permission this time.

Grabbing the white coverlet off the bed as he left, Kyril ran down the stairs two at a time, spreading the blanket over the body as he passed. Someone else could deal with the dead. Lady Westerby was long past either censure or absolution.

By the time he made it back to Evenburg, it was nearly lunchtime, but Ramsey was nowhere to be found. Kyril delivered the hopefully incriminating vial to the physicians attending the king's sickroom, handed Lady Westerby's final words to Lord Caspar, and went off in search of his friend. When even the tower proved empty, Kyril turned his weary steps toward the garden, another favorite haunt in times of distress. He was not forced to endure the shrubberies for long. A familiar voice hailed him from the balcony off the Great Hall—Ramsey, beckoning for him to come up.

Kyril did not bound up the stairs quite so energetically as

usual. A night without sleep was beginning to wear on him. As he walked up the steps, considering what he would choose to tell, he tripped.

The moment of uncharacteristic clumsiness brought him to his knees halfway up the stairs, and left him only a hair from catching himself with his face. Ramsey made his way across the balcony and peered down at his friend.

"Kyril, are you drunk?" he asked curiously.

Kyril paused to consider without bothering to get up. "Possibly," he answered thoughtfully. "Though mostly with lack of sleep. I promise I bought more than I drank last night."

Ramsey raised an eyebrow. "You're making me doubt your honesty and your sanity, brother." Ramsey's tone was doleful. "Get up before I'm forced to call for a physician."

Kyril grinned and started to push himself up. Then stopped. Picked up something that rested at the end of one of the stairs. Something small, that glittered like gold in the sunlight. "That's odd." He eyed the object as he got to his feet and continued up the stairs. "Pretty though."

"What is it?" Ramsey had already walked to a bench and sat down.

Kyril followed him and held out his hand. "I'm not sure," he answered, frowning, "but I'm guessing someone is missing it. Looks like a personal keepsake of some kind." He opened his hand and placed his find in Ramsey's palm. And had the unsettling experience of watching his friend's face drain of expression as he stared at the thing—a tiny, sparkling, golden stone horse.

A look of panic came into Ramsey's gray eyes as he lifted them to Kyril's face. "Where did you find this?" The prince's voice was nothing but an anguished whisper, his face pale and set.

"On the stairs, just now." Kyril stared at him. "Ramsey, what is it? Do you recognize it?"

The prince nodded, his expression reflecting something that looked far too much like despair. "It was hers." Ramsey's shoulders, his hands, went limp with shock. The tiny golden horse tumbled to the ground, still giving off sparks from the sun. Mute but indisputable evidence to the truth.

"Kyril." He repeated that anguished, heartbroken cry. "It was hers!"

Still confused, Kyril dropped to a knee next to Ramsey and gripped his shoulder. "Whose, Ramsey?"

His prince looked up at him, utterly shattered. "Embrie." He whispered the name hoarsely. "And Elaine. Kyril... I've been a blind fool. They were the same person."

CHAPTER 16

*P*rince Ramsey Donevan Tremontaine sat by a window, feeling lost, rudderless and empty. Despite his resolution to live up to his office, he had never wished so badly to escape his life. Before all this, he would not have hesitated to spend half a day riding in the Kingswood, sorting out the chaos in his head. But even if his current situation had allowed such a thing, it would have brought him no peace. Not anymore.

He would have to remember her. Be puzzled by her. Feel betrayed by her. Want to see her and ask why. Find out what had driven her to do such terrible things.

It was so hard for him to superimpose the two women in his mind. Embrie's honest vulnerability and impetuous temper, with Elaine's incisive questions and penetrating wit. How could they have been the same?

In some ways, he had seen it. Recognized something in Elaine that resonated with him in the same way Embrie had. And perhaps the problem was that he had idealized the latter in his head. Made her into something she could never have been, except in his own imagination.

The question was really whether he would choose to do anything about it. He could order a search. Ask questions at every house within riding distance of the Kingswood. It was sure to turn up something.

But did he really want to know? Was he prepared to face her and ask those questions? He wasn't sure he could. It would be so much simpler to forget she had ever existed, let his heart and his hopes die quietly from the crushing blow she had dealt him.

But did he owe it to his father to know more? To find out anything she could tell him about the conspiracy that so nearly destroyed everything he loved?

In a way, it already had. Destroyed his admittedly too-innocent belief that the evils of power and politics had left his kingdom untouched. Destroyed his faith in the kernel of good he had always believed Rowan still possessed. Perhaps even destroyed his father. He wasn't sure he had the courage to look Embrie in the eye and do what he must. Not with any dignity. Perhaps he was not as ready to be king as he had hoped.

There was a knock on the door. Quiet but frantic.

"What is it?" he answered wearily. He had hoped for a few more undisturbed moments.

"Mortimer, Your Highness. May I speak with you?"

Ramsey groaned silently. Mortimer was incredibly efficient, but sometimes fussed overmuch on matters that did not seem very important to Ramsey. Like the color of linen for the formal napkins. Or the available supply of lettuce. He hoped this time it was actually something important. Perhaps a problem with Ramsey's instructions from yesterday.

"Come in, Mortimer."

The stern-looking older man entered soundlessly and shut the door behind him, greeting his prince with a rather too formal bow. He looked... excited? How odd.

"How can I help?"

Mortimer actually stammered. "Y...y...Your Highness, I must ask your permission to make a change... in staffing."

Ramsey lifted an eyebrow. Since when did it require his permission? Ah. Since his orders that no one be in the castle if they were not known to be trustworthy. It made sense. But...

"Mortimer, under the present situation, it seems this person must be very important for you to take such a risk." Ramsey knew the steward would take his meaning.

"Your Highness," Mortimer explained carefully, "I have tried —many times—to secure this woman's services for His Majesty. She is a cook without peer, Your Highness. Nothing I offered seemed to move her and I had given up hope... I thought it might be a special surprise, for His Majesty, when he recovers..."

Ramsey almost frowned, but sighed instead. Mortimer had been devoted to his father for years, but he was also devoted to the renown of the House of Tremontaine. Which meant having the best of everything. If this woman was the best, Mortimer would not rest until her reputation enhanced that of His Majesty's table.

"And are you satisfied that she is not a spy? Someone who might wish to do my father harm?" Ramsey asked.

Mortimer twisted his hands together momentarily. "That's the thing, Your Highness," the steward answered, with some worry. "She says she will accept the job, today, but only if she can speak to you. Alone."

Ramsey stared at Mortimer in consternation.

"I thought perhaps you would... er... see what she wants? Decide for yourself..."

Ramsey finally understood. The steward wanted badly to hire her, but he did not want the responsibility if she proved to be untrustworthy. So he had brought the problem to his prince. Trying not to be annoyed, Ramsey glared, just a little, at Mortimer, for having put him in such a position. And on such a day.

"Very well, Mortimer. I will see her. But not without guards outside the door at least."

The steward smiled happily. And with a great deal of relief. "I have already taken the liberty of procuring the guards, and the woman is waiting downstairs. Shall I show her up?"

Ramsey put his face in his hands. He should have known. Mortimer sometimes took competence to hitherto unheard of and highly annoying levels. "Yes, Mortimer, you shall. But please, warn her to be brief. This is very much *not* the day for lengthy complications."

Mortimer nodded briskly and left, with what Ramsey imagined was probably a cackle of glee as he closed the door. Ramsey had never observed the austere old man cackling, but he had learned long ago not to place much confidence in the outward demeanor of servants. As a rule, they hid far more than they showed. Considering the depth of Ramsey's failures in judgment of late, it would not surprise him to learn that Mortimer was hiding a wife and seven children in the castle larders.

It took only a few minutes for the steward to return, but when he did, Ramsey had already seated himself behind his desk and assumed his most practiced air of majestic irritability. It usually encouraged petitioners to make themselves as brief as possible.

The woman who entered behind Mortimer, however, did not

look inclined to be hurried. If there existed a more inflexible-and implacable-looking person, Ramsey hoped never to meet them. She was short and widely built, perhaps a bit younger than Mortimer, with gray hair and an uncompromising expression. No smile lines. Ramsey began to suspect she lacked a sense of humor altogether. Perhaps food was not all that amusing.

"Your Highness"—Mortimer had his blank face on again —"may I present Mistress Vianne?"

Ramsey nodded gravely after the woman dropped a curtsey that was as correct as it was perfunctory. A stickler for the letter of propriety, he imagined. As if she knew her duty and refused to give even a tiny bit more of herself than was necessary. He gestured for her to sit down, and excused Mortimer.

When the door had closed he returned his gaze to his guest and found her watching him with at least as great a measure of assessment as his own. Her eyes were intense and somehow disapproving. Ramsey actually caught himself wondering whether he had done something wrong.

"Mistress Vianne, you must know how irregular it is for me to conduct interviews with potential members of the staff." It would not do for him to be questioning his own conduct when he meant for this woman to be questioning hers. Ramsey tried his best to look stern. "I agreed to see you as a favor to Mortimer, who has faithfully served my family for most of his life. Please, if you can, make this brief. As you may have guessed, I really have very little time and far too many demands on it."

The woman seemed neither dismayed nor hurried by his slightly irritated tone. She merely withdrew a stack of papers from her reticule and placed them on his desk, in front of her. Clearly not within his reach. Her expression did not change.

"Your Highness." Her voice sounded as inflexible as she looked. "I need to tell you a story."

Ramsey kept his jaw from dropping only with great effort. "I beg your pardon? Madam, need I repeat—"

He may have dispensed with courtesy but she seemed quite willing to follow his lead. She actually interrupted him.

"Your Highness, it's about a girl." She pressed on before he could collect his wits and silence her completely. "Her name is Trystan Embrie Colbourne."

And suddenly Ramsey forgot whatever he had intended to say. "Did you say Embrie... *Colbourne?*" His wits deserted him in a rush as he made the connection.

Colbourne. As in Anya? Merciless blonde with the mercenary mother? A mother who had given no indication that she possessed more than two daughters? Memories swirled until Ramsey felt dizzy... Embrie, weeping... speaking of her tormentors... Her reluctance to return home... Her illegitimacy...

"Very well, Mistress Vianne. You have my attention."

"As I said, Your Highness, her name is Trystan. And she is my granddaughter."

~

A few minutes later, Ramsey had abandoned his chair and stood by the window, his hands clenched on the sill, his mind seething with fury... and shame, as he remembered his own thoughtless words on the balcony. He may have wished to disbelieve the tale he had just heard, but he had been left without that option. The cook had been wise enough to bring proof. Proof that Embrie's choices had been a desperate fight for her own freedom, rather than a deliberate act of betrayal.

He could not pretend that her choices had been good ones, or that their consequences had not been terrible. But she had been placed in an unthinkable situation without friends or family to turn to and she had acted. Intended her actions for good. Ramsey was painfully aware of how greatly he relied on the wisdom of those he loved. Without that, would he have done any better? Could she have done better if she had known what he now did?

"Why did you never tell her?" His tone was fierce. Evidently, his protective feelings were experiencing a resurgence.

Vianne, to his surprise, squirmed ever so slightly under his scrutiny. "I made a promise, Your Highness. I had others to protect, and Lord Colbourne did not hesitate to make threats in order to safeguard his secrets." She hesitated. "I do not pretend that I have not regretted it. And never more so than today." She dropped her head, stared at her lap, and then continued.

"There is something else. I cannot guess at whether my Trystan has lost your regard to the point that you no longer care what becomes of her. But either way, you should know."

Ramsey bent a piercing gaze on her bowed gray head, apprehension taking up residence in his stomach.

"Trystan left me last night to return to Westhaven, to retrieve something of value. She left a note, saying she would be back by dawn." When the cook lifted her head to look at him, there were tears in her eyes, and a quaver in her voice. "She has not returned."

Ramsey stepped firmly on his panic and tried to consider the information rationally. "Mistress Vianne," he said carefully, "I feel I should inform you, in the strictest confidence of course, that one of my agents paid a visit to Westhaven this morning. I regret to report that Lady Westerby is dead. She appeared to have been injured in a struggle of some sort. We are unsure with whom. Could it be possible..." He did not finish the sentence.

"Your Highness," Vianne asked sharply, "what precisely are you asking?"

"Whether you think it possible that Miss Colbourne might have, even accidentally, become involved in an altercation with Lady Westerby that resulted in the latter's death."

Vianne favored him with another of her measuring looks. "I believe, Your Highness, you are really asking whether my Trystan might have murdered Lady Westerby and fled rather than face the consequences." She did not sound impressed.

"I do not believe I suggested anything of the kind, Madam, but should you feel inclined to answer that question I will not prevent you."

Vianne actually seemed grimly pleased. "The answer, Your Highness, is no." She inclined her head thoughtfully. "Could she have accidentally caused Lady Westerby's death? I presume the answer must be yes. But murder?" She shook her head. "Trystan has survived for six years in the same house with my mistress, Lady Colbourne, and her daughters. Though you may think it impertinent in me to say so, if those three could not drive a girl to murder, the task must be deemed impossible."

Ramsey gave a short, unamused laugh. Having met the women in question, he could not disagree with her rather grim logic.

"And in any case," Vianne continued, "I am confident that she would never have run away without returning to tell me first. Even if she had somewhere to run to." She looked at him rather pointedly. "Though I suspect, if she had, she would have run there any number of times in the past three years, rather than continue to suffer her stepmother's sovereignty."

Ramsey considered this with growing agitation. The cook could be mistaken, of course. But she had known Embrie all her life. Compared to his brief meetings, hampered as they had been by the need for secrecy, he must consider Vianne's knowledge of her to be superior. Her conclusions were likely as close to accurate as they were going to get. Naturally, the woman had a vested interest in convincing him that her granddaughter was innocent. But if she believed otherwise, why inform him of her absence? Why risk so much in coming to tell him unless she truly believed Embrie to be in trouble?

Worse yet, what if Vianne was right? What if someone had taken her?

Thanks to Lady Westerby's final letter, most of the members of the conspiracy had been identified and were either being watched or questioned. None but Lord Fellton had been willing to claim any knowledge of Elaine and the part she had played in the near-success of their schemes, let alone their failure. He had a strong suspicion that Lady Westerby had confined the knowledge of that part of her plan to as few people as possible, for obvious reasons. Herself, Lord Fellton, and Rowan.

Rowan had known.

With a growing sense of dread Ramsey contemplated what Embrie had told him that night on the balcony. That his brother had given her a paper. A blank one.

Lady Westerby would have told Rowan enough to help him identify their "agent." And Rowan had been the first to push Ramsey towards marriage with Elaine, by eliminating Hester. The older prince would have known the purpose of Ramsey's invitation to her that night. And Rowan's near-immediate disappearance indicated that he had very likely learned of the plot's failure.

Might he have returned to Westhaven in search of the one who had ruined his bid for power? Even if he had laid their failure at Lady Westerby's door, for her choice of the girl who had eventually betrayed them, he might have risked an appearance there. And if he had found what he sought? What if Elaine had walked in on him as he took his revenge on his former ally?

Rowan would not have bothered to kidnap Elaine without cause. If Ramsey's deductions to this point were correct, the girl would not have gone with him willingly. And there could really be only two reasons for Rowan to force her.

He might have intended to repay her for her betrayal. To take her life more slowly and painfully than Lady Westerby's. Or he might have hoped to trade her life for his, believing that someone would care enough to ransom her. He might even be counting on Ramsey to do so.

Rowan had always seemed to know what Ramsey was thinking or feeling, sometimes before Ramsey knew it himself. Could the older prince have guessed that even after the plot had been revealed, Ramsey might yet care what became of the woman who had betrayed them both?

Ramsey had little choice but to place his hope on the very thing that had frequently made his life miserable: his brother's uncanny ability to twist Ramsey's thoughts and emotions to meet his own ends. Embrie's life could depend on Rowan's belief that Ramsey still harbored feelings for her.

That he had feelings was certain, but Ramsey himself wasn't sure if he knew what those feelings were. His only certainty was a sudden, desperate fear that left him staring wordlessly across his desk. At perhaps the only person in the kingdom who loved Embrie enough to share that fear.

~

Once again, Ramsey called his personal council together. Lizbet, Caspar, Brawley and Kyril. This time, he told them everything, from his first meeting with Embrie to his conversation with Vianne. When he finished, there were tears in Lizbet's eyes.

"Donnie, you idiot boy, how could you not tell us?" She almost sounded angry with him beneath her tears. "We could have found her... done *something*!"

Ramsey just looked weary. "Aunt Lizbet, I think you know why I couldn't. Why I didn't. And right now we don't have time for explanation or blame. We have to find Rowan!" Helpless anger rose in his throat. "If he has indeed taken Embrie, I believe he hopes we will try to rescue her. That we will be willing to trade her life for his. But I doubt he will wait forever. And in the meantime..."

Speculation choked him. If only he could believe that his brother would not harm her. Perhaps the heaviest knowledge he had gained these past days was the realization that he had no idea what horrors Rowan was capable of. He could no longer claim to know what depravities Rowan would sink to. It galled him. Burned him. Sickened him. But the boy Ramsey had grown up idolizing was gone. Perhaps he had never been. All that was left was a beautiful, conscienceless monster.

A monster who intended to use the girl Ramsey... what? Loved? That wasn't the right word. Cared about? It seemed he still did. Perhaps even admired and respected in many ways. He had feared for her safety. Hated those who tormented her. Envied her courage and determination. She had moved him to anger, to laughter, and to tears. He felt as though he had truly lived during those short times he had spent with her, and part of him had died when she betrayed him. And if he was to get up in the morning with hope instead of despair, he had to find her. To tear down the secrets that had grown up between them and begin again. But squarely in his way, as he always did, stood Rowan.

"I'm sorry, brother." Kyril did not bother with his title, ignoring the fact that others were listening. "I should have tried harder to find him. Done something…" His hands were clenched and his face was pale. "I've failed you." He sounded miserable.

"Shut up, Kyril," Ramsey rubbed weary hands through already disordered hair. "You may be my brother in all but name but if you say something so patently ridiculous again I will be forced to commit violence against your person."

The object of his wrath gave a strangled sound that was probably supposed to be a laugh.

"We'll find him, Your Highness." Brawley's calm assurance was, Ramsey believed, entirely unjustified. "He can't survive without servants, and where there are servants, there's gossip. Wherever he's gone, it'll get out eventually."

"And what if he's gone for the border?" Ramsey knew better than to believe his brother would do what anyone expected. "That Caelani ship off the coast… what if he had more contacts than that? He could be halfway across the kingdom by now!"

"With an unwilling passenger?" Kyril's brow was furrowed in thought. "Ramsey, I cannot believe this Embrie would be submitting tamely to Rowan's threats. She's intelligent, and not easily intimidated. He won't find it easy to drag her anywhere."

"And if she's drugged?" Brawley pointed out. "There are a

number of ways to subdue a person that have nothing to do with threats of force."

"And still others that don't involve subduing at all," Lizbet chimed in. "Rowan is a charismatic and overwhelming person. It's entirely possible he could have convinced her to go with him with no need for threats."

Ramsey shook his head. They were wasting time. "None of this matters, and you all know that," he stated flatly. "No one has ever been able to outguess Rowan. He's got a head start and we have no chance of predicting his intentions. If he wants us to find him, we will. If he doesn't, the best we can do is start looking."

Kyril chuckled suddenly, an incongruous and not particularly humorous sound in the tension-filled room. "You know," he mused, "I think we're all guilty of permitting Rowan to convince us of his own invincibility." Ramsey's brows lowered but Kyril didn't give him a chance to respond. "On the night of the ball, I was joking with Ela…" he broke off with an apologetic expression and corrected himself, "… with Embrie, and she said she felt like Rowan wasn't a person at all, but a 'malevolent spirit,' I believe she called him." Brief, rueful expressions appeared on everyone's faces. The characterization seemed only too apt. "She also made the observation that we talk around him, rather than about him. I believe she was more right than she knew. Our efforts to protect the crown by covering up his scandals have allowed him to become larger than life." Kyril's eyes narrowed and his jaw clenched. "I think it's time we stopped."

"What do you propose?" Caspar asked in his quiet voice.

Kyril's answer was simple and fierce. "The truth."

≈

And so the truth was told. Like any proclamation of the crown, it went out by messenger to every town in the kingdom, to be posted for all to read. A single page, it briefly detailed the history and crimes of Prince Rowan Calloway Tremontaine and called for him to be found and submitted to justice. It included a writ of arrest. Lizbet had penned it herself, and Ramsey was grimly awed by the power in her appeal. Rowan had never had many friends outside of the merchant nobility, and would have even fewer when the extent of his indiscretions was known. If he was, as they believed, still within the borders of Andar, he would be seen, and hopefully reported.

In the meantime, a search began. Every available body that could be spared was sent out, by pairs and triads, to every place Rowan was known to frequent. His hunting lodge was searched, his belongings sorted through and his friends questioned. Even those who might still claim an acquaintance with the disgraced older prince proved very willing to speak candidly, no doubt a bit terrified by the growing call for Rowan's head. None of them, however, were very helpful. They knew nothing, had seen nothing, heard nothing. Rowan, it seemed, had entrusted his plans to no one.

The days lengthened. News grew scarce as those sent out drew nearer the borders of the kingdom. The king still hovered between life and death, and talk grew of passing the crown to Ramsey simply in the interest of business.

It was not an insult to King Hollin. Despite the previous unrest, Ramsey's father had been well-loved by most of his people and the outrage over his attempted murder was very real. But no kingdom could go on for long with no one to guide it. The uncertainty alone was beginning to renew the tension between the guilds and the palace. Ramsey had been aware of the danger when they chose to publicly acknowledge the truth of the king's condition, or at least so he told himself. He had not, however, been ready to acknowledge the consequences. That he could be forced to accept the crown while his father yet lived felt like treason. Like disloyalty. And yet, he did not know how long he could hold out.

~

It was in the midst of this torturous waiting and indecision that a visitor came to Evenburg. A full five days had passed since Rowan and Embrie's disappearance, three days since Lady Isaura Westerby had been proclaimed a traitor and given a traitor's burial: an unmarked grave in an undisclosed location. About mid-afternoon, Ramsey had retired to his office after a painfully stilted meeting with the guild representatives and his father's council to discuss the crown.

Those five days not been kind. He had difficulty sleeping, and rarely ate. When he could, he sat by his father's bed, or played with his cousins, but his heart seemed gone. He had seen Lizbet watching him with love and concern, but he hadn't even the strength to reassure her.

Ramsey was sitting at his desk with his head in his hands when the knock came. He groaned. "Yes?"

"You have a visitor, Your Highness." Mortimer sounded as proper as ever, but Ramsey had known him long enough to hear a certain… tone, in his voice. "One of those you left instructions about."

Ramsey felt a brief surge of interest. He had indeed left instructions should certain people come calling. Certain people who had yet to play their part in this drama. After a brief discussion with the steward, he settled himself behind his desk to await the interview.

The woman who entered was one he knew by sight alone. He had technically never met Lady Malisse Colbourne, and, frankly, had never wished to. He knew enough about her to doubt his ability to control his temper in her presence.

She was, he found, astonishingly small. And disconcertingly young. Lady Colbourne did not appear to be much past thirty. Her blonde hair was demurely coiffed and she was dressed quite affectingly in black. She seated herself at his invitation and gazed at him beseechingly with enormous blue eyes. It might have presented a better picture if she had not reminded him so forcefully of her terrifying daughter.

"Your Highness," she began, drawing a handkerchief from her reticule and discreetly dabbing her soulful blue eyes, "I am so grateful you have agreed to see me. I come to you upon an errand of some delicacy."

Ramsey schooled his face to stillness. Even a degree of polite interest. Under the desk, his hands itched to wring the woman's neck. "Indeed, Madam?"

"Yes, you see… well, I'm sure you recall my daughters, Anya and Darya, whom you were so kind as to invite to your recent masque?"

Ramsey nodded, when he realized a reply was expected.

Malisse went on. "Though it may not have come to the attention of Your Highness, I have, in fact, a third daughter."

Ramsey permitted one eyebrow to rise. "A younger daughter, I presume?"

"No, Your Highness, Trystan is in fact the eldest. And," she hastened to add, "in truth, the girl is my stepdaughter, the child of my late husband, Lord Percival Colbourne." Ramsey nodded as though in understanding. "I have always," she continued, with a small, emotive sniffle, "hoped that she would see herself as one of my own daughters. Have always done my best to treat her as such. But…" She cast down those enormous blue eyes for a brief pause before glancing up at him through long, dark lashes. "The poor child did suffer so at her father's death, you see. They were so very attached to one another." Another dab at her eyes with the hankie. "She frequently suffers from such profound depression of the spirit that it quite overcomes her reason and"—Lady Colbourne favored him with an imploring look, filled with long-suffering and anguish—"I have had no choice but to protect her from the severe agitation of being much in company."

Ramsey's hands tightened into fists. He reminded himself that his mother would never have approved of him giving a woman a black eye. "I see, Lady Colbourne. But—" It seemed he was doomed to interruptions.

"It has been such a burden, Your Highness. I'm sure I need not tell you what a mother suffers when her child is unable to enter fully into the joys of life! And then, when the masque was announced and I knew she would be unable to bear up under the strain of attending…" An actual tear made its solitary way down that flawless porcelain cheek. "I could scarcely rise from my bed for wondering what to do. And then, well, it seemed such a great blessing, Your Highness, when a woman I had always considered a friend came to me with an invitation." Lady Colbourne's eyes pleaded with him to understand. "She wished Trystan to stay with her, so that my dear girl would not be subject to the crushing disappointment of realizing she would be unable to attend the most exclusive entertainment of the season. And I thought…" She lifted her hands and sighed. "I thought she meant well. I thought it would be such a wonderful opportunity for my poor, sad child."

"It was not, I take it?" Ramsey felt the need to play his part in this little charade.

"Oh, Your Highness, how could I have known? I swear to you, I had never a suspicion, and I was so distracted with preparing my Anya and dearest Darya for the ball, that I could not have been expected to realize what she was-"

"Lady Colbourne," Ramsey interrupted with very real impatience, "I presume there is a point to all this?"

His visitor gave a little sob and buried her face in the handkerchief. "Your Highness, my poor Trystan was staying with Lady Westerby! Our closest neighbor! And I have not seen her since I heard… oh, the horrible news."

At this point, the woman gave herself over entirely to weeping. Ramsey sat back and watched her for a moment, impressed despite himself. A pity, he thought nastily, that she was too old for Rowan. They would have made quite a splendid pair.

"Lady Colbourne, I fear you find me somewhat confused." She looked up at him through tear-drenched lashes. If he hadn't known better, he might have found it affecting. "Am I to understand that you have misplaced a daughter?" She nodded pathetically. "And am I further to understand that this daughter was staying with a woman who died *five days ago*—a woman known to have planned and committed acts of violence and who died by a hand not her own—and you are only now expressing your concern?"

Lady Colbourne met his eyes with a bit of a start, the beginnings of worry in her expression as she heard the censure in his question. "Your Highness, I beg you will not think less of me as a parent." She nearly stammered in her haste to explain herself. "I assumed she was hiding, afraid to come home, and that she would eventually return to the bosom of her family. I never dreamed…" A flutter, of handkerchief and eyelashes. "Never! That anything might have happened to her." Her eyes fell. "I confess I may also have been a trifle concerned, that someone might assume, though we have always been staunch supporters of His Majesty, that we had, in some way, been complicit… but never! Please, Your Highness, I implore your assistance in finding my dear girl! I cannot but think she may have met with some sort of accident, or desperate persons, and be in dire need of rescuing! She is so delicate, so easily upset! I shudder to think of what she might be suffering."

With an effort, Ramsey restrained his fury. He remembered the girl he had chased across the downs. Who had firmly refused his help because she feared for her secrets. Who had faced him on his own balcony and stood her ground in the face of his rage. Who had dared to tell him the truth he had not wished to hear.

Trystan Embrie Colbourne was neither delicate nor easily upset. Nor, he finally realized, was she likely to be in dire need of rescuing. With the part of his mind that was not seething with anger, Ramsey silently thanked the creature across the desk for reminding him that the woman they were searching for was both tenacious and intelligent. She had, after all, survived her step-mother. Embrie might be the only person he knew who was prepared to survive his brother as well.

"Lady Colbourne, perhaps I should assure you that we are both aware of your daughter's existence and doing everything possible to recover her." He received a sharp look of inquiry, which he chose to ignore. "I also feel it necessary to inform you that I claim some acquaintance with Trystan and will therefore be giving the matter of her whereabouts and her history my full attention." Even Lady Colbourne was reduced to uncertainty by his cold stare. "You are, of course, sincere in your wish to have your stepdaughter returned to you?"

Malisse gathered herself enough to look shocked at his tone. "Your Highness, of course, we will be most relieved to know she has been found and will return to us!"

Ramsey eyed her for a moment, then nodded, reached into his desk and produced some papers.

Lady Colbourne eyed them, unable to completely disguise her trepidation. "I... don't understand."

"No," Ramsey answered softly, "I'm sure you don't."

"Wh...wh... what are those?"

"Perhaps you would care to glance over them?" Ramsey knew he sounded sinister and didn't really care.

His guest picked up the paper on top of the stack, ran a hurried gaze over its contents, and turned into a different person. There was murder in the blue eyes that looked at him now, murder and a tiny hint of fear.

"Where," she spat furiously, "did you get these? I keep them locked up. My private papers! And they're lies! Forgeries! I can call my barrister. He'll testify to the fact that all of it was left to me!" Ramsey leaned back in his chair and crossed his arms.

"Yes, Lady Colbourne, I'm sure he will," he answered her coolly. "But I find myself wondering why you guard forgeries so closely. Especially when they appear to be genuine originals with the signatures and seals of witnesses. Dated the day before your late husband's death! Do you care to dispute these facts?"

The blonde woman seemed to consider for a moment, her hand tightening on the incriminating papers briefly before she seemed to relax. "It doesn't really matter, you know." Her voice was once again calm, her smile white and even.

"Oh, doesn't it?" Ramsey's question was soft and dangerous.

"Of course not!" she snapped contemptuously. "The girl is nothing but a by-blow! The child of some woman who caught my husband's eye while he was traveling. Some whore who had the nerve to arrange for the baby to come to him when she died, and he, being a sentimental fool, took her in and pretended she was his!" She laughed then, a cruel, mocking sound. "We all knew, of course, but he never let anyone speak of it. And he had the nerve to tell me I must raise the creature with my own daughters!" She assumed a look of long-suffering martyrdom. "Of course, I acceded to his wishes, and did my best with her, but blood, you know, will tell. She's been nothing but a burden to me, and then, when he died? What should I find but that he's made half his estate over to her!" A snort of disbelief. "As if he thought anyone would permit an illegitimate child to inherit! You can be sure I went to my barrister and he assured me that I was the legal heir. Without proof of her legitimacy, not a penny of the estate could go to that wretched brat!"

Lady Colbourne favored him with a self-satisfied smirk. "Of course," she continued silkily, "I have said nothing, even now. I cannot wish for my husband's memory to be tainted by such a scandal. And if... when, she is found, I trust that Your Highness will see fit to restore her to us without reference to the unfortunate truth. It would a great pity if Lord Colbourne's legacy were to be overshadowed by the disgraceful behavior of a child who hasn't the wit to appreciate that her circumstances should have left her on the street!"

Ramsey smiled. It was not a nice smile. Without removing his eyes from Lady Colbourne, he reached into his desk once more and produced another paper, old and much folded. "Perhaps,

Lady Colbourne, you would do me the honor of perusing this other document. I assure you, it is as genuine as the first."

She took it. Unfolded it. And sagged visibly in her chair. Her perfect porcelain complexion seemed to age before his eyes as she looked at him with an expression of un-comprehending blankness. "It's not true," she whispered. "It can't be true. Percy hinted once or twice, but there was no proof..." She froze. Realized too late what her words had implied.

"Why, Lady Colbourne, nothing more to say?" Ramsey's tone grew mocking as he rose to tower over her. "Did you forget to mention that *this*,"—he pointed to the paper—"is the scandal you truly wished to conceal? Perhaps even more than you wished to disinherit your stepdaughter!"

The blonde woman's mouth opened briefly, and shut. There was bitter resignation on her face as she rose to her feet. "Excuse me, Your Highness."

"Sit down!" Ramsey rarely had occasion to use such a tone and was a little surprised when Lady Colbourne obeyed. "You will be excused when I have finished and not before. Your disregard," he stated coldly, "both for the demands of the law and the duties of kinship, disgusts me. I intend to see the full weight of the law applied to your judgment whenever we are able to ascertain your daughter's whereabouts. In the meantime, Lady Colbourne, might I suggest that leniency could be in order if you think yourself capable of following a few, very simple instructions."

The once-disdainful widow nodded, without looking up. Her expression, for once, was stripped of pretense. There was nothing left but defeat.

CHAPTER 17

The feeling of grim satisfaction Ramsey derived from his confrontation with Embrie's stepmother was all too short-lived. Too soon, the pressures of waiting reasserted themselves. Two days he waited, paced, pretended to keep busy, failed to eat, worried about his father, watched for returning messengers. Two endless days, and nights that brought little to no sleep. A week had passed since Rowan and Embrie had disappeared. Ramsey had almost convinced himself to stop hoping when the letter arrived.

It came in the hands of a courier, who had ridden hard for three days on his way from the town of Zell, last outpost on the northeast road that led through the mountains—mountains that guarded the border between Andar and Caelan. On the outside of the letter was penned in a strong, ornamental script, "Prince Ramsey Donevan Tremontaine." The writing was unmistakably his brother's.

Ramsey's hands shook nearly as hard as the courier's legs as that mud-spattered young man collapsed into a chair. Knowing the importance of what he carried, the courier had ridden almost the entire distance without stopping except to change horses and eat.

The courier stopped gulping water long enough to explain. "I put up the message, Your Highness, in the center of town," he said hoarsely. "And waited. Folks were getting upset when they read it. Best I could tell, the mood was ugly. Folks out there have always been loyal to His Majesty." He took another drink. "About a day after it went up, I was ready to leave, head back. Came out to my horse, found this tucked in my bag." He shrugged. "Never saw who put it there, Your Highness, but it looked like something you'd need to see."

Ramsey agreed. "You've done well." He gripped the messenger's shoulder briefly, and was answered by a shy dip of the head. "Get some rest."

He did not stay to chat, but nearly ran to Lizbet's office and entered without knocking. His aunt was sitting on the floor talking quietly to her son, yet swiftly dismissed Parry when she saw Ramsey's expression. He broke the seal and read silently what his brother had written. Without a word, he handed it to Lizbet and walked over to the window with a quick, nervous stride. She watched him but did not press him, only read the letter for herself.

To My Beloved Brother and Future Sovereign, Greetings,

It can hardly have escaped my notice, brother, that there has been, of late, a stirring of sentiments amongst the general populace which are hardly flattering to either my person or my reputation. I cannot pretend to remain unwounded by the spurious claims being both proclaimed and promoted with commendable industry in every community along my road. Imagine if you can, brother, my sorrow at the discovery that the liability for these upsetting and injurious rumors lay, not with those of my enemies as have frequently stooped to fallacious accusations, but with my beloved family, whom I have ever counted amongst my staunchest defenders and allies. It falls beyond my scope to conceive of the transgression which has effected this material change in your affections for me, but I find it in me to believe, wholeheartedly, that your wish, dear brother, to resolve this painful breach in our friendship is as fervent as my own. I hope you will forgive me for not accompanying this letter, as it has, strangely, become both difficult and tiresome for me to travel. My heartfelt plea must be that you will consent to join me here, in this delightful, if somewhat provincial, location, that we may attempt, with dignity and forbearance on both sides, to resolve whatever matter has proven so ruinous to the intimacy which has always characterized our relationship. I beg you will exercise both haste and discretion, dear brother. Allow me to assure you that it would prove quite immeasurably distressing to both of us should our failure to resolve these differences result in irreparable harm to those whose loyalty to our fair kingdom has ever been above reproach.

As I am well able to offer you the hospitality of my establishment here in the fair city of Zell, I would be quite thoroughly offended if you felt it necessary to burden yourself with the distractions of retainers or baggage. It would, I am convinced, be entirely to the benefit of all should you arrive both swiftly and without accompaniment. Until such time as I am privileged to embrace you once again, I remain,

Your Fondest, Most Obedient Elder Brother,
    Prince Rowan Calloway Tremontaine

"That *bastard*," Lizbet muttered under her breath as she finished reading. "At least he makes himself clear: come alone or she dies." Ramsey still said nothing. "What are you thinking, Donnie? How will you answer him?" She paused to consider, her chin in her hand, one finger tapping her pursed lips. "I suppose we could counter-offer. Send an entourage to a safe distance and negotiate. I'm not certain I feel comfortable with a flat refusal."

"No," said Ramsey.

"No, what?"

"No, to all of it," he answered. "Kyril was right. Rowan is neither omniscient nor perfect, but he is smart. We have no way of knowing where he is or how entrenched he could be by this time." For once, Ramsey felt sure of himself. "He will not risk capture, nor will he compromise." His mouth twisted, as if tasting something unpleasant. "At least, he never has before. I believe," he continued after a thoughtful moment, "we must do as he requests."

Lizbet's mouth fell open, then her brows drew together in anger. "Absolutely not! Donnie, I will not permit you to endanger yourself. Remember what he's done! What he hopes to do! Do you really think he will hesitate to harm you? That these feelings he claims to harbor are genuine?" Her face was quite red by that time, but the tirade stopped when she realized Ramsey was not going to fight her.

"Aunt Lizbet, I love you," he answered quietly, "but this is not for you to permit or otherwise." He strode towards her and took her hand. "This is mine to answer. I am his brother and I am Father's heir. It is past time for me to face him, as a man and his future king, and put this issue to rest." He smiled at her sadly. "This game he plays is now between us alone, and I am not entirely a fool... he has taught me well, since we were very small.

I think that I can ensure my safety, and, by going alone, I endanger no others."

Lizbet looked at him, tears pooling in her eyes.

Ramsey had no desire to hurt her. She might be his aunt, and very nearly his mother, but she was also his advisor, and now he needed her to accept that role above the others. To support his choice, even if part of her still saw him as a boy who needed her.

She closed her eyes, and nodded, just barely, in acknowledgement. "Your Highness," she whispered, "let it be as you say." Before she could open her eyes, Ramsey took her by the shoulders and shook her. Surprised, she glanced up through her tears.

"Cut it out, Auntie," he chided firmly. "Yes, I intend to be overbearing and have my princely way this time, but that's no reason to give me this 'as you wish' nonsense. You're still my voice of reason, even if I occasionally choose not to listen to you. No doubt to my eternal detriment."

Lizbet wiped her eyes, smiled weakly, and smacked the back of his head with fervor. "That's right, foolish boy, and if Brawley gets to hear of this you'll be in twice as much trouble."

Ramsey groaned. "I know," he admitted. "I should probably find someone to sit on him. Unfortunately, right now, I need you to gather as much of the council as you can, and at least one of the barristers. I'm going to need an expert to draw up a legal document. Also, send someone to prep a horse and food for three days' ride. Money as well. I'll be taking the courier route and changing horses as often as necessary, but I'd rather not spread my identity too widely as I go." His lips twisted. "Charging my expenses to the family coffers might bring more notoriety than I'd care for."

Lizbet had to agree. Outside of Evenleigh, Ramsey's face was not well known. Unaccompanied, he could likely travel in anonymity across much of the kingdom.

With so much to accomplish and time being short, little speech passed between them as the hour of departure grew near. Ramsey spent a considerable period closeted in his rooms with the barrister and councilors, and emerged slightly after lunch, dressed for traveling, bearing one bag and two sets of papers. The atmosphere in the hall outside his rooms was tense, though it contained only two people: his aunt, trying to look nonchalant, and Brawley, not trying at all.

"This is not happening, Your Highness." Brawley's teeth were clenched and his jaw muscles appeared near frozen. His eyes flashed with more anger than Ramsey had ever seen from his friend and captain.

"Brawley." Ramsey acknowledged him evenly. "I appreciate your concern but I don't believe I asked for permission."

"No." The older man's voice was hard. "You didn't. And neither am I."

Ramsey sighed, and glared a little at his aunt. "Aunt Lizzie, I thought we agreed someone was going to sit on him."

Lizbet gave him a pointed look. "Nobody agreed on anything, Donnie. I'm not stupid enough to get between you two, but I happen to agree with Brawley."

"Alone, Brawley." Ramsey tried patience. "The note said alone, and that's how I'm going. I'm not risking anything else."

"Yes, Your Highness, you are." Brawley would not be cajoled or convinced this time. His hard, clipped words betrayed cold fury. "You're risking the heart and soul of this kingdom and I am *not* going to allow your father to wake up and find out that I let you! You can imprison me for treason or you can shut up and let me come, but those are the only options."

"Brawley," Ramsey groaned, his voice rising in frustration, "I'm not doing this because I suffer from a manly need to prove myself, and I'm not trying to be some kind of martyr. But I can't let my brother hurt anyone else! I don't want to make this an order, so why must you test me?!"

"Because you're practically my son!" Brawley roared back. He stopped, chagrined, and went pale as he realized what he had said. He had obviously not intended the words to be out loud.

But he had very clearly meant them. There was stunned silence in the hall. Ramsey found that his mouth hung open and closed it, overwhelmed by astonishment. When he blinked, his eyes stung suspiciously. A glance at Lizbet confirmed that she, too, was holding back tears.

His voice quiet and raw, Brawley tried to explain. "I'm sorry, Your Highness. I meant no disrespect. But if you went out there alone and something happened to you, I don't think I would survive it." The older man's expression was calmer now, but Ramsey could hear the plea for what it was. "My *life*... all of it that matters, nearly every waking moment, has been about protecting you. About making sure, not just that you survived, but that you would be ready to be king. A good king, and a good man. And with this one decision, you could make it—all of it —meaningless."

Ramsey could not remember feeling so much shame.

Twenty years, he had known Brawley. And when he thought about it, he had learned as much, or more, from the captain of his guard as he had from his father. Not that King Hollin had been a disinterested parent, but he had, by necessity, been a busy one. It had been Brawley who picked him up after childhood scrapes, Brawley who taught him to control his temper and look out for those weaker than he. Given him his first sword and taught him to use it. Protected him from Rowan until he was big enough to defend himself.

It was not that Ramsey held no affection for his captain, quite the reverse. He had simply never realized the depth of what lay between them until Brawley pointed it out. Nor had he bothered to consider what it would mean to Brawley if he died. Brawley's whole life had been spent in the service of his king. Brawley was unlikely to ever have a wife, or a son of his own. He had committed himself wholly and completely to the Tremontaine princes, and in truth, Ramsey realized, had as much right to be there to confront Rowan as anyone else. Perhaps more.

"All right," he heard himself say.

"What?" Two voices answered him in shocked unison. Brawley looked as though the rug had been pulled from under him. He had probably been prepared for a drawn-out campaign.

"All right. You can come."

Lizbet, he could see, was smiling and crying and trying to hide it. Brawley just looked at him stoically and nodded terse acceptance. Their eyes met, suspiciously red on both sides, as understanding and apology passed between them. After twenty years, nothing more needed to be said.

Once Brawley took his leave to prepare for departure, Ramsey turned to Lizbet. "So much," he said lightly, "for my brief foray into autocracy."

His aunt patted his arm. "I'm sure you'll get better with practice," she offered kindly.

Ramsey snorted. "I'm sure as long as you and Brawley are around to cut me down to size I run no risk of becoming a dictator. Even," he added, "a benevolent one."

"Wisely spoken." Lizbet inclined her head modestly. "Now

why do I feel from the expression on your face that you are about to attempt it anyway?"

Ramsey just looked sad. "Because this time we both know I'm right." His sigh was wrenching and heartfelt as he handed her one of the sets of papers that he carried. "This is my insurance, Aunt Lizbet. It's not fair and I wish I didn't have to, but every one of my father's councilors agrees."

She glanced over the first page as he spoke, and the sound of her indrawn breath was as painful as he'd feared. "Oh, Ramsey, no." Her face was white and drawn. "He's so young. And we've tried so hard to keep him out of all this."

Ramsey wanted to make this easier, but there was no glossing over the truth. "Yes, he's young," he replied gently, "but how young was I when my life turned down this road? He has you, and he has his father. He's a strong boy, and a smart one. And," he added, "if all goes well, this will never come to be. But for now, I need to do this. For our family, and for Andar."

Tears ran once again down his aunt's face, but she nodded. Despite what Ramsey knew had to be deep misgivings, she would understand why he had to do it. And as his advisor, she probably applauded his decision. As a mother, he doubted she could feel anything but pain.

~

There was little more to do. It was not long till Ramsey and Brawley stood in the bailey, their horses saddled, bags packed, saying their goodbyes. Ramsey had passed by his father's room, and stood for a quiet moment at the bedside, fighting for words. A simple farewell. The reason for his leaving. A promise that everything would be better soon. But in the end Ramsey left without saying any of it. The truth was too miserable to be spoken aloud and he could not bring himself to offer platitudes, even to a man who could not hear them.

It was not a comfortable trip. Ramsey had never considered himself particularly addicted to luxury, but he gained a great deal of respect for his couriers on that ride. The weather was not always dry, the food was always terrible, and even when they stopped to rest, the pounding of hooves seemed to rack his body. He was grateful that their pace left no opportunity for speech. It was doubtful that either of them would have known what to say.

Three days after they left Evenburg, thoroughly filthy and exhausted, the two men trotted into the thriving border town of Zell. Tired as he was, Ramsey's heart kicked uncomfortably when he realized how close he was to confronting his brother. How close he was to Embrie.

Ramsey really had no idea how Rowan expected this meeting to proceed. Would the older prince make an attempt on his brother's life? Try to bargain for his own? And how would they find him? No doubt Rowan had a plan. Ramsey just wasn't sure he wanted to wait for his brother to carry it out.

They dismounted in front of a likely looking inn, close to the center of town. It was early afternoon, and foot traffic was fairly thick. After days of endless riding with no sounds but the drum of hooves, the miasma of scents and sounds was somehow overwhelming and disorienting. While Ramsey was still blinking to clear his head, a man materialized in front of him. A man both he and Brawley recognized.

Porfiry had been Rowan's valet for, well, ever, or at least since Rowan had been old enough to choose his own servants. A wiry little man with hard, dark eyes, Porfiry gave Ramsey a nasty, crawling feeling every time they met. This time was no different.

"You were to come alone." No preamble, no honorific, no expression.

Ramsey bottled up his surge of anger and smiled coldly. "Well, we don't always get what we want, do we?" He looked down at Porfiry from his somewhat superior height. Ramsey had never been one to flaunt his advantages, but he figured there was a first time for everything. "I didn't come here to bargain with lackeys. Take me to Rowan."

Ramsey expected some kind of argument or evasion. The valet didn't even blink.

"This way." Porfiry did not wait to see if they obeyed, merely turned and walked away.

"Seems awfully sure of himself for a pipsqueak in service to a traitor," Brawley observed thoughtfully.

"So he does." Ramsey narrowed his eyes and took a deep breath. "Too bad we have to put up with it. For now."

Leading their horses, they managed to follow the frequently disappearing figure of Porfiry as he made his way through the mid-day crowd to the outskirts of town. Eventually, he ducked down a side street past the nondescript frontage of what appeared to be a run-down, unused warehouse. They went around the building, to a tiny side door, where the valet stopped.

"Only the prince goes in." He appeared unconcerned by the fact that the two men weighed as much as four of him and neither of them looked particularly placating.

"We go together or not at all," Ramsey replied, "and your master doesn't have to like it."

Porfiry shrugged, unruffled, and opened the door. They tethered their horses, shared a significant glance, and went in.

The door opened directly on a steep stair, probably leading to apartments over the workspace below. Brawley, of course, insisted on going first. The stairs ended at a landing, with another door. Brawley didn't hesitate but pulled it open and stepped inside. Ramsey followed.

The space beyond was largely empty, but for dust, broken crates, and what was obviously a makeshift living space. It was lit only by a single dingy window. There, gazing through the smudged pane with an expression of pained beatitude on his angelic features, was the man they had come so far to see.

Ramsey's heart gave a brief, aching thud. There was no sign of Embrie.

"Where is she?" His voice sounded harsh in the silence.

Rowan turned to regard him with a quizzical smile, his person as unrumpled as though he graced a drawing room, rather than a dingy warehouse. "She?" The butter-smooth voice sounded genuinely confused. "Who is 'she'? I confess, brother, I had hoped for a rather more affectionate greeting."

"I don't give a damn what you hoped." Ramsey was too tired to be conciliating and too worried to play games. "I'm here for Em... Trystan, Elaine, whatever. I'll ask again, where is she?"

Rowan's expression grew sad. "I don't know what you must believe of me, Ramsey," he responded mournfully. "I asked only that you come alone, that we might discuss our differences like men... like brothers! And you have denied me!" He shook his head, the picture of wounded dignity. "It pains me, this distrust that has grown between us. And worse, it seems. You would accuse me of... what?" He appeared genuinely confused. "Abducting young women against their will? Hiding them in warehouses?" Rowan laughed. "Acquit me of such foolishness. I am, I believe, wise enough to know that such accommodations as these would never suit a member of the gentler sex."

With a supreme effort of will, Ramsey took a death grip on

his temper, though his hands fisted of their own accord. This was, perhaps, Rowan's favorite game. To anger him beyond reason and then pretend it was Ramsey's fault.

"By all means then, brother." Ramsey forced his voice to remain even. "Tell me of our differences. Tell me what you want from me. Tell me why I am here. But know this:"—the temperature in the room fell sharply with his next words—"I know exactly what you have tried to do and what you hoped to gain. Your morals disgust me as much as your methods sicken me and I am ashamed to admit that I once admired you. There is nothing you can say, or do, that will change that."

"Oh, Ramsey... Ramsey..." Rowan's soft laugh trailed off into the silence. "You always were a poor, idealistic boy. As for what you think you know... I ask you, what have I done? What great crime have I committed?" He held up a hand to forestall comment. "Our kingdom was on the verge of chaos. Father's policies simply weren't addressing the needs of our people. If they looked to me for hope, what was I to do? Ignore them? Pretend I had no duty to allay their concerns?"

Ramsey was stunned. Did his brother truly expect him to believe he had acted in innocence?

"When the most vocal among Father's detractors began to grow violent," Rowan pointed out, "I had no choice but to join them. Attempt to decipher their plans. Hope to counter them in time."

Ramsey nearly exploded. "You tried to kill our father, Rowan! I have proof!"

Rowan raised one elegant eyebrow. "Proof, little brother? What proof? Someone told you? Someone overheard someone else?" He snorted. "Even you are not such a fool as to believe that traitors are truthful when caught. And, after all," he added softly, "our father isn't dead, is he?"

"Near enough," Ramsey snapped, feeling slightly rattled by the sheer reasonableness of Rowan's arguments. "And whatever you claim, Rowan, you left! You ran rather than face me after that business with Miss Ulworth."

Rowan's eyes widened fractionally. "Business with… Ramsey, I thought you would thank me!" Confusion radiated from his face. "I thought to save you from marriage with a woman who could never love you as you deserve. What else could a brother do under the circumstances?"

Ramsey was left with his mouth hanging open. He knew… *knew* that his brother was guilty, beyond all doubt. Rowan had conspired against the king and fled when the plot was exposed. But his explanations… they all sounded so plausible. So simple. They made all of Ramsey's suspicions seem weak, products of an envious imagination. He glanced at Brawley. The older man just stood there, watching Rowan, his arms at his sides, no visible expression on his face. No help from that quarter. Rowan had successfully deflated his accusations within moments, obviously well prepared for everything Ramsey had come to say. A little too well perhaps…

"As you say, Rowan. Perhaps I should have thanked you. And perhaps I will thank you yet." Ramsey held up empty hands in a gesture of helplessness. "You have answered my accusations and attempted to allay my fears. Except"—he folded his arms firmly and stared pointedly at his brother—"for one. Rowan, where is Elaine?"

It was such a small thing. A tiny twist of the lips. An infinitesimal betrayal of what lay beneath the polished surface. But it was enough.

"Which one, brother?" The mocking tone returned to Rowan's voice. "I could be wrong, but I could have sworn there was more than one."

"The one you kidnapped at Westhaven, Rowan. Not the one you had stolen from her home and planned to murder." Ramsey's own lips twisted into a sneer. "Or have you planned to murder so many girls that you can no longer tell them apart?"

Rowan regarded him coolly. "Still you persist in believing the worst of me." He shook his head, as if in disbelief. "I never intended to murder anyone! Elaine Westover was safe, under the protection of my men, when they were set upon without justification by your overzealous guards. As for the other," he continued more softly, locking gazes with Ramsey, "she was nothing but a lying, conniving, grasping little bitch and I ensured that she will never trouble this kingdom again."

He laughed again, softly and derisively at the shock Ramsey could not manage to hide. "Oh, didn't you know, little brother? Everything she told you was a lie, concocted to save her own skin. And if you must have a murder, perhaps I should tell you that I found her standing over the body of Lady Westerby, after she killed her to cover her own guilt."

The blood left Ramsey's face and his hands shook. His brain stuttered. Embrie. Dead. Embrie. Dead. Rowan had killed her. His own brother had killed her.

"Poor Ramsey." His brother's consoling tone was a rasping buzz that cut through the fog of his pain. "Did you love her, little brother? Believe her pitiful, pathetic stories? You always were too gullible." He laughed yet again, as if in triumph. "Oh yes, that one was quite the actress. She knew exactly how to play you. A professional, in more ways than one, if you take my meaning."

It was a blatant insinuation. And a terrible mistake. Ramsey's head lifted and his mind cleared. A painful grief lurked just out of reach, but it had been buried under the weight of resolve. Rowan had betrayed himself at last.

"Such a lovely story." Ramsey clapped slowly in mocking appreciation. "And how gratifying it must be to paint yourself in the role of savior. I might even have believed you, until that last little bit. You might have succeeded in blinding me once again. But I fear," he said, somehow sounding calm and collected, "you are quite mistaken in your assumptions."

Rowan did not move. For the first time, he appeared less than perfectly in control.

"I know who she was, Rowan," Ramsey said softly. "I met her, long before Lady Westerby convinced her to come to the ball. Her name was Trystan Embrie Colbourne, and she was a lonely, frightened girl, without any friends or family to turn to. Not a spy and definitely not a killer. And you, brother, have just confessed to murdering her."

~

For perhaps the first time in Ramsey's memory, Rowan seemed to have nothing to say. His eyes glittered oddly in the poor light, his entire body tense and still. The silent moments passed, and Ramsey found himself afflicted by uncertainty. What would his brother do now? Continue to assert his innocence? Or accept that his character had been tarnished beyond repair?

When Rowan finally moved it was a slump of defeat. He turned slightly to the window and his beautiful, golden face fell. A sigh, deep and moving, could be heard even where Ramsey stood, watching him carefully.

"Rowan," he said finally, "why did you call me here? If you

believed yourself so innocent of wrongdoing, why hide as though you were guilty? What do you want from me?"

"I wanted you to disappear." Rowan's answer fell from his lips like a curse, soft and deadly. "I should have been king. And I could be, even now. All I would have to do is rid myself of you." His pale face was focused, intent, and a tiny bit flushed. "Of a brother who has been nothing but a pestilence in my life since the day he was born."

If Ramsey had not prepared himself for that admission days before, it might have been staggering. Now, it only ached. Without even a hint of outward reaction, he removed a roll of papers from inside his shirt and proffered them to his brother.

"Not just me," Ramsey told him with grim satisfaction. "You would need to rid yourself of a few other people as well. You see, I guessed where your ambitions might lead you, and took the precaution of naming an heir before I came." Rowan looked startled. "Parry is a blood relation, even if he isn't Father's line. He'd make a good king, and Lizbet would be an excellent regent." Rowan's flush grew deeper and his lips thinned. "I suspect, however," Ramsey continued thoughtfully, "that if you ever showed your face in this kingdom again she would not stop to be diplomatic, but would settle for shooting you through the heart without question and without mercy." It was not an exaggeration and both of them knew it.

"So, I'll ask you one final time," Ramsey persisted, "what did you want with me? Did you suppose I would forgive you? Offer you a pardon? Permit you to convince me of your innocence? Or hope that I would agree not to subject you to the crown's justice simply because you're my brother?"

Rowan's expression fell. He said nothing, but looked at Ramsey with a strange expression of pity. Some emotion crossed his face. He seemed tortured, but resigned. And then, without a word, he moved.

It was so fast, Ramsey did not realize what had happened for several moments. Rowan stood there, one hand still outstretched in the motion of throwing. He had put his hand to his belt… lifted… thrown… something glittered… Ramsey turned to where his brother's eyes were yet fixed on the stolid form of Brawley. Still upright, still silent, but with a bloom of red on the fabric of his coat, where the golden hilt of Rowan's dagger stood out from high on his chest.

CHAPTER 18

*R*amsey's paralysis was broken when Brawley began to slump. He reached his captain's side only just in time to prevent him from collapsing entirely. Lowering him carefully to the floor, Ramsey ripped off his coat and placed it under Brawley's head, not once glancing at his brother. A moment's investigation was enough to ascertain that the blade was lodged just beneath the collarbone, too high to have pierced the heart and too close to the shoulder to have damaged the lung. It was bleeding fast however, and Ramsey dared not remove the dagger for fear of making it worse. Brawley's face was pale, but he clung to consciousness.

"Ramsey," he said the name hoarsely, and perhaps for the first time. "Your back, Ramsey," he whispered. "Watch your back." He lifted his head slightly to look into the eyes of one of the men he had nearly raised, while the other watched from across the room. "You must not worry for me, boy. Let me be and get yourself out of here alive!"

"Damned if I will," was the only answer he got, as Ramsey cut off his captain's sleeve, slicing through the material to bare the wound. Balling up the resulting shreds of linen, he pressed them firmly around the dagger, hoping to slow the bleeding. Grabbing Brawley's other hand, he brought it up and held it in place of his own, hoping Brawley would have the strength to hold the temporary bandage in place. Then he stood, wheeled around, and crossed the room with a swift economy of motion that might have stunned those who considered him little better than a clerk. His hands were at Rowan's throat before either of them had time to blink.

Ramsey slammed his brother back against the wall and pinned him, with his hands, his weight and the unrelenting force of his cold gray gaze. For all that Rowan was taller and heavier, for a moment he was as nothing before his brother's rage.

"You bastard!" Ramsey snarled furiously. Rowan was still and pale and utterly composed, even in the face of murderous wrath. "Why?! He loved you! We all loved you! Why?" Ramsey screamed at Rowan as though he could force an answer from him, but the elder prince remained unmoved. Only the slender, compressed lines of his lips betrayed his tension.

"I'm terribly sorry, Ramsey," he whispered finally, with the smallest of smiles, "but I did tell you to come alone."

Ramsey grabbed the front of his brother's jacket and hurled him sideways.

Rowan did not really resist, and fell to the floor a short distance away. When he sat up, he was still smiling. "I think," he added, "you will find that when you think about it, all of this is your own fault. You were too busy riding around moping to help Father, too selfish to ask Hester what she really wanted, too infatuated to see through Elaine's masquerade, and too afraid to meet me alone." Ramsey could only clench his fists and breathe.

One breath at a time, in and out, as Rowan's voice droned on. "I was only trying to help. Even when you convinced Father to disinherit me in your favor, I wanted nothing more than to ensure that our kingdom would thrive." He rose to his feet. Held up both pale hands in supplication. "And I was rewarded by suspicion and threats. Even now," he continued, sounding grieved, "I am forced to resort to violence, to protect myself from my own brother!"

"I'll only ask once more, Rowan," Ramsey forced himself to remain still. "What do you want? Tell me quickly. Before I decide to kill you here and now."

Rowan actually laughed. "You seem to genuinely believe that such an action lies within your power, little brother," he answered, sounding vastly amused. "I am forced to admire your self-confidence, if not your judgment," he added dryly. "As for what I want, it's simple. If the crown is indeed beyond my grasp, I wish to be gone from here." He shrugged, seemingly unconcerned with such a minor setback. "There are other lands, other opportunities, and I prefer not to dwell on failure, but to look forward to possibilities."

"And what," Ramsey replied coldly, "makes you think I would allow you to simply ride away, unhindered and unscathed?"

Rowan appeared surprised. "Why, brother, I had not thought you so cold-hearted! Perhaps you have not yet noticed that you have a choice to make." He smiled beatifically. "Poor Brawley is not likely to survive long without care. And I am quite unlikely to permit you to simply bind me and haul me back with you like a prize boar. In fact, considering that Porfiry is waiting downstairs with a crossbow, I begin to suspect you are outnumbered."

Ramsey remained silent, trying not to betray his chagrin. The situation was, in fact, looking less than ideal.

"Should you," Rowan continued, "choose to give me what I want, I will simply disappear, never to trouble this fair kingdom again, and you, dear brother, will be left to tend your faithful retainer and return home."

"I suppose," Ramsey replied mockingly, "that eventually you will get around to answering my question. What is this thing that you so desperately want?"

Rowan bowed with courtly elegance. "A writ of passage, of course," he answered with a flourish.

Ramsey fell silent, thinking. A writ of passage with his signature and seal would permit Rowan to circumvent the warrant that had gone out for his capture. He would be able to cross the border, unhindered. Once outside of Andar, it was unlikely he would ever be caught. His crimes would go forever unpunished, and he would be free to wreak destruction on some other, unsuspecting kingdom. It seemed unthinkable. But...

Rowan broke in on his musing. "And in case you find the faithful Brawley's life insufficient motivation to abandon your plans for my demise, I find it within myself to offer you this, as well." Rowan reached into his shirt and produced a vial on a chain. A vial filled with a dark, murky liquid. Ramsey's heart raced with a sudden, frantic hope.

"And that is...?" He managed not to betray his anxiety. The golden chain dangled negligently from Rowan's elegant fingers.

"Why, it's Father's antidote, of course."

Ramsey looked up, startled, into Rowan's eyes, and read only sly triumph. And Ramsey knew, finally, that he'd been beaten.

Rowan could be lying. Probably was lying. But Ramsey could not possibly take that chance. If there was hope for his father, he had to try. He had always known he could never bring himself to kill his brother outright. Now, with two lives hanging in the balance, he had no choice but to let Rowan go. With a brief glance back at Brawley, who watched weakly from behind them, he nodded.

"I believe you know what choices you have left me, Rowan. Very well. Your writ of passage. In exchange," he continued resignedly, "you will agree to leave. Now. Leave this building, leave this town, leave this kingdom. You will not attempt to harm me, or Brawley, before you do so. You will summon a physician for Brawley on your way out of town. And"—his voice grew harder than flint—"you will never again cross the border back into Andar, or I will see you dead. Do not imagine that I will hesitate to give that order."

Rowan looked calculating, but only for a moment. He had always known Ramsey a little too well, and this time, he seemed realize there would be no pushing him further. "Agreed."

From the pile of belongings on the floor, Rowan produced the necessary items: paper, ink, quill, candle, and wax. Ramsey lifted his personal seal from beneath his shirt, where he carried it on a chain. The document took only a few moments to write. The writ permitted free passage to Rowan Tremontaine and his servant, but only for two days. The writ would then expire and Rowan would once again be a hunted man. It also specified that the writ be destroyed when the two men crossed the border. Rowan's mouth twisted briefly, bitterly, at this provision, but he made no objections. When it was signed and sealed, the brothers carefully completed the exchange. The moment Ramsey grasped the vial he placed the chain around his neck and returned to Brawley.

The older man's consciousness was clearly slipping. Blood had saturated the torn cloth and continued to seep from around the dagger. While Ramsey fashioned a better cushion for his head, Rowan was gathering his few belongings and readying for travel, a slight smirk pulling at his mouth. Ramsey ignored him until the older prince descended the stairs, at which time Ramsey descended in his wake. Porfiry still waited at the bottom, but this time he held the reins of their horses. Apparently, Ramsey thought wearily, the servant shared his master's prescience.

"A physician, Rowan," he reminded as his brother mounted up. "For Brawley's sake at least, do not fail in this."

"Why, Ramsey," Rowan returned mockingly, "why would I do otherwise? Did you suppose I meant for Brawley to die?" He shook his head, a gentle remonstrance. "You must think me a monster." Then he added, softly and warningly, "If I had wanted him dead, that dagger would have been in his heart."

Ramsey suddenly felt like weeping. His only brother, by now perhaps his only family. And this was their parting. Perhaps the worst of it was that Ramsey hoped it was forever.

"Go, Rowan," he said finally. "Get out of my sight and out of my kingdom. Know that I dream of the day when your memory no longer troubles me."

"Oh, but Ramsey," Rowan answered sadly, "of course I will trouble you. You will wonder every day from now until you die whether you judged me fairly. You will wonder whether you should have let me live. You will wonder whether I was truly guilty, or whether you wronged me terribly. Every time you sit on my throne you will think of me and when you are old you will ponder what I have done with my life. And you will be afraid, Ramsey, of the answer. You will fear that I may indeed find other lands and other opportunities, and that I will come back, some-day, for what is mine."

He leaned down, then, from his saddle and looked straight

into Ramsey's eyes with implacable coldness. "And I will come back, brother. I swear to you I will come back."

Without another word, the beautiful golden prince straightened in his saddle and rode away, never once looking back. It was not until he had disappeared around the corner that Ramsey realized he had been holding his breath. Letting it out in a rush, he closed his mind to thoughts of Rowan. They were too raw and painful to contemplate, and he had no time to spare. He would see Brawley settled, ensure that he would be cared for. Then he would ride back the way he had come, without pausing for rest unless he fell out of his saddle with weariness. He would go home. Try to save his father's life. And mourn for Embrie's.

Almost without thought, his hand crept into his pocket, and drew out the tiny golden horse. A feeble ray of sun caressed it, struck sparks from its polished surface. He had brought it, hoping they would find her, daring to believe she would be unharmed. That he would be able to at least restore her treasure and return her to her home. Now, it mocked him, with the knowledge of his own helplessness, and with memories of what he had lost. His fault... her fault... none of it really seemed to matter now. Clenching his fist around the horse, Ramsey returned it to his pocket and went back upstairs to wait for the physician.

≈

On the high road to the north, about two days' ride from home, Kyril Seagrave was in a foul mood. He had set out from Evenburg in company with a single guard, five days before, and was now both deeply weary and impossibly filthy. Most of his search had been conducted in rain and mud, they had been forced to sleep wherever night found them, and their inquiries had turned up precisely nothing. Kyril felt as if he had questioned everyone in Andar but the dogs, with no more helpful result than a handful of quizzical looks and a great deal of head scratching. Rowan had apparently disappeared entirely, and as for kidnapped girls... Kyril might as well have been hunting unicorns.

At least he was now alone with his surly, ill-humored thoughts. The guard had been left behind with a physician the previous morning after coming down with chills, no doubt from their bad habits of riding into rainstorms and sleeping in puddles. He had been a decent enough companion, if unimaginative, but the man had been badgering Kyril ever since they left Evenburg with one, all-consuming idea. They must search The House.

It quickly became apparent to Kyril that his partner had been one of the two men responsible for discovering the real Elaine Westover. The unfortunate fellow was now convinced that the false Elaine must necessarily be hidden in the same place.

Kyril had scoffed none too politely at the idea. Rowan was hardly the sort of person to behave so predictably or foolishly. He was far too canny to use the same retreat twice. But The House was located not far off their road, and when the miserable, sneezing guard had made one last plea, Kyril grudgingly agreed to at least look. It wasn't as if another layer or two of mud could make much difference. And he was able to justify his capitulation by reasoning that no one had thought to look there yet. Perhaps Rowan might have known it was the expected thing to do, and therefore that no one would have expected him to do it.

Growling under his breath at the uselessness of his errand and the ridiculous circularity of his thoughts, Kyril had followed the guard's directions. Afterwards, he intended to return home by the most direct route possible. Home, to a bath, and hopefully to good news. Surely by now, someone else had been luckier than he. Even if Kyril himself didn't quite know what that luck might entail.

He hardly even knew what to hope for. Finding Rowan, certainly. That was a given. Rowan was the only one left who might, if he chose, be able to save the king's life. And after Kyril had spent several sleepless nights considering ever more inventive methods of making Rowan's existence as miserable as possible, he would be greatly disappointed if he never had the opportunity to put any of those rather brilliant ideas into practice.

Embrie, however, was another matter. Had it been Kyril's decision alone, he would likely have left her to her fate. He was not entirely happy with Ramsey's decision to trust her, and found himself bitterly unwilling to forgive what he still saw as her betrayal. But his friend very clearly still cared about her. Still believed in her. Kyril would hope for the best for Ramsey's sake, even if he intended to ask some very pointed questions once she was found. If she was found.

Despite his wandering thoughts, Kyril had been watching closely enough that he was able to identify the landmarks the guard had mentioned. A strange old tree hanging over the road. A broken sign with a few meaningless letters half buried in the mud. And a track, barely visible, leading back into the trees.

In his haste to complete what he still considered a useless search, Kyril almost missed the footprints. If his mud-spattered bay gelding had not suddenly stumbled, leading Kyril to dismount and check for signs of injury, he might not have seen them at all. But he did, and the single set of prints pressed neatly into the mud from last night's rain were too fresh and too strange to ignore. The road had been deserted for miles. There were no towns. No farms. Only one house that he knew of and the prints appeared to have originated from there. They came down the track out of the woods and turned down the road away from him. Small prints. Light ones.

It might have been nothing. There could be a perfectly reasonable explanation for someone to be traveling down the road on foot in the middle of nowhere. But Kyril was nonetheless afflicted with the unexpected sensation of hope. Mixed with chagrin. The guard may have been right all along, and he could have saved them days of searching. Remounting, Kyril spurred his horse in the direction the unknown, small-footed person had taken.

His pursuit was not long. The road curved twice, narrowed as it bridged a swollen river, and then widened abruptly to reveal a long, flat stretch ahead. A stretch that was occupied by a solitary, cloaked figure trudging on foot through the mud. Kyril pressed his horse forward until he drew even with the strange pedestrian, who stepped off the road and turned to face him as he pulled the gelding to a halt. He was greeted by a brief indrawn breath, an almost involuntary sound of surprise.

"Lord Seagrave?" The voice under the cloak was female. Its owner pulled back the deep hood to reveal a face that was at once familiar and not. Chestnut hair. Amber eyes. A pale, slender face with a somewhat pointed chin. Despite the differences from the picture in his memory, Kyril knew at once that he had found half of what he searched for.

He felt an immediate surge of disappointment as he stared at her, comparing her face with Elaine's. Wherever Rowan was, it was now even less likely to be here. The girl was probably no better than a decoy, whose purpose was now finished. This thought was followed by an even stronger surge of anger, that she was alive and alone when everyone had assumed her to be with Rowan, a suffering captive rather than a willing companion.

The girl watched in silence as Kyril struggled with conflicting emotions. He wanted so badly to hate her. If only she had cried. Tried to defend herself with overwrought explanations. Made a bid for his sympathy. Then he might have been able to justify it. But the wary expression in her eyes, the weary tremor in her shoulders finally defeated him, deflating his anger and transforming it into a sort of resigned bitterness, tinged with pity. She was obviously cold, tired, hungry, and miles from anywhere familiar. And she was regarding him without much sense of hope.

"A long way from home, aren't you, Elaine?"

She looked briefly dismayed, but that emotion seemed to pass, leaving only exhaustion behind. "That, Lord Seagrave, would require that I actually possessed one, a point on which I am no longer certain," she answered, her voice sounding rougher than he remembered.

Cursing himself for lack of courtesy, even to a woman whose character he doubted, Kyril dismounted and offered her his water flask. She hesitated, but only briefly, then murmured her thanks. Thirst was no doubt a much more pressing concern than pride.

Kyril watched her as she drank, then spoke again, disappointment sharpening his questions. "You claim no home or family, then? Did you steal a name because you had none?"

She darted a glance in his direction, clearly unprepared for the pointedness of the question. There was no way for her to have known that they had uncovered her identity.

"If you knew my family, My Lord, such as it is," the girl finally replied, a bit dryly, "you would realize that they do not care for sharing. Names or houses. You might also find it evident that any house which contains them ought necessarily be disqualified for consideration as a home."

Kyril, having met the Colbournes, could admit to the justice of her statement. But he hardly expected her to acknowledge the connection, so he was rather surprised by what she did next. Sighing and closing her eyes for a moment, she turned to face him and looked directly into his disapproving eyes.

"Perhaps," she offered, squaring her shoulders bravely, "it is time we were properly introduced." His eyebrows shot up. "Lord Seagrave, my name is Trystan Colbourne, and whatever you may think of me, I am, I confess, very pleased indeed to meet you." She gestured to the road in both directions. "Though I suspect I would have been pleased to meet highwaymen under the circumstances."

Kyril could not help a short laugh at her honesty. So this was the Embrie his friend had fallen for. Though he noticed she was careful not to mention her middle name. "I suppose I am honored, though somewhat confused," he replied, politely evasive. He suspected Ramsey would not wish him to reveal the source of their information. "I thought I had met all the Colbourne ladies, and you, I am certain, were never among them. Another branch of the family, I take it?"

"Ah, no." Her twisted smile suggested painful secrets. "I was not considered suitable for polite company." Kyril eyed Embrie, wanting more than ever to dislike or disbelieve everything about her. But he had already begun to catch a glimpse of what had captured Ramsey's attention.

"Are you certain you claim the Misses Anya and Darya as sisters?" he inquired, watching her carefully. "I shudder to think that someone apparently considers *them* suitable for polite company."

His companion was surprised into a laugh of genuine amusement, quickly muffled. "I see you've been introduced," she responded, her amber eyes twinkling with humor. "Though it's decidedly impolite for me to say so."

For another moment the two watched each other, Kyril wondering how much of what he knew was safe to reveal. This Embrie somehow managed to look uncertain, hopeful and resigned all at the same time.

"How the devil did you get out here anyway?" He needed to find out whether she knew anything of Rowan's whereabouts, and it might be interesting to see how much she was willing to tell him.

"As to the method of transportation," she answered, "I confess I could not say, having been unconscious for the entire journey." She hesitated, watching him as if trying to decide how much of the truth to tell. How much he would be willing to believe. "Until this morning I was bound and locked in an empty house, hoping someone would find me."

Unsurprised, and unconvinced, Kyril nodded to indicate at least surface acceptance of her statement.

"It was suggested to me," she continued, "that the house was the same one which was used to confine..." She trailed off awkwardly, but it was enough.

The guard had been right, and perhaps Kyril should have guessed it. Rowan's twisted sense of humor had probably found it amusing to use the same location. Especially if, as Embrie suggested, she had been a prisoner and no one had ever thought to look there.

"It might ease your mind to know that we suspected you had

been kidnapped, rather than run away," Kyril offered finally, a trifle bewildered by his own benevolence.

Embrie seemed startled by this revelation but accepted it. "I confess I had hoped that my kidnapper, at least, would draw pursuit. It seemed foolish to suppose that anyone would be displeased by my disappearance."

Kyril very carefully did not take up that thread of conversation. While he might be curious about the death of Lady Westerby, this was probably not the time to ask.

"Prince Rowan?" he asked shortly, though he already knew the answer.

Embrie nodded. "He left shortly after I woke up."

Kyril looked at her curiously. "How did you get away?" Her answer might prove telling. If someone had rescued her she would not now be trudging her solitary way down a deserted road.

Embrie looked at him ruefully and lifted her hands so that the edges of her cloak fell back. Her wrists were wrapped in torn, bloody strips of cloth. "I got tired of waiting," she said.

Kyril swore and grasped her hands, pulling them down to see the extent of the damage. There appeared to be deep gashes on both arms, and some were still bleeding.

"There was a window," she explained. "When I realized no one was coming I managed to break it and used the shards to cut the ropes on my wrists."

And with that, the last meaningful bits of Kyril's suspicion drained away. He could choose not to believe her words, but it was beyond even his ability to deny the evidence of her blood. They were clearly wounds of desperation. Whether or not she had gone to that house by choice, she had remained by force, yet another victim of Rowan's cruel machinations.

"How long were you there?" Kyril was startled to feel his anger rising once again, but no longer directed at her.

She seemed to struggle for a moment with remembering. "Six days, I believe. At least that's how long I was conscious. His Highness left what he claimed was enough food for five days, then said he thought someone would find me by then." She closed her eyes for a moment. "He laughed when he said it. I could not tell whether or not it was a lie."

Her eyes opened then, and she grasped his arm without warning. "Lord Seagrave, I know you have no reason to believe me, and I have no way of knowing whether it was the truth, but, before he left, Prince Rowan told me something." Kyril gestured for her to continue. "He said that if I was rescued, I might wish to tell someone—the King, His Majesty, is poisoning himself! There is a weak tincture of henbane in his gout medicine that is causing his illness. If he stops taking it, he will very likely recover."

Kyril froze, but his thoughts sped on. The girl could be lying, but to his own surprise he was prepared to guess that she was not. He might have thought the whole performance an act, but for her lacerated wrists. If someone else had damaged her, she stood to gain a great deal of sympathy by reporting it truthfully. And while it was possible that she had known of the poison beforehand and now chose to attribute the revelation to Rowan out of a desire to clear her own name, that possibility took nothing from the import of her words. If they were true... If the king still lived...

"Can you ride?" he asked seriously.

She nodded, but did not at once move towards the horse. "Lord Seagrave,"—her voice was flat—"this is a matter of the king's life. You will get on faster if your horse is less burdened. Perhaps you should consider leaving me. There will be other travelers, and even if there are not..." She shrugged, a curiously defeated gesture.

"Enough, Miss Colbourne," Kyril admonished with unwonted sternness. "In the first place, you can't possibly weigh very much. And in the second..." He frowned slightly. "His Highness Prince Ramsey would never forgive me if I left you."

She looked startled. Then pale. "I had imagined His Highness would prefer not to encounter me again," she responded, quietly and miserably. "He can hardly care what becomes of me now."

Kyril eyed her sharply, but by then he had prepared to mount his horse. Swinging into the saddle, he offered her a gloved hand. Still watching him with some trepidation, she grasped the proffered hand, not without wincing, and pulled herself up behind him.

"His Highness," Kyril offered, as he turned his horse back the way he had come, "seems concerned with your welfare for some reason." The sudden movement of the horse nearly unseated his passenger and forced her to grasp his cloak to avoid being left in the mud. "You probably ought to hang on, you know." He turned his head to look at her. "I promise not to shower you with unwanted attentions if you promise not to dump me off and steal my horse." A small glimpse of his characteristic humor, it seemed to both of them like a peace offering. Not exoneration precisely, but a willingness to be something other than at odds. The girl... Embrie... flushed under his scrutiny, but nodded, and put her arms very carefully around his waist.

"You should know, however," Kyril added, "that whatever His Highness may choose to think with regards to your past or your actions, I don't appreciate being lied to. You made me like you and then you betrayed my brother. The upshot of it is, I'm not at all certain that I approve of you."

The girl behind him sighed. "Lord Seagrave," she answered solemnly, "I suppose I should tell you—I'm not certain I approve of me either."

∾

It had been a less-than-ideal week. Trystan could remember nothing between hearing Rowan's voice whispering in her ear at Westhaven, and waking up, wrists and ankles bound, slumped in a chair that was the only furniture in a cold, empty room. She had felt sick, with terror and probably with whatever she had been given to keep her unconscious. At first, she was not sure if she wanted anyone to hear her. But as the hours passed and no one came, she began to call for help.

After a while, Prince Rowan had unlocked the door and entered the room. He had worn a strange smile as he watched her, perhaps hoping for a reaction. When she gave him nothing but a cold stare, he had laughed at her. Taunted her with hints of the scene left behind them, of the probable deductions that would be made when Lady Westerby's body was found. He spun a complicated web of poisonous half-truths that briefly made her feel ultimately responsible for the deaths of Lady Westerby and King Hollin, the collapse of the House of Tremontaine, and eventually a crushing invasion by foreign forces. If she had... If she had not... When her head was spinning sufficiently and her guilt threatened to crush her, the prince had retreated, but Rowan's mocking laugh had echoed in her ears long after he departed, leaving food, water, and a dreadful responsibility in his wake.

For a time, she believed he was still in the house, listening, hoping she would break. Eventually, she had managed to remember that she was not personally responsible for all the world's evils, but it did not stop the silence and uncertainty from wearing away her patience and resolve. She had called for him. Screamed at him. Used some rather inventive language if her memory recalled correctly. Eventually, she had realized that he was truly gone. And that she was truly alone.

Despair had descended with a vengeance. The door was solid, both locked and barred. There was a window, but it did not seem to open, at least not with the weak and awkward motion available to bound hands. She had carefully hoarded the food and water. Tried to eat it slowly. Tried not to think about it dwindling, and what she would do when it was gone.

The nights had been the worst. Cold and terrifying. Every noise had seemed fraught with doom. It was, she realized now, a miracle she was still herself, still sane. The memory of Vianne had held her together when nothing else could. Vianne, telling her that she could bear whatever was necessary. That she was stronger than anyone knew. She had clung to those words fiercely, believing that someone would come. Believing she would have a chance to tell someone what she had learned about the king.

On that last day, as she kicked frantically at the window, Trystan had wondered if Rowan had told her about the king's poisoned medicine only so the knowledge could drive her mad. To torment her with the belief that she could save him if only she could get away. It had nearly succeeded. But she had gotten away, through sheer bloody-minded obstinacy, and a flat refusal to believe that a window would not break if you kicked it hard enough. She had left a lot of blood behind, but had taken her knowledge and her sanity with her. Rowan had not defeated her.

And for now, as she trotted down the road behind a man who despised her, it would have to be enough. She had liked Kyril

Seagrave a great deal, but she had forfeited the right to his trust. A fact he had proven by returning briefly to the house she had left. He searched the premises thoroughly, looking, she presumed, for proof, both of her captivity and Rowan's absence. The latter seemed evident by the complete lack of anything to indicate human habitation, outside of the small room with a broken window. That room contained more than enough to corroborate her story, from the putrid chamber pot to the sickening red stains on the floor. They were larger than she had remembered. Large enough that even Kyril was visibly shaken. He shot her a sharp, considering look, but said nothing.

After that, he had wasted no time returning to the road. The urgency of her news outweighed all other considerations, apparently even Kyril's doubts about her integrity.

Now, bouncing uncomfortably behind his saddle, there was little to distract Trystan from an endless litany of rather hopeless speculation. Such as wondering what awaited her back at Colbourne Manor. It was probably where she would end up, if Lord Seagrave permitted her to go her own way. Now that he knew who she was, that Elaine was really Trystan Colbourne, would he tell Ramsey? Would Ramsey try to find her? She could only hope not. Whatever was to happen now, her part in it seemed done. She had told everything she knew, and though it could not fully redeem her, perhaps, if the king recovered, it could lessen her guilt. Not in her own mind, of course. That kind of forgiveness would be much harder to come by.

There was, naturally, still the problem of what was to become of her after going home. Vianne had not seemed inclined to let her stay. Malisse would be unlikely to let her remain in the house, especially when she learned that Trystan had exposed a link between the Colbourne name and the plot against the crown. For now, however, Trystan's mind kept returning to the small but undeniably comforting thought of her room, her bed, and the oblivion of sleep. Malisse was not going to keep her from that. At least not without bodily violence, which was hardly a suitable method of resolution for a well-bred woman.

There was a part of Trystan that knew she would eventually be forced to face Prince Ramsey again, as herself, with no masque, no pretense, no lies to hide behind. She couldn't decide whether she would rather face execution or be relieved to have it over with. So instead of dwelling on the painful lack of certainty in her future, Trystan focused on the fact that, for now at least, she was safe. She closed her eyes. Eventually, the motion of the horse ceased to matter, her head fell forward, and she drifted into sleep.

CHAPTER 19

The day of Ramsey's return to Evenburg was warm and sunny. The spring rains had at least paused, and the whole world seemed green and cheerful. There were birds. And squirrels. Ramsey knew there were squirrels because he had nearly ridden several of them down in his haste to discover if his father still lived. The world seemed so dark, he wondered how it could have the nerve to have squirrels. He also wondered whether the bizarre meanderings of his brain were chiefly the result of grief, worry and guilt, or having gone five days with almost no sleep. Or perhaps all of the above.

Ramsey suspected that the squirrels fled not from the haste of his passing but from terror at his appearance. Filthy, unshaven, rumpled and disordered, with gaunt cheeks and bloodshot eyes— it would be a wonder if they let him in the castle gate. And behind all these pointless musings ran a single, stark thought: my father is alive. It repeated itself. My father is alive. It would be true by virtue of his conviction. He would not let it be otherwise.

He had lost his brother and he had lost Embrie. He would not lose his father too.

The clatter of Evenleigh's cobblestones under his mount's hooves was nothing less than sweet music. He made his way swiftly to the gates of Evenburg, not even pausing at the guard's challenge. Dismounting nearly proved his undoing. The world spun as his feet hit the ground and his vision temporarily darkened. Even as he hastily grabbed at the saddle to hold himself up, Ramsey heard the sound of guards approaching at a run. Straightening and glaring balefully was enough to establish his identity and set up a yell that echoed oddly around his already disordered brain. Prince Ramsey had come home and it seemed the whole castle felt the need to be loud about it. Blinking owlishly at his bags, Ramsey decided he didn't need them and started inside, only to be instantly intercepted by a smiling (*smiling?*), bowing Mortimer.

"Your Highness-" the steward managed to get out before Ramsey was nearly bowled over by a brown-haired female missile.

"Lizbet?" It was indeed his aunt. His giddy aunt. She was beaming at him so happily there were tears in her eyes. "Aunt Lizbet, I have something…" Ramsey began to remove the chain from around his neck, to hand her the vial he had carried so swiftly across the kingdom, but his aunt was too fast for him.

She clasped his shoulders firmly in her small hands. "He's going to be all right, Donnie! He's going to be fine!"

Ramsey's jaw dropped. "Then… the physicians, they… Da is going to be all right?"

Lizbet nodded, tears now streaking her flushed cheeks as another person skidded into the entrance hall and stalked toward them, scowling furiously.

"Ramsey, you brainless idiot! You're lucky nothing happened to you because if it had I would have killed you myself!" Kyril embraced his friend briefly but fiercely, then pulled back to look at him with an appalled expression. "Ramsey, you look like death. What's happened?"

"Not here!" Lizbet pushed them both towards her office.

"Wait!" Ramsey looked at both of them uncertainly. "You're sure? Father is not going to die?"

Lizbet snorted. "At least not anytime soon... not of anything except surliness and frustration, that is. Come, Ramsey. You can see him after we've talked."

Ramsey let himself be led, almost too confused to grasp the truth. His father would live. When they reached his aunt's office, he sank into a chair with a groan and dropped his face into his hands.

"Ramsey," Lizbet asked suddenly, a note of worry in her voice, "where is Brawley?"

Ramsey looked up at them bleakly. "Still in Zell, I hope," he answered, trying to hold back exhausted tears. "Rowan..." a half-sob choked him, born of relief, anguish, and too many sleepless nights. "Rowan put a knife in his chest." Kyril swore violently, and Lizbet exclaimed in shock, even as she put her arms around her nephew and held him as tightly as she would one of her own children.

"He wanted to keep me from following him, wanted to force me to let him cross the border, so he stabbed Brawley and gave me this..." The golden chain dangled from Ramsey's fingers. "He said it was Father's antidote." Another sob ripped out of his chest. "I had to let him go! I couldn't stop him. I had to let him go." Ramsey's voice shook. "He made me believe that it couldn't be as bad as it seemed and then..." He looked up at his aunt.

"Embrie's dead," he whispered hoarsely. "Embrie is dead and Rowan killed her."

Kyril snarled in terrible fury, crossed the room in an instant and knelt in front of Ramsey. He took his friend's face in his hands and forced his prince to look at him. "Ramsey," he said slowly and firmly, as though speaking to a child. "I don't know what Rowan told you, but it was a lie. Embrie is alive. I found her and brought her home."

Ramsey just stared at him, uncomprehending, his expression raw and terrible.

"Ramsey! She. Is. Alive."

The truth finally found its way through the fog, through the wreck of Ramsey's mind and heart, to resonate joyfully beside the news of his father's recovery. Incongruously, the tears he had tried to hold back finally broke free in horrible, tearing sobs. He had not cried like that since his mother died. Even as his shoulders shook with the strength of his emotion, he realized that his primary feeling was now that of relief. Suddenly, the day no longer seemed the worst of his life. It might not have made the top ten. Ramsey could even find it in him to be glad there were squirrels.

"Ramsey," his aunt said finally, despite her own tears, "I believe whatever you have to say can wait. I will see to it that one of our best physicians is sent to collect Brawley immediately. I will make sure your father knows you are home. You"—she narrowed her eyes at him—"are going to bed. Now!"

Ramsey remembered that he was tired. The world was not entirely right, but it was far closer to right than he had believed for the past several days. And everything that was not yet right could wait for him to...

He only made it back to his room with Kyril half-carrying, half-dragging him. Foster eventually showed up to lend a hand, and together they put the prince to bed. Kyril pulled off his friend's boots and handed them to Foster, who carried them out of the room with an expression of appalled distaste.

A smile crossed Kyril's face as he crept out of the room and left Ramsey to his sleep. There could not be a great deal wrong with the world when a valet could spare such extreme malevolence for a pair of mistreated footwear.

$$\sim$$

It was a very strange homecoming for Trystan.

Lord Seagrave left her at the crossroads nearest Colbourne Manor, mounted on a borrowed horse. They had been largely silent for the final part of their ride, somewhat of inclination and somewhat of necessity. A second horse, borrowed from a crown courier station, had greatly accelerated their progress, especially once Kyril realized that his companion could match any pace he set on horseback. After that, their speed had, for the most part, precluded conversation. What conversation did pass between them had been polite, but strained. Lord Seagrave had not seemed inclined to answer questions, and Trystan had been far too aware of his disapproval to press him.

She arrived at Colbourne Manor just before lunch time, sore and filthy from head to foot, though her bandages at least were clean. Kyril had paused their journey, in the face of her protests, long enough to have her lacerated wrists seen to by a healer. The woman had given both of them a dark look, but asked no questions, only cleaned, stitched and bound up the wounds. Trystan hoped it would be enough. She had enough explaining to do without being required to address the matter of her injuries.

Trystan left her horse with the same lazy-looking man who had driven her to Lady Isaura's for tea that memorable afternoon, several lifetimes ago. His expression of suspicion disappeared when Trystan pointed out the crown brand on her mount's shoulder and suggested there would be dire consequences if he failed to treat the animal with care.

Upon leaving the stable, Trystan's feet turned automatically to the kitchen entrance, but changed course at the last. She wanted Vianne to know she was home, but, more than that, she needed to show Malisse that the old Trystan was gone.

Since her departure, Trystan had known both terror and pain. Experienced both exultation and dread. In truth, she could no longer imagine being frightened of Malisse or her threats. Her stepmother's power to intimidate seemed so small, so paltry, that Trystan could not even summon the energy to care what she was going to say.

Trystan knocked forcefully on the front door, not without a wince. Perhaps she should have kicked it instead. The door swung open in the firm, businesslike hand of... *Hoskins?* Trystan's eyes went quite wide with surprise and then crinkled in a silent laugh. The distinguished-looking older man was looking at her as though he had seen a ghost. A very familiar, very welcome ghost. Trystan suppressed the urge to hug him. It would have embarrassed him deeply, so she settled for grasping his hand—carefully—in welcome.

Noting the bandages crossing her palms, Hoskins raised an eyebrow at his employer's wayward child.

"Long story, Hoskins," she answered wryly. "But before you

say anything, I need to tell you how very, very glad I am to see you back." The gray-haired butler bowed with great propriety. "How did you…"

There was no need to say more. Hoskins drew himself up with an air of satisfaction. "It seems the mistress had some complaints regarding the competence of my successor. When she was forced to turn him off and experienced some difficulty in securing the services of anyone else, I was only too happy to agree to resume my position." A conspiratorial smile lurked at the corner of his mouth. "And may I say, madam, how very glad I am to see you returned to us."

He raised one eyebrow as voices suddenly echoed into the entrance hall. One of them, at least, was unmistakable. Malisse. Trystan and Hoskins looked at each other, dispensed with propriety and rolled their eyes in unison.

Malisse had obviously not been aware of the identity of her caller. She took a single step into the entryway and froze, staring at the filthy apparition before her.

Trystan waited calmly for the diatribe to begin. She expected a certain amount of haranguing would have to take place before she would be permitted a bath. What happened next shocked her.

Malisse walked forward, never once looking into Trystan's eyes. Her face seemed carved from granite as she approached, gave a stiff nod of greeting, and addressed Trystan in a modulated, well-bred voice. "Welcome home, dear child."

Trystan's mouth was not equal to the self-control demanded of it and dropped open.

"We will be lunching shortly," Malisse continued, "but I'm sure you will wish to bathe and rest. I will have a tray sent to your room, unless you have other preferences."

Trystan just looked at her stepmother. She could not even begin to guess how she ought to respond. Was this Malisse's idea of a joke? "Yes, I certainly do want a bath, and food, but I'm quite certain I can see to it myself, Stepmother."

A false smile, bright as the sun and nearly as blinding, answered her. "Oh no, my dear, I wouldn't hear of it. Just go on up and I'll arrange everything. So pleased you have returned!" As though the limits of her politeness had been reached, Malisse abruptly whirled and disappeared.

Trystan stared after her, then turned to Hoskins, whose expression could only be called a smirk. He shrugged, but said nothing. Apparently she was on her own in deciphering the mystery of her stepmother's behavior. Perhaps Vianne would know, and Trystan would ask her, but first, that bath. No doubt Hoskins would spread the news of her return far faster than she could do so herself anyway.

Trystan made her way up to her room, grimacing as tortured muscles protested the long flight of stairs. She thought it seemed as though her stepsisters' doors shut abruptly as she approached, but it seemed ridiculous to suppose they might be spying on her.

Her room, to her relief, was just as she had left it. At least it appeared to be, until she opened her closet, hoping to find some clean clothes. She found rather more than she'd bargained for. An entire row of unfamiliar dresses hung there, plus four pairs of what looked like new slippers placed neatly on a shelf. They appeared to be her size, but that was absurd. Had Malisse acquired a guest in her absence? And why would she put Trystan back in her own room if it was already in use?

Feeling increasingly disturbed but too weary to do anything about it, Trystan answered the knock at her door to find that her bath had begun to arrive. Perhaps her powers of discernment would grow if she was clean.

One bath, a change of clothes and a nice lunch later, Trystan went to look for Vianne. When she arrived in the kitchen, all activity stuttered to a halt. Everyone stared, but no one said anything until one of the kitchen maids, a girl named Grita, approached.

"Begging your pardon, madam, but can we be helping you with anything?"

Trystan frowned. "Where's Vianne?"

Grita grinned, clearly unable to hide her glee. "She's not here, Miss Trystan. She doesn't work here any more."

Trystan's mind ground to a stop. Vianne? Not here? Impossible. She would never leave Colbourne. Unless… Just as a wave of righteous fury began to rise, Grita went on.

"She took that job, at the palace. Went off a little over a week ago. We ha'nt seen her since."

Trystan tried to process this information and failed utterly. Vianne had turned down the palace job three times. She knew all about Trystan's entanglement with the royal family. What had possessed her to take that job now, of all times?

Trystan was beginning to feel as though the whole world was turned upside down. The true test, she decided, would be at dinner.

Which, when it came, was really no help at all. Anya claimed a headache and remained in her room. Darya merely shot sullen glances across the table and Malisse seemed determined to make minimal conversation about polite nothings. Every attempt by Trystan to approach the subject of the changes in the household were met by evasion or simply ignored. Nothing was mentioned about her own past or future. Trystan was sure that the restraint must be killing her stepmother, but the irritating woman showed no cracks in her facade. She said good night before the dessert course was brought in, taking Darya with her. Trystan guessed she didn't trust Darya not to talk when her mother's back was turned.

Trystan went to bed shortly thereafter, pleased to be back in her own room, but extremely disturbed by the disordering of her former life. That life had frequently not been pleasant, but it had been predictable. This strange new place felt even less like home than she remembered.

She fell asleep wondering whether it was all just a dream.

Ramsey slept for some time. When he finally cracked his eyes and yawned, it was to a strange and bright new world, a world suffused with a feeling of leftover urgency, like there was something he was supposed to be doing, but he couldn't remember what it was. Or where he was. He looked around, blinking, until he established for certain that he was in his own room. It was morning, though he couldn't remember it being night when he went to bed. For that matter, he couldn't remember going to bed. Which explained why he was still in his clothes. Filthy, unwashed, unshaven... the sheets.

Foster was going to kill him.

And with that, the events of the past few days fell on him with all their dragging, suffocating weight. Rowan. Brawley. His father. Embrie. With that final thought, most of the weight lifted again, and for the first time in what seemed like weeks, Ramsey felt almost happy about getting out of bed.

Opening the door of his bedroom, he was greeted by the at

once severely disapproving and genuinely welcoming face of his valet. Foster was obviously happy to see him. He was not happy to see his master's clothes. Or the state of his hair. Or the bewhiskered wreck of his face. He was also clearly feeling peeved at being left behind while his employer went gadding about the kingdom wearing wrinkled shirts.

It was a full hour before Ramsey escaped, bathed, shaved and attired in miraculously laundered, un-rumpled clothing. He had been forced to admit to himself during the past week that as much as he disliked most of the trappings of his royal life, he had learned to appreciate the strange luxury of being clean.

The halls seemed smaller than he remembered as he tried to walk quietly towards his father's apartments. It was early yet, and few people were about, which was fortunate, as Ramsey was not interested in answering any questions before he accomplished this first, most important task.

He did not really even know what he was going to say to his father, only that he had to say it. The king needed to know the truth about his son. His sons. Even Ramsey could tell that what had passed between him and Rowan had changed him. He didn't know how much, or even if the changes were good ones. Only that he was a different person than he had been.

But when he entered his father's room, something held him back. The king was awake and sitting up, enduring an examination by Emersen, his personal physician. Hollin's eyes were bright and his temper fully recovered, if the curses he directed at Emersen were any indication. But he was changed as well, just as surely as Ramsey.

The robust and fiery king, who had never been less than equal to any challenge, had diminished. He looked a wreck, true, and had lost a great deal of weight, but it was not only the physical effects of his ordeal that Ramsey marked as he crossed the room to hug his father.

King Hollin had aged. Not merely in body, but in spirit. Some part of his spark, his tenacity, had gone, and Ramsey knew with a deep, aching sort of grief, that he was unlikely to ever get it back.

So they talked, but not so much of truth, and Ramsey felt desperately old as he realized he was shielding his father. Not that he intended the king should never know what had happened between his sons. Hollin was king still, and he must know what threats his kingdom would face. But for that day and that time, Ramsey chose to bear the burden of truth alone, and in doing so, began to grasp something of what the future would hold. Saw the inevitability of growing up to protect the person who had always done the protecting. A person who would very likely resent the notion that there was anything he needed to be protected from.

So Ramsey did not trouble his father with all the available facts. Instead, they spoke of the attempt on the throne, and discussed its outcome. They briefly discussed the necessity of trying the conspirators and determining their punishments. Of Rowan, Ramsey said only that he had fled the kingdom. Of Brawley, he said that the captain had been injured, but did not mention how. And of the ball? It didn't seem like there was much to be said. He was not yet married, and hadn't particularly thought about it in days. And his father, mercifully, did not press him on the subject.

～

The king very carefully did not ask any of the questions he wished to ask of his sole remaining child. He had been apprised of the situation in part by his sister-in-law, and knew much of what Ramsey did not tell him. About Rowan, about Brawley, and even about a girl named Embrie.

The boy looked terrible. He had aged, not so much in body, but in spirit. So much of his energy, his hopefulness, had gone and the king wondered sadly whether his son would ever fully recover.

The boy was obviously spent, mind and heart alike. If Ramsey was to mend at all, it would take time. His father intended to be certain that he had that time. Promised himself silently that his son would be shielded from the worries the kingdom now faced, for as long as it took. He would give suitable instructions to Lizbet, who would be suitably delighted to carry them out. Ramsey would be protected, even if he didn't like it, even if he didn't know he needed to be. That was a father's job, and King Hollin was grimly determined not to fail in it. Not this time.

~

After leaving his father, Ramsey made his way to Lizbet's apartments, where he played quietly with Parry and Prisca while he waited for Kyril and Caspar. When everyone was assembled, with the painful exception of Brawley, they shared their stories of the past few days.

Ramsey grew still and his jaw clenched as Kyril explained how he had finally discovered Embrie's whereabouts, and what she'd had to tell him.

"Would it have killed him, eventually, if we hadn't found out the truth?" he asked, thinking of his father.

"The physicians believe it would have worn him down in time," Lizbet said, "though it's hard to know for certain. The dose was small enough to keep from killing him outright, but large enough that he was nearly comatose, with hallucinations and convulsions at times. The healers were able to purge him, and the symptoms stopped within hours."

Ramsey blew out a long breath. Knowing he had done what was necessary did not prevent him from feeling like an idiot when he realized that the swift and torturous ride back to Evenburg had been an exercise in futility. Perhaps the only good to come of it was that he was home, where there was obviously a great deal to do. With the king barely able to cope with basic tasks and Lizbet frighteningly overworked, his help was desperately needed.

"Ramsey," Kyril began tentatively, "about Embrie…" Ramsey looked at him steadily. "She doesn't know that you have made the connection, between her and Elaine. I thought perhaps you would want to tell her that much yourself."

Ramsey was silent. What did he want? He was hardly sure himself.

Kyril continued. "I wanted very badly to hate her, Ramsey, and I won't apologize for it. I liked her and she betrayed you, and that is not an easy thing to forgive." He looked thoughtful. "But, on our ride back, I think I saw enough to realize why you believed in her. Why you decided to trust her, even when it made you look a fool."

Ramsey was startled for a moment, then grinned sheepishly. He likely had looked a fool.

"I'm still not entirely certain I approve," Kyril went on seriously, "but I hope you'll at least talk to her. You both, I think, deserve a chance to be happy, in spite of what's happened."

Ramsey filed that thought away for future consideration, then told his family what had occurred in Zell. He left out nothing, even admitting to his own doubts, his willingness to believe that

Rowan told the truth about his motives. "I wanted him to be innocent," he sighed finally. "Wanted it so badly that some part of me heard what he said and made it make sense. It was all true, to a point. No one died. The conspiracy was exposed. I thought it was possible that he might have just wanted to help."

"How did you finally decide not to trust him?" Kyril asked.

"When he told me he had murdered Embrie," Ramsey answered honestly. "He claimed she had been manipulating me from the beginning. I might have believed him, if I hadn't met her, before all this started. Rowan had no way of knowing that we were acquainted. That, in some ways, I knew her better than I knew him. It was his one miscalculation." He grimaced. "I know it seems silly and weak of me, that it took such a thing to convince me he was a villain. I knew he was liar. I have more reason than anyone to know his weaknesses, his enjoyment in others' suffering, his talent for manipulation. And I fell for it all over again."

"You're his brother!" Lizbet broke in heatedly. "You'd be more unnatural if you didn't want to believe the best of him."

Ramsey just looked sad. "And yet," he said, as much to himself as to the others, "I still don't know what to believe. What were his motives, truly? What were his goals? What did he really expect to gain from all this? In the end, people were hurt, but the conspiracy was exposed with remarkably little damage. And the thing of it is, the thing I will never be quite sure of is this—did he plan to leave me this way? Questioning him, questioning myself? Never quite able to be certain what was real and what wasn't?"

"It's exactly the kind of thing he would do," Caspar put in levelly, "but I hope you won't allow it to poison you."

"Unfortunate choice of words," Kyril added with unrepentant cheerfulness, "but I agree. Rowan obviously wanted you to doubt yourself. Spend the rest of your life looking over your shoulder, wondering if you made the right decision."

"And you did." Lizbet, Kyril and Caspar spoke in unintentional unison, sparking surprised laughter from all four of them.

"Personally," Lizbet said dryly, "I'd like to think I would have eviscerated the bastard, but that's speaking as a mother, not as his brother and the future king. What you did showed both judgment and restraint and"—she folded her hands and glared as though daring anyone to disagree with her—"I'm proud of you."

Ramsey acknowledged her compliment with a smile and a slight bow. "So what now?" he asked, not really expecting an answer. Back to work. Back to life. Pick up where he had left off and try to move on. The other three looked at each other in confusion.

"What do you mean, 'what now?'" Kyril said, pretending to look surprised by Ramsey's question.

"Yes, what do you mean?" Lizbet echoed slyly.

Ramsey looked from one to the other. "Am I missing something?" he asked, wondering what they all knew that he didn't.

"Obviously," Kyril responded promptly. "Ramsey, it's clear to all of us that you have a very important meeting to arrange. We are not going to arrange it for you. But there is too much unfinished business between you and a certain young lady and we're all tired of living in suspense."

Ramsey frowned. "I'm not sure I'm ready."

"Do it anyway," Lizbet interrupted with a stern look.

"Before you lose your nerve," Caspar put in, his eyes twinkling behind his spectacles.

"And before you stop eating, lose your figure and die of despondency," Kyril added, nodding sagely.

Ramsey found he was growing nervous just thinking about

it. What would it be like, seeing her again? Would she even want to see him? Once she found out that he knew everything? Even if she did, they could never again be simply Embrie and Donevan. There were too many barriers between them, and the innocent honesty of their fledgling friendship had been crushed.

And yet, Ramsey knew his friends were right. He needed to see her. And he would do it soon. If only everyone would stop looking at him with those identical expressions of smug anticipation.

~

When Trystan finally opened her eyes, the sun was high and bright, and for one shining moment she was suffused with a sensation of warmth and well-being. That moment fled like a rat before a lantern when she reflected on yesterday.

Hoskins was back. Vianne was gone. Malisse was being inscrutable. There were dresses in her closet that were not hers and a horse in the stable that wasn't hers either. It was enough to make her consider rolling over and going back to sleep. Until a sharp ache from her arms reminded her that she probably ought to get up and change her bandages, at the very least.

It took some time to acquire ointment and clean linen and rewrap her wounds, which appeared to be healing nicely. Afterwards she chose one of the unfamiliar dresses to wear, reasoning that it could always be washed and returned to whomever had left it.

She went downstairs and tried to locate her family, but was informed by Hoskins that they had all gone out. It was early for a morning call, and Trystan reasoned grimly that they had been purposefully avoiding her. Not that she intended to complain, but it was hardly a behavior that could continue for long.

A feeling of restlessness settled over her as she wandered aimlessly about the house. It was ridiculous to suppose that she could settle back into her old life, with its numbing lack of purpose, after the past weeks. There was nothing for her to do, no one for her to avoid, and the sudden absence of any source of terror left Trystan feeling rather bereft.

More than anything else, she wanted to see Vianne, but she could hardly trip blithely up to the castle gate and ask for her. Nor was there anyone else she could talk to. Without quite realizing it, she was pacing from room to room, muttering to herself when Hoskins finally pulled her aside.

"Miss Trystan," he suggested with a significant glance, "perhaps you should consider that a certain gray hunter may be sadly in need of exercise."

Trystan did consider it. She had only just returned from two straight days of riding. She hardly needed more time in the saddle to remind her of her aches and bruises. On the other hand, it wasn't as though she was helping anything by wearing holes in the carpet. Perhaps a ride would get her mind off her strange circumstances. It was, at any rate, worth making the attempt.

She returned to her room to change into her trousers and boots and was soon trotting off toward the stables with a brighter outlook.

An inquiry directed at the disgruntled stableman confirmed that someone had indeed come for the borrowed horse quite early that morning. He had made no inquiries, only collected the animal and left. Trystan wasn't sure why the news should disappoint her, but it did.

Brushing off the man's attempts to assist her, she soon had

Theron saddled. He was a bit flighty from having gone unridden for so long, so she was forced to accept help while mounting. In the end, it was just barely after noon when she trotted off into the warm sunshine, determined to forget the memories and decisions that plagued her and simply enjoy the day.

~

It was not long after lunch that Ramsey's inexplicable sense of dissatisfaction finally drove him out of his rooms. He couldn't focus on work and he couldn't sit still. Unwelcome memories kept intruding on his attempts to concentrate, crowding out every rational thought until he was forced to abandon all pretense of productivity. Kyril stopped in just as he was about to resort to throwing things.

"You've had a rough week," Kyril noted, which to Ramsey seemed an inexcusable understatement. "Why not get out of here, go for a ride?"

Ramsey gave him a disbelieving look. "I believe that's what I spent most of the past week doing," he responded blightingly, "and I really have very little inclination to climb back into a saddle until sometime next year."

Kyril folded his arms and raised an eyebrow. "Then, by all means, throw yourself out a window instead. Anyone with half their wits can see you're dangerously close to doing yourself an injury. Do us all a favor, get out, clear your head. Besides," he went on, with a bit more sympathy, "you need the break. This hasn't been easy for anyone and least of all you."

Ramsey groaned, but the more he thought about it, the more he thought Kyril might be right. He really had no desire to haul his aching body back into a saddle, but at least this time he needn't ride at a breakneck pace across half his kingdom. A gentle ride, perhaps to the Kingswood and back. It might permit him to sort out the mangled mess of his thoughts. Whether it was a flash of intuition or the spark of memory, before he left his rooms Ramsey paused a moment to slip something into his pocket. For some reason, carrying the horse with him seemed like the right thing to do.

CHAPTER 20

Trystan could not tell whether it was guilt or longing that guided her, but it seemed no accident that she found herself riding across rolling fields in search of a certain stone wall. She felt infinitely older than the girl who had last sat there, kicking her heels and twirling her reins, enjoying the sunshine and the company. That girl had had a future. Not a very pleasant one, to be sure, but there had been a sort of comfort in its lurking presence.

Now, she felt as though she was waiting. Trystan wasn't even sure for what, only that something about her adventures, if that was even the right word, seemed incomplete.

She found the wall, or perhaps Theron did. Sliding off, she stretched aching muscles and groaned, tied Theron's reins to his saddle and allowed him to graze. The wall was warm and solid… a little too solid for an abused backside, so she leaned against it and slid down to sit on the tall grass of the pasture. It too was warm, and soft, and smelled like summer. Trystan smiled and closed her eyes. She laid her hat on the grass beside her and pulled out her hairpins. An afternoon this perfect should not have hairpins in it. When her hair was loose and decidedly less itchy, she leaned her head back against the wall and thought about nothing. The droning of insects, the stirring of a slight breeze and the warm sun on her face conspired to lull her to sleep as Theron grazed peacefully nearby.

~

The only warning she had was the dull thud of hoofbeats, intruding on her dreamless nap. Jerking awake, she looked around for Theron and was appalled to realize that he was gone. He had never left her before, and obviously was not as well-trained as she had believed.

Trystan was considering cursing her stupidity when the sound of an approaching horse filled her with sudden relief. Of course. He had only disappeared over the rise in the hill, not run away. Jumping to her feet, she started towards the sound of hooves just as her quarry came into view.

It was not Theron. It was an all too familiar bay horse, bearing a brown-haired, gray-eyed rider. He approached at a walk and pulled up when he drew even with her.

She could not look.

Did not want to see him.

Especially did not want to see the look in his eyes when he recognized more than just Embrie. For what seemed a very long time, the only sound between them was the wind through the grass.

"Lose something?" His calm question made her wince. He dismounted and walked towards her as she fumbled for an answer.

"My horse, apparently," Trystan managed to find words and congratulated herself on sounding reasonably normal. "He's never seemed inclined to wander off..." Her voice promptly wandered off as Donevan drew nearer. And nearer. She glanced at him, caught between terror and curiosity. His face was calm, though his eyes betrayed some indecipherable emotion.

"I may have found what you were looking for," he said, by this time standing directly in front of her. He reached down and took her hand. Turned it over. Trystan's heart faltered when he placed something in her palm. Something warm and familiar.

Her golden horse. When she looked down and realized what he had given her, the last of her hopes finally died. He knew.

Trystan curled her hand into a white-knuckled grip, closed her eyes, and turned away. She could not even look at him. Could not bear to see her betrayal reflected back at her. Tears began to spill from her eyes as she stood miserable and silent on that sun-warmed hill.

"I'm sorry," she whispered, almost too quietly to be heard, an apology to herself as much as to him.

"What are you sorry for?" he asked, with surprising gentleness, still standing only a step behind her.

"Everything," she replied, brushing at her cheeks and wishing he would leave her to cry in peace. Wishing she never had to face him again.

"I'm not."

Trystan did not answer, but stiffened in surprise when he closed the distance between them and placed his hands on her shoulders.

"Embrie, please look at me." He turned her around, gently but inexorably. "I'm not sorry," he repeated, his hold on her shoulders both warm and strong. "I've never been sorry that I met you. Not for a single moment." His eyes were clear and honest, and Trystan could not withstand their scrutiny.

She pulled back and glared at him through her tears. "Don't lie to me, Donevan... Your Highness... whoever!" Frustration and humiliation choked her. She couldn't even call him by the right name. "You called me a bastard," she stated flatly. "And a scheming, treacherous fraud." Donevan winced. "And I won't pretend you didn't have every right to. So don't you pretend you're not sorry that I lied to you, betrayed you, and nearly got your father killed."

The object of her scorn only folded his arms and gazed at her without rancor. "Yes, you did all those things," he admitted. "And I confess I'm only just beginning to reconcile what I know of Embrie with everything Elaine has said and done. But there was no excuse for what I called you. No excuse for the way I acted that night you came to tell me the truth." He held up a hand when Trystan tried to interrupt. "No, please, hear me out. I was cruel, vindictive and utterly unjustified in my behavior," he told her firmly. "You need to understand, the only reason my father is *not* dead is because I met you."

Trystan looked up at him in confusion and saw confirmation in his face. Somehow, he believed he was telling the truth. She dropped her eyes, refused to ask her questions, and he went on.

"The only reason I am alive and the conspiracy that threatened this kingdom is not, is because I met you." He stepped closer then, his voice wavering oddly. "And while I am infinitely grateful for those things, I am even more grateful that I had the chance to know you—to be astonished, delighted and captivated by you—before all of those things happened." Trystan made a brief, strangled sound of disbelief, but he forged on. "Otherwise, I might have believed my brother when he told me you were a heartless mercenary. I might have believed in the possibility that you had murdered Lady Westerby and fled. I might even have been convinced that you lied to me about my dancing."

Trystan was startled enough that she almost laughed. He had been able to make her laugh, nearly from the first moment they met. It was one of the things she liked best about him. One of the things she was trying very hard not to remember, because if she did it would end with her crying over things she could never have.

"I admit that I lied," she said finally, into the silence, "but never about your dancing."

She thought about lies, and about truths. And while she was no longer lying to Donevan, she knew that in wishing he would go away, she was lying to herself.

She did not want him to leave. She wanted to spend what remained of forever smiling whenever she looked at him across a room. She wanted to talk to him about everything and about nothing. To laugh with him at the ridiculousness of life and cry with him at its inevitable sorrows. She wanted to run her fingers through his endearingly rumpled hair and make him happy when he was sad because the thought of him being sad broke her heart. And most of all, she wanted to take back every moment of her life since that afternoon in Lady Isaura's sitting room.

But that could not be. Any more than she could suddenly become fashionable, wealthy and legitimate. Any more than she could truly be forgiven for all that had passed between them. Donevan was grateful because things had ended well, but if they had not, it would still have been her fault. And because she respected and cared for him now more than ever, both as a man and as the future king, she had no choice but to ask his forgiveness. It was a painful and difficult thing to do. At least it would have been, not so very long ago. Her pride, Trystan thought wryly, had undergone a rather drastic reduction of late. Perhaps it would not stand in her way after all.

She managed finally to look firmly into Donevan's eyes as he stood there, so close, waiting for her to speak. "I know I have no right to ask, let alone expect to receive," she told him, so quiet and diffident that the breeze nearly carried her words away. "But I can't pretend that I don't want your forgiveness. I have tried, since I realized what I had done, to rectify my mistakes. I know it will never be enough. That trust, once broken, is a difficult thing to mend. But," she forged on, looking into the distance over his shoulder, "I'm going to ask. Because I need to find a way to forgive myself, if I am to rebuild some sort of life from the disaster I have made of it. And if I am ever to forgive myself, I need some sort of hope that you might someday forgive me as well."

Her voice trembled and her lip quivered. Tears hovered, threatening to fall as she looked at him bravely. "Prince Ramsey Donevan Tremontaine, I have injured and offended you deeply and I am more sorry than you could ever know. Will you... could you ever find it in you to forgive me?"

Prince Ramsey Donevan Tremontaine closed the distance between them with a single step and took her pale, upturned face between his hands. A feeling of disbelieving joy shook her from head to toe as he gently brushed away her tears with his thumbs.

"Embrie, you beautiful, ridiculous girl," he told her softly. "What I've been trying to tell you is... I already have."

≈

Ramsey hardly knew what he had intended, coming out to the

wall, on that particular day. Or even what he had hoped. But when he saw her, eyes ringed by shadows, face drawn by sorrow and fatigue, every last doubt he harbored fell away.

Her reaction to him was perhaps inevitable. Anger, remorse, embarrassment. It must have taken an unbelievable degree of courage for her to face him. That courage, he thought wryly, was the only part of her character he had never had reason to question. And when she asked for his forgiveness, with heart-wrenching dignity, it took everything he had not to drop down on one knee and beg her to marry him right then and there. But he couldn't. Not because he didn't want to, but because there was something else he needed to do first.

When he said that he had forgiven her, the look of joy and relief in Embrie's eyes was almost painful. But there was a shadow still. So many questions remained. The matter of her illegitimacy yet lay between them. And there was a story he needed to tell her. A story he had been longing to tell her for days, one that would hopefully put all those questions to rest.

"But you-" She started to say something, probably another apology.

Ramsey met Embrie's objection with a finger across her lips. It was time to tell her the rest. "Shush," he admonished, with mock sternness. "The truth is, I've been wondering whether you would be willing to forgive *me*. I should have tried to find out why you did what you did. Instead, I had to find out when it was nearly too late. And," he added, "from a most unexpected source."

"What do you mean?" she asked, confusion written plainly on her face. "How could you have found out? No one else knew about my stupidity except Lady Westerby, and-" She broke off, and pulled back from him a little. "You must have thought I'd killed her."

"No," he said simply. "I didn't. Not really. But I did ask." He watched her intently as he said it. "I asked the one person who might have reason to know." At her look of trepidation he could not help raising the question. "What did happen that night? If you don't mind telling me."

Embrie sighed, but unbuttoned her collar to show a ring of fading bruises. "Lady Westerby's coachman must have told her what happened when I was at the palace. When I went back that night, to look for my horse, she found me. Tried to..." The memories were obviously unpleasant, but she went on doggedly. "I tried to get away, and we ended up at the top of the stairs." Embrie shuddered visibly. "I don't know which was more frightening: her hands around my throat or looking at her body after she fell down the stairs, wondering if she was going to get up and try again."

Ramsey felt sick. In part because he knew what had happened next. "And then Rowan?" he asked, unable to stop himself.

"And then Rowan," she answered softly. Then shrugged, as if to shake it off. "I suppose you know what transpired after that."

"Yes," he admitted, catching her hand in his and pulling back her sleeve to reveal the bandages on her wrist. Kyril had told him of her injuries but he was still somehow unprepared for the sight of them. "Yet another reason why I feel as though I am most truly in your debt."

She pulled away again, obviously uncomfortable with his scrutiny. "What I want to know is," she interjected quickly, "how did you find out all of that? How could you have known I was at Westhaven that night?"

Ramsey had wondered when she would get around to asking. She had to have been curious, especially when Kyril had told her nothing. "I take it Lord Seagrave was less than forthcoming," he said in a lighter tone, hoping to put her more at ease.

"Lord Seagrave," she answered, with a touch of her old sarcasm, "is apparently far more discreet than anyone gives him credit for."

Ramsey laughed, relieved by her attempt at humor. "I'll tell you," he replied carefully, "but it's a bit of a strange story. I think perhaps you should be sitting down when you hear it." She gave him a look of equal parts curiosity and disgust, but was willing to be led back to the stone wall. As they neared it, Ramsey remembered her injuries and stopped her. "With your permission," he said, and when she looked confused, he simply picked her up and set her gently on top of the wall. Embrie turned rather pink and said nothing as he sat next to her and began his tale.

"I had some visitors, while you were away," he began suddenly. "Two, in fact. But the first was probably the most important, as well as the most shocking." He watched Embrie closely as he continued. "I'm sorry there's no way to prepare you for this, but… the first visit was from your grandmother."

Embrie just looked at him as though he were insane, if not dangerously so. "I'm not certain about very much these days," she replied cautiously, "but I'm quite certain I haven't got a grandmother."

Ramsey smiled at her, but it was a sad smile, at the thought of how many years had been lost to lies. "Yes," he responded gently, "in fact you do. And you've known her for most of your life." He stopped, letting her think, letting her discover it on her own…

"Vianne?" She gasped in shock. "That's absurd! Vianne could not be. My father never..."

Ramsey nodded in confirmation. She needed to know the whole truth. "Yes, Vianne," he said, hoping she would be willing to hear him out. "She never told you because your father threatened to act against her family if she did. I believe that hiding it became a habit that was too hard to break, even when your father died."

Embrie's mouth opened and closed a few times before she managed to speak. "How could I have had a grandmother all this time—right in the house—and no one knew?" It was probably a bit much to absorb. Not just the fact of it, but the pain of realizing how badly she'd been lied to.

"But wait." Embrie's brows had drawn together in furious thought. "When she came to you with this story, you believed her? Why would she have bothered, knowing how implausible it would sound?"

"She brought proof," Ramsey answered, bracing himself for the next revelation. "Papers, some taken from a locked box hidden in your stepmother's study, and one that Vianne had secretly kept for years."

Still stuck on "grandmother," Embrie was obviously not yet coherent enough for "papers." Ramsey forged ahead as carefully as possible, trying to make himself unmistakably clear. "They were quite important papers. In fact, one of them was your father's will."

Embrie looked neither surprised nor concerned. She had, he suspected, put the matter of her inheritance behind her several years ago.

"And the other," he went on slowly, "the one in your grandmother's possession, was a certificate of marriage."

"Of marriage," Embrie said slowly, cautiously. "Whose marriage?"

"Your father's," Ramsey said quietly. "Not his second marriage, but his first." When Embrie's face went pale he picked up her hand and grasped it firmly. "Embrie, your father was married to your mother. He let everyone believe otherwise, even lied to his closest friends, because he could not bear the humiliation of having anyone know that he had married a kitchen maid."

～

Trystan felt herself stop breathing. The whole world seemed to be spinning around her. The rough stones under her thighs, the dull ache in her wrists, and the warm pressure of Donevan's hand were the only things that seemed real.

She had a grandmother. Vianne was her grandmother. And her parents had been married. For an instant she felt a blinding surge of anger. How could they have let her live like that, believing she was alone, for so long? But the anger drained away as quickly as it had come. She knew too well the power of a threat. Had let Malisse rule her with threats for years. She was in no position to judge Vianne.

"So after Vianne convinced you of who she was, she told you what had happened to me?" Trystan managed to ask the question in a more-or-less normal voice. Donevan was still watching her with evident concern. He had no doubt known this would not be easy for her to hear.

"She had guessed at some of it," he answered, looking relieved that she had weathered the news. "And thought, correctly in some respects, that I was her only chance of getting you back alive." He squeezed her hand gently. "She risked a great deal for you, you know. I believe she's always loved you, but never had much of a chance to show it."

Trystan shook her head. "The truth is, she's always shown it; I simply never recognized that love for what it was." A tear threatened, and she blotted it with her sleeve.

"Your grandmother," Donevan admitted, "is a rather terrifying woman."

Trystan smiled in spite of herself. The image of Vianne terrorizing the prince of Andar with a wooden spoon was an oddly appealing one. "I've never found her quite as terrifying as my stepmother, but she can be intimidating," Trystan agreed.

"Speaking of Lady Colbourne," Donevan added.

Trystan shot him a quick look of dismay. "Do we have to?" she muttered darkly.

"She was my second visitor," he confessed. It earned him another disbelieving look from Trystan. "I believe her intent was to contain the scandal she knew would arise when it was discovered you had been staying at Westhaven at the time of Lady Westerby's death."

That definitely sounded like Malisse. She would have been furious at the need to protect her good name from her stepdaughter's misdeeds, but she would have risked it. "If she knew what happened, why has she..." Trystan considered for a moment. "She has been suspiciously polite ever since I returned." She turned to Donevan, hoping for an explanation. "Did you...?"

Donevan actually laughed, with evident satisfaction. "I did," he answered. "I told her that I knew who you were and I showed her the documents your grandmother provided. She had guessed," he added, "about your parents. Your father hinted, but never told her the whole story—how he and your mother ran away together when he was young and foolish, and she died shortly after you were born. Malisse chose to assume the worst when your father never produced proof, and then, after he passed, she saw a way to profit from that assumption."

"What did she stand to gain?" Trystan wanted to know.

Donevan's look did not bode well for Malisse. "Your father's will left half of his estate to you, Embrie. By simply declining to contradict the general public rumors of your illegitimacy, your stepmother was able to control his entire fortune herself. It was a despicable fraud, and by the time a judge is finished with her, I suspect she will come to regret it nearly as much as she should." He pressed her hand again. "You should know, however, that my barristers have confirmed that you are, in fact, an astonishingly wealthy young woman."

Trystan was rather tired of losing her powers of speech, but it was a lot to learn about oneself all at the same moment.

She was forgiven.

She had a grandmother.

She was not illegitimate.

And she was quite disturbingly rich. It all felt so unreal, so very wrong somehow.

"I don't feel like I deserve it," she burst out, before she could think better of it. "All this good, when I've done nothing but make horrible decisions."

Donevan was silent for a moment. "My aunt said something similar to me, not so long ago," he finally answered. "She wondered what I would have been like, had it not been for my brother." He looked off into the distance thoughtfully. "I think she was trying to say that I didn't deserve his blighting effect on my life. But when I thought about it, I realized that I wouldn't care to change anything."

425

Reaching across the space between them, Donevan tipped up Embrie's chin and looked into her eyes.

"Life is too precious for regret," he told her. "Remorse and forgiveness are important, yes, but not regrets. Because in the end, we affect each other in unforeseen ways. No one would have chosen the path you have walked. But if it had not been for all the misunderstandings, all the suffering, and yes, the betrayals, we would not be sitting here today." Trystan tried to protest, but he stopped her. "The plot would have gone forward, and you would not have been there to stop it. My father would likely be dead. They were planning to kill me before they decided that marriage would be preferable, so I would be dead as well, and Rowan would be king. Your grandmother would have had no reason to come out of hiding and your heritage would never have been revealed."

He smiled at her, and suddenly, Trystan felt as though the entire world had come out from behind a cloud.

"So you see, perhaps we should thank Rowan, after all," he finished, dropping his hand and sighing, "for making all of this possible."

Trystan sensed a sort of melancholy when Donevan mentioned his brother. "What happened to him, then?" she asked tentatively. "To Rowan, I mean."

Donevan's lips twisted. "He's gone," he replied simply. "In the end, I saw him for what he was and I let him go."

Trystan wanted to comfort him as he had done for her, but she'd had so little experience either offering or receiving such a thing that she found herself holding back. "Do you miss him?" she asked quietly. "Or hope he will return?"

Donevan shook his head without hesitation. "I exiled him," he answered grimly, a note of resolution in his voice. "Forever. As the prince of Andar I promised that he would die if he ever set foot in this kingdom again. But…" He hesitated. "Yes, in a way, I miss him. I miss the boy he was, and the man he could have been." His voice grew tight and harsh. "And I wish I had never known what it felt like to want to kill my own brother."

Trystan did reach out then, to clasp his arm in sympathy. Donevan looked at her in surprise and answered by placing his other hand over hers. Their eyes met, and this time they held.

"Embrie." Donevan did not move, but his tone and expression changed, to become both humorous and hopeful. "My brother is gone. My castle is turned upside down. My father is a cantankerous wreck and my kingdom is in shambles. And after all this trouble over the small matter of one masqued ball, it seems I am still in need of a wife."

Trystan's breath caught. Her heart threatened to jump out of her chest and her brain went dead.

"I'm not asking for an answer right away," he went on, dropping his gaze to the top of his hand where it rested on hers, "but I am going to ask the question. I don't care about your money. I don't care about your family. I don't even care that some people are going to question my sanity when I tell them." He drew a deep breath. "And what I'm hoping to tell them is that you have agreed to marry me."

Trystan felt tears and laughter rising together as he finished, and said the first thing that popped into her head.

"That didn't sound like a question."

Her prince looked at her and raised a disbelieving eyebrow. "Are you, Trystan Embrie Colbourne, going to quibble about language at a time like this?"

She nodded, not quite managing to hold back a smile that threatened to split her face in two. "Your Highness," she answered around her laughter, "I intend to quibble quite strenuously about whatever I choose for a very long time to come."

His answering smile was lopsided and perfect.

"Besides," she added with an irrepressible twinkle, "you haven't even told me why you want to marry me."

Donevan subjected her to a mock glare and slipped off the wall. He came to stand in front of her, took both her hands in his and addressed her.

"Embrie," he said, quite seriously this time, "some weeks ago we stood here and I accused you of seeing me, perhaps more clearly than I saw myself. And you answered, by speaking of all the things you could not see. Things that we concealed from each other to protect our secrets. Since then I have decided that I no longer wish to have secrets from you. So I will tell you what you wished to know. Starting with this: what I love, now and forever, is you." Trystan stopped even trying to hold back her tears. "What I fear is that you will never be able to trust me enough to love me in return." Donevan's gray eyes held a depth of sincerity that banished all possibility of doubt. "What I hate is those people who have used you and countless others for their own gain. What I envy is my aunt Lizbet and her husband, whose lives have given me hope that marital happiness is not impossible." Those eyes crinkled in a smile that would have melted a far more resistant heart than Trystan's. "I live for the day you say you will marry me, and I would not hesitate to die if it would keep you safe. And I get up every morning with hope, rather than despair, because I believe there is a purpose to everything we have done and everything we will do. That purpose, I believe, has conspired to bring us together and so, I ask you, Trystan Embrie Colbourne… will you marry me?"

Trystan's laughter and tears could not really have been separated. "Your Highness," she answered through those happy tears, trying and failing to hide the depth of her emotions by matching his solemn demeanor, "I would be pleased to accept your proposal."

His Highness did not bother to hide anything. He picked her up off the wall and whirled her around while she shrieked with laughter. When he set her down, however, his face was stern.

"Miss Colbourne," he admonished with mock severity, "I have not given you permission to address me with such irritating formality. I believe I told you my name is Donevan."

"Yes," his wife-to-be responded, smiling sweetly, "but now that I know it irritates you, I will be sure to refer to you as 'Your Highness' as often as possible."

His answering laugh warmed Trystan to her toes.

"Then I can see," he said, smiling back and taking her upturned face between his hands, "that I may have to resort to underhanded tactics." And he kissed her.

EPILOGUE

$\mathcal{I}$t was not a lavish wedding, at least not by the usual standards of the nobility. The bride wore simple white satin, which made her look washed out and did nothing for her long, unbound chestnut hair. There were roses, but only because it was summer and they were easy to come by. The bride did not particularly like roses.

There were very few guests in attendance. Not because no one wished to be there, but because the groom had not bothered to invite very many people. The king, of course, sat in the front row, the suspicious glint of pride in his eyes not quite masked by his unwavering expression of kingly dignity. The bride's grandmother did not appear to smile either, though the people who knew her best would have asserted that she was dangerously close to tears. Next to her, looking severely uncomfortable, was a bearded, gray-haired man with his arm in a sling. Several parties speculated that his disgruntlement may have arisen from a dispute about the necessity of weapons at a royal wedding. The groom's aunt also sat close at hand, shedding copious tears and clinging to the arm of her beaming husband, while the groom's cousin was observed putting something unpleasant down the back of his sister's dress, the nature of which has yet to be discovered.

There were a few other guests, relatives of the groom and friends of the bride, many of whom it was rumored were no more than servants, although this was never actually confirmed. And far to the back of the modest hall where the ceremony was performed, one might have even seen a small woman veiled heavily in black. Though it was popularly believed that she was in fact the bride's stepmother, the woman would never admit to having been present, thereby forcing interested parties to gossip endlessly about the matter whenever she was absent.

The bridesmaid, a stout, dark-haired young woman with a pronounced tendency to giggle nervously at every turn, appeared to approve of the proceedings, though in truth, she generally appeared to approve of everything. Especially the groomsman. That young, blond nobleman took great pains to avoid his female counterpart and seemed, though not overflowing with congratulations, grudgingly pleased with the groom's choice and perhaps, it must be said, a trifle jealous.

After the ceremony, the clearly happy royal couple rode away together on a singularly fine bay horse, if only as far as the royal coach waiting for them on the outskirts of town. The groom admitted sheepishly to having given instructions for the second horse to be returned to the stable, as the ruse seemed to have worked so well for him on the occasion of his proposal. His princess scowled with no conviction whatsoever at his temerity and promised retribution, even as she admitted to herself that she had no actual objection to sharing a horse.

Predictably, their next few months were not so simple as fairy tales would make them. There were plenty of protests, complaints and dissenting opinions. There were even those who speculated that such a marriage, founded upon such strange circumstances, could never last. These obstreperous persons were quite studiously ignored by anyone intimately familiar with the events that had brought the prince and his princess together. No matter how strange or how brief their courtship, they had learned the hardest lessons of love long before they said their vows. And though their ever-afters would bring them both happiness and tears, they would choose to face those moments together. Which, in the end, is all that even a fairy tale could ask.

THANK YOU

Thank you for reading! I have loved writing this series and getting to know its characters and I hope you have enjoyed going on this journey with them. For more of their adventures, check out the rest of the series, or sign up for my newsletter to be the first to find out about new releases.

http://kenleydavidson.com

If you loved Traitor's Masque and want to share it with other readers, please consider leaving an honest review on Amazon or Goodreads. Not only do I love getting to hear how my stories are impacting readers, but reviews are one of the best ways for you to help other book lovers discover the stories you enjoy. Taking even a moment to share a few words about your favorite books makes a huge difference to indie authors like me!

OTHER BOOKS

The Andari Chronicles is a series of interconnected fairy tale retellings that evoke the glittering romance of the originals, while infusing them with grit, humor, and a cast of captivating new characters. *If you enjoyed the world of Andar, be sure to check out the other books in the series:*

The Andari Chronicles Reading Order:

- *Traitor's Masque*
- *Goldheart*
- *Pirouette*
- *Shadow and Thorn*

http://kenleydavidson.com/books

ABOUT THE AUTHOR

Kenley Davidson is a story-lover, word-nerd and incurable intro-
vert who is most likely to be found either writing or hiding
somewhere with a book. A native Oregonian, Kenley now resides
in Oklahoma, where she persists in remaining a devoted pluvio-
phile. Addictions include coffee, roller coasters, more coffee,
researching random facts, and reading the dictionary (which is
way more fun than it sounds). A majority of her time is spent
being mom to two kids and two dogs while inventing reasons not
to do laundry (most of which seem to involve books).

www.kenleydavidson.com
kenley@kenleydavidson.com

ACKNOWLEDGMENTS

This book, like many others, is not simply the product of a writer working in isolation. From its inauspicious beginnings as a spur-of-the-moment NaNoWriMo project, this story has become what it is because of people who love stories and refused to let me give up on this one. After all of the time and the work that have gone into making a long-held dream a reality, I feel it is entirely necessary to point out some of the people without whom Traitor's Masque would be nothing but the name of a file on my computer.

First and foremost, I would express my love and appreciation for the fantastic guy who did the design and layout for the book, and who also happens to be a pretty amazing husband. He refused to stop asking me when I was going to write a book, and when I agreed to try, he wouldn't let me quit, even when I was sure no one would ever want to read what I had written.

Likewise, my family are at least partially responsible for this moment. They read my first draft a chapter at a time, and loved it enough to beg for the next chapter, and the next, until I realized it was time to write "The End." To Mom, Dad, Tiffany and Chandra—thanks for being my first and most demanding fans!

After the first draft was completed, I might then have never let it see the light of day, except for the encouragement of my first beta readers, who happen to be some of my favorite people in the world. To Kylie, Janie, Mary, Wanda, Carol, and David—just remember, this is all your fault! You made me do it!

To my last-minute proofreaders, Chandra and Chris—I am profoundly grateful both for your skills and your willingness to wade through the minutiae in order to make this the best book possible.

And last but not at all least important, I offer up deepest thanks to my editor, Janie Dullard at Lector's Books, who is not only my favorite editor but a fantastic friend who I can't believe I haven't actually known forever.

Made in the USA
Columbia, SC
29 November 2019

84054864R00267